Bomber's Law

The Friends of Eddie Coyle (1972)
The Digger's Game (1973)
Cogan's Trade (1974)
A City on a Hill (1975)
The Friends of Richard Nixon (1975)
The Judgment of Deke Hunter (1976)
Dreamland (1977)
A Year or So with Edgar (1979)
Kennedy for the Defense (1980)
The Rat on Fire (1981)
The Patriot Game (1982)
A Choice of Enemies (1984)
Style vs. Substance (1984)
Penance for Jerry Kennedy (1985)
Impostors (1986)
Outlaws (1987)
The Sins of the Fathers (1988) (U.K. only)
Wonderful Years, Wonderful Years (1988)
The Progress of the Seasons (1989)
Trust (1989)
On Writing (1990)
Victories (1990)
The Mandeville Talent (1991)
Defending Billy Ryan (1992)

Bomber's Law

A NOVEL

GEORGE V. HIGGINS

A JOHN MACRAE BOOK

HENRY HOLT AND COMPANY NEW YORK

Henry Holt and Company, Inc.
Publishers since 1866
115 West 18th Street
New York, New York 10011

Henry Holt® is a registered trademark of Henry Holt and Company, Inc.

Published in Canada by Fitzhenry & Whiteside Ltd.,
195 Allstate Parkway, Markham, Ontario L3R 4T8.

Library of Congress Cataloging-in-Publication Data
Higgins, George V.
    Bomber's law: a novel/George V. Higgins.—1st ed.
        p.   cm.
    "A John Macrae book."
    I. Title.
    PS3558.I356B66   1993
    813'.54—dc20   93-26006
                                                       CIP
ISBN 0-8050-2329-1

First Edition—1993

DESIGNED BY PAULA R. SZAFRANSKI
Printed in the United States of America
All first editions are printed on acid-free paper.∞

10   9   8   7   6   5   4   3   2   1

Bomber's Law

1 The early-morning, late-November sun began to come in low and slow and cold and pale over the railroad bridge at the Dockett Street commuter-train stop on the Dedham–West Roxbury line, cheap-glittering the dirty windows on the southerly side of the yellow cinderblock auto-body shop—the sign on the roof in tall, hollow, red-plastic letters read: BUDDYS' YOUR BRUISED CAR'S BEST BUDDY—and Dell'Appa writhed in the passenger bucket seat of the blue-and-white Chevy Blazer. He exhaled loudly.

"Keep yah shirt on, pally," Brennan said complacently in the driver's seat. "Some days he's early and some days he's late, and most days he isn't: he's on time. I assume he must go in early sometimes, and then sometimes they have him come in late. But naturally, I never know; it's not like I'd know in advance. It isn't like they're tellin' me. Call me up and say: 'Early, tamarra. Tamarra he's goin' in early.' So I never know, the day before, which day is gonna be which. So, you wanna see Joey—which, I assume that you do; I think you *better,* since you're gonna be the one follows the guy now—you gotta come early. Be patient. Stay late. Or else you just ain't gonna be sure.

"You guys, you young guys, you ain't got it right; you don't understand: these guys don't follow our schedule. They don't care if we'd rather stay up late. They don't make their plans to suit us. So, we're gonna follow them? Fine, so we follow them, they can't stop us, we want to do that. But then we play by their rules then. We don't like it, the hours they keep? That's all right with them. They don't give a shit. It's not like they ask us to do it, they come 'round and said: 'Please, follow me.' "

"Ah, fuck you," Dell'Appa said, "yah big sackah sententious *shit.*"

"*Oooh,*" Brennan said contentedly, sipping on the narrow spout on the locking brown-plastic cover of his Dunkin' Donuts mug of coffee, "*there's* a big one, all right. Got to write that one right down here now, so I don't forget it. Look it up right up, I get home. What was the word you said there? 'Sen-*tent*-shush'—that right? Have I got it right there, what you just said? Just how you spell that word anyway?"

Dell'Appa scowled but he did not say anything.

"Yup," Brennan said, "it's a great thing, I know, bein' a real college guy. My kid-brother Dougie, he's one of you guys, too, he's got a college degree. I may've told you this, did I? As matter of fact, he's got two of the things, first the first one and then he got a master's. I guess prolly though his can't be as good, probably, the first one that he got, I mean. As good as the one that you got. Because that would explain what I didn't get, when he did it I didn't get it.

" '*Another* one?' I say, that's what I say to him there. 'Jesus Christ, Doug, you already got one of the things. What the hell you need another one for? They're like tits; they're like balls? You're supposed to have two? You look silly with one? Is that it? You've got one and you think it looks funny? For Christ sake, look at me, *I* haven't got one, I haven't got *any,* and I always felt pretty good. Like I was doin' all right, pretty much on top of things. And I always did pretty good.'

2

But he says no, this next one's the master's, the computer science thing there." He coughed. "I guess it's all right, you can stand it," he said. "If you like all that school shit, I mean."

Dell'Appa drank from his large cardboard cup and did not say anything. Brennan had parked the Blazer at the westerly curb of the southbound lane of the approach to the overpass. Except for the windshield the Blazer's glass was 80 percent sepia-smoked all around, so that those inside it could see out, imperfectly, but no one could see in except by peering over the hood, and a dark-blue curtain on an overhead track behind the seats concealed the cargo area even from front view.

"I said to Brian," Dell'Appa had said to his wife, Gayle, the night before, "I told him. I said: 'Brian, you know you're gonna hafta surplus that fuckin' Blazer submarine when Bob leaves, when he finally does retire, and let him take it with him for a buck or maybe ten. No one else's gonna want it. No one else'll ever drive it. The fuckin' Blazer's as much his's the shell is, belongs to the turtle. By now it's probably gotten so it even smells like him, practically livin' in it like he does. So, I dunno, do turtles retire? Probably turtles do not. Just keep right on turtling along, 'til the day they drop dead or something. Well, okay then, when the turtles *die*, when a fuckin' turtle dies, does another, younger, *working* turtle come along and take his house? Take his old shell and use it? I don't think so, Brian. I don't think turtles do that. Bob built the goddamned fucking thing, put the skylight in the roof, made the periscope box with the mirrors —has anybody ever actually used that? Used that periscope? Actually stuck the box out and taken pictures through it? I never heard of him, and I sure know I'm not gonna. I'd feel like a *fool* doin' that. And Con Cannon isn't either. Johnny Finn, anyone, nobody will. No one but Bob wants that goddamned thing, so let him be the one to fuckin' have it. Get it the fuck out of here. It's an embarrassment.'"

"My theory is," Brennan said, "and not just about Dougie either —Buddy down there, Buddy Royal? And you? All this applies also to you. My theory is that once you start doin' a thing, you know, it's like you got used to it, somethin'—you keep doin' that thing all the time. So like if it's going to school that you do, then that's what you do: go to school. And the same with Buddy, all right? You see what I'm sayin' to you here? He's runnin' that chop shop down there. He's always been runnin' that chop shop; he's been runnin' that chop shop for *years*.

" 'Oh no, it's not a chop shop. Body shop. Body shop. Body shop.' *Right*. Now can we just cut the shit here please now? Buddy Royal buys stolen cars. And he cuts them up and then he sells the parts, through the midnight auto supply. Four-thousand engine? Eight-thousand engine? Buddy can do better for you. Just tell 'em what you need, and it doesn't matter, and he'll have a guy he can call. 'BMW,' he'll say, that's what you want, 'Corvette,' 'Porsche,' don't matter. Whatever you want, Buddy can get, run you about fifty percent. Maybe a third, if you're lucky—he likes you. Could go as low as a third, you're buying steady from him. Bucket seats? Radios, tape decks, and that shit? Yup, Buddy can get that for you. Transmission, rear end, fuel-injection system? Custom wheels, five grand a set? Certainly can, no trouble at all. 'We're here to serve you, is all. Just tell us, whatever you want.' And he's been doin' that, years.

"So, we know this. We also know this, for years we've known that he's doin' this. And we know, all right? How the AG would feel, we grab Buddy, he calls a press conference." He deepened his voice. " 'We're cracking down now on organized crime and what makes insurance rates sky high. Today we have broken a stolen-car ring that rooked Bay State drivers out of millions of dollars a year.' The guy would've come right in his own shorts if we'd've ever done something, actually let him do that. Well then, so then, why didn't we, then? Why didn't we goddamned bust Buddy? It isn't like we didn't know. Well, I'll tell you why: he wasn't important, as important as what else we had. He was just too far down on our list."

Brennan laughed, making a short rough sound like a big unhappy dog complaining about being pushed out of doors into a cold rainy day. "So now Buddy's number, it finally comes up. We got the wire in on Buddy."

"And then, so what happens?" Brennan said. "I'll tell you what happens: *nothin'* happens. Not one *thing* inna whole fuckin' *world*. Two weeks ago fuckin' Wednesday this is, we get the fuckin' wire in, so we're on our second one now, I guess, must be, and so far we haven't got shit. Must be some guy in New Hampshire or something's givin' better prices for fresh hot new Corvettes or something

4

these days, because our good friend Buddy ain't seen *squat,* is what our little friend hasn't seen. Which is Buddy's fuckin' *luck,* of course, but it's also the same thing with us. It's just our fuckin' luck, too.

"We've been after Buddy, what? Two, three, five years? I don't even remember, it's been so long. So long he's been in there, doin' what he does, and we always knew he was doin' it, and so'd everyone else. Cop stops a guy speedin', he ran a stop sign; no brake lights; some damned thing like that, he didn't get a new sticker, he's writin' the guy up and what's the guy say? What does the guy always say? Well, he doesn't like it, gettin' a ticket, he doesn't think it should cost him, but it's gonna cost him, he can see that, so what can he do about that? He can give the cop a small ration, his shit, because what has he got to lose now? He's already gettin' the ticket.

"And what does he say, when he wants to do that? They all say the same fuckin' thing. They say: 'Hey, Ossifer, sir, 'stead of bustin' our chops, we're just mindin' our own fuckin' business, jackin' up our insurance like this, whyn't you guys sometime go'n get Buddy Royal? You know who Buddy is, right? Guy under the bridge there, hot-car operation? *Sure,* you guys know all about that. So then whyn'tcha do something to him, 'stead of givin' all of us here a hard time here? What is he, some friend of yours there? Like that mechanic over in Holbrook there, good friends with alla the cops, and the Staties then finally go in and bust him, receivin', the stuff that he had his friends go in and steal there, while all his good buddies on the police force're standin' guard, lookouts for him. Buddy got somethin' like that there with you guys?'

"Now lemme ask you this: what're you gonna say? What're you gonna say to this guy? Are you gonna say: 'Well, yeah, sure, we know, we all know what Buddy is doin'. But Buddy's low level, he's not a big guy, he isn't priority with us. We only go after the big guys, you know? The Francos and bad guys like you that run stop signs. We haven't got time to chase Buddies around. He isn't big enough for us.'

"You gonna say that to a guy, this guy that's been bustin' your balls? So he can just go and call up some talk show and say, he'll probably use his own cellular phone, phone he's got right in his car—maybe forgot to stop at a stop sign, or get a new sticker there, but he remembered, get that phone in all right: 'You know what this cop just said to me? He said sure they know, you *bet* they all know, what goddamned Buddy Royal is doin' and what it ends up costing us, and he said, he told me, that that doesn't matter, they don't even give a good shit. What they care about's who's got his sticker, his new inspection sticker, not the guy who is cutting up cars. "He's just a fuckin' *annoy*ance. Some kind of a nuisance or somethin'." ' Yeah, you do that and you won't get thanked.

"But *then,* then we finally *go* in and *do* it," Brennan said morosely, "Buddy's number finally comes up, like you knew that some day it just hadda. And then what do we get? A guy jerkin' his chain is the game highlights of it, some guy who's got no respect for him. Because most guys, you know, they don't dare to say to him: 'Hey, Buddy, you little piece-ah shit.' Because you know, well, maybe you wouldn't, but he thinks he's a real desperado. Capone in his mind's not as big as he is, John Gotti or Raymond, any of them guys. No one's as big as Buddy Royal. Well, maybe Capone, but the rest of them guys? Buddy eats their lunch all the time. If you take Buddy's word for it, I mean, but you'd be a fool if you did, because he is completely full of it.

"But most of the guys that he does business with, they're not gonna say this to him. They're not gonna say to him: 'Buddy, you asshole,' because then he might get mad at them, you know? And this they don't want to have happen. Because, let's say, you tap out onna weekend. All teams that you bet on, every one won, they all won but they lost onna spread. And on Settle-up Day, which's Tuesday, like always, your book's gonna wanna see money. None of your fuckin' excuses, all right? You're gonna get healthy next fuckin' week, he'll just carry you over 'til then? And the this and the that and the other, all if he'll just carry you? 'Uh-uh, *sorry,* no-no, can't do that. Nobody runs no tabs here. Management policy here.' And so then, what do you do?

"Simple. What you do there is, you get somebody's 'Vette, somebody's pretty-new 'Vette that you saw his blonde honey there out drivin' one day, you're just goin' downah the store, and you take it to Buddy and Buddy will take it—it's just like you went to a bank. Bada-*bing,* bada-*boom,* you got four or five grand, go see Mike the Book and he's happy. He's happy; you gave him the dough you owed him. You're happy; you're not gettin' beat up. And Buddy is happy, he's got a new 'Vette, so *he's* gonna make a few bucks. Everyone inna whole world is happy again—'cept for maybe the guy had the 'Vette and his honey. Those two people, they're probably not. But everyone else is, and that includes you, and that's why you give Buddy no shit, piss him off so he doesn't forget it. Because you always know where Buddy is, where he is going to be, because if you ever needah, you can sell him something, and this is good thing to know.

"But not this guy," Brennan said, "this guy that called him up, I forget which day now, I forget which day it was now. I think that it might've been last Wednesday there, Wednesday or Thursday or something. Anyway, this guy does not give one good shit about *anna*-thing, anna-thing in the whole world. He must have a trust fund or somethin', it's like. Or maybe some oil wells or something. Because when Buddy starts in with his usual routine, like he does always does, alla time, every time that he gets onna phone, the first thing he does is he warns the guy. 'Now be careful now what you say here. Because this line's tapped, you know. They're after me here. So be careful what you say on it.' "

"How's he know the line is tapped there?" Dell'Appa said. A Boston inbound commuter train made up of stainless-steel-rib–sided passenger cars salvaged three decades or so before from the shells of moribund New England railroads expiring in the lethal embrace of Conrail, pulled by two antiquated GM diesel engines—ex–Boston & Maine; New York, New Haven & Hartford—demeaned in their fourth and fifth decades of sturdy service by broad midriff stripes of faded purple paint, Easter egg–accented with yellow, passed under the road and stopped briefly at the Plexiglas-shielded, aluminum-framed passenger platform next to the tracks emerging from the southeasterly side of the bridge.

Brennan craned his neck to look in turn at each of the semi-trailer-size outside rearview mirrors he had mounted on the leading edges of the doors of the Blazer. He saw no one. The train started up again almost at once and pulled away. He looked at his watch. "Six forty-three," he said. He nodded. "Looks like this's a regular mornin', he's goin' in at the regular time, the time that he usually does."

"Meaning: seven forty-eight," Dell'Appa said resentfully.

"Usually, yeah," Brennan said, settling back again into the seat.

7

"That's when he usually does. But like I say, you're never sure. Sure in advance is what I mean, exactly what he will do. What is is if he misses the ones that come before that—well, not *misses,* exactly, because if he wasn't here to take a particular one, any particular train, it wasn't like he *tried* to, tried to make it but he didn't; it's because he didn't *want* to, want to take it, take that particular train. Because that's the way he usually is: regular as regular clockwork. But if they're up early for some reason, like Joey hasta be somewhere or something, some distance away from here, or it's one of those unusual days, like I say, unusual but they do happen, when he himself hasta be in early himself. And then it's been known to happen that he will catch one of the earlier ones. So that's why we hadda be here. In case he did that today. Because then otherwise you wouldn't've been here to see Joey, when he comes by here with him."

"Yeah," Dell'Appa said, folding his arms across his chest. "Joey. I *thought* it was him we were after. This Buddy shit, I didn't know from. So we really are here to see Joey."

"Well, you have to do it," Brennan said. "You know you have to do that, if you're gonna be followin' the guy, see what the guy looks like and so forth. And his car, and so forth and so on."

"I know what a goddamned old gray Cadillac Sedan de fuckin' Ville fuckin' *looks like,* for Christ fuckin' sakes," Dell'Appa said. "Honest to Mother of *God.*"

"Well, sure, but not this one," Brennan said, "not necessarily his one, you don't, because those things, they don't all look alike. Especially when they get that old there. It all depends what kind of care they had taken care of them along the line there, you know? *After* they were new. Everybody knows that. You know that. It's when they're all brand new, before anybody hardly even drove them, then they all look the same. Like each other. But now, eight, ten years later, well, the paint and all that stuff? That's when it all depends. And consequently they don't all now, they don't all look the same at all now. So you couldn't be sure if you had the right one, if I didn't show you which one."

"Bob," Dell'Appa said slowly and softly, "I know the guy's registration, remember? I know the numbers, the numbers that're on the registration and the license plate that he has to have attached to the rear of the vehicle in a prominent and easily visible position, right? I *know* all those things; these things I already know. So if I went to the place where he ordinarily goes, where he *always* goes, in fact, every morning after he leaves here, and I saw that gray Cadillac four-door hardtop with that fucking license plate on the fucking back bumper of it, then I would know I had the right car. Simple as that, Bob; simple as that."

"Yeah," Brennan said, "but you wouldn't know for sure if he drove it there, if he was the one drove it there. He could've just had someone else just drive it there for him, and he went off someplace else, with someone else, do something, and ditch his tail while he was doing it, something he didn't want us to see him doing. Or maybe just to take a day off from having us tail him. He could've done that, you know, too."

Dell'Appa groaned.

"I know, I know," Brennan said, "but this's still the sort of thing that you got to keep in mind on these things. It's not just the old slash-and-burn, you know, here; you go in, you do this, you do that, and then *boom*, it's all over—you're finished. Nothing at all like that here. This kind of thing, this thing that we're doing here, what you've got to be is, you got to be very methodical about it. Got to be very methodical about it at all times."

He made a broad smoothing motion with his right hand. "*Patient*, that's what you've got to be with this stuff here. Always've got to be very methodical, very patient. Always keep your mind at all times on what it is that you're doing. Focused. Got to be focused at all times. Got to say: 'All right now, am I sure of this here? Is this the right thing to do here, right here at this point in time here? Is this what I ought to be doing? To get where I want to be going in this, well then, is this the right way to go?' And also: 'Am I really sure about this?'

"That's what you have to do, all the time in this. That is what we have to do. Because that's the only way you can ever be sure, we can ever be sure. About any of this stuff you're doing." He nodded. "So, yeah, I know, so you hadda get up. And you don't like gettin' up, right? Well, who does? You tell me who likes gettin' up. No, you can't, because nobody does. But so, neither can I, so I certainly can't blame you for that. But trust me, I know what I'm doin', and even though I know you don't trust me in this, believe me, I know what

I'm doin'. And just sittin' here like this, sittin' right here, like we're doin', all right? This's the best way to do it."

Dell'Appa sighed. He had closed his eyes.

"Yeah, I know, I'm borin' you," Brennan said. "Well, that's the trouble with you guys. Alla you young guys're like that. You think, you're all, you're all just like that kid there, that Leno kid there on TV. They threw Johnny Carson off of there, and then look what happened to them. They throw Carson off and they put the kid on, and then so what happens then, huh? The other kid gets all mad, am I right about this? And so what does he do then? He *quits.* That's what he's gonna do, at least. So that's what I mean about that. They started out there, they had Carson and Leno and also the other kid there, they say: 'Right, this's goin' too good. Things're goin' along 'way too good around here. We gotta find some way, fuck up. I know, I got it. I know what we do: we dump Carson and that oughta do it.' So they did that and by Jesus it did it. Now what've they got, now they did all of that? They got Leno is what they've got: Leno. Carson's gone and the other kid, too. The other kid's packing his bags."

"Tell me how Buddy Royal knew his phone was being tapped," Dell'Appa said, his eyes still shut. "That at least sounded interesting. The gear that we use now's very low-voltage drain, and the drain's only during a call. So how'd he find out we were on? How'd the guy know? Tell me that. Somebody tell him or something? We got a leak in our pail? Oughta find out who it is, if we do, find out as fast as we can, stick a soldering gun up his ass."

"He didn't *know*," Brennan said. "Buddy didn't know we had the wire."

Dell'Appa opened his eyes. "You just told me he did know," he said. "You just finished telling me, two, three minutes ago, that Buddy Royal told the guy who called him up last Wednesday or Thursday, you weren't sure, that his line was tapped. You just told me that yourself."

"That's what I'm tryin' to tell you, you asshole, for Christ sake," Brennan said. "That's what it is about Buddy—he always told guys that stuff. Like it made him a big man, he's warnin' them: 'Everyone's after me here. That's how fuckin' big a guy *I* am.' But he don't actually know that we're on, even though we now actually are, and we're hearin' him tell guys we are. But he's been tellin' 'em that stuff for years. It's not like it means anything.

"Anyway, to this guy it sure doesn't. This guy calls him Wednesday, I mean. And Buddy tells him, and he isn't impressed at all. He says: 'Like who is this, Buddy? Who do you mean? Who is it that's after you now?'

"Well," Brennan said, "you would've thought, the way Buddy reacts, you would've thought at least he must've been sittin' bare-ass onna throne, takin' a good shit himself, and some guy that maybe owed him a thrill or two, maybe just give him a tickle, figured out how to get a cherry bomb under there, right about under his balls, and that's when he set the thing off. Because Buddy yells, and I mean, really *yells:* 'Just what the fuck do you mean? What the fuckin' fuck you mean by that? You know who I mean, you fuckin' asshole, you know who I mean when I say. I mean, I mean the State fuckin' Police. And the FBI bastards, and all of them fuckin' guys there. Plus all the insurance company snoops, and the snitches and private assholes. Cocksucker. That is who's after me there. Who the fuck else would it be? The fuckin' Rat Patrol, maybe? Saint Catherine's Bugle Team there?'

"Oh, he's as mad as a hornet," Brennan said. "He's practically frothin' the mouth. You can almost see him, hoppin' around there, face gettin' all red—he's a very excitable guy there—bangin' his hands on his desk, and this guy is laughin' at him. I mean: actually laughin' at him. You can hear him over the phone. 'Shit, I don't know,' the guy says. UPS, maybe? A COD package? Bunchah guys from the bakery or something? Kid that brings overnight from the post office? How the fuck should I know? What I hear, could be just about anyone.' "

"I'm not following you," Dell'Appa said.

"What?" Brennan said.

"I don't get it," Dell'Appa said.

"Don't get what?" Brennan said. "What the hell're you talking about?"

"What the hell'm *I* talking about?" Dell'Appa said. "What the hell *you're* talking about is what the hell I'm talking about."

"I don't get it," Brennan said.

"Goddamnit, Bob," Dell'Appa said, "the bakery truck guys, and the UPS guys, and the mailmen and *all* of this shit. All of this shit that you're tellin' me, that the guy that called Buddy on Wednesday said to him that got him so hugely pissed off. I don't get it. It doesn't make any sense to me, not the slightest bit of sense at all."

"Oh," Brennan said. "Well, okay, see, I guess, I thought you knew, just like everybody else in town. Knew."

"Well then you thought wrong, then," Dell'Appa said, "because, and you're really about the last person inna world I oughta have to tell to keep in mind this, but I'm not like everybody else in town because I haven't been in town with everybody else, all right? Remember that. For the past eleven months I've been out in Hampshire County with the cows 'n sheep 'n pigs; anna chickens, ducks 'n goats; anna bull dykes in Northampton and anna gays in all those towns, all that happy horse-shit stuff. Ever since they figure out there's somethin' funny goin' on in the treasurer's office there, right? And the books're gettin' cooked in the county office, right, 'member? So I haven't been around town, 'long with everybody else, and as a result I do not know what the rest of them all do. So you have got to tell me."

"*Suure*," Brennan said. "But just let's keep in mind here who it was, whose fault it was, that you got picked and sent out there to do that little job. It wasn't my fault, Harry, boy. I was not the one. It was you, made that choice easy. You made it easy for them. You picked yourself out."

"You know, Bob," Dell'Appa said, "there's about, oh, probably there's about six hundred things that you can't do at all, that you're just fuckin' lousy at. But high up on that list of things, of anybody's list of things that you can't fuckin' do at all, right up near the top of it there's an entry that says: *lying*. You're about as good a liar as I am a deep-sea diver, except I've got no experience at doing deep-sea diving, and you have got a shitload when it comes to telling lies."

Brennan turned his head and stared at him. He drummed the fingers of his right hand on the steering wheel and ran his tongue slowly back and forth on the edges of his upper front teeth. After a while he nodded. "Okay," he said. He turned again and faced forward, looking out the windshield. He nodded once more. "Okay," he said, "got that straight: so that's how we're gonna have it. That is how it's gonna be, then. How it's gonna be 'til I get through and you've got the whole show to yourself. Now you've made it back and this's how you want it played."

"Just how the fuck did you think I'd want it played?" Dell'Appa said. "Just what exactly what the fuck did you expect to happen, huh? Did you think when I came back here—and there was never any doubt of that, but that I would be *back,* Bob, except maybe in your dreams—I'd come back like Saint Francis, meek and mild and kissing flowers? Up yours, pal, if you did expect that, that was what you did expect."

"I really didn't know, you know," Brennan said, arching his eyebrows and tapping the steering wheel with the first two fingers of each hand. "I said that to Margaret. When I first heard you were coming back, I went home that night and told her, that was one the things I mentioned, that we talked about that night, and she said: 'Oh, what do you think? How will he react? How will he react to you?'

"And I said, I told her, I said: 'Margaret, I don't know. I've got no idea at all. It could be that he's changed a lot, that this whole thing's changed him, he will've grown up some and we'll get along just fine. Or it could be that he's thought it over now and sees just whose fault it really was. Or it could be he'll come back here and he'll just want it to be ignored. And whichever way he wants it, well, that's the way that it'll be. I'm on short time now, and so to me it doesn't matter. I could get along with Stalin, I think, all the time that I've got left. So we'll do it like he wants to do it, way that Harry wants it done. And that way when the time comes to go out, I'll go out quiet, no beefs with anyone.'" He looked sadly at Dell'Appa. "And that was what I said to her," he said. "That was what I said."

"Bullshit," Dell'Appa said, in a voice like something he'd found rumpled and forgotten on the floor at the back of a closet. He put his head back on the rest and closed his eyes. "Like I said, you've got no talent for that. Finish telling me all about Buddy Royal. I don't think you're making all that up. Some of it, maybe, not all."

The sun had appeared washed-out and whitish over the Blue Hills to the east and Brennan sucked on his coffee-mug, his shoulders slumped and the folds of his grizzled facial flesh hanging slack around his mouth. "Aww," he said at last. "It wasn't really very much.

Buddy's first wife left him, 'count of he would beat her up. But he was not like most of those guys, only hit her, it don't show, belly, back, like that; he hit her where it *would* show, 'round the eyes, the nose an' mouth, knock a couple teeth out—like he was *proud* of it, the little rotten piece-ah-shit.

"And then so she finally left him," Brennan said. "His first wife finally left him, and time goes by and this and that, he finds another woman. Guess she didn't hear the news. Or then again, may be she did, she did hear the news, but she figures: 'This's cake. I can handle this guy.' And if she did that, if that was what she did to him, well, I guess that she was right—she does handle him."

" 'S she do?" Dell'Appa said.

Brennan pulled his shoulders forward, dumped his body off to the left, raised and lowered his eyebrows, exhaled through closed lips, tilted his head, and said: "Hey, what can I tell you? She fucks other guys, 's what she does. *All* of the other guys there.

"You really can't blame her," Brennan said. "She was honest with the guy. That's what she told him she would. Before they got married, she changed her mind, changed her mind three or four times, they hadda keep puttin' the weddin' off there. Because she keeps tellin' him, she wants to do, 'stead of marrying old Buddy here—and this's the new bride we're talkin' about now, Buddy's new wife that he wants her to be—is marry the rich jerk that she was screwing, before she met Buddy, all right? And then started in screwin' him. Go and marry the boyfriend she had before Buddy and come home from the honeymoon, I guess, and get settled in, the new husband and so forth, send her clothes to the laundry and so on, rinse out a few pair-ah fresh pantyhose, and then get right back down to business.

"The daily routine, that's what you need, the week-to-week daily routine. Everyone knows what to expect. Screw Buddy afternoons before the rich-jerk new husband gets home from where he goes every morning to make all the money he makes. But not *every* afternoon, darling; only *some* afternoons. Three a week, I think. Or maybe it was three this week and two next week, and three again, week after that. Because apparently Buddy's not the only new boyfriend she got after she turned the rich-jerk new boyfriend into the old boyfriend. She's got to think about keeping the other new boyfriend, the new-

14

new boyfriend, I guess, happy, too, and that's what the other after-noons a week are gonna be for. I'm tellin' you, this's all very compli-cated.

"Well, at first everybody's being very sympathetic, 'Poor Buddy,' all of that shit. Finally falls in love for real, the real thing, the poor guy—and keep in mind here, Buddy's no colt here here; guy's gotta be up close to sixty, and this dame of his, that she's so hot to trot, she's a good fifty-five herself there—"

"A *real* good fifty-five, from what you're tellin' me here," Dell'Appa said.

"She's pretty lively," Brennan said. "Anyway, he won't listen, ev-erybody's tellin' him: 'Forget about about this broad. You won't dare to leave the house, she'll be havin' someone in. You're better off without her. And he wouldn't listen. Know what he does? He wears her down. And she does marry him. And then when they get back here, from where it was they went, well then, just like she promised, she is doin' it, porkin' every guy in town. And that's what that guy Wednesday meant, about all the deliverymen and all that kind of stuff. He meant that all those guys he mentioned, they're all fuckin' Buddy's new wife, while Buddy's down the shop."

"How'd Buddy react?" Dell'Appa said.

"Well, like you'd expect an actual normal person to," Brennan said. "Like somebody knocked the wind out of him. It was almost enough, damned near enough, if you knew the guy's a bone-dry, hard-ass, chop artist, steal his own mother's car if it was a red 'Vette and he had a guy needed the parts, make you feel actually sorry for him."

"It almost makes you wonder, sometimes, doesn't it?" Dell'Appa said. "If maybe, where these borderline guys like Buddy Royal're concerned, if maybe we shouldn't just leave them alone, right where they are, and let them torment themselves. Makes each others' lives hell on earth, just like they'll do if we don't. Buddy's action, what you say he's doing there? What he's been doing for years. If we caught him, what'd he get? Eight or ten, if he got that? Out in the sunshine, three or four years? Do that like he waits for a table. But if we just leave him, leave him where he is, look what his own friends'll do, make him feel like a turd on the ground. And it works like a charm, too—they do it. Just like a fuckin' charm, it does.

"So maybe that's what we oughta be doin' here, Bob, you think? Huh?" Dell'Appa said. "Just goin' around here and sizin' up guys and seein' what their friends do to them. If they've got enough trouble without us, goin' to all the expenses."

" 'Expenses'?" Brennan said.

"Well, *yeah,*" Dell'Appa said. "It's expensive, catchin' guys, collecting evidence. Taking it before grand juries, gettin' the indictments. Tryin' them if they want trials—those judges make real money. And then puttin' them in jail, is that it? That what you got in mind? That costs like holy shit. And these here're parlous times, you know? Nobody's got no money. The taxpayers, you know, we ought to think about this thing. Maybe they are better off if we do like I just said. Identify the guys who're already getting such a bunch of shit from all their friends, and life in general, too, they just don't justify the cost of putting them in jail. The kind of guys, you put them in, they look around, say: 'Thanks. I got to thank you guys. This really is a whole lot better'n the shit I had at home.' Makes you feel pretty stupid."

"Fuck you," Brennan said.

"I'm *serious,*" Dell'Appa said. "Maybe that's what we should do with our friend Joe Mossi. 'Stead of sittin' here shootin' the shit about Buddy Royal and stuff. Run a profile on Joey. Look at it and then decide if we want to do this. One way we come down it, we say: No, Short Joey goes. This guy is a bad actor, not a good citizen at all. Look what he does for a living: he kills guys on order. This is no way to behave.'

"But then again, maybe we don't. Maybe we don't say that. We take a look at what we got and say: 'Hey, he's all right. True, he does kill guys for money, but look at the guys he kills: very lousy, low-rent guys. "Riffraff," you might say. If he didn't kill them then we'd have to deal with them, and look what that would cost. And plus he's good to his brother. Get Joey onna telephone, I wanna talk to him. I think I see a way here, Commonwealth can save some money, we throw him a little work.' "

"Okay, you wise prick," Brennan said, "turn off the faucet, okay? At least get a look at the guy this morning, I know you're not goin' off blind on this thing I been workin' so hard for so long."

"Tell you what," Dell'Appa said. "If and when the guy does show up this morning, I will take a good look at him, all right?"

"That's all I am askin' from you," Brennan said. "That is all I am askin' from you here."

"And if he doesn't," Dell'Appa said, "if he doesn't, well then, I won't."

2 "You know, I got to really say, Harry," Brennan said, "I really got to say I think you must've gotten outta the western part the state there just about the nick of time. Is all I got to say."

"Why?" Dell'Appa said. In front of them to the south, on the other side of the bridge, informal, irregular processions had begun, plainly purposeful men and women long experienced in the workday routines, advancing down the hill without expressions on their faces, clustering obediently though restively at the traffic light on the curb at the corner where Dockett Street intersected with a four-lane boulevard connecting to the east with Route 9. They waited there until the crossing signal lighted, advancing en masse when the white light said WALK as though blissfully convinced that no Massachusetts driver had ever disregarded a stop light or would run that one that day.

Brennan was drinking coffee. He furrowed his brow over the Dunkin' Donuts cup, but he did not lower it from his mouth. Behind the Blazer to the north, more commuters just as impassively trudged up the rise to the crest of the bridge, the minority choosing to walk in the street, eddying around the Blazer, and then down toward the inbound-train platform.

"I said: 'Why?' " Dell'Appa said.

Brennan lowered the cup perhaps an inch from his lower lip and said: "I heard you." He raised the cup again and resumed drinking.

The night before, Dell'Appa had told his wife over a dinner of roast chicken at their kitchen table that Brennan had not changed. "He hasn't changed a bit," Dell'Appa had said. "Two weeks ago today, I come back. I've been away eleven months, give or take a week. Far as Bob's concerned, I might as well've been away eleven years, or've just stepped out for eleven minutes and come right back in again. Wouldn't make any difference to him. I went in there two weeks ago, everybody else's givin' me the meet-'n-greet; 'Hey, whaddaya say, huh?' 'Glad you're back'; 'How was it out there?'; 'Feel good and so forth?' Not Buffalo Bob, not him. Comes in, sees me, says: 'Harry,' and goes into his office. Next time I see him: this morning. Not one other time until today, not once in the past two weeks.

"Today. Comes in ten minutes late, that's also still the same. Says: 'Mornin', Harry,' to me. Puts his coffee on the table—there's always a pot making, and he always brings his own in—hangs his raincoat up, sits down and has it while he scans the night shift's raw stuff for anything that might be good. When he finishes, he leans back, looks at me and says: 'Gotta see a man today. Couple guys, in fact. Nothin' to do with what we got, what we'll be workin' on. Prolly just as well, you think? Give you a better chance to read the files, get you up to speed. Listen the tapes, if you wanna.'

"I don't know what the hell," Dell'Appa had said to his wife, "what the hell in God's sweet name he thought I'd been doin' for the past two weeks while I waited around for him to hand over the Mossi

19

case, if I wasn't reading it. Brushing up on my Shakespeare, perhaps? Not that it still wasn't just fine by me, another day without him. A day without Bob Brennan, any reason at all, is a day full of sunshine, made by the Lord. But apparently my last for a while. He's pickin' me up at the office tomorrow at oh-six-ten-oh-my-Gawd hundred hours—that's six-ten A.M. to you slugabed civilians—to go to a place that's about an eight-minute drive away and stake out a train stop where our wary quarry's not very likely to be—is, indeed, almost certain *not* to be, at least according to the files that Bob Brennan had much to do with creating—until sometime not too soon after seven-thirty A.M. So what's the explanation, if there is one, for this transparently irrational behavior on the part of two highly trained, genuine crack troops—none of your recent merger assimilees from the Registry and elsewhere, but the real-McCoy, honest-Injun, Massachusetts State cops?

"Simple: Robert Brennan happens to be one of these crack troopers, and he's in charge of this little outing. Robert *likes* irrational plans. Robert's the strangest piece of work that's walked the earth in all the years since Grendel's dear old mother died. If in fact she did die, now that I think of it. Maybe there's something to this reincarnation stuff. She came back in a Brennan-suit for this life, to rest up for her next confinement."

Gayle had laughed. "No scoffing, now," Dell'Appa had said. "It could be, you know. There are more things in heaven and earth than're dreamt of in your philosophy. There have to be. That's the only way anyone could possibly and plausibly account for the existence of Bob Brennan."

She studied him for a while. "It could be he knows, you know," she said. "It could be he's figured it out. Oh, not exactly *what,* of course, what is going to happen to him. But that something probably is. Something probably is."

"What," he said, but it was not really a question. "I never said I was going to do anything to him."

"No, you haven't," she said. "No one ever said you weren't careful."

So Brennan was not yet ready to answer. This meant he would not speak again until he had "done some thinking." He had once excused himself from responding at once to a staff meeting speaker's request for suggestions and comments on a new proposal by explaining soberly that he had always "had trouble every time I triedah think an' talk at the same time, and I would like to think some about this, if that's okay with you. Before I talk." No one else at the meeting had disputed Brennan's admission that he found it difficult to think while simultaneously doing anything else. "Such as, for example," Dell'Appa had said to Gayle that night, "chewing gum. Smoking. Or walking." Thinking for Brennan was a task that could require considerable time; Dell'Appa therefore looked at his watch.

It was a stainless-steel-braceleted Seiko quartz chronograph with a tachymetre bezel and three small dials inset: three timers, with a stopwatch, each function activated or concluded by means of a button on the side of the case. He had bought it for $250 ($100 off usual price, according to the Filene's Basement ad in the Boston *Commoner*) at an after-Christmas clearance sale three Januaries before, while still righteously seething at having been measlied the previous Christmas Eve when the gifts were handed out. Having decided to get even, but having been quite unable to think of a suitably expensive present that he had truly coveted without even knowing it existed, and therefore indisputably should have received, complete with a big red bow attached (though probably not the Porsche 911 Carrera 2, German racing silver, that in fact he really did want; as grouchy as he was, he was prepared to concede that the price, around $73,000 the way he wanted it equipped, made any expectation of that particular gift at least arguably unreasonable), he had waited for a sign that would show him what to do, waiting as patiently as a prudent soothsayer would cast lots repeatedly, seeking absolute confidence that success would certainly result from the crucial military action he would then recommend to his short-tempered, homicidal emperor.

He was cautious about such matters for a reason. Friends from work and college classmates after they first met Gayle often complimented Harry later on having married well above his station, relying on nothing more than the incontestable fact that she was so extremely smart and cheerful that five minutes after they'd been introduced to her the eighteen-or-so extra pounds she had accumulated at her hips and on her chin, neck, and upper arms (mostly during the complete inactivity medically enforced upon her during her pregnancy with Roy but had never seriously addressed since) had vanished in the magic of her wit. Their good-natured insults were meant to chafe him a little, but not to mask their genuine envy, in which both Gayle and he later wallowed.

But still, while it was never easy being married to a clinical psychologist whose father, a university hospital chief and professor of orthopedic surgery, permitted his affectionate family (there were four more doctoral degrees, all Ph.D.'s in the liberal arts, among Gayle's siblings; her mother's was in biology) to refer to him at festive gatherings as "the family mechanic," defending himself by terming them collectively "my home-bred, muzzy-headed coven," it was especially hard for Harry when striking back at any slight, real or imagined, inflicted by one of them. He managed generally to hold his own, being faster if not as profound, but he did so only by always taking great care. The choice of retaliatory action had to be precisely perfect. Otherwise his just resentment, and he along with it, would be made into objects of still more and further fun.

The watch was perfect. He had known it the instant that he saw the picture of it. He had gone and bought it gladly that same morning, before he went to work, so that he might accustom himself to its new heft on his wrist during the day, and then in the evening he had worn it casually but still ostentatiously home, having rehearsed precisely what he would say when Gayle spotted it and quietly reproached—not: bitterly scolded—him for having been financially so selfish.

He had planned to reply calmly, but still to remind her firmly that for what had been the third year in a row he had laid out nearly nine hundred dollars on gifts for members of their family, every dollar of it plundered from cold, rainy, windy, dirty, highway-repair-detail overtime, stolen out of his limited free time (that would have to be done delicately, too; Gayle had been very reluctant to suspend her developing counseling practice when her ob-gyn doctor had placed her under pregnancy house-arrest by warning that she would almost surely miscarry, as she had twice before, if she did not accept confinement, and she remained extremely sensitive to the fact that following doctor's orders, and then carrying out their own decision that she should stay home with the baby for the first three or four crucial years, had shoved all the family financial responsibilities onto Harry's shoulders—but he would do it, nonetheless). From that family in return he had received a dark-blue terry-cloth bathrobe, three three-packs of Jockey shorts matched with three three-packs of Jockey vee-neck tee-shirts, and a set of long-handled, chromium-shafted, wooden-handled utensils for his summer use at the Charm-glo pro-pane grille (the purchase of which had taken him four months to clear from the MasterCard statements), on the redwood deck he had built with his own cut and blistered hands (pre-fab lumber kit and other materials: ten deadly fatiguing months on the MasterCard) in the backyard of the house he owned with Gayle in Whitman, near the above-ground pool (on which he was still making monthly pay-ments on the home-improvement loan from Southeastern Bank for Savings, and would be for another four years).

"I know, I know," he planned to say, wrapping up his defense, "my inner child slipped his restraints, went out to play today. But even an old mongrel dog gets to take a run off the leash now and then. Can't keep him tied up *all* the time."

Gayle had noticed the watch the instant that he entered the kitchen that night, inspected it closely, pronounced it very hand-some, kissed him on the cheek and said she was glad he had bought it, "since you really got stiffed this Christmas. Last couple or so Yules, in fact." He had therefore kept his speech to himself. Gayle had outsmarted him again, but he was actually pleased. She was *so* quick and *so* good at it, finessing him like that, completely fair and square. Skill that great had to be admired, even by its victim, espe-cially when the good-sport victim came out of the exchange with a fine new watch that helped to ease the pain.

The watch read 6:55. Therefore none of the commuters converg-ing on the bridge—most of them in tan raincoats, open, unbuttoned and unbelted in the unseasonably mild late-November morning, showing almost jauntily in the slanting sunlight of dwindling autumn solid red and plaid melton zip-in linings, backdrops for perfectly presentable, businesslike flannel suits, or sports-jacket-slack or -skirt ensembles, carefully purchased at discount stores and outlets located in the Boston suburbs alongside secondary four-lane feeder roads tied in to the southerly arc of Route 128—was likely to interest Brennan or therefore Dell'Appa. Another fifty-three minutes still remained before the scheduled arrival of the 7:48 that most days interested Short Joey Moss, a/k/a Short Joe Mossi; Joseph John Mossi; Joe the Moss. So it would be all right to stay relaxed for a while and heckle Bob Brennan some more. "*Awww*, 'd you miss me all that much? I'm real touched."

"You're touched, all right," Brennan said, "the same way my mother says my sister-in-law Laura's touched. In the head. Six sandwiches short of a Holy Name picnic, three players short of a ball club. That Laura, boy, she is something. My youngest brother did all right, selling those computers I still don't understand, even though I use the things—not because I like 'em, no; it's because I hafta, just like everybody else that's over forty, doesn't like the things at all but also doesn't have no choice—and they got this real nice house over Quincy. Bought it when the price was right, and I mean: *really* right. Back the late Seventies, you know? Before everything explodes there, prices go right through the roof; then ten or twelve years later, after all the suckers pay them, get in hock up past their balls, down the prices come again, ka-boom, ka-boom, ka-boom. And now the banks're goin' under; we're all really inna shit. It doesn't make no sense to me. Makes no sense at all.

"But this place that Doug has got, over Quincy there, it's really a beautiful setup. A truly elegant setup. Like something outta one of those magazines, you know? The shrubs and the trees, and all kinds of flowers? Just by lookin' at them you could tell: they'd be worth all kinds of money today, even if prices are down. Just by themselves, they'd be worth the big money, 'f you went out and tried to buy them now. So, they had this house a few years, much too big for just them, and then finally they had a family, Laura finally admitted it: Yup, they saved up dough enough so that even if Dougie does keel over with the heart attack—Doug's thirty-eight, and a heart attack for him's about as likely as Arnold Hammenegger gets one; kid's in the gym and on the treadmill every single day, watchin' his diet like he was one of those bony fashion models with no tits at all and less ass— well, Laura and the new Dougies will be perfectly all right. Financially, at least.

"Before that it was like . . . before that she was obsessed or something, saving up their money, every dime she got her hands on. Which was every dime he made, unless he went haywire out on the road and had a cup of coffee and a sandwich or something. Because

24

otherwise he brought every penny home—and Doug, like I say, makes good money. So that was quite a few dimes there.

"Now, you got to let me put this in perspective here. As long as I remember, the one thing Doug's always really wanted, ever since he was just a little kid, was a little powerboat. Not like the rest of us: cars. Trans Ams, the IROC Camaros, what-have-you. Later on, of course, Lincolns, Cadillacs. Nope, what Dougie wants is a boat. Not a great big one now; one of those things that looks like it has to belong to some billionaire Greek or something, screwin' the movie stars on it. Nope: This's the kind you keep onna trailer, under a tarp, 'side the garage—got the neon-blue finish with the sparklies all through it— 'til it's summertime again, and it's time for boats again. Then you hitch it up the car, the weekend, take it down the ramp, put it inna water and you cruise around all day. Sun starts going down, you bring her in again. Put 'er onna trailer, take 'er right back home. You don't actually ever *go* much of anywhere, so the fog comes in or it starts to rain or something, well, there's no real problem; you just turn 'er around and go home like a bat outta hell.

"Myself, I got to say it looks pretty boring to me, but Doug's the guy who's paying for it, right? With his money that he earned himself? Should be all right if he likes it, and he does. Hell, he *loves* it. So, what's the damage, huh? Nobody gets hurt. Just riding around like that—heck, it's basically the same thing we did with our first cars, back when we were stupid teenagers. We filled them up with gas and drove around town all night, split a couple six-packs, maybe, sure, three or four of us, but we didn't get shitfaced and we didn't get stopped by the cops, and we talked about how we'd been getting laid. Which of course we hadn't been; we were all just talking, lying to each other. We'd've been actually doing that, actually out getting laid, well, that's what we would've been doin' those nights. 'Stead of spendin' them all, ridin' around, wastin' gas and tellin' big lies.

"But: we all knew, we all understood what was going on, and that's why we didn't mind it. That's what made it all right. When we said how we were getting laid, and how we got into Joanie's pants, what we were really sayin' was that we sure would've rather been getting Joanie's pants off and getting into Joanie 'n riding around with a bunch of the other guys that also weren't gettin' laid, drinkin' the beer and tellin' the lies, but Joanie, any Joanie, wouldn't even go out with us, any one of us. And we all knew it. Hell, we knew it so good we never even bothered asking her, any Joanie, even to go out. So what it was, it was: 'Just shut up and gimme another Bud there, okay?' Right? But, if there was no way inna world that you were ever gonna fuck Joanie, at least the other guys you knew weren't fuckin' her either, weren't doin' any better with the girls that *they* didn't dare ask out, and you weren't by yourself every Saturday night, without a damned thing to do.

"Well, that's basically what it is Doug's doing now, he's out riding around in his boat. Except of course Doug now's getting laid, of course, on a regular basis, even though he did have to get married to do it, just like the rest of us did. Mostly found out we hadda do, 'f we ever planned to get laid. On a regular basis, I mean. I think that's what every guy hasta do, finally, he faces up to the facts. Maybe he's rich and maybe he's handsome, maybe there's dames all around. But sooner or later, he'll have to face it: for regular sex, if that's what he wants, he is gonna have to get married. The dames got it worked out that way, a long time ago, and that's how we get it: on their terms. Or pay for it there, you know, right? Or else we don't get it too often— this's 'fore all the broads would put out, at least if what I heard was true, but which don't matter now again, I guess they stopped again: AIDS.

"So anyway, that's how it was and so on, and Doug hadda wait for the boat, when there really wasn't no reason. But: so what, huh? Now he's got it. And what's it cost him? Five thousand bucks or so, the trailer and the boat. Six, he goes whole hog. Doug made that much easy; he had double that to spill. But Laura? Nothin' doin' with the boat, until they had the family, and no family until they saved up about as much as that old Jean-Paul Getty guy there. 'Uh-uh,' Laura says to him; Dougie told me this, and I even heard her say it to him once or twice myself. 'Not if you want a family, like you're always sayin'. We got to save our money, if kids is what you want.'

"Well, there's no two ways about it: Doug is pussy-whipped. Laura must be real dynamite, he gets her into bed, suck a goddamned golf ball through a hundred feet of garden hose, you ask her right. 'Cause what Laura says to do, that's what Dougie always does. It's kind of embarrassing, actually, seeing your own brother, kid you grew up inna same house with, acting like that around her. That's

. . . well, she *is* his own *wife* I mean, right? After all, they've been married for what, almost fifteen years now.

"You see a guy Doug's age," Brennan said, "he starts acting goofy like that around some dame, it's got to be the new girlfriend he just got. She's probably about nineteen or so, *va,* va-va; *va,* va-va; *voom.* And also real bright, of course, too. 'Meet my new receptionist, Heather.' She's gonna answer his phones for him now, really add some class to his office. Soon as he teaches her which end is which, you listen here, at this end and you talk in there to that. And then just hope she never forgets, doesn't get confused, when she's out front in the office and there's other people there, that what she's got in her hand there is a telephone you just put up *to* your mouth and not some other thing that you put right *into* it and then right down your throat. So sure, okay, it's kind of funny, guy that's at least middle-aged, he looks a little silly, hard-on's almost tearin' through his pants like he was a teenager again, but you're really not surprised. The wives that also know him, his friends' wives, okay? *They're* not even that surprised, or mad. Guy finally makes a lot of money, he can rip the sweet stuff off? It's not like he was the first one, took what he could never get. This thing goes on all the time.

"But this other thing, that Dougie does? Guy's still ga-ga, about his own *wife?* Makes no secret of it? Don't see *that,* that often. Kinda like makes a guy nervous, you know? Your wife happens to be there, sees him acting like that around his own wife, which naturally my Maggie does, family get-togethers and all, all you're gonna get for a week after that's the old deli special, my friend: hot tongue in the mornin', cold shoulder at night, and do what you want with your pickle, my friend—just don't try to serve it to her. Doug and Laura, all their kissy-face and oh, sweetie-pieing? They don't make it easy on the rest of us, they go around acting like that.

"But still, they're happy as hell; anyone can see that. And nobody can argue with that, am I right? Nobody can argue with that.

"So that is fine, they saved the money, they had the kids, and now they're all happy and all. Dougie's got his boat and now the kids're growin' up. Oldest one is nine. And they can start doing things that up 'til now they've been, you know, they've been a little young. Such as for example the Hallowe'ening, there. Trick-'r-treating, right? This year they can do that.

27

"Except," Brennan said, "except that one of the things that every-body in the family notices, right off, everyone but Doug, that is, is that Laura . . . when the kids first start getting old enough to do some things on their own, like go on pony rides or get started down the Y—they got a real nice Y over Quincy, very nice Y there, lots of activities—they have a hard time doing that, because Laura's com-ing too.

"Now I don't mean she's the same as all the other mothers that drive the kids the Y and then sit up in the bleachers and watch them get their lessons. I mean what she does is butter up the instructors from the day she signs the kids up, and she makes sure the swimming teacher that they actually draw knows she's got her Red Cross badge. Laura's a certified lifeguard or whatever they call them. And then, when her kids finally start, who's inna pool with them? Well, the young teacher is of course, but so is Mummy Laura, in her old teen-age bathing suit with the Red Cross badge sewn on.

"Now I can tell you, pal," Brennan said, "Laura's maybe still a damned good-lookin' woman for a woman her age, and she is. But she still *is* her age, you know? And she's still had the three kids now, since she was the Y teacher's age, which I never knew to make a woman's figure better-lookin', unless she was 'way too fat when she got knocked up and her doctor said she either hadda lose a lotta weight or else she would lose the kid, and she got scared enough to do it. But that was not the case with Laura, and the long and the short of it is that as far as she's concerned, there's also a few years gone by since she came home after the prom and didn't actually tell her mother that she finally let Doug use one of his prong-ons for what God meant it to be for. But of course she didn't have to tell her mother, did she? No, because her mother already knew. She knew the minute she saw Laura come in through that the door. She was very pleased that night, Laura's mother was. When she saw what'd happened, that she'd stayed up hoping she would see, well, she felt pretty doggoned good. Smart young girl her daughter'd turned out to be. Learned her lessons well, especially the ones her crafty old mother'd taught her, without saying a word. Just like her own mother taught her."

Brennan chuckled. "We can kid ourselves all we want," he said.

"It don't change a goddamned thing. They all learn it from their mothers, and that's how they get what they want."

"Which is what?" Dell'Appa said.

"What is 'what'?" Brennan said.

" 'What they want'?" Dell'Appa said. "You took that turn kind of fast on me there. Sorta left me alone at the crossroad."

"Well," Brennan said, "husbands, of course. Men. That's how they get a man to agree to take care of them and support them and protect them, and help them make babies. They can make fun of us as much as they want, but unless they can get something from us—either we inject it with the tool that old Mother Nature gave us or else we lope our ponies into little plastic shot glasses, and then some doctor shoots it up into them with a big hypodermic needle like they knock the cows up with—it's hopeless. Outta the question. They can't make any babies. And after they've made the babies, or just plain-old *gotten* old, so they start to sag and so forth, and no man'll look at them, and support them, and protect them in their old age, well, that's when they'd better've played the cards right, done what their mothers trained them to do back when they were perky little virgins with their pointy little titties: grabbed back then what they need now by trading what we wanted then for what they were gonna need later. So they have to—that's how they get those things. But they're just foolish, silly, if they think they can pretend afterward, after they had those kids, that they still look the same's they did when they were young. In bathing suits. No matter how much they want to. It isn't gonna happen. Unless they have plastic surgery there—I don't know anyone who did that, but I guess I wouldn't know if I did, would I, if she got any kind of a job—it doesn't matter at all. How much they want it to be. But that's what Laura was doing, with the swimming thing, and it wasn't happening. No way.

"My mother doesn't think that Laura even noticed. That it's dawned on her even now. Because the same exact thing happened with the pony rides, which're supposed to be the way the kids ease into it, get used to riding horses. So when they get a little bigger, they won't piss their pants and cry, maybe, they get put up on a horse."

"Sounds like a pretty good idea to me," Dell'Appa said.

"Oh, it is," Brennan said. "I was growing up of course, and the same with Doug and all the rest of us, and also the other kids we knew, hung around with after school: none of us, none of us had any trouble, learning to ride horses, not a bit. Because we didn't. It was completely outta the question. What it cost back then, rent a horse an hour, it was half what my dad brought home.

"He was in charge of Produce there, down the A and P. Thirty-one years, until one day they just announce they're gonna close the place, and then the big day comes, and a buncha guys in trucks drive up and boarded her right up. The good old A and P. 'The Great big Atlantic and Pacific, goddamned, no-good, double-crossin', son-of-a-bitchin', Tea Company.' That was what he always called it after that, when he come home at night after he'd been out there all day onna street, like all the other days after his store shut down: lookin' for another job. Not havin' any luck.

"It wasn't anything that complicated, so no one could understand it. He was too old. He knew it himself. No one was gonna hire a guy in his position then, not for the work he did. Almost sixty, a job in which you got no choice, you got to lift those crates? Fat chance. It wasn't gonna happen. You couldn't really blame those guys, the hiring guys, I mean. Men back then, in their sixties, most of them back when he was that age looked like over seventy today. Those store managers took a close look at him and they said themselves: 'Uh-uh, no part of this guy. He comes in, he lasts three weeks, and then: "Uh-oh, I hurt my back." And he goes off to see his doctor, that he went to grade school with, and the next thing that we're hearin' is that he's disabled. On our insurance plan. Which is where he's gonna stay, the next twenny years or so. Guys like this guy don't get better. Once they get disabled the only best thing left that they can ever hope to get is the one where they get dead. And when they're on your insurance, that can seem like it's taking a very long time. A hell of a goddamned long time.' So it's: 'Sorry, we got nothin' open just now. Drop by some other time.'

"But that isn't what they mean," Brennan said. "What they mean, what they meant then: that they never dared to say, and they never would today. Because then they would get sued, if they said what they meant: 'Not today, old buddy, nope. Not in our lifetimes. You're over the hill now, Granpa. Road-kill. Dead meat. Fossil City and long gone.' Even though Dad never would've done that, pretended he was hurt if he wasn't really hurt. He was the type of guy that wouldn't even fake a real bad cold into a case of flu, take three or four days off and maybe catch up on his sleep. He was 'way too honest. To him that was just stealing; my father didn't steal.

"But those strangers that he talked to, that were interviewing him? Had no way of knowing that. You couldn't blame them at all. But you still couldn't blame him, either. There wasn't anything he could do. It wasn't anything he'd done. It was just something that'd happened and then gone on and left him there, helpless, where he stood. He maybe smelled like beer those nights, like he didn't come straight home? Well, that was the reason. He knew what he was up against, and what he could do about it. Nothing. So on the way home he'd stop off at Sweeney's. Sweeney's at the bridge. It's gone now, years ago. Sweeney's ain't there any more. It got torn down. But it was there then, and he liked it. All of them old guys liked Sweeney's. Sweeney was an old guy himself. Shoot the shit with his old pals, my father would, all of them still pissed off, too, the stupid thing the company'd done to them and all their friends. After all those years. In jobs they were proud of, doing work that they did well. That was the last one for them, too, for most of them at least. Last job they ever had. Dad never got another one, 'til the day he died. Tried for over fourteen years, but he died unemployed, and at least ten or a dozen of those years, he could've done a job. It was really sad. A man, I think a man that wants to, and's in good health and all, I think he should be allowed to keep his job 'til he decides he wants to quit. Not 'til some young wise guy that he never even saw but who knows everything, of course, says: 'Everyone this old or older is too old to work, so boot their asses out.' "

"Isn't what you mean," Dell'Appa said, "that he died retired? Not that he was unemployed? He must've been well into his mid-seventies by then. They must've had pensions, the retirement plans and all."

"Oh, sure," Brennan said, "they had those. They had the pensions. Nothing like Fat City, no, but they were union men. So, yeah, they had their retirement pay, and their Social Security. It wasn't like he and Ma were destitute or anything. House was all paid off. There were six of us kids, but only four of us in school. Rest of us all were working. Still living at home, sure, we all were. Either 'til we got

31

drafted, the boys, or made up our minds to enlist. And the two girls out fishin' for marriage proposals, even though they were both still in school, but still working part time after school and on weekends. We were all paying our way. Dad and Ma had no reason to worry. They were all right as far as the money, as far as that was concerned.

"So: No," Brennan said, "it wasn't that. It was the job itself. It was not having the job. Dad'd always had one of those, ever since the Japs surrendered, he got discharged and came home. When he got laid off, it was like he'd been beaten himself, worse'n the Japs ever were. By his own people, people he fought to protect. That's what he couldn't get over: Americans did this to him.

"When he still had the job, which he did until we were mostly all grown up, like I said, he was a different kind of man. He was proud of himself. Oh, sure, he was always griping that he should've had more money. Or some big promotion with a nice raise that some young college boy'd gotten should by rights've gone to him. But just the same, he knew what he was then. And whether you and I now'd look at what he did back then and say: 'Well, it wasn't all that much, throwin' cabbages around,' well, that doesn't really matter now. And it wouldn't've mattered then, either. At least not to him. Right or wrong, he was proud of what he did, proud of the job he had, and that he did it well.

"And so he was also proud of the money that he earned, and that was the end of horse questions. Those were honorable wages he brought home. Dollars that he worked for so he could take care of his family. As he'd promised he would do, and as a man did anyway, if he was a man. So how those dollars got spent, what they got spent for, that was also important. They couldn't be wasted. What they went for had to be something just as honorable and important as his work that'd earned them. Because if it wasn't, well then, he was a fool to be taking the whole thing so seriously and working so hard to bring those dollars home. So, when he figured out that for working that same hour that one of us would spend riding the horse, half of what he made would've gone to pay that horse, Dad got good and mad. He hit the roof. 'I will be damned,' he said, when the question came up that once—I think it was my sister Amy was the one that brought it up—'I will be damned if I will work half of every hour, or half of any goddamned hour, just throw away thirty goddamned minutes out of my damned life that I will never see again, to pay a stupid god-damned *horse* to work for only twice as long.' And that was the end of it. Never come up again in our house, least that I ever heard.

"But Doug, like I say, he's done real good, and this is a different generation. So his kids're now gonna learn how to ride. The horse could be making as much as, oh, one of us is, even one of those so-called major-league ballplayers you got now—two-million-a-year, two-thirty-two banjo-hitter who lets the easy grounders go right through his legs, and when he does catch one, throws it over the first baseman's head into the dugout, and then shoots off his mouth to the press about how it wasn't his fault. It wouldn't matter to Doug. Those kids, to Doug: it's like they're, you know, the British royal family there, fuckin' dummies they are. But, something along that line, right? Prolly grow up chasin' foxes and stuff, screwin' everyone but their own husbands and wives, the ones they're supposed to be screwin'.'"

"I still don't see anything wrong with it," Dell'Appa said. "The horses, I mean. Maybe not with the Royal Family either. I woke up every day, had to look at one of those dames over my newspaper and my morning coffee, I think I might run around. And considering how I look, how I am most mornings, I dunno as I could really blame a dame who got so bored she couldn't stand it, and then fooled around on me.

"But, your brother's young kids learning horseback riding? Sounds just great to me. All this screaming bullshit about the yuppies and their kids: the ballet lessons; private schools; the gymnastics, vacations, and music lessons; blah blah blah: 'These kids're growin' up spoiled.' Well, so what if they are? I wish when I was growing up, my parents'd had that kind of money, spoil the ass off of me. Buy me computer games and stuff, take me to Disney World. But okay, so they didn't. Shame on them and shame on me. I still've done all right, I think, even with my dee-prived childhood. I checked my head this morning, I got out of bed, and it's still screwed on nice and straight. But, would I've liked it better, if my folks'd had the money so that they could buy me everything my little heart desired, and so that was what they did? Go to Boston, or New York, even, every Saturday, and wall-to-wall FAO Schwarz? Leavin' nothin' but the shelves and my orders for next week? You bet your ass I would've. I would've gone apeshit for that, if I'd grown up that way. So, you can afford it? Fine. If you can, and if you want to, then by all means do it. If you got the money, and your kids appreciate it—because not all of 'em will; some of them're little shits, just like some grown-ups are—but if they can have a good time and then still be nice kids after-wards, well, take 'em to Saint Louie, Louie, take 'em to the fair."

"That isn't what I'm sayin'," Brennan said with weariness. "If you'd ever give me a chance to finish, you'd know it isn't. The swim-ming lessons and the riding lessons, all the other stuff: I'm all for that, all right? I agree with you. What I'm trying to tell you is that when Doug and Laura's kids go swimming, go to learn to swim, Laura goes swimming too. When the kids're gonna go onna pony rides, and so they're putting on their black *jackets,* and their special tan *pants,* and their hundred-dollar fancy *boots,* and their special little *black hats* that look like the derbies there, but they're really hard hats you could wear on a construction site and have a whole bucket of hot rivets drop on your head from thirty stories up, without gettin' a hair outta place, guess who's also putting on the whole damned horsie uniform? Laura is, is who. By the time Dougie's little family's all ready to go down the Blue Hills Reservation there and ride the little ponies, they've got on enough horse-clothes that cost a whole shitload of money that if you put it all together and used it to buy a horse instead, you could buy at least one of them that maybe wasn't quite fast enough to beat the other horsies in the tenth, the dogfood race, onna card at Upsan Downs, but still can walk and eat and shit, and then you'd have your own. Your own living, breathing horse. You could ride him any time, in your own old clothes and your big brother's hockey helmet. Any time you liked.

"And that is what I mean, that's the sort of thing I mean. That's what Laura does, that's the kind of thing she does and she did on Hallowe'en. And then ten days later, the same thing. It didn't make no sense the first time, made no sense at all, so naturally, first chance she got, the first excuse she had, she did it all again. The woman isn't right. She gets all excited and so forth about something new that she's going to do with the kids, and how great it's gonna be for them, that pretty soon she's completely forgotten what it really is that they're gonna do, and why it was gonna be so great for the kids. And then all she can think about is all the new things she's gonna need to do this, and how many of them. And that's what they always end up doing: getting dressed up in new outfits, messing around with a bunch of new gadgets, and making no sense at all. And she did it again, Hallowe'en."

"What: 'she did'?" Dell'Appa said.

"With the toilet paper," Brennan said. "Doug goes off to work this particular morning, just before Hallowe'en, and I guess it seemed safe enough. Laura's acting normal, right? Normal as she ever does. She's making breakfast for the kids, and they're all excited, like little kids always get 'fore Hallowe'en, about what they're gonna be, what they're gonna go as, how they're gonna be dressed up when they go out Hallowe'en—nothing wrong with that. So Doug goes out, gets in his car, and he goes off to his office. And he puts in his regular day's work, prolly makes thirty grand, maybe forty; goes from there to the gym, works out an hour. Then he showers, gets dressed, and goes home. Where he gets a little surprise. The big red maples, both sides of the driveway, the shrubs and the dogwoods, all that stuff? Every single *tree*, every single *shrub*, every single anything that's in that goddamned yard and's got a branch on it that isn't right down on the ground: every goddamned one of them is draped with toilet paper."

"Toilet paper," Dell'Appa said, "hanging from the trees and stuff?"

"You got it," Brennan said. "Seems that after Doug left for work, Laura and the kids got so interested, talking about the costumes that she's making for the three of them, just the kids, now for Hallowe'en —so far as I heard, I don't *think* Laura's planning to go out with them wearin' a tall, pointy black hat and a long pointy nose, ridin' on a carpet-sweeper or something, although I could be wrong on that— that they lose all track of time and the kids miss the school bus. Well, two of them miss the school bus and the other one misses the kinder- garten minivan. So Laura has to take them. In her new BMW wagon."

"*Hey,*" Dell'Appa said, "nice, but *nice*. That's a pretty pricey item."

"I'm here to tell you," Brennan said, "it lists for over forty grand there, and by the time you get through adding on the sales tax and the luxury and all that other crap, you're gettin' a lot closer to fifty'n

I'd feel comfortable being. Where the cars're concerned, well, it isn't like it is with the boats, with Dougie; where cars're involved, Doug doesn't stint.

"But it's really kind of funny, you know? How often those kids of theirs're missing buses alla time now, since Doug bought it. When Laura had the Audi sedan, the kids never had this trouble. The buses came at the same times—nothing's changed on that. And Laura back then always had the kids all ready, waiting for their rides. No big deal. But since the Bimmer comes her way, well, nobody can get started now in time to catch their bus. My own suspicion is—I don't mind telling you this; I would not say it to Doug—that once they really did miss the buses; the first time, they actually did. So that time it was legit. Laura really hadda do it; she didn't have a choice. But then, she did it that time, my guess is that she happened to spot someone that she really doesn't like, looking that new car over and getting the old slow-burn on. I mean: really jealous. Eating their belly out. And that's where this all comes from.

"I don't mean that it's just Laura," Brennan said. "That's not what I'm saying to you here. It's all women. Women in general. Women're really mean like that, much worse'n we are, about those kinds of things. They're much quicker to notice it when something that they're doing, that they've got a perfect right to do; something that nobody's got any right to stop them from doing; but just the same there really isn't any need for them to be doing that particular thing right then, and that particular thing at that particular point in time— putting makeup on, but doing it right at the table in the restaurant, maybe, instead of going to the ladies' room—is really getting on someone's nerves? It's really getting their goat. Well, a woman'll notice that, always. And the minute, hell, *the second,* that she does, bang, that's it. She's gonna do it some more. A lot more. Even if she's finished, and doesn't need to, do it any more. If it's the lipstick-and-makeup thing, she's gonna put on so much of it, and screw around with it so long, that if you timed her without seeing what it really was that she was doing, you would think that she was grooming a big old poodle for a dog-show on TV from Madison Square Garden. Or maybe a whole horse, for a horse-show."

Brennan paused and reflected. "I think it's because when a woman deliberately does things that she knows'll really get on somebody else's nerves, really yank their chain for them, there is usually not the slightest chance that the person that she's pissing off like that is gonna say to her, like they would to you and me, and sincerely mean it: '*Oh*-kay, that creases it. If you do that once more, I'm gonna get out of this chair, which I don't wanna do because I got my feet up and I'm all nice and comfortable, and I'm gonna haul off and hit you so hard inna mouth that when your first grandchildren start getting born, they'll all need Polident too.'

"I'm not talkin' about the Buddies of this world here now, the Buddies that whack their women around for no reason. Or the hookers that fight worse'n men do, the street-whores protecting their corner. They got nothing to do with this here. What I'm talking about with respectable women like Laura, an' it doesn't matter if they're black or white, is . . . I'm not saying they should get bopped when they deliberately piss other people off. What I'm saying to you here is that they don't even ever get warned, you know, *threatened,* with a good shot upside the head, if they don't cut it out and start behaving themselves. Not that either one of us'd ever do it, go ahead and actually *do* it or anything, hit a woman like that, I mean, but still, the way things are it's not even something that they even have to even, you know, even *think* about. So as far as they're concerned there isn't any reason to behave themselves if they're having any fun at all when they're *mis*-behaving. See?"

"I'm not sure," Dell'Appa said. "Lemme sleep on it, get back to you on it in the morning."

"Well," Brennan said, "on their way to the various schools, Laura and the kids apparently see this house where there obviously lives somebody as nutty as Laura. And that other nutbag'd already gone and draped the trees all over with the toilet paper, and it took them awhile, Laura and the kids, to figure out it's supposed to be, in the dark with some lights on it people're supposed to think it's Hallowe'en ghosts. In the trees, and they think: 'Wow, what a real great . . .' "

Brennan leaned forward fast in the seat and stared at the outside rearview mirror. Dell'Appa looked at his watch. It read 7:09. "Nope," Brennan said, relaxing again, "that's not him. I thought it was him for a minute, comin' to catch the seven-fourteen. He's done that some times. But today isn't one of them, I guess."

37

• • •

"*Yeah*," Gayle said slowly, that night at the table, turning her knife back and forth beside her plate and frowning at it, drawing the word out as though it had been an extremely fine thread of some delicate fabric that would fray and then break if pulled too hard, "remember back before Roy was conceived, when we were still living in Brighton? And I was still doing my training research? Remember that patient I had? That mild mousey young woman from Everett who dressed like she was Miss Jane Marple in real life, and looked like her, too, even though she was fifty years younger, but then turned out to have that, well, rather unusual habit?"

"Sure," he said, "the cockgazer-spinster. Male subway riders were complaining. She wanted what she didn't have. But, geez, Brennan? I doubt that it's that. The old bastard does have four kids."

"Oh," she said, "not penis-envy, no. *Money.* But it amounts to the same thing. His younger brother's success is something he doesn't have. But he can't be jealous of it, as he could—and most likely would—if someone else had it. No, no. To disapprove of Dougie's big money would disapprove of himself, if he did that. He'd be a jealous big brother. So instead he disapproves of Doug's pretty wife—and I'll bet, I would *bet*, his good wife's plain, and he ignores her—but he puts it in terms of her conduct. And now even his mother agrees."

Dell'Appa didn't say anything for a few minutes. "*Yeah*," he said, "yeah, that could be."

"Now, Natty Bumpo," Gayle said, slyly smiling, "wanna talk about how come he's so glad to see *you* back from your wilderness days? Since you claim you mean him no harm?"

"I didn't say that," he said.

3 Late Monday afternoon Lieutenant Dennison had been careful in all respects. "No need for hastiness, Harry," he had said to Dell'Appa. "No call for concern. Take your time. Proceed calmly. Be of the best possible cheer. People and things change so constantly, but so gradually, that when—heck, because —we're around them all the time, we don't even notice what's going on until the whole commotion's over. And then, when we start trying to figure out just when the whole rigamarole started, and what we've got on our hands now, we get slam-dunked again. Our watches're no good. The calendar's what's called for. And when we do get the main time-frame sorted out, well, we have to deal with the inner clock.

"See, while everything else was changing, so were we. We were changing too. You've been gone almost a year. A whole year that Bob's spent adding to that file, Short Joey's file. While you were out of here, loose in the woods by yourself, as far as he's concerned—because you weren't where you could see him, watch him like a hawk, and he wasn't watching you, because he couldn't see you either—during that year he was changing. Just like the file that he was working on was changing. And like you were, too, yourself. Independently of one another. So was I.

"Well, there's no need to get all lathered up when that happens, let alone when it finally dawns on you that it happened. Take your time. Like I've had to. Like we all've had to, one reason or another. I've got a brand-new house."

"What was the matter with your old house?" Dell'Appa had said. "The house in Canton, right? With the sunken living room, picture window, overlooking the golf course? One good strong lefty golfer with a nasty slice, you're getting fresh air up the ass? I thought you and Tory liked that house. Never understood quite why, but I did get that impression."

"And you were right," Dennison had said. "We liked it very much. But we don't live in it any more. Because we changed. Or we got changed. Against our will. Amounts to the same thing, I guess, although I'd bet if it was your idea, you'd like it a lot better. Lemme give you directions to the Dennison ancestral home we now occupy in Westport.

"You've got to bear with me now," he had said. "This's no exaggeration. Don't get the idea that anything I'm telling you maybe ought to be discounted by at least a dime, most likely a quarter, even fifty-percent, maybe, off the sticker-price. I know how it's going to sound to you by the time I get through: as though somewhere along the line I must've gradually begun to take leave of my wits. You may've been pretty sure we were on the same planet when we started out, but you'll be absolutely certain when I'm finished that somehow I went into a time-warp you didn't happen to notice, and we've come out in different spheres. The only reason you can still see me and hear me is because I did manage to insert myself into a geosynchronous orbit. But I will sound like I'm no longer on earth. Because that's the way it sounds to everybody—it's the way it sounded to me when it'd first happened, or I first began to realize it'd happened, and I tried telling it to myself—just to see how it would sound.

" 'Well, no, it's not actually our house. Well, it is our house, *now* anyway, but that wasn't what it was supposed to be. It's really just the way it sort of worked out. See, this house, where it is and all, this, well, it wasn't our idea. It was never our idea to buy it is what I mean. Which, as a matter of fact, we didn't, although we're certainly buying it now and we're going to be, and not only for the foreseeable future either; also for the unforeseeable one beyond that. Buying it, that is. For nine more years. At least. Heck, we didn't even want to move into it, but we more or less had to, and now the reason we moved in, the lady we moved in to be with, well, she isn't around anymore.

"Here or anyplace else, really; we had her cremated and scattered her ashes on the wind, room-service, you could call it, for the Buzzards of the Bay, if there're any still alive. Because that was what she wanted, and one way or the other, whatever Virginia wanted was what you always ended up doing. It shifted, of course, the wind did, while we were right in the midst of doing it, sprinkling Virginia, I mean, so some of her got blown back into our faces—ashes-sprinkling and -scattering. They're like peeing, I guess: never sprinkle to windward; always sprinkle to leeward. Otherwise you'll get a good faceful of the dearly departed. 'Depart*ing*,' I guess I should say, 'dearly depart*ing*,' and none too gracefully, either. Damned gritty customer, Virginia was, not only when she was alive and but then also after, *especially* after, we'd had her crispy-crittered. She did have that streak of cussedness, she did. She probably *wanted* sprinkling her to be a big pain in the ass, too. Just like she'd always been herself, at least when she had a choice. But it doesn't matter. Not now, anyway. What matters now, when what we'd naturally like to do is move out of the goddamned ark we didn't want to move into in the first place, is: we can't. We might as well be in chains.'

"Now you have to agree with me," Dennison had said, "the whole story's plainly preposterous. Completely true, in every respect, of course, but still: sounds completely preposterous. Prisoners. Of our very own house. Which of course it actually isn't, never was and never will be, because it's not a house we ever wanted. For a house to be *your house,* in the actual meaning of the term, it has to be, right from the very beginning, a house that *you* really want. And this one that we've got, we never did. At all. But we're stuck with the damned thing, just the same."

"Cannon said it looks like a horror-movie set," Dell'Appa had said. "He told me one day when he had to do something in Pittsfield and stopped by for a beer with me in Northampton on his way back here. He said you and Tory'd had him and Jackie to dinner and it'd been a hell of a bad night, thunder and lightning, all that shit, and he said when he first saw that house: 'I thought I must've taken a wrong turn along the way, and I was at the Bates Motel.' He said Jackie said to him: ' "Well, okay, but just dinner. That's all I'm stayin' for. Brian may claim this's Tory's mother's house, but I have seen the movie there, and I'm takin' no showers in *that* joint." '

Dennison had laughed. "Well," he had said, "I wouldn't argue with him. I don't agree with him, but I wouldn't argue with him. To me it looks more like a big Mediterranean-seaside villa designed by somebody, some architect, who knew exactly what the classic design of that genre called for, and understood that his client had a very precise picture of the finished structure in his head, exactly corresponding to the classic design. So the designer, quite prudently, followed it devoutly, and no doubt his client was delighted. And the architect certainly was not.

"Oh, as a professional he most likely felt a certain sense of satisfaction; it's the pro's job, once he takes it on, to carry out the client's wishes, not his own, and there couldn't've been any question but that he'd done that, in spades. Because there's no mistaking what it is, or what it was meant to be: a three-story, mauve stucco villa, with claret trim around the windows and doors, and a maroon terra-cotta-tiled mansard roof—which is, not so incidentally, a hellishly-expensive bauble to maintain and repair, all those little hooks and wires holding everything in place like the guts of a Swiss chronometer, until the weather inevitably does to the whole arrangement exactly what New England weather would do to a Swiss watch if you left the guts of it exposed outdoors for a year or so. The first one or two hooks and wires let go so the whole thing starts to slide off and go crashing down piecemeal into the shrubbery.

"It's perfect, you see," Dennison said. "It just isn't perfect for here. What it would be absolutely perfect for would be a choice site on the lower slope of a Côte d'Azur corniche with southeastern exposure to the ocean. An exact copy, in other words, of the mansion-house where the designer's client had spent his halcyon, wealthy boyhood, the eldest child and only son of an international merchant who'd made himself princely-rich by means of his shrewdness in the selection of rugs, woven in the Land of the Peacock Throne. Rugs that he purchased by the bale, cheap, for resale in units, at retail-expensive, to people with far more cash'n brains back home in America.

"No, the trouble with the house wasn't then and isn't now with *what* it is; the trouble's all with *where* it is. Adriatic, Mediterranean: either one of those would've been the ideal place for it. Wouldn't've mattered in the slightest. But smack-dab in the middle of a Bristol County, Massachusetts meadow—slightly rolling, very pretty, very pleasant, very Fairfield Porter, or maybe Fairfield County—especially in springtime when the wildflowers're in bloom—well, even though it's in Westport and you can smell—and sense—Buzzards Bay to the south, it's a good mile and a half from the harbor. So much for any hope of seeing open water. Which's fatal, for a house like this one. It *has* to overlook the water. No option. Mandatory. You can't have a house as tight-assholed as this on any site where the surroundings—the terrain and vegetation, no matter how spacious and open they might look to some Bronx tenement refugee, someone who'd grown up in a city—'re going to give even the slightest hint that something may be closing in on you. But that didn't matter. That fact didn't matter and neither did the architect's opinion, which I can state with assurance even though I never met the chap and don't even know who he was. The architect knew, one this good would've known this, had to've known this, that if you build a house like that, in a place like that, where you cannot see the ocean from a minimum of one major window in every important room, every room where anyone's going to spend any amount of time, and then you go and live in it long enough, sooner or later you will find that you've begun to lose your mind. But that's the location that our architect's customer owned, and the one he'd picked, and where he wanted his dream house to be built, which carried a certain amount of weight in the decision: he was, after all, the fellow who was going to be paying for the fucking thing. The first time it got paid for, at least. So it didn't matter to him that everyone who lived in it after he got through with it would begin to lose their marbles fairly soon after they moved in."

43

"Communications with the spirit world, all that sort of thing?" Dell'Appa had said.

"Well, sure," Dennison had said, "but in the old lady's case, that was nothing especially new. She'd started having regular conversations with dead people right after Tory's father died. Only well-known dead people, though. Virginia was very picky. About everything."

"Well, that's not uncommon," Dell'Appa had said. "Lots of widows that my mother knows, friends of hers that've lost their husbands, they have those kinds of conversations. She brought it up one night when Gayle and I were over for dinner, my father was griping about some trivial thing or other—she'd left the porch-light on all night or something, and he was saying he'd have to give some more thought to getting a divorce if it happened again, part of their standard routine—and she said she supposed he'd gotten so he liked nagging her so much he'd come back and do it after he was dead. Like his old friend Mike was doing to Rose now. And my father didn't like that at all."

"Death's never been his favorite subject," Dennison had said.

"Uh-uh," Dell'Appa had said, "not by any means. He just clams up when it's mentioned. I think making a good living, doing something he thought he might like to do, and being good at it; I think all of that was probably only part of the reason he went to law school. The other part was that he figured there must be a loophole somewhere in the rule that says we're all gonna die. Death and taxes, right? The two inevitables. The inescapables. But taxes aren't, inescapable, at least not all taxes, when you come right down to it. They're not all inevitable, I mean. A good many of them can be avoided, if you're careful and determined. Lots of loopholes in tax laws. So then, if it's possible that a good lawyer can show you a way to skate around the tax law, maybe a good lawyer could also find an escape hatch in the death law, and help you duck around that. Of course you'd probably then find out that for tax-purposes it'd still be better if you died, say, by the end of your current fiscal year. 'If all else fails, you might even consider hiring that batty doctor out in the Midwest who helps people kill themselves. Not that I'm suggesting you're incurably ill, or anything that disagreeable, not at all. In your case, it would be purely for tax-purposes.'

"Not that my father'd do that. He's 'way too conceited. That's what I think really ticks him off about death: the possibility that the world could ever get along without him, now that he's been in it. He's the type that wouldn't be discouraged by the fact that no other lawyer's ever managed to find a way to get around death. He'd most likely figure that's just because until now there hasn't been a lawyer who's been as smart as he is. So, if there *is* a way out of death, and anyone's going to find it, he of course would be the boy who would do it. Hasn't yet, as far as I know, but I'm sure he's still working on it, there, boy. But anyway, if your mother-in-law and your father-in-law were close . . ." Dell'Appa had said.

"Uh-uh," Dennison had said. "Well, no closer'n any other couple that's been married over thirty years, I mean. And besides, the conversations she started having—or started admitting she was having, after he died; could be they weren't something new. Just something she'd thought she'd better keep to herself until he died; didn't want him to have her put away. But her people on the Other Side, in the Great Beyond? After he died, and they had their meetings with her, they didn't have him along with them. He wasn't one of her callers. Far's she ever let on to us, at least. If he did attend, he apparently didn't have much to say. Or if he did, it didn't seem to have made a real lasting impression on her. She didn't allow him any more airtime after he was dead'n she had when he was still alive. Not that there was anything new in that. She never had been all that interested in what Stan had to say, anyway, even back when he was alive, right in the same room with her.

"So: no," Dennison had said, "it wasn't the house, when she got the house, that the dead people'd started talking to her. That'd been going on for a long time. I dunno as you could properly classify what she had with them as *conversations*, though, come to think of it—so far's I ever heard, they only talked to her; she didn't talk to them. At least not in the beginning, and I don't think after that, either. If they ever did let her have a two-way hook-up, send as well as receive. I don't believe so. If they did, she never let on. When she told us about something she'd learned, say, from Douglas MacArthur or somebody, it was always what this particular famous dead person'd had on *his* mind to say to *her*. 'Mister Poe,' for example."

"As in 'Edgar Allen'?" Dell'Appa said.

"The very fellow," Dennison said. " 'Mister Poe told me that he served in Battery H of the First Artillery at Fort Independence on Castle Island under the name of Edgar A. Perry, and rose to the rank of lieutenant,' she told us. 'This would've been in Eighteen-and-twenty-seven, he was there, when he was eighteen years old. Mister Poe said that while he was in Boston some of the other soldiers told him about how another young lieutenant by the name of Robert Massie had been killed in a duel on Christmas Day ten years before, and his friends had become so angry that they got the other man drunk and took him down to the dungeon in the fort and chained him to the floor and then bricked up the wall and went away, left him in there to die by himself. And Mister Poe said he wrote a story about that, he did change it somewhat, but he didn't say what it was. So I wouldn't know about that.' "

"You're shittin' me," Dell'Appa said. " 'The Cask of Amontillado'?"

"*Hey*," Dennison said. "For the love of God, Montresor, *I* am not shitting you, man. The late *Virginia* may be shitting you, posthumously using me as her helpless cat's paw, but I am not shitting you." He smirked. "Besides, it checks out, some of it. That's how old Poe was, when she said it happened, and he did enlist here, under an alias. And they did find a skeleton, chained to the floor of the fort, in a four-brick-walled room with no entryway, back in Nineteen-oh-five. It was dressed in a full uniform. Tory went to the library one day and looked it up. *After* Virginia, told us."

"Would your mother-in-law have done something like that," Dell'Appa said.

"Looked up stuff like that, just to goose us?" Dennison said. "Or maybe remembered it from something she maybe heard when she was a little girl, about the body being found? Put it this way: if she'd thought of it, and she was bored, yeah, she might've gone to the trouble. But she didn't need to, she didn't need that stuff; she kept us hopping with no effort at all.

"But anyway, that was the sort of encounter that she seemed to have with the dead people. What Mister Poe or another one of them'd had on his mind to say to her. Not what she might've had on her mind, to've said to him. Which would've gone to show, I guess, that they were just as smart as she always claimed they were. Her consultants, I mean, as she referred to them. On the Other Side—that was the only address she ever gave us, where they could be reached. Where she could reach them, at least."

He had paused. "And that's another funny thing, I just thought of now: all of her consultants, least all the ones I ever heard about, all of them were dead, famous, *American men. White* American men: no minority-group representation at all. No affirmative action on the Other Side, I guess. No dead famous foreigners either. And, come to think of it, no dead famous *women* in her little circle. Huh. Have to mention that to Tory tonight, give her chain a little tug, here. Wonder if she's ever noticed that, no dead women've amounted to enough to interest Virginia, not while they were alive."

"Won't get you anywhere," Dell'Appa had said. "She'll just come right back at you and say the reason was her mother's generation'd been brainwashed, growing up, to ignore what women did."

"Yeah, probably," Dennison had said. "Anyway, though, Virginia had a lot of faith in them, her invisible pals. She told us how badly Mister Parker felt, Mister Harvey Parker, that he had no way of knowing, when John Wilkes Booth checked into his hotel back in April, 'Sixty-five, why he was practicing his pistol shooting nearly every day at the shooting gallery down the street, and what it was he planned to do when he got to Washington only ten days later. She said that Mister Parker always felt that if he'd only known, Mister Lincoln might've lived.

"And they also gave practical advice, her visitors did," Dennison said. "She said in fact they were the ones who told her how to get the house, so at least we know who's to blame. They told her how to bet. What numbers to play in Megabucks. When Tory found out she was doing that, writing down the numbers her consultants recommended to her during their visits, or seances, whatever they were, and then having Lucy buy the tickets for her twice a week, when she went to the store to do the grocery-shopping, well, at first Tory thought—and I thought, too—all this nonsense was some of Lucy's doing. That Lucy'd been filling the old lady up with a big daily ration of some of that old Creole black magic, bayou-ragtime-voodoo she'd most likely brought up north with her all the way from old Metairie. Maybe had the old lady usin' dream-books to choose numbers, same's she did herself. Next thing, we figured, old Mama-Doc Lucy'd have Virginia sacrificin' goats or something, hoodoo-voodoo on the back porch, every moonless night. So that was the first thing that came to our attention: this nice little old lady, looked like she was living out the string of a perfectly-ordinary, commonplace life in her nice peaceful little white house on a nice, quiet, tree-lined street in Taunton, well, it began to look as though she might not only've gone 'round the bend at a pretty good clip but then'd kept right on going, and'd traveled a good distance down the track beyond it, in fact, before we'd begun to catch on. Kind of frightening, it was. We had some thinking to do.

"See," Dennison had said, "Tory got Lucy in to help her mother out. It was just temporary, after she had the hip replacement operation. Someone to fetch and carry for her while she couldn't get around. Found her through an employment outfit, an agency that the doctor's office recommended. Specialized in that kind of thing. Just 'til she got back on her feet.

"Wasn't 'til a good deal later," Dennison had said, "we commenced to find out Lucy hadn't been wholly in agreement with those terms. What she'd had was what they call one of them-there 'mental reservations whatsoever' that the fellow with the Bible always asks you if you're hiding, when you take an oath to serve, so help you God, and you're not supposed to be. Holding something back, something you're not telling him. As though you'd admit it to him if you did have one, and it wasn't broad enough to cover keeping it a secret itself. Lucy's mental reservation would've been broad enough for that. She sure hadn't seen any reason to mention it to us when she first came. Course at the time we didn't even have a Bible with us, not that we would've thought to ask. She didn't surface it until after the business with the lotteries came to light, when we started paying a bit more attention to what was going on between the two of them those happy days, in that little house. Then it sort of dawned on us, what'd really been going on. Lucy hadn't been gettin' any younger herself, when Virginia'd been discharged from the hospital to convalesce at home. Hadn't been for some time, in fact, certainly not by the time she showed up to work for us. And full well did she know it, too, did old Lucy know this."

Dennison had gentled his voice, introducing a mourning tone and elegiac cadence. "Yes sir, Lucy'd been a mite footsore herself, right from the very beginning of her stay with us. That was how it'd started to look. Kind of *tired,* you know? *'Tarred,'* that's what she called it. 'Ah'm *tarred.* Go an' lay day-own a wahl here, an' ray-ust.' Way you'd be bound to get, you'd been like her, just bummin' around all your whole, entire life. No security to speak of, not a bit. Sure couldn't live on what the government was gonna give her when the day come, she couldn't work no more. Knew that much. Had friends, tryin' do that, goin' hungry half the time, put out their homes, them's had 'em, not that many of 'em did, they worked so hard to get. Spent their *whole lives,* just like her, gypsyin' from place to place, this job to that one, then thuh othuh one, never settlin' down. Now they'd gone and gotten old, and jus' *look* the fix they're in.

"And that was another thing we two dopes hadn't noticed until then," Dennison had said, in his normal tone of voice. "Lucy was no fool. She maybe hadn't brought a degree from Tulane up from Loozyanna with her, but she was smart enough to know a good thing when she stumbled into it, and smart enough after that to do her level best not to stumble out of it. So in the natural course of things Lucy'd already seen to it she and the old lady'd become pretty attached to each other. When Tory first tried to suggest to her mother, maybe Lucy should be getting in touch with the agency, thinking generally about where she might be going next—Lucy's services not being free, gratis and for nothing, by any stretch of the imagination, and the old lady's means being very far from sufficient to support a live-in maid, cook, or whatever the hell it was Lucy'd managed to become by then, in addition to covering her own expenses of living by herself, well, 'Ginia—which was what Lucy called her—raised a fearful stink.

"Didn't make the slightest bit of difference at all to Virginia that Lucy'd been getting paid, when she first came, out of medical insurance limited to reimbursement of the cost of her convalescent care. Or that now that she was up and about, on her feet again, the insurance people were going to say she'd finished convalescing, and so those payments'd run out. Which meant: therefore so should Lucy.

"No sirree Bob, 'Ginia wouldn't hear of it. She and Lucy'd gotten by all right, and they'd continue to get by. They might have to economize some, she realized that—cut down on the number of pay-perview movies they ordered up from the cable-TV people, most likely, that sort of thing. But they'd be perfectly all right, just the same, and if what Tory was concerned about was *her* inheritance, that her mother might be going through that, if *that* was what was *really* on her mind, well, Tory and I—somehow I'd become a party to this discussion, in her mother's estimation, despite the fact I wasn't anywhere near the place that day, I was fifty–sixty miles away and had no idea it was even going to take place—well, we could just face up to the fact that Tory's father'd left that money to *her,* his poor dear widow, first and foremost, so if there was anything *she* needed, or *anything she wanted,* after he was dead and gone, well, she was to have it, without a second thought. And it was only if—'Capital *If,'* she said to Tory—there was something left after she died, that Tory was to get anything, anything at all. So we, Tory and I, 'the two of you,' was what she said, we could 'just stop worrying about that, and mind your own damn business for a change.' "

"And did you?" Dell'Appa had said.

"Of course not," Dennison had said. "It was a mighty tempting offer, sure, but one we couldn't even think about. We couldn't do that, couldn't've done it even if we'd wanted to. Tory's an only child, no one else to take care of her mother. As Virginia'd been herself, an only child, so she had no sisters or brothers of her own who might've helped to look after her. Tory's father'd had a couple of sisters and a brother, but none of them lived around here and they'd never had much contact with their brother or his wife, even when Stan was alive. Stan's brother didn't even come to the funeral. His sister, Katherine, said he was laid up in Tucson, which was where he'd retired to, with phlebitis in his right leg, and that may've been true, I suppose. Although Virginia made it pretty clear she didn't think so. But the long and the short of it was that Tory was it: if she didn't look after her mother and her interests, who else was there around who could be trusted to do it, and'd also actually go through then, and *do* it? No one, that's who.

"Not that I blame anyone," he had said. "Not for one minute do I blame them. One of the reasons, one of the principal reasons, that it costs so much to hire and then keep people to take care of the elderly is because it's no damned picnic taking care of the elderly all day. It's a lousy, rotten job, that's what it is. The patients're sick and they're frail, and some of them're just plain downright mean. They're queru-

lous, and demanding, and unhappy. A good many of them deliberately spend a good part of every day rolling around in their own shit.
They haven't lost control of their bowels or their bladder. They're not
incontinent at all. They soil themselves and mess their beds out of
sheer cussedness, because they've got a mad on at the person taking
care of them and know how much that person hates cleaning up shit,
and cleaning the shit off of them, or they do it because what they'd
really like to do is shit on the relatives who put them into care, but
the relatives know what they're thinking and're too smart to come
within range."

"Pure spite," Dell'Appa had said.

"Spite, pure and simple," Dennison said, "and Virginia had it in
spades. The only way we could ever figure out to get ourselves a fifty-
fifty chance of her doing what we actually wanted her to do was by
convincing her that we passionately wanted her to do the opposite.
And then, if she decided to do anything at all—which was never
guaranteed; she was very clever, and she'd long since figured out, or
good old Lucy'd told her, that her scheming daughter and her wicked
son-in-law might not be above pulling some reverse psychology on
her. So unless she was completely sure that we sincerely wanted her
to celebrate her eighty-second birthday by taking up sky-diving or
bungee-jumping, she might not only refuse to rent a parachute or a
long rubber-band; she might not do anything at all. But if we did
convince her that we truly thought something was an absolutely
rotten idea, then there was at least an even chance that what she did
decide to do might turn out to be what we'd actually had in mind.
What we'd thought she ought to do in the first place. But we never
could be sure. There was always that lingering uncertainty. It was
like batting against a young Nolan Ryan–type pitcher in a night
baseball game with no lights on: you're up there in the dark with just
a thin stick to use to defend yourself against a fastball coming at you
at a hundred and six miles an hour, and the crazy-wild kid who's
throwing it's got no more idea in this world where it's going'n you've
got, when he rares back and lets 'er rip.

"So for, say, Virginia's last eight or ten years in this vale of tears,
well, not every day turned out to be exciting, but still, when you woke
up in the morning, there was always the distinct chance that things
might all of a sudden *get* pretty exciting. There was always that

exhilarating possibility. Along with the knowledge that if there was an uproar in the making, you'd be hip-deep in the middle of something else that was really important to you when you first caught wind of it. 'Up to yo' *ass* in alli-ga-*tors*,' as I heard old Lucy say once.

"Which was another thing about dear Virginia: Not only was what she'd just now decided she absolutely had to have done always extremely important; it was also, invariably, extremely urgent. It had to be done *right now,* because the man with the backhoe and the front-end loader was waiting at the door for her decision on whether she wanted the entire county dug up, and unless she told him within two minutes that she did and he should get to work, he'd start up his flatbed and take a long-standing offer that he'd been putting off for years to dig up Rhode Island, from Pawtucket all the way down to Westerly, and her big chance'd be gone forever—she'd never see him again.

"See, she always started with the element of surprise in her favor, like an enemy fighter pilot diving down out of the sun to attack your fuel-tanker. You could never be sure whether she'd call you, on any particular day, and she knew this. So whenever things got too dull to please her, she'd capitalize on it and confront you with a full-blown, rampaging crisis already well underway before she'd made up her mind to call you about it. To do something about it right off." Dennison had snorted. "I said she lived in Taunton? That was wrong; I should've said she lived in Ambush.

"Anyway," he had said, "after Stan'd died, and she'd had the operation, and Lucy'd dug herself in, there was one area in particular where we could always be completely confident that we had no idea at all what she would do next, and that was betting on the Massachusetts State Lottery. We knew she would most likely do it, but only if she felt like it. We didn't know what made her feel like it. We couldn't keep track of it. There wasn't any pattern. She didn't really have any system, although naturally she claimed she did. She'd bet the three-digit and the four-digit Daily Numbers, exact order, any order, all those variations, but she didn't bet them every day, and on the days she did bet, almost never the same number two days in a row. The way I guess most gamblers do: choose a number and that then becomes *their* number, their birthday or the registration on their car, and then they stick to it for years, day in, day out, until they die. But not Virginia. If it was the same number she'd bet the day before, she very seldom bet it in the same way. It was never clear to Tory what'd prompted her to do yesterday what she had no intention of doing, wouldn't've heard of doing, today. Unless it was something one of her consultants, one of her spirit-visitors, 'd suggested over-night. And of course, as you might've guessed, there was absolutely, positively, no way in the world of ever knowing how much she'd bet, or whether she'd won or lost.

"It was Instrument Flight Rules all the time when you flew with her, and your instruments were always on the fritz. She might or she might not bet Mass Millions, or Mass Cash. Then again, she might decide to pass up all those big-jackpot scams and instead have Lucy get her a whole wad of those evil scratch-'n-sniffs, the instant-game cards, insidious little sucker-bets they peddle to the clinically-, patho-logically-, terminally-ignorant pigeons, at a buck or so a whack— they've got one that goes for *five*, dude, five whole fuckin' dollars, for a sucker bet—our good old, righteous, 'One and Only,' Con-man-wealth of Massachusetts, at the top of the ethical game. Good old Reverend Cotton Mather must be spinnin' now, boys, screamin' in his crypt there like a double-overhead full-race cam on a Top-Eliminator Fuel-A dragster when the Christmas tree goes down and it's runnin' low on oil. 'When the Mafia does it, it's criminal, boys, and it's your damned job to go out there and catch 'em. But when Holy State does it, it's all right. It's grand. It's the purtiest thang inna world. 'Cause our intentions are good, and our hearts, they are pure, and you can believe this, law says so, and we are the ones write the laws. So we just can't ever be wrong.' But regardless of what Vir-ginia's choice turned out to be, you wouldn't've known in advance, and you couldn't've known, either. Because she didn't. And *that* meant you'd never know from day to day or week to week, month to month or year to year, how much she was spending. Read: losing. How much she'd won if she won. So consequently you had absolutely no way to estimate how much she'd be likely to throw away next week, next month, or next year, on this gambling obsession of hers. And that was just what she wanted.

"The old bat was crafty, you see. She may've been daffy, or head-ing in that direction, but she was still very sneaky, just as devious as she could be. Her Stanley'd been an accountant, an accountant to the rich. Well, some of those rich people were also dotty, and many times he'd served as a court-appointed conservator for some old bastard millionaire who'd gone silly over his twenty-year-old housekeeper and was about to deed to her—or him; not all of the dotty old moguls were men, and some of those who otherwise resembled men liked the sweet boys just as much as the softheaded old ladies did—his mineral rights to the whole of Venezuela if this new sexual toy'd promise to French-kiss and hand-job him to sleep at his naptime every day, until he went to meet Jesus. Virginia knew all about the dodge that the heirs-expectant used then, thank you very much; her late Stan'd received many a retainer after some mogul's nervous relatives'd been to court and convinced a judge that their poor old Uncle Bosely'd lost his marbles, and really needed a keeper or he'd give the ranch away. Virginia'd have none of that foolishness. Tory might know to the penny how much Stan'd left the old lady, and she might know, too, how much it cost Virginia to live—docs, medicines, home maintenance, heat, lights, and so forth—but until she could prove to a judge that what Mom was pissing away on Lucy's pay, and Lucy's keep, and the Lottery, all together'd reached critical mass, the point where it was endangering her ability to remain self-sufficient, no self-respecting person in a black dress on any bench in a court of law was going to rule that the old lady'd forfeited her God-given right to make as big a reasonably-limited damned fool of herself as her time on earth permitted.

"And so, to our low-grade despair," Dennison had said, "the old lady did persist in her bad habits, shrugging off our more-than-occasional heavy hints that the Lottery's a mug's game, appealing only to the innocents who think that three-card monte's a square shake, and they know they'll beat it some day, maybe Tuesday will be, their Goodnews-day, and then one Wednesday night, just as we sat down to a late dinner in our old new, or former modern, house, that we actually *liked*,—the one we'd picked out for ourselves, in convenient Canton—the old bat called up and told us she'd just won the fucking thing."

"No shit," Dell'Appa had said. "She won the Lottery?"

"No shit," Dennison had said. "And no kidding, either. Virginia, bless her heart, hit a Quik-Pik Megabucks for three million American dollars. Apparently the consultants' vision of the future wasn't sharp enough to let them see ahead of time exactly what numbers would come up, but it was zoomed in good enough to tell them when Virginia's stars and planets were so perfectly aligned that the Lottery machine itself would pick the winning number for her, if she made nice and asked it. And so that was what she'd done, or she'd had Lucy do: Ask the simpering machine to pick a winner for her, and that's precisely what the dear, dear thing'd gone right to work and done. To the lilting tune of three million smackeroos. Guess it pays to have Poe in for tea. Or maybe it was U. S. Grant who told her. We never did narrow it down there."

"If it was Grant, by God," Dell'Appa said, "it wasn't tea she had him in for."

Dennison laughed. "No," he said, "but it didn't really matter. She enjoyed them all, all the people who climbed up into her spiritual tree-house. And she did win three million bucks. Hard to argue with results."

"Paid out over twenty years, right?" Dell'Appa had said.

"Right," Dennison had said, "but it gets a little more complicated than that. What they do, the people at the Lottery, they buy annuities for the winners that over the course of those twenty years will deliver equal annual payments that add up to the amount of the jackpot. For three million, it's a hundred-fifty large each year. But that's before taxes, State and federal, which get deducted first, before the winners get their checks. In Virginia's case, what they figured'd be about right to *de*-duct and *with*-hold was fifty-two-five K, leaving a net check of ninety-seven-five. Which, with the interest rate where it was when Virginia scored the booty, would've been the annual yield on a little over one-point-two mill, not three million, if you'd invested the money in a solid twenty-year mortgage. Not only does the State con you into making the sucker-bet in the first place; if by some prank of fate it turns out you actually won, you get conned again on how much."

"But still, wholesome walking-around money," Dell'Appa had said. "Nine-seven-five ain't no whale shit."

"Oh, most certainly not," Dennison had said, "but the plot, as dey say, continued to ticken, dere, and it developed that the check that Virginia would get each year after taxes would be forty-eight, seven-fifty."

"As in forty-eight-thousand, seven hundred and fifty dollars?" Dell'Appa had said. "If I am not mistaken that would be precisely half of the ninety-seven-five left in the pot after the taxes came out."

"Exactly," Dennison had said.

"You're not gonna tell me," Dell'Appa had said.

"Do I need to?" Dennison had said. "For the record, okay, maybe I should. But it's really not necessary. She said she and Lucy'd agreed to split their tickets, any winnings that they got. 'One of us wins, we both win,' Virginia said. 'Neither one of us loses alone.' "

"Very cosy," Dell'Appa had said.

"Oh, absolutely heart-warming," Dennison had said. "Although actually, if it'd just been that, the two old ladies turning into high-rollers, advised by Alexander Hamilton and FDR, in their sunset years, it would've been just fine. And it was unquestionably very nice for Virginia and for Lucy, too, as long as Virginia was alive, because it meant that what she'd thought all along she could do, but couldn't really've managed, on what Stan'd left her for money—support Lucy living with her—she now really could do. And that made her happy, which from our selfish point of view was also a very fine thing— happy old people're just like happy middle-aged people, and happy young people, and happy-dear, little children: much less trouble to their kinfolk than unhappy old people. No, the real trouble didn't begin until later, after Virginia'd cooked up the house idea and decided there was no reason why she couldn't finally have, at seventy-nine, the house she'd always wanted since she was a blushing bride and she saw it one day with her husband, because his client owned it and Stan'd had to drive down to it to see the man. And goddamned if it wasn't for sale, didn't just happen to be on the market, asking-price: four-hundred, twenty-five-thousand, breathtaking, American, dollars."

"My," Dell'Appa had said.

"I should say so," Dennison had said. "Now, praise God, by the time Virginia began to hatch this harebrained plot of hers, we'd managed after much exertion to get it through her head that the Lottery folks hadn't really screwed up, and she more or less understood that she hadn't really been supposed to've gotten her whole mill and a half in one swell foop, and the way that they were proposing to pay her off was not only the way they paid off all the big winners, every time; it was also perfectly legal. She still thought it was also a perfectly rotten trick to pull on the people who bought tickets on million-dollar raffles thinking they would get a million dollars all at once if they should win, and I've got to say that even Tory and I found it pretty hard to argue with her on that point, but she did still have it straight that that was the way they were going to do it, and it was not against the law. So, when she found out that the castle of Chillon was for sale, the very same house that she'd visited with her Stanley back when his rich-oddball rug-merchant client was not only living in his dream-house but running his business from it, she went into the whole adventure knowing that she'd have to get a mortgage. Which for a woman in her very late seventies, even one who's just hit the Lottery for a one-half, after-tax share of almost forty-nine K a year, is no mean trick to pull off. For some reason or another, bankers and other lenders—even those extremely-shifty fellows doing business out of low-rent, store-front offices in cinder-block shopping plazas that aren't quite making it and depend on late-night, home-shopping channel, cable-TV advertising to drum up business for them—for some reason or another all of these people are very reluctant to write twenty- and thirty-year paper for people much past, say, forty birthdays or so.

 " 'They say they won't consider anything over ten years, even though we've got all that jackpot money,' she told Tory. See, the cock-and-bull story she'd dreamed up for our benefit then was that she and Lucy were both going to be on the mortgage, so whatever the monthly payment turned out to be, each of them would be paying half that. And the plan was that she would make a will leaving Lucy enough from her share of the winnings to cover her half of the mortgage if she turned out to be the one who died first—which it sort of figured she would be, since Lucy at the time was a spry young seventy-two-year-old, as lively as a squirrel. But for some reason or another, which Virginia never did manage to explain to Tory's complete understanding, Lucy didn't want to be listed as co-owner on the deed, which we both thought was kind of a strange attitude for a mortgage borrower to have, even when the borrower was an igno-rant, unsophisticated, simple elderly lady from the bayou country. I mean, commit yourself to paying two, maybe three, thousand dollars a month, debt and taxes on a great big fancy house, and then turn around and say you want no part nor share of ownership? That you could pass on to your dear kinfolk? Well, hard as we found it to believe, according to Virginia that was Lucy's wish. She wanted it instead all to go to Tory and me, when she went to Jesus, if Virginia'd died first. Partly because Virginia'd be putting what she got from the sale of the Taunton house, that Tory'd expected to inherit someday, into the Westport Disaster, and partly to show how much she admired us, for taking care of 'Ginia.

"Flattering? You bet. It almost like to turn our poor fool heads. But it still didn't, you know, make a lot of sense to us. At least not until we were sure we were where Virginia couldn't possibly hear us, and then we just busted out laughing. Just goes to show you, I guess: if you're gonna start slingin' the shit, you should get started early in life. Not when you're seventy-nine.

"Well," Dennison had said, "that wasn't the way it actually was, of course. What Virginia was doing was scheming to buy the house by herself, for her and Lucy to live in. The real-estate taxes down in Westport on that monster were about the same each year as the tax bill on her house in Taunton, rates and assessments being lower down there, so that came to about two hundred bucks a month. On a fifteen-year mortgage, ten-and-a-half percent, fixed rate, that left Virginia about thirty-eight, thirty-nine hundred a month from her annual Lottery check, which meant the maximum she could finance, using every dime of it, would've been just under three-hundred-fifty grand. Total. Her place in Taunton was free and clear, in good shape in a nice location; even though the market was depressed at the time, she figured to clear somewhere between ninety-five and a hundred-fifteen if she could find a buyer who could find a bank. So that meant that as a matter of fact she wasn't being completely unrealistic, not financially at least, when she proposed to buy a house that cost as much as the castle did. Actuarily? Common-sensibly? Sure, she was nuts. Bonkers, bananas, out of her everlasting tree, even to dream of such a thing. But mathematically, arithmetically, there was nothing wrong with the idea at all.

"So, there being no logical way to argue her out of the idea, Tory got involved too. In the inspection tour and then the haggling, I mean. The sellers, the late owner's grandnephews, put up a stiff struggle. It would've been a lot more convincing if they hadn't been a couple of guys who had their own lives all set up in Syracuse and Washington, hadn't already sold off the remains of the rug business to one of their late uncle's competitors, and 'd had at least some interest in uprooting themselves and their families so they could live in Westport, Massachusetts, but they held out for a while before they finally came down to three-sixty-five. Which, after Virginia put most of what she got from selling her own house into the down payment, meant she and Lucy had a monthly payment of between thirty-one and thirty-two-hundred bucks a month. For her, an old lady with her Social Security, the pension Stan'd left her, not to mention their savings—old Stan'd been careful; Virginia'd been known to suggest, as a matter of fact, that he was rather 'close with a buck'—that was a comfortable expense, if it happened to be how she wanted to spend her own money, and it was.

"So she did," Dennison had said. "That was six years ago, and everything went along just tickety-boo for a little more than three years, Virginia and her companion just as happy and contented as could be. And then, contrary to all expectations, Virginia's included, Lucy up and died. Just keeled over in her chair one fine spring afternoon while they were watching Judge Wapner, mooning over how cute his court officer there, Rusty, was, and what a nice smile he had, and boom, that was the end of her. It was also when things started to get complicated. For us, I mean.

"It would've been all right if Virginia when that happened'd still been living in the house in Taunton. Where she'd lived for over forty years. Friends all around who knew her, lived close by to her. The man down at the drugstore'd known her twenty years. The kid who'd used to mow her lawn, shovel out her walks and driveway; he was all grown up, of course, and now he owned the gas station and took care of her car. Police chief'd been with D Troop when I joined this outfit. Tory and I were less'n a half hour up the road, and if something'd happened to her, one of those people would've found out in a jiffy and called one of us right up. She'd been protected there.

"But now," Dennison had said, "in this goddamned house that she'd bought for herself, all the way down in Westport, for God's sake, she was out there all by herself. Out in the meadow alone, without another soul living close enough to her to even notice if her lights'd come on? Well, that wasn't so good. They don't have much crime down there, and the place's so far off the beaten track it's pretty unlikely any roving, thieving bastard looking for a rich old lady, living by herself, to break in on and steal from, 'd ever happen to see it. And sure, her health was good. She could look after herself, and we did know some people who'd look in on her every so often, let us know if she seemed to need us to do anything. But it was still awful lonesome for her, down there all by herself all day, with no one else to talk to, most days, after Lucy died. *Real* tough for her when the winter came that year, short days, got dark so early, and the wind just howlin' through there, sounding colder'n it was. She stayed over with us at Thanksgiving, the Wednesday night before and then through the weekend, Tory went Christmas-shopping with her, and it was pretty clear, to me at least, she wasn't in all that great a hurry to get back down there to Westport. Tory sort of revamped her schedule after the holidays, so she could get down there once or twice a week, take Virginia out to lunch or maybe meet her some place, make sure her car was all right, maybe get some shopping done, take her to get her hair done. But it was still a pretty makeshift arrangement. We didn't talk about it to her, and she didn't talk about it to us, but there wasn't any use trying to kid ourselves: it was only going to last as long as it lasted, and that'd only be until something came along and happened, meant she couldn't be alone all the time like that any longer.

"She'd always said when her time came she'd go in a flash, 'just like that'"—Dennison had snapped his fingers—"because that's the way it'd been with everybody else in her family, all of them died of heart trouble. And that was the way she wanted it, too: 'That's the way to do it, you ask me' was what she said, but when it finally happens, it doesn't always happen like you want it to, or like it happened every single time one of your cousins died. And it didn't, exactly, with Virginia, either, although she never really did get to the point where you'd have to say: 'Well then, no use pretending any longer about this. This woman's just laid up, can't take care of herself anymore.' It was more of a gradual thing, things just gradually getting harder and harder for her, until it was finally clear to everyone that either we were going to move in with her down there, which neither one of us of course wanted to do, or she was going to have to move in with us up in Canton—and she didn't want to do that."

"So how'd everybody decide it was going to be you two moving down there?" Dell'Appa had said. "I mean, I know it sounds sort of cold-blooded and everything, but it'd more or less seem to me . . ."

". . . that it'd make more sense for the *two* people who're probably going to be around longer to stay put where they are, and have the *one* person who probably isn't going to be around for at least a whole lot longer move in with them, right?"

"Right," Dell'Appa had said.

"Right," Dennison had said, sighing. "Well, I'll tell you the reason. Tory's as good a daughter to her mother as she is a wife to me and a mother to the kids. Tory's a good woman. And I'll do anything for Tory that she ever asks me to, unless she's lost her mind or something that she wants would kill her. Which I do not think will happen. But the reason we moved down there wasn't because Tory saw that as part of her duty to her mother and asked me, and I agreed to do it because I'm in love with Tory. It wasn't even because Tory's mother put the heat on and commanded us to come, because to give the woman credit, she was almost as reluctant to have us make the move as we were to do it.

"No, the reason was much simpler and a good deal less attractive than any of those other possibilities would've been. It was just what my good rabbi predecessor, the sainted Bomber Lawrence, told me when I first came on the job, what the simple explanation almost always is for so many of the lousy things that everybody, even good guys, nice guys like you and me, and good old Bobby Brennan—hell, even Bomber Lawrence—always seem to end up doing. We've always got good reasons for the things we did, but nobody wants to hear them when the things we did were good. It's just the bad and stupid things we do that our friends want reasons for, and for that kind of thing the Bomber reason always is: 'We did it for the money.' There isn't any decoration and there ain't no colored lights. There isn't any gravy and we're out of salad-dressing and we got to face the facts and just take 'em as we are. We did it for the money."

"Right there, now," Brennan said, hunching forward in the driver's seat so that he completely blocked any partial view Dell'Appa might have contorted himself into sharing in the mirror.

"What's he wearing?" Dell'Appa said.

"Ah, the usual," Brennan said offhandedly.

"Oh," Dell'Appa said, "so he's wearin' *'the usual.'* Well, that certainly clears it right up for me, doesn't it? Case I might've any doubt in my mind, some lingerin' confusion about what the guy is wearin'. Since, you know, I've never seen him before today, and I still haven't seen him today yet, either—thanks to you sittin' there, like Buddha or Jabba the Hutt there, hoggin' the whole view like you're doin'. But now at least I know: all I got to do, I get back the office tonight and I sit down to write my report of the day's adventures with you and Uncle Wiggily, Squirrel Nutkin, all the guys—Peter fuckin' Rabbit—is put down that even though I never did get a good look at any of them, any of the usual suspects, I'd still know them anyplace now. In the dark in a coalbin at midnight. Because I had your guidance in this. Right."

Brennan did not turn his head or say anything and Dell'Appa saw no reddening at the back of his neck; Brennan was ignoring him again, just as he had deliberately nonexisted him during Dell'Appa's rookie year in street clothes, when he had managed to make himself the senior non-com whose hazing Dell'Appa most despised. But now there were at least two differences: Dell'Appa, sitting with Sergeant Brennan in the Blazer three years after that first year in plain clothes, had a sergeant's badge of his own in his pocket; he had thus long since outgrown any motive, without acquiring any new inclination, to grovel for Brennan. "Any Brennan," as he put it that night to Gayle, "or any other bastard under the rank of Detective Lieutenant Inspector. Let the word go forth from this time and this place, to all the Brennans in all the world, no matter what their names are: 'Party-time was yesterday. Now is payback time. Fuck all you guys. Fuck all your horses. Strong letter follows. Harry.' Should've just called him an asshole right off the bat, 'stead've wastin' valuable time."

Dell'Appa cleared his throat and selected his testimonial voice, a bit heavy on the self-important-timbre pedal but nonetheless very serviceable, not only for giving evidence to jurors assembled in poorly miked, acoustically dead courtrooms but also for goading an overbearing former tormentor in the privacy of a truck cab, when he chose to overlook whimsical changes in status made in the passage of time. "For the Uncle I'll write: 'of the usual height, the usual weight and all that stuff. The usual hair and the usual eyes; in the usual colors, I think. Wears the usual clothes in the usual way; the usual *feet*, in the usual *shoes*, stickin' out of the plural end of the pants, the end at the bottom, you know? And the usual belt through the usual loops up at the singular end, of this very usual garment.' Dupe verbatim the same brilliant rundown for Squirrel, and then all I got left to do is rerun it just once more, for Peter. I'll be on my way home like a blue streak tonight, boy—no greased lightnin' was ever this fast."

That did the job. It made Brennan's neck good and red. He sat back suddenly and hard in the driver's seat, turning his head to focus on Dell'Appa the baited-bear scowl and career-threatening glare that had intimidated so many tenderfoot detectives in so many years gone by. Brennan had done more than merely overlook the years and the changes they had worked; he had nullified them by his own act of will, just as a fat man enables himself to graze comfortably out of the refrigerator by first gearing up the confidence that calories consumed while standing don't count in the day's total tally. He said:

"Just what the fuck is the matter with you, kid? The *fuck* is the matter with you? Your third week back inna real world with us, no more king of your own little hill, no one knows *what* you're doin' out there inna woods, or maybe you're just doin' nothin', and now here you come back where you'll hafta work, and you know it, and you're acting like the job's a zipper with the sharp teeth there, that we yanked up real fast and caught your cock in it. What was it, old buddy, that what it was? You can tell Bob. Bob's your old pal. Cry your heart out right here on my brotherly shoulder. You leave somethin' sweet 'n precious out there in those woods? Or maybe some sweet behind's what it was, a Little Red Ridin' Hood, maybe? Your own little Goldilocks-sweathog, all sorry and sad, all alone inna weeds, when she heard her hero was leavin'.'"

Brennan shifted his tone into a whining simper. "*Poor* baby-Harry. Those big meanies called him up, and they said: 'Okay, back to work. We need you back home-base, chop-chop. Wrap up that whipped-cream assignment you promoted for yourself, shouldn't've existed in the first place, not for a Boston-based trench-grunt, at least. A Springfield accountant, yeah, maybe, the eyeshade and pocket-protector, but no job for a genuine cop. One with all those *yew-neek* skills that you've got, that you bring to the same job we've been doing without them, pretty damned good, too, all of those years before you came. Cost the taxpayers arms and legs, too, of course, all of those *special* unique skills. But: hey, doesn't matter, not anymore, now it's all over and done with. Just get your candy ass back in here Monday morning, fit for normal duty. You've screwed around all that you're gonna now, out there inna bushes, the milkmaids.'

"And so as a result now you're gonna sulk, workin' under men senior to you. Who can see if you're doin' things right, and'll *say* something to you, you're not. That what it really is, Percy? Well, tough fuckin' shit, you fresh little prick, 'f you don't like takin' orders again. Suck it up, candy ass, then suck it in, and then if you still don't like how it actually works, go on sick days. Claim 'nervous exhaustion.' "

Dell'Appa did not say anything for what seemed to him like several minutes, if not several hours, being absolutely certain that if he allowed himself to reply at once to Brennan's sneering he would surely incite himself further, beyond the limits of his ability to control himself. His voice would rise into a roar to the point at which the rush of hearing himself saying what he'd wanted to do for more than a year, and wanted again to do now, would be more than enough to impel him do it. He really would haul off and break the man's jaw. He knew that, but he also knew, even more surely, that that was far more than he would want, in calmness regained later, to have to know that he had done.

So there was some relief, to find that out. Somewhere along the time-line he had passed along with birthdays a milestone of increasing genuine maturity, without even noticing it. He really did not want to emerge now from his anger to find that he had acted on it while it lasted, and had broken Bob Brennan's jaw. It was a year or three over fifty, and with the rest of Brennan it would have been pensioned off some time back, in the days before the retirement age went up to fifty-five. Most likely that jaw was dry shingle brittle, furnished with dental appliances—Dr. Morse called all dental plates and bridges "appliances," including those he had fashioned for Harry to replace the three right upper and two lower teeth knocked loose by a sixteen-year-old Wellesley rich kid in the Mowglieh Tigers Rap Concert riot in his second year on the force (no more than two or three seconds before he had backhanded the kid with his long baton and hospitalized him with a fractured skull; the kid had recovered, after nine weeks in bed, his parents muttering about lawsuits until they heard about Dell'Appa's firm intention to reciprocate and as his lawyer put it to them: "Take your fucking house for what your druggy little bastard did."), thus causing Harry and Gayle ever after to call them his "maytags"—that a single solid shot would easily shatter and jolt off the shrunken lower gums, ramming sharp pieces of flesh-colored tough plastic at strange angles into the soft palate, making deep, jagged entry wounds. It was good to discover that causing grave bodily harm to Bob Brennan or even somebody like him, however delicious anger made the prospect, was no longer the sort of thing likely to be done by the kind of man Dell'Appa had always intended to be, some day; had worked hard to become, and now apparently had some reason to believe himself to be—even though it was the first thing that had come into his mind. He had already made a good start on beating Brennan senseless with his mind. There was no need to do anything more, especially if it involved risk.

During Dell'Appa's silence, Brennan breathed heavily across from him, plainly meaning to convey by means of labored, noisy inhalations and exhalations the falsehood that he too was in the mood for a fistfight. But his pale-blue eyes would not meet Dell'Appa's gaze and stay locked in, despite his efforts to steady them; their shiftiness gave him away. That was also good; it meant there was no danger Brennan would stupidly throw a sucker punch if he somehow got the erroneous idea that Dell'Appa had been distracted by something or someone outside the truck. So for Dell'Appa the appropriate tactic was therefore to find a way to occupy his mind and his time until the appearance of a subject of sufficient common interest to warrant (and also explain) total disregard of what had just happened, and open a fresh conversation.

Beyond Brennan's left shoulder, entering Dell'Appa's field of vision from the left, the sidewalk commuter procession on the other side of the roadway now presented among the almost-uniformed office-workers a man whose costume and behavior did not match the generic description. He carried an oxblood attaché case, the elegant two-inches-slim model favored by many of the other morning walkers, but he did not carry it in the same way. He flourished it in the carefree, loosey-goosey manner of an adolescent boy idly but still elaborately tricky-dribbling a basketball on his way to a playground court for a pick-up game of Horse. He swung it back and forth in patterns alternating between tight figure-eights and straight fore-and-aft arcs, each variation traveling about eighteen inches, first beyond and then behind his right knee. This required the other pedestrians to slow down and hang back to allow him to lead, or veer wide if they wanted to pass him, so that he would have plenty of room. But Dell'Appa observed no frowns of annoyance or exchanges of insults and gestures between the non-conforming man and the briefly-detouring pedestrians. Everyone involved, first in creation of the inconvenience and then accommodation to it, seemed to find it an ordinary, unremarkable feature of the daily walk to the 7:48.

The unusual man also tried to walk with the loose-jointed gait that gifted young athletes either possess from birth or acquire by considerable practice, but he couldn't bring it off, despite all his obvious planning and effort and someone's fairly considerable expense. He wore premium-grade high-top sneakers. Dell'Appa recognized them as a brand of footgear he had seen aggressively and repeatedly advertised by relatively-young and highly-muscular, to-him-generic celebrities, during prime-time network telecasts of professional sports. They wore the sneakers and pretended to glide through heavy workouts while shouting provocatively, superciliously, or contemptuously at each another and also anyone who might be watching.

Those lithe people on TV mildly annoyed Dell'Appa. They were apparently known and admired so widely and well (though not by Dell'Appa or any one of his friends; Gayle said he had only to be patient, predicting that when Roy was a year or two older, he would update Harry's education much more thoroughly and often than he could possibly wish, "at eighty or a hundred bucks' tuition per pair," she said, "every time his feet grow another half-size or some kid who's two years taller takes a rebound away from him") that their full names, cavalierly unstated in the ads, had obviously been deemed superfluous by the sneaker-maker and his advertising outfit. This meant that the advertising people had talked the manufacturer into paying the performers truly enormous sums of money for the antic services filmed for the ads that in turn cost so much to broadcast. And those combined expenses of production and broadcast exposure explained why the sneakers had to be priced at retail out of the reach of anyone except celebrities so recognizably richly-famous (except by Dell'Appa and his friends) that they didn't have to buy them; according to the sports pages in the newspaper, the sneaker-manufacturers who hired the scintillating people to make the ads also gave them carload-lots of the footwear for nothing.

Which in turn meant that Harry was right and the whole exercise was a charade. The manufacturers had no reason to care at all what sort of people wore the sneakers out into the real world, what they did once they were out in it, or even if anyone actually did put on those fancy shoes and go out. For the manufacturers it would be perfectly all right if all the flashy damned things that were purchased for real money, or shoplifted out of heavily-insured inventories, remained forever thereafter in the gaudy boxes, shoved 'way to the backs of darkened shameful closets, so long as the well-funded escapees from reality and normally-functioning sanity in sufficient numbers first underwent mood aberrations sufficiently severe and persisting long enough to cause them to march in columns of bunches into mall-stores and cough up the listed prices that not only paid for the stars and the ads, but made the sneaker-people very rich indeed.

So, while the man on the Dockett Street bridge wearing that particular pair on that pale, bright November morning certainly would not have been one of the typical buyers projected to the maker by the media-buy people who devised the TV-ad campaigns; would plainly never be able to enjoy whatever wonderful athletic advantages the maker had engineered into the footgear; and looked like a pathetic fool wearing it in public, all of that would have been a matter of complete indifference to the sneaker-maker. Either the feckless man himself had gullibly purchased the shoes, or someone whose reason had been overcome by generous love for the sneakered man (unless it was weariness of his wheedling and pleading) had paid over the cash for those cruel shoes, supplying the props for a pitiable show and at the same time making the charade a rousing triumph by giving the maker his profit.

The unusual man lacked style. That would have been entirely bad enough if he had not been able to perceive it when he saw it, but he had an additional misfortune: he was just bright enough to recognize style, to notice grace and study easy confidence, so that in time he had come to believe that if he could learn to display those gifts in the same careless manner as the blessed who possessed them, he would then have the gifts themselves—and then he would not be *different,* at least not in the bad way, anymore. So he was trying to fake it that morning, as he had on many others and would on many more, and he was failing, as he always had and always would.

He wore black, heavy-gauge, cotton-twill pants, baggy in the seat, and a blousy, bulky, black, tanker jacket showing a neckband teaser of neon-scarlet sateen, most likely a reliable indication that the jacket was reversible to red-flag to the whole world any in-your-face mood that might overcome its wearer. But Dell'Appa, his anger at Brennan now having receded sufficiently to permit him to think rationally about matters other (and more complex) than bashing Brennan in the teeth; having instantly perceived that this man, his short black hair graying at the temples under the White Sox black-wool cap shielding his happy face, was too white and too old ever to have been prudently allowed, "pastly, presently, or futurely" (as Dennison liked to say when split-infinitively-importuned "to just at least *think*, okay?" about a transparently-stupid, cockeyed course of action he had quite rightly just summarily rejected—by saying: "not a chance" —and would never authorize, "unless first overtaken by a fit"), by anyone who loved him to risk having any mood like that in a public place, now gradually and belatedly realized that the man was too flat-out handicapped as well.

He was wearing that entire ensemble to the train-stop in exactly the same jauntily-hopeful mood that boys ten and under wore their Red Sox hats and jackets, and brought their fielder's gloves, to see games at Fenway Park: so as to be prepared to step right into the starting lineup and serve, should some pregame disaster disable the whole team and require quick assistance from the foresighted boys, to avoid the otherwise-assured (and profoundly-ignominious) disgrace of forfeit (the boys themselves were fully aware that the fantasy was utterly preposterous and so claimed that they brought the gloves "in case of a foul ball," not even risking the ridicule of their friends by admitting to indulgence of the fantasy, but in secret they harbored it just the same). The man was wearing what his wardrobe offered as his best clothes, and he was carrying the accessory that the other people, in their best clothes as well, recognized as a credential establishing that the person in possession was indisputably a competent adult, on his way to do serious work. In the similar but not identical, nearly-congruent, adjacent world where Dell'Appa now perceived the misfitted man really lived all his life, happy and content, everyone was about ten years old, at most approaching eleven, and he along with all the people whom he met each day in that world, on the Dockett Street bridge or anywhere else that he might take his private planet, would remain at that age forever. Which would be until the day he died, most likely smiling that same serene smile. "Is that him?" Dell'Appa said. "Is that guy there the guy, our guy? The retardate next to the curb?"

"Yup," Brennan said with combined grimness and sadness, "that's Danny all right. You're lookin' this minute at the safest helpless person in the whole United States. At least 'til the day comes that Short Joey dies, Daniel Mossi's as safe as an angel. And probably at least as happy. Anywhere he goes, he's welcome. And everyone who knows Short Joey knows he'd better be, because as dumb as he is, Danny-boy can talk.

"See, if somebody's bad to him, bad to Danny," Brennan said, "well, years ago, some guys were. They were making fun of him one day and stuff, and one thing led to another and the first thing you know they've ended up gettin' him to take his pants off and go to the store bare-ass. There were these two guys, couple short-hittin' DPW guys, common garden-variety bullshit artists, thought they were some kind of wise guys because they'd faithfully punch in down the State garage every morning, and then they'd adjourn to the poolroom in the Square and spend the whole entire day down there, gettin' the taxpayers' money to do it. They even had their own custom pool cues they kept there, ivory grips and plush cases, all that stuff. Far as they're concerned, the Public Works there, that was just something they did every day, like havin' a coffee before work, only they got paid for the coffee. But the poolroom was where their real jobs were. And then there was one day when *that* even bored them, gettin' paid for hustling pool. So Danny comes in, and that's what they did to him. With the pants, I mean, and I guess they come to regret it.

"They'd already gotten themselves drunk on beer, this day when he comes in, and it's just early afternoon. Women out inna stores, shoppin', kids outta school for the day, all kindsa people around, your normal day, but in the poolroom I guess it was slow. No pigeons around they could hustle. So they decide that what they'll do is play this little trick on poor old dopey Dan. Now keep in mind what I told you: This's a good many years ago, before word gets around what Joey can do, what he *will* do if somebody crosses him, and also before Joe and Danny caught on. So, when these two guys, these assholes, start in tellin' Danny if he takes his pants off—and this's January, mind you, I think it was, good and cold anyway; no day you'd want to be out with no pants on, even if that was your ambition—and then he goes out of the poolhall, and down the street, oh, maybe a block and a half, to the newsstand the Greek used to run there, along with the Numbers 'til lunch, the Greek'll be real pleased to see him. This is what they're tellin' Danny, and Danny, bein' an idiot, somethin', he's believin' this shit. They tell Danny if he goes in and shows the Greek his bare dick and his ass, the Greek'll be Danny's friend ever after. Give him Luckies for nothin', Dan used to smoke those, or else maybe he was gettin' them for Joey, I dunno, but they're gonna be free from the Greek. The Greek'll take Danny the ballgames. He'll take Danny to Paragon Park, which was still open in summer back then—hell, still existed, too; now it don't even do that anymore—and they'll ride on the big Ferris wheel.

"You can see what these two guys, these two assholes, 've got in mind they're doin' here: they're insultin' the Greek, usin' Danny. Well, like I say, this's all years ago, before Joey and Danny catch on that bad people will try to hurt Danny. 'Bad people': the fact that there're bad people around don't come as news to Joe, being as there's some would say he's already one of them himself, or gettin' there, at least, and the gentlemen he works for are not universally admired. But the bad people he works for and is working to become one of, they are not bad people like these damned ditchdiggers are. The bad people that Joey knows, that always treat him right, they are not the rotten type of people that humiliate the helpless, mortify the weak, and really hurt the poor bastards who they know can't hit them back. And Joey thinks, he is *convinced,* that that's not the same thing *at all.*

"Well, that night, after the Public Works guys do that to Danny, he goes home and tells it to Joe. How he did what they told him and went to the Greek's, left his pants and his Jockey shorts back in the poolroom men's room and went down the street in the daytime as bare as the day he was born. And the Greek went berserk, Danny goes into the store, his dick bobbin' around and he's freezin'. The Greek, he knows that Danny's not bright, that he didn't think this thing up. Somebody must've made him. So the first thing the Greek does, he gets a blanket from the back and he gets Danny all wrapped up there and then he calls the cops. To come take Danny home. And

71

pretty soon, they do that. The cops come to the store and they see what is going on, and they take Danny home. But first they gotta follow procedure, naturally, so they take Danny down the emergency room, get him examined and so forth. Make sure he didn't get exposure or something, and that nobody did anything else to him after they talked him into takin' his pants off but before he goes out in the street. Don't want somebody suing the City there, sayin' the cops should've done something, they didn't make sure he was all right. And this takes some time, naturally, like hospitals always do there. But finally they get all the test-results, and he's all okay, and it's safe to take Danny home.

"So the cops do that, they drive Danny home," Brennan said. "He goes in the house and Joe's home, a cop goes in with him, and that's when it begins: the routine the two of them've been following ever since the cops that day hadda bring Danny home. Ever since then, if you do something to Danny, that Danny doesn't like, he'll go home and he'll tell Joe. And Joe will listen, very closely. He does not go off half-cocked. But if when Dan is finished and Joe's got no more questions for him, if Joe decides he doesn't like what Dan's just finished telling him, what he says to Joe you did, or you got him to do, well then, the next Mossi you see will be Joe, and he'll be in a really bad mood. Which is never a pretty sight, I hear. In fact what I hear is that if Joey's really pissed off, it could even turn out to be your very last sight on this earth. The last thing you ever see.

"Those two guys from the poolroom, for example: for some reason or other that night, after Joe finds out from Danny and the cops what'd happened to his retarded brother that day, well, it must've made him thirsty or something. So Joe decides that what he's gonna do, after hearin' that, what he'd really like to do was go out for a beer. And he just happens, you know, to drop in at that very same place where Danny was that afternoon. Reasonable enough, since it's right there in the Square, short block or two from his house, and the two jokers from the DPW by now're back from the State garage there, after their hard day's work punchin' in inna mornin' and then out, in the late afternoon. They're in there and they're even struttin' around a little, shootin' their mouths off, you know? Proud of what they did to Danny that day, tellin' anybody who'll listen, and there's quite a few in there who will.

"There's a lotta other people in there, in fact," Brennan said, "when Joey comes in the door. And nobody bats an eye, right? Well, why should they? Joey comin' in for a beer's nothin' outta the ordinary. It's a regular neighborhood bar. No one's surprised, they see Joey—he lives inna neighborhood, right? They always see him around. And where else you expect, he would go for a beer? Normalest thing in the world. And besides now, keep in mind what I told you: This's before the word really gets out, and everyone knows what Joe does. Then it's not like today, when he comes inna room, all riled up with the fire in his eye, anna strong men head for the exit.

"So he goes in, like I say, for a coupla frosties, bagga chips and a Slim Jim or something. And those two guys, the two assholes from the afternoon, they're in there. Well, naturally, one thing an' another, they all say 'Hello' an' 'How yah doin'; 'Hey, howzit goin' there, huh?' each other, including of course them and Joey. Why wouldn't they, huh? Them and Joey, all say hello to each other. It's not like they did something to *him,* they did what they did to his brother that day. Not the way that they see it, at least. Danny's over twenny-one, isn't he? So he's an adult, way they see it. What they did to Danny, they did to *him.* He wants to do somethin', to get back at them, well fine, then, let him—let him, and see how far he gets. But Joey? Why would he have a beef? They didn't do nothin' to Joey. The way those guys see it, they're all right with Joey—never did nothing to him. All knowing each other like they do, all bein' the same neighborhood. Hey, these guys known each other for years. And they're talkin' and so on, you know how it is, just shootin' the shit back and forth, nothing unusual at all perfectly run-of-the mill thing, that's all. And nobody's paying attention.

"And then, *bang,* that's when it happens. One minute the three of them're just standin' around, like everybody else, drinkin' the beer, just the usual shit, and the next thing you know, it's the goddamnedest thing, the assholes're takin' their pants off. Right out in public, son-of-a-gun if those two DPW guys're not all of a sudden pullin' their pants off, just as fast as they can, right out in fronta the bar. Alla customers standin' around, men, mostly men, but some women're in there with them too, and all them there lookin' on, starin' right at 'em, you know? And they get their pants off and then they pull down their shorts, and now they're just standin' there, their limp dicks inna breeze, like they always wanted to do that, what they just did, ever since they can remember. They always had a secret wish to stand around with no pants on in the neighborhood bar down the Square. And now there they are, they're actually doin' it, just like they always've dreamed of. But now it's like that's all that they knew—they dunno what they wanna do next. Everything gets very quiet.

"But that's when Joey says somethin'. He says somethin' those Public Works guys. That nobody says later they could hear at the time, even though they're all standin' right there next to them, no more'n five feet away. But not a soul hears what he said. And then the Public Works guys, completely bare-ass now still, both of them go over the pool tables, inna middle of the room, and bend down over them, and they beg Short Joey, absolutely fuckin' *beg* him, to take their personal, monogrammed, customized pool-cues outta the rack onna wall where they put them, and ram them right up their bare asses."

"Mercy," Dell'Appa said. "I assume Short Joey would have none of this disgusting, perverted business and told them sharply to stop all their foolishness and put their trousers back on at once."

"No," Brennan said thoughtfully, "as a matter of fact, he did not. I suppose it was a matter of Joe being such an obliging guy, you know? He was always well-known for that. If he happened to see that you needed some help, and he was the guy that could help you, well, he'd pitch right in and help you out, even without bein' asked. Always been that way. You could ask anybody. They would all tell you that. He might think that what you want is kind of strange, maybe even a little kinky, but if you're a friend of his and it wouldn't hurt anyone else, well, he would do his very best to make sure that you would get it. So, if these two guys both wanted him to take their own pool cues and stick them up their asses for them, well, they were over twenty-one, adults too, just like Danny—who was he to argue? They got their cookies that way, what business of his was it?

"And so he went and he did it. Shoved those sticks up them so far it looked like they hadda be gonna come right out of their mouths, or their noses or something, any minute there now. They're both screaming, of course, at first, when he first does it to them, starts it up them there, they holler pretty good, but when he really gets that wood up there good and deep, well, from what the people said it was like someone's getting murdered. All kinds of stuff gushing out of their mouths, vomit and bile and so forth, and blood just *spraying* out of their ass. Things tearing an' rippin' an' breakin', inside. Like they were two fountains of blood. They said they wanted him to help them out with this? Well, they come to the right guy for that. Short Joey helped them out, all right, and when he's got them things in as far as it looks like they'll go, then he gets the chalk and he goes around to where their heads are, and they're both passed out now, alla pain I suppose, and chalks their noses for them, right there."

"Jesus," Dell'Appa said.

"Oh, I'm here to tell you," Brennan said. "Those DPW guys never got their rocks off like that before, or *since,* is what I think—now that they know the kinda chances they both took. They hadda both go to the hospital, in fact, emergency surgery there for internal bleeding. And a good thing they did, too, people said; those two guys could've died there, I guess, and the docs were surprised that they didn't. But they didn't complain. Never complained. Not then and not afterwards, either. Not one word did you hear out of those guys, not a peep did they say about Joe. Some people afterwards, I understand, might not've known all the facts in the thing, told them they should file complaints there, charge Joey with A and B, maybe even DW there. Which I suppose a pool-cue would be, a dangerous weapon, I mean; if a cigarette is if you use it on purpose to burn another person, I would think if somebody else took a damned pool-cue and rammed it hard right up your ass, rippin' your guts all apart, that would be A and B, all right, and that pool-cue'd be the dangerous weapon. But nope, they just didn't look at it that way, not those two DPW guys. They just said: 'Nope. Wasn't that way at all.' Way they told it, it was something they'd asked for, asked for themselves, something they'd decided that they wanted done one night when they'd had too much to drink. And pretty obviously now, after what happened, well, they wished they didn't. But it was all still totally their own idea."

"Remarkable," Dell'Appa said.

"Oh, you bet," Brennan said. "But that's a big part the reason, anyway. Why what Danny does when he's in a place, well, it's always perfectly great. No matter what Danny does. He could whip out his dick and pee on the floor, or shit in the umbrella stand, if they had one. That would be just as all right. Just let Joey know, if Dan ever did something like that—which in fact I don't think he has, ever; if he did, nobody I talked to ever heard of it, or at least mentioned it to me—and Joey will discipline Dan. But don't take it out on Danny yourself, because that is what Joey don't like. And nobody in his right mind wants to do something Joey doesn't like. So that's how safe our Danny is. Daniel Mossi is so safe I doubt it's even ever crossed his mind, how helpless he really is. Or would be if it weren't for his brother. We all should have brothers like that."

"Good Lord," Dell'Appa said. "And this is the kid the file says is 'slow,' 'slow or slightly retarded'? People can talk him into taking all his clothes off and walking downtown naked, and would if it weren't for his brother, and this guy is 'slightly retarded'?"

Brennan sighed. "Yup," he said, "the very same. He's the guy that they mean."

"Jesus Christ," Dell'Appa said, "he can't have much more than an eighty-I.Q. Just hearing that story, or just looking at him: Either one'd tell you that easy."

"He's not sharp," Brennan said hopelessly. "There're some things he can do, but not very many, and if you want him to be able to do one or two of them for a few hours in the morning, a few more in the afternoon, you'd better not expect him to do any more than that. You ask him to do three or four of the things that he can do, you're gonna confuse him. Screw up his confidence. So then he panics, right? And when he panics then he can't do anything, any of the things that he actually did learn how to do, in the special classes that he went to. When he gets upset he seems to think that what you want him to do is all of the things he learned to do, only all at once. And he can't do that."

"Have we got any idea, any kind of hard numbers at all, just how retarded he is?" Dell'Appa said.

Brennan shrugged. "I dunno," he said. "I never actually asked anybody, I guess, 'least not that I ever recall now. Never saw any reason to. What'd be the point? Poor kid's a dummy. What difference would it make, he's this grade of dummy or that kind? 'A dummy's a dummy's a dummy,' I say, and if he's a dummy, that's it.

That's what he is, and that's that. How bad off he is doesn't matter. There's nothing I know of, 'll cure man of that, so he won't be a dummy no more."

"Geez," Dell'Appa said, as the man in black with the attaché case reached the apex of the bridge, about even with the front bumper of the Blazer. "You wanna be careful there, Robert, make sure all that milk of human kindness you've got washin' around in your gut there doesn't curdle and upset your tummy."

5 "Hey, for what it's worth, I feel sorry for him," Brennan said. "Naturally I do, like anyone would. But: 'for what it's worth,' and that ain't a hell of a lot. What good does it do him, or anyone else, if I feel sorry for him? Even if *you* feel sorry for him. Big-hearted fella like you are, how much good does that do the guy? Not much, if it's me that you're askin'. Sure, it must be tough on a person, be simple like that. Know you're not right and you never will be quite right, no matter how much school you go to. And really tough, too, on the family—his mother and father, I mean. I'm sure glad my own kids were all all right. Go through your whole life, all the rest of your life, after something like that's happened to you? Wonderin', maybe, it's something you did, you or your wife was the reason? Don't envy the people that that happens to. Must be a terrible thing.

"But what does that do for anyone here? Me or you feelin' sorry, for Danny or them, sorry for any of them. His poor mother, Teresa? She died years ago, Eighty-two or so, maybe; eighty-three, might've been. I dunno—somewhere in there. People feelin' sorry for her, she had the idiot son? Didn't do her much good when she's still alive, sure won't do her any good now.

"And his father, Luigi," Brennan said, "he's still alive there, at least. I guess. As far as I know, at least. I didn't hear yet that he died. But he's livin' now, over Don Orione, cross the Tobin Bridge there, and from what I hear, he doesn't know anyone now. Even people like Joey and Dan, that still go out there to see him. Which they do, give them that, once a week. Credit where credit is due. One's a dummy and the other one's a major-league hood, but they're still his sons, only two kids he ever had, and they don't need anyone tell them: They know what they got to do. Nope, nobody needs to remind them. Every week out they go, year in an' year out, Dan and Joey drive out to see Pop. Even though Pop stopped tearin' pages off the calendar some time ago, and can't tell you who they are, these days. Or who anybody else is, either. His two sons're just a paira movin' bodies that now and then come between him anna the sun, in the summer, he's sitting out on the deck; inna winter the light from the room lamp, they got him inside where it's warm. So sometimes he's in their shadows a while, like he was being eclipsed there, but that's about all their visits mean to him. Danny most likely don't notice much difference—though maybe he does, I dunno.

"Poor old Luigi, hard-workin' guy every day of his life he could still make it down to the shop? All those brutal years he had, mouth's all fulla nails, he's hammerin' heels; day in and day out, he's half-solin' shoes, fixin' handbags, and why does he live this shit life? It's all he can do, know how to do, to take care of his family and feed them. Including a defective kid, that will stay that way for forever.

"And now where's Luigi, after all of that grim shit? He's in the same exact fix himself as the kid was, and the dummy's out there most likely believin', he's takin' care of his dad. I dunno. A person didn't already believe in God, I dunno as I could argue very hard with him he really oughta start, when you see a thing turns out like that.

"But that's the way it did turn out, though," Brennan said. "It did turn out that way. So that leaves the two boys, Short Joey and Dan, able-bodied at least, an' Joey's the one that's in charge. Danny sure couldn't be. But Joey's also got some problems of his own, it comes to taking over from his mother and his father, takin' care his little brother that can't take care of himself at all. Joe is the oldest, which would mean that even if he wasn't in the kind of sometimes-noisy work he's in, the risk'd still be there.

"Think about it for a minute," Brennan said. "Suppose if Joe, instead of bein' what he is, if he was just a farmer, say, kept two pigs inna pen, maybe some chickens for eggs and a big dinner every so often, and a herd of cows out in a pasture. Down in Plympton or someplace. And his idea of a big time was goin' a Grange meeting, or watchin' 'Wheel of Fortune' or something. Instead of being what he is, 'Short Joe Mossi outta Boston, guy that never messes up,' he's a bog farmer down in Carver, plantin' cranberries, and every night after his dinner, he's got to watch TV. Because he's got this mammoth secret crush on Vanna White, on 'Wheel-a Fortune'? It wouldn't make no difference, really. Odds'd still be that he dies before his brother, because Danny's six years younger'n him. It's not just in the point-spreads that the numbers are the game—they're also the game we all play, as a general rule. So that would still be bad enough, if Joey was a farmer, because what difference does it make? The question's still the same: What does Danny finally do, when Joey's not around? As he most likely won't be, some day down the line, when Danny's still all hale and hearty, a big strong healthy idiot with twenty years to live. I don't know the answer to that.

"But now we go and we plug in the other thing, the thing that makes it even worse: Joey's not a farmer. It's worse'n if he was. Sure he doesn't take the chances, he's famous about that—and that means 'any chances,' God forbid the foolish kind. He does not go off half cocked. The thing you always hear about him—an' this's from the guys that know, who really *oughta* know—if someone brings up his name, is that Short Joey gets the call when the job is sensitive, and by that I mean—or I mean *they* mean, that is—it is *really* sensitive. That call he always gets. Because he *is* the man, the man that takes no chances. Unexpected things don't happen on a Joey job because that's why it's Joey's job: So that kind of thing won't happen. But still you and I and the lieutenant, and all the other Good Guys who're after Joey's ass, who've been after it for years, every single one of us knows and so does Joey, too, that no matter how you plan things, how you never take a chance: When you're doing what he does, you are never really sure. Never absolutely sure.

"So that's the second thing with Joey, Joey's second problem where his brother is concerned. His first one is he's older, so some day he might not be around while Dummy Dan still is, and his second one . . . well, his second one is really *two* more, when you come right down to it. Problem Two and Problem Three. Problem Two is that his work is not the kind of trade where you can ever be completely sure you took no chance at all. You maybe didn't take any chances that you spotted, and you've been at it long enough so when you look something over, you see most things that can go wrong. But that still might leave something that is so completely new that you didn't recognize it and it slipped right by you there. And the longer that you've been at this, or been at anything, the likelier that is. To happen, that is, come along and fuck you up completely. Something new you never noticed, because it was brand-new to you and you did not know what it was.

"So there's that," Brennan said, "and then there's the second part of Problem Two, which is Problem Three, which is us. All of us. All the people that're on the other side from you, if you happen to be Joey and you do what a Joey does. We don't approve of what you do, and when I say that what I mean is that we *really disapprove.* We dislike what you do, pal, we don't like it, big-time, and who you do it for, and why he's paying you to be around in case he needs it done again, like he did before. And what you get for doing it, the money that you make, and all the years you've made it? That stuff pisses us off, too. So much so that we've reached the point where we'll take either one of you, or anybody else around that can give us one of you, and then we'll use the one we get for a game of ferret-legging. And if it turns out you're the player in that dandy game, when it's over you will wish that you were never born.

"Now," Brennan said, nodding toward the rearview mirror on the leading edge of the driver's-side door of the Blazer, "if you are that poor bastard, with all that on his mind, and as always you would like to get your first look at anyone who might turn out to be the newest cop on your case, before this newest cop can get his first look at you, what you would do this morning would be the same exact thing you've done every other morning since the first time you drove down here and you saw this Blazer here. Because you never know in advance if this one is the morning that the newest cop, the new kid 's picked out to be the first one that he shows up to watch you on your own block.

"So, every single day what you would do is, you would take your foot off the gas in your Cadillac car and you would creep up nice and slow behind me sitting here, and you'd take a nice long look into my mirror, to watch me watching you. And you'd take your sweet time doing it, just like you've also done, every single day, tying up the traffic and not giving a good shit when civilians get pissed off in the cars behind you, because you never do. Because while you've seen me many mornings, you also know how cops behave—after all these years of having cops watch you, you know almost as much about cops, if not more, than the cops who've been watching you—and when one knows you burned him, years and years ago, and besides, he's getting stale, chasing you around—so stale his genius-boss now even agrees —there'll be a new cop on your case. And you'd like a fast first look at him, before he gets his first at you. Which if he's in my truck with me —as he's liable to be, so I can play spotter for him, handing you off like a football—you might be able to sneak that look at him right from my mirror, if the new guy doesn't duck."

"I take it Short Joey approaches," Dell'Appa said, turning his upper body and reaching for the door handle to unlatch and open it, so as to step out and down onto the retrofitted stainless-steel running board, release the passenger seatback, and enter the rear compartment of the truck to hide behind the curtain.

"You take it correctly, Kemo Sabe," Brennan said, grabbing him by the left forearm, "but 'Kemo Sabe' this morning means: 'Shit Head,' because you are not taking it smart."

"I thought the drill was, I got into the back and peeked out through the curtain when he came," Dell'Appa said.

"It was and it is," Brennan said. "But the way you're s'posed to do it, you're gonna see if you can do it without gettin' your big fat ass alla way outta truck so you're lettin' Short Joe get such good a look at it there he could measure you for new shorts, custom-made, if he wanted. And then, when you're sure he's finished doin' that, seeing what you look like from the back, then givin' him a nice close look from a different angle of you: a nice profile, from the front, make sure he gets your best side, while you're leanin' back outside the truck, before you get back in. Okay?"

"You told me," Dell'Appa began, "you told me back the office—"

"I know what I told you," Brennan said. "I told you this guy is good. He's been at it a long time, and no matter how good you are, or how careful you are to be good, sooner or later he'll make you, he'll burn you, and more likely sooner'n later. But I also told you—I remember I did, my Alzheimer's so far's in control; not like that poor bastard's, our good mutual friend's there, that you never did get to meet—the longer you stay invisible to him, the better off we all are. Now what you gotta do is crawl over the console and get in the back, there, right now. He's stuck at the light down by the fire-station, some fat crossing-guard broad picked his car first in line to stop all the cars for the brats. So, just shut up and get in there."

"We should've practiced doing it this way back in the garage," Dell'Appa said, contorting his upper body away from the seatback, releasing it forward and then crawling over it into the rear compartment, his buttocks and legs sliding awkwardly, painfully and noisily over the molded seatback and the transmission console, his booted feet hitting the underside of the dashboard.

"Wouldn't've made any difference, we did do that," Brennan said calmly. "You would've been just as clumsy back there inna garage if we had, and then, you wouldn't've been any less clumsy here. You're too big for this mission. Practice wouldn't've changed that. Practice wouldn't've made you smaller, cab bigger. The only other way we could've done it would've been for you to ride out here in the back, and stay in there the whole time, like somebody's cat in one of them big tan plastic hampers that they put them in to ship with the luggage on airplanes, they go on the family vacation. And I didn't think you'd go for that."

"You were right," Dell'Appa said, dragging his feet into the back and turning to draw the curtains closed to a narrow slit behind the seats.

"Of course I was right," Brennan said, looking at Dell'Appa in the inside rearview mirror. "I'm always right. But you're all set now. As soon's he gets a little closer to us you can take the whole show in."

Daniel Mossi had just reached the stairs leading to the railroad tracks and the platform and started down them when the crossing guard waddled officiously back to the sidewalk in front of the fire station, waving disdainfully to the motorists to proceed.

"The gray Caddie?" Dell'Appa said, peering through the sepia film masking the glass of the window set into the rear door of the Blazer, "assuming it *is* gray, of course, seeing through this glass so darkly. The first car in the line there, comin' up the hill? That the Caddie I'm s'posed to be watching?"

"You know," Brennan said, "it's a funny thing. I was thinking, the other night, I got home, I got a beer, I just found out you're coming on: This case's been part of my life. Which is how come I know so much about Short Joe and his family, and how their lives've been: because I hadda. I had to learn all I could about them and how they lived their lives. Because their lives're becoming part of mine, you know? It's almost like I—we—grew up together, me and Joey and Dan, like we were the kids from two families that lived right next to each other while everybody was young. Except that we *didn't* grow up next to each other, me and Joey and Dan, and we've been staying in touch with each other much better'n I did with the kids that I actually knew, when I was a kid myself, I was growing up next to, and much more I bet'n Joe and Dan did, with the kids that they used to know.

"Except maybe not Joe. Kinda work that he does, those guys're like each other's family. A lot of them grew up with each other, you know? And lots of them really are cousins. Hell, 'the Mob's' what we call it, or 'the Mafia,' and so do they—they do that. But sometimes they also, they call it: 'the Family.' And for lots of them, that's what it is.

"Well, that's how it's startin' to be with me," Brennan said. "I'm beginnin' to feel like I joined it. This family that all these guys got, I've been on this case for so long that I'm now in their family with them. I think they will miss me now, when I'm gone. Things just won't be the same. You'll be onna job some day, tailin' Short Joe, sittin' outside some cheap diner, and he'll come out, look around to make sure, you didn't duck out on him there, while he was in havin' a western-on-white, with some tea, and it'll hit him. He'll come over to the car, tell you roll the window down. He'll lean on the door edge and he'll say to you: 'Harry,' he will say to you, because of course he'll know what your name is, fifteen minutes after you take the baton from me, that is if it even takes him that long, fifteen minutes, 'you do a good job on this, Harry. Takin' nothin' from you here. Good solid professional job. But I got to tell you, Harry, it's just not the same. The way it was, the good old days, when Bob was on my ass. Bob was like a guy I always knew, by the end of it. "My associate," you know? I kinda miss the guy. You ever see him, tell him I said: you was to say hello for me.' And then he'll walk away, and you'll roll the window up . . ."

"And maybe wipe away a tear I couldn't hide," Dell'Appa said. "A furtive testament to an enduring furtive friendship that overcame all odds."

"Fuck you," Brennan said. "You know how long I've been on it, how long I've been on this case? When I draw this assignment—not this time, no; this's the first time, years ago, I mean, we first started tryin' to make him; back then—I first pull the Joe Mossi file, it was a half an inch thick. That's all it was at that time. Now Joe's never been a virgin, at least not for very long. That's not what I'm sayin' to you. Ten minutes at the most, 'til he got the deal sized up and picked out which side to be on. He's always been a player, the git-go, busy a very long time.

"But when I pull Joe Mossi's file, that first day I ever see it, little do I realize what it is I'm really doing. I'm starting a whole new career; that is what I am doing. Morning papers that day, I remember this, had a big-deal, front-page story. Some big-wheel, hot-stuff bankers, politicians, businessmen, they all got together and they had this great idea: they're gonna bring the Tall Ships back. The Tall Ships back to Boston, that created such a big stir when they first come years ago? Well, they're gonna come again. These big blowhards're gonna make 'em. Make a fortune for the city, tourists, TV, all that crap, throw a great big party, too, fireworks and everything? Every hotel'll be jammed, all the restaurants, too. And pretty soon, like always—you know the first day this'll happen, 'cause it always does—there's all these people yelling, all these *other* people, and they are pissed because they're not the ones that thought of doing it. Bringin' the Tall Ships back. And in Boston, we do this, this's what we do. We didn't think of it? It's no fuckin' good then. Can't be just, no fuckin' good. You can ask anyone that, and they will all say the same thing: 'We didn't think of it? It ain't no good. It's somebody rippin' you off.' So they were all sayin', just exactly like they always do: 'It's all bullshit. Never happen. You're just blowin' smoke up our ass. Just another phony scam, shake the money tree for you.' And that goes on for a long time, back and forth and so forth, seems like it's never gonna end, these bastards, you know? They *enjoy* it. They *like* doin' this to each other. And if it does, well, it won't matter: no one'll remember what it was all about. Not by then anyway.

"Yeah, but well, it didn't. They did come back, the Tall Ships did, even more'n came the first time. And wall-to-wall people came too, from the Cape Cod Canal alla way the Canadian border there, seems like from TV at least, all stompin' around, spendin' their money, gawkin' at all the old boats, and the whole wingding's so big a success that no sooner'n all the Tall Ships leave town again, the second time, there's talk starting up to bring 'em right back. 'Ohh, this's great. Canned beer ain't even this good. We should do this every year. Or maybe every three years, you can't get them every one.'

"Okay, maybe they're right. Maybe we should. And thanks to you, and thanks to me, and thanks to lots of guys, God knows how many guys, Short Joey's file's much smaller now. And you know why that is? Because now it's all computerized, and that little disc is *thin. But,* if you had it all typed up, like I done for myself and I recommended you doing too, that file is now *two* folders, at least, and they're about three inches thick. But Joey's still out on the loose, same's he was back then. We may know everything about him but if onions screw up his digestion and whether he farts at the movies, and spoils everyone else's night out—and if we don't know, it's because we don't wanna. But as much as we know, he's still on the loose, and it's us that're still poundin' sand.

"Well, okay, we ain't got him. We worked a long time, and we didn't. But we're not finished yet. We're still gonna get him, if he doesn't just fool us, and die. Okay, so we do it. I'll grant you that the time bein'. Say we get Joe, and now Joe doesn't talk. Which Joe *won't;* I don't care what the brass says. So Joe goes away for all day and all night, and he never gets out again. Is the operation that he worked for, is it outta business? Maybe, that day comes, it will be; I tend to doubt it, myself, but yeah, it is possible. But it won't be because we nailed Joey. Or, take the opposite thing, if you want: he does talk. He still doesn't go free. 'What he's done, in his lifetime,' the head headhunter says, 'he's a vicious beast, he is. A very dangerous man. For that he's got to do some time, at least, and by "some" I mean "a lot."'

"So Joe goes away anyway. Say he draws ten. That's minimum three-to-five inside, they don't hit him 'habitual, organized criminal; racketeer-mobster; real heavy-duty bad actor. For that stuff you get something extra. Say: twenny to life, two or three times, each one on and after the others. Forget thoughts of parole—do it all. Say "Good night, boys and girls," now, blow good-bye kisses to them. You won't be at their wedding receptions.' Well, what happens to Danny, 'f that happens to Joe? Either one of those things?

"Same thing that'd happen if Joe should die of the natural causes there, right? He could have a heart attack, too, you know, just like a judge or a priest. He's still on the butts, the serious butts; he's smoked Camels for most of his life. That isn't good for him, from what I hear. So Joey could get sick from that. And then what happens to Danny? Who takes care of Danny when Joe's in the can, or Joe's in the ground? We got him or Saint Peter did? I'm telling you, and you can quote me: If we get Joey and put him in jail, take him out of the play, we're also taking his brother, Danny, and we might's well face up to that. If Joe goes to jail, Dan goes to the home. The hood and the dummy run as an entry: lock one up, you lock 'em both up."

"Well," Dell'Appa said from the back, "but that isn't so anymore. We don't lock up the functioning ones anymore. The ones that at least get around."

"Yeah, I know," Brennan said, "and that's sorta what's worrying me. They've got their freedom now, but lots of times that seems to mean they're free to die on the street, and so that's what they tend to do. I'm not really sure I want to be one of the nice helpful guys that finally helps Danny do that. By putting his brother away."

The faded-gray Cadillac Sedan de Ville creeping up to and alongside the Blazer now showed by the tattered condition of its phaeton vinyl roof and the chalky oxidation of its painted finish more years and less upkeep than had been apparent when it stood motionless 200 yards away. "Yeah," Dell'Appa said, "well, if you can sorta park the weight of the world somewhere else off of your shoulders now for a few minutes and give me the play-by-play on this Brillo-padded, bullet-head that's coming up behind us now, well, that would not go bad at all."

"Yeah, Harry, yeah, I know," Brennan said. "Make all the fun you want, the cheap cynicism of youth there, buncha tough guys that never earned toughness, think it's just issued to you with the badge, but I'm tellin' you, when you're my age and you've been at it this long, you're gonna start to wonder if all the things that you did, while you were carryin' that badge and all that hard-boiled attitude, whether they were right."

"Up yours, all right?" Dell'Appa said. "Let's just try to do the job."

"Well, then," Gayle said, sharing the last of the wine into their glasses as he returned to the table from racking the dinnerware in the washer, "that makes it even plainer, doesn't it? Seems to me it does. What Bob's going through—and as much as you dislike him, he's still not immune to time's passages and so forth—'s a very familiar syndrome not only to but among clinicians themselves. I suppose it's sort of a variation on the Heisenberg Principle, about disrupting the system that you simply have to measure by the very act of measuring it. What you told me about him suggests to me that as he approaches the end of his career, his police career at least, which is often very hard for people, especially men, in the kinds of occupations that in the minds of most of the community define the individuals engaged in them—as the jobs of policemen and firemen do—he's collided with the reality that when he's done as he thought he was supposed to, 'changed the community' in some way, 'made it better,' it's now apparent to him that he's also 'changed the community' as well, quite involuntarily, even inadvertently, in a way that 'made it worse.' So, when he now wonders whether it would really be appropriate— 'ethical,' or 'moral,' as he'd most likely see it—to incarcerate the older, vicious brother. If by so doing he, or you, or anyone acting in either of your places, would thereby unavoidably diminish the life of the younger, retarded brother. So what in effect he's doing is not compensating in advance for the loss that he expects, and the loss that will indeed come, as he would probably think he is, if he's at all self-referential, but questioning the basic validity of his entire career to date. And this is very hard for him."

She paused. "I know you don't like him, Harry," she said, "and I think you've got very good reasons not to. But that doesn't alter the fact that Bob Brennan right now is an extremely troubled man. A deeply-troubled man."

"Look," Dell'Appa said, "if he is then I'm sorry. Not *very* sorry, just: sorry. But that's not what's on my mind now. What worries me's not how he feels, but what he may've done to feel better, that he shouldn't've done. Or, equally scary, far's I'm concerned: what he might not've done, that he should've. Mistakes and misjudgments: everyone makes them—we all deal the best we can with them. But what if his conscience's told him to do something the law says he can't? Or excused him from doing something he should've, so then *I* wind up in the shit—tell me: then what do I do?"

"I don't know," she said. "I can always describe what I see in the data. I can't always prescribe how to change it."

He took a deep breath. "Okay," he said, "so much for that then, I guess. I just wish I felt like I had Brian with me, though. Beyond here, I think there be dragons." He paused and swirled the last of his wine once. "I know you think that I'm after Bob," he said, frowning, "even though I never said that. But even assuming that you're right, I do not want him to've done this. As much as I hate him, really despise him, I do not want to come around an ordinary corner on an ordinary day and trip right over unavoidable evidence, fuckin' *proof,* that Bob Brennan has done or is doing something that is gonna fuckin' ruin him, if anyone finds out—and he knows that it will, and I've been looking. I do not want that, Gayle. I want him to go in peace, and I will tell you honestly that I am scared to fuckin' death it doesn't matter, what I want. At all."

6 "I've got to admit," Dennison had said, "that sort of shook me up, when it first dawned on me one night while I was paying the damned mortgage, writing out the monthly check for the payment that we can't afford to make, on this house that we don't want, that the reason I am doing it proves the Bomber Rule is right. Or put it this way, at least: As many times as I've applied it to somebody's behavior that I just couldn't understand, my own or someone else's, it's never failed me yet. Time and time again, when there's just no explanation for why someone did something, you'll find if you look far enough, dig deep enough, wait long enough, that, yes, there *is* an explanation after all, and it's: money. The Frogs've got 'cherchez d'argent'; Bomber's got his Reason; and both of them are right. Right there, on the money.

"Virginia mostly did all right by herself for the first couple years after Lucy died on her. The two of them'd had time enough to locate most of the emergency services—oil-burner repairman, snow-plow man, stuff like that—that a person dumb enough to buy a house'll usually need in the normal course of things, so when something went wrong that had to be fixed right off, and needed a genuine repairman or a guy with the right equipment—like a truck with a plow on it—to do it, not just some handy-dandy, all-purpose, rechargeable adult daughter or a clumsy son-in-law but someone who actually knew something about fixing a busted sump-pump or getting a garbage disposal unit running again, she had one she could call.

"Like I say, her health was good. Plus she'd had a certain amount of practice, living by herself, in the years after Stan'd died but before she'd had the operation on her hip and Lucy'd come in. She didn't *like* being by herself again, not by any means, but it wasn't new to her. We gave her a season ticket to Megabucks for Christmas—because quite naturally after she'd won it the once there was going to be no way ever afterward of talking her out of faithfully betting it twice every week until doom finally cracked—so that cut down considerable on her need to get out to the store. Tory got down to see her at least one afternoon a week, not all that easy to do, even though it sounds like it would be, not if you're trying to start up your own small business at the same time and you've still got your family responsibilities, too. As Tory did and does. And they talked every day on the phone. She was functioning. She could handle it.

"She could handle it," Dennison had said, "but she could only handle it as long as she could handle it, you know? She was not the type of person who ever would've faked it, laid a guilt-trip on somebody to get something that she really didn't need, just because she craved attention or something. But she also wasn't stupid. When she got to the point where she really did need help, or else she was going to end up in some truly serious gravy, she knew it, and she wasn't too proud to admit it.

"And that's where the money came in," he had said. "That cock-and-bull story she'd told us about how she and Lucy were buying the house together? Well, it hadn't been one-hundred-percent-pure, total bullshit. There was considerable truth to it. The deal they'd worked out really did protect what was Tory's rightful share of her father's estate that Virginia'd sunk into the house. If what the two of them'd figured was what'd likely happen, if things'd really turned out that way, with Lucy the survivor, she would've had enough money to pay rent to the bank every month that would've come to her half the mortgage payment. For as many years as there were left to run on the mortgage—*and,* on top of that, since Lucy'd never shown any signs of wanting to live like the queen of England, more'n enough to take care of her for as many more years as she turned out to have on this earth.

"Now, give the old biddies credit here, that setup would've handled the whole thing very well. Tory and I could've stayed right where we were in Canton, paying Virginia's half of the mortgage, if she died before it was paid off, out of her Megabucks checks. And Lucy could've stayed put too—her Megabucks money would've covered her half the rent easy and still left her more'n enough to live on. Then, when she kicked the bucket, Tory would've inherited the whole house of horrors, and we immediately would've turned right around and sold the goddamned thing for whatever the market would've brought.

"*But,* with Lucy dying first, and leavin' her Megabucks checks to some niece or other down of hers down in ragin' Cajun country, well, that made it an entirely different bag of cats that we had on our hands. Virginia had enough to pay the whole mortgage and cover all of her other expenses, but it was going to be a real tight squeeze. What she actually had, income from all sources, would've been just barely enough to do both, if you really stretched it. And that was the real problem that we all had to face: the stretching. She just didn't have any slack at all. One heavy, unexpected expense, like a new roof, or one more small but steady, regular expense, some new prescription'd keep her breathing but that'd cost as much to refill every month as the payment on your first car did; some other article she simply had to have: either one'd do it, just sink the whole thing. The minute she needed anything more'n a cleaning lady dropping by three, four hours a week—because this's still a great big house we're talking about here, keep in mind, even though there's only one person living in it; even though some rooms're vacant, closed off in order to save heat, that doesn't mean they still don't have to be opened up and dusted every now and then—that'd be her camel's-backstraw. She'd be in over her head.

"She was trapped, and because she was, so were we. If she paid the whole mortgage, she'd need help with her overhead. If she covered all her medicines, her normal incidentals, plus the food, and the car, the insurance; the phone, heat and water, lights and so forth, well, then, she'd need help with the mortgage. Which we'd be in no position to give her. Not with the kids' tuition bills, and not on top of what it was costing us to live in the house in Canton. We just couldn't do it, even with both Tory and me working—and we're not living in any kind of luxury that I'm talking about here either. There was just no way that we'd ever be able to swing it. It just wasn't going to be possible.

"Well, what all of us were really hoping, of course, that none of us of course'd even so much as hint at, especially Virginia herself—was that when it happened to her, well, it would just happen, like a bolt out of the blue, and then it'd be over with. But of course that didn't turn out to be what happened."

"I wonder if it ever does," Dell'Appa had said.

"Of course not," Dennison had said. "Or at least, not often enough so anyone'd be anything more'n a fool if he relied on it happening that way. If it did there wouldn't be any such thing as a motor-vehicle fatality, let alone forty-five or fifty thousand people getting killed that way every year. Everyone'd always wear their seatbelt. Nobody'd ever get himself reeling-shitfaced and then get behind the wheel. When your wife was out in the old family car, just coming up on a crosswalk, the brakes wouldn't all of a sudden let go on her. And there wouldn't be a school bus stopped there at that very moment, letting all the little kiddies out to run into the street, right in front of her. Everybody's timing would be perfect, every time. If there were two ways that a given thing could happen, one that'd be disastrous and the other a fine beach day, we'd all have lovely golden tans. Melanoma'd be unknown. Disasters wouldn't happen. Casualty-insurance guys'd starve, and there'd be no more venture capital to put up more office buildings than anyone'll ever use.

"In Virginia's case," he had said, "what she was praying for was a nice, neat, thunderclap of doom, but when her number was starting to come up, her choice turned out to be out of stock and on back-order. What she got instead was a gradual, almost imperceptible, deterioration. Just a normal slowing-down that none of us probably even would've noticed if we hadn't all been braced for it, on the lookout like hawks to see if it would happen. And maybe that's got something to do with it too. You think? If there was the slightest chance, an *outside* chance, a longshot, that a bad thing might not happen, in any case like this, the fact that everyone still knows it might and can't get it out of their head, that that maybe brings it on?"

"Like one of those self-fulfilling prophecies there?" Dell'Appa had said.

"Yeah," Dennison had said. "Maybe everybody's force field or something like that, maybe the worry waves just go out and cause sympathetic anxiety-vibrations, tremors, that kind of thing, in the cosmic milk, so you get whitecaps kicking up in the cereal bowl, washing your karmic Wheaties all over the sports section and the funnies while you're trying to read them."

"I don't think so," Dell'Appa had said. "If that could happen, then counting on something to happen the way it really should, under normal circumstances, the way you wanted it to—say, that Larry Bird's back really hadn't gotten so bad that he really was gonna have to quit the Celtics while he was still pretty young—then more things'd happen that way. The amount of hoping for the good re-sult'd always reach critical mass 'way ahead of the anxiety and dread that the bad one might be already underway, and anyone who both-ered to look around'd see a lot less grief."

"I suppose," Dennison had said. "Anyway, there was this one Sunday we drove down there—one of Tory's favorite woodland sprites was opening his first shop of his very own, down in Somerset, throwing what actually turned out to be a very elegant, summer-Sunday champagne brunch—big tent with flowers on it in the yard out back, lobster salad, chicken salad, leg of lamb, roast beef, local trio playing show-tunes—all of which we would've missed except that in addition to needing to stay on good terms with people like David, in her line of work, she also really does think a lot of him, so she thought we ought to go. And then after that we drove over to see Virginia.

"I can 'see it now,' " Dennison had said, deepening his voice. "My father used to watch that show, Edward R. Murrow, when I was a kid. 'See It Now.' Sunday nights at first, and then later on they moved it, some night during the week. Murrow cured him, cured my father, of smoking. For a while. Murrow got lung cancer, and he was the one that always had a butt in his face? Well, as long as he was all right, and you could see him every week if you didn't think he was, then all the scare-talk about smoking had to be just a bunch of bull. But then, when the word got out, he was dying of it? My father said: 'That does it,' and he quit. And it was hell. He was in Hell himself and he always was real generous so he took us all along, everyone who lived with him and everyone he worked with. And then Murrow died anyway, which was just the kind of thing my father'd been hoping for, *any* kind of thing that'd give him an excuse to quit his quitting, and he said: 'Well, fuck it, then,' and started up again."

"That what killed him?" Dell'Appa had said.

"Sure," Dennison had said. "Along with all the other things, I mean, that a person gets going wrong with him when he gets to be ninety-one. He lived for over thirty years after Murrow died, and when he finally did get into the speed checkout line, well, I think he died of basically the same thing that Tory's mother died of. Only in his case I think there was a greater amount of sheer wilfulness in it. During the last year or two of his life he spent a fair amount of time complaining that the only friends he had left who weren't dead were getting silly. But since he really only had one left, Peaches Cassidy, what that actually meant was that when he forgot to call Peaches over in Norwood to remind him they were driving out the next day to the alleys on Route Nine in Framingham, to watch Don Gillis tape the 'Candlepin Bowling' shows—two or three, back to back, that the two of them'd watch again on TV when their Saturdays came up; they never missed that show—Peaches'd get nervous. He'd start to think Dad was losing *his* marbles, call him up and ask him: 'You still doin' all right, Jake? Not gettin' simple on me, I hope.'

"But then Peaches had the heart attack that killed him, and about two weeks after that, Dad had one of his own. Course I think a sprained ankle would've done it. If his heart hadn't attacked him, he would've found something else to die of. He'd just reached the point where he'd lost interest in the whole thing. It was time for him to go. People know that, feel it or something, recognize it right off, too, what the signal means. And it's like they just sort of excuse themselves, get up from the chair in a room where something's still going on, isn't over yet, and just leave. Answering a summons that only they could hear. If you didn't happen to be paying attention, you wouldn't even notice they'd gone until you got up yourself, and since most of the world isn't paying attention when most people vacate their places, hardly anyone usually notices. And not many of those who do notice remember for very long afterwards.

"Virginia was different," Dennison had said. "She wasn't as old as Dad was, of course, but she grew up in a generation where women who were strictly wives and mothers really didn't make a lot of friends, of their own. Not after they were married. After that the female friends they had, except for the women who lived next-door to them, were the women who were married to the men who were friends with their husbands. The next-door women never liked their husbands, and the husbands always knew this, sensed it, so they of course didn't like the next-door women.

"But, see, they couldn't very well just come right out and say it. That that was the real reason why they never wanted to have anything socially to do with Joe and Isabel, like take in a movie, maybe, or just go out for a pizza or something for a change some night, instead of just staying home all the time and cooking dinner every night all the time, the same old thing, old thing, old thing, always the same old thing. They couldn't say it because their wife was absolutely right when she said it seemed as though they always got along all right with Joe, swapping tools and stuff back and forth with him on the weekends, and when it was only a matter of sitting down over a couple beers after they finished waxing the car or cutting the grass on Saturdays, they seemed to like each other well enough.

"Because they knew if they did that, did come right out and say it, that the reason that they didn't want to go out with Joe and Isabel was because Isabel didn't like them and they knew it, they always knew it, knew it the first day they met the broad, and they didn't like her either, their wife would feel like she had to defend Isabel, or whatever the woman-next-door's name happened to be, and the only way she'd be able to think of to do that most likely would be to attack her own husband.

"She might even actually come right out and say that there were lots of times, as a matter of fact, when she'd thought to herself that if Isabel didn't like their husband—which Isabel'd never come right out and actually *said,* mind you, but if she had've done that—well, she had plenty of good reasons not to like him. Always being so rude to her and acting like she didn't even exist, they couldn't even see her when she saw them in the yard in the morning and said hello to them or something. Which would promptly make him just as mad as she already was, so that he would say something like: 'Yeah, in that goddamned yellow house-dress that she wears all the time, and that blasted kerchief she's always got on there, tied around her head. She ever take that damned thing off and *wash* it? I don't care if she is your friend. I can't stand that woman.' And then the two of them would have a good fight, when all she'd been trying to do was get out of the house and the kitchen for one night and talk to somebody besides him for a change, and he was just so selfish that he never understood that she needed to get out after spending all day in the house. The upshot of which would be that neither one of them would get laid at all that night, and most likely not for the next week or so, either, until finally one of them got so horny that the fight was over with because it had to be or else no one was ever going to get laid again. Well, *fuck* that. Which no one of course said aloud then, but they muttered it deep in their hearts, boys, they said it deep in their hearts.

"So what the husbands did was find a *different* reason to explain why they didn't like the next-door women. And the one that they generally came up with was that the women next door were stupid. As in fact they quite frequently were, and their wife would have spotted this already by herself, so she would have a pretty hard time defending Isabel, and would therefore maybe not even try. She would not be happy, but she wouldn't be all pissed off, either, with a big hair across her ass that'd be there until the snow flew and the Christmas lights went up, and at least there would still be at least a possibility—maybe not too good a one but still a possibility—that when a man came home from work he might get laid that night.

"So once the sun went down or when the weekends came, these women who were wives and mothers never socialized with the next-door women who were doing the same thing. They were just daytime friends, and those're not the kind you keep.

97

"The years began to mount up, and the husbands started dropping off, one by one. And therefore so did most of the friendships of their grown-up years. They vanished, *poof,* into thin air, the same as all the friendships that they'd had when they were girls, and they were friends with other girls who went to school with them. Or when they were young women and they'd worked together with them in the same stores and offices. The ones they shared all those secret giggles about boys with for quite a while, and then with the ones that they knew later: knowing nods and smiles about young men. Not much later they got very jealous of those disloyal ones, though, the little bitches who stabbed their best friend in the back, by getting their engagement ring *first,* before their best friend did—'Never speak to *her* again.' Back when they were young, before they found their own husbands—those friendships that they'd had back then just disappeared. Like blocks of dry ice melting; not even a dirty little puddle on the floor to remind you they'd been there.

"It was sort of a paradox, really. You had all these women who'd followed the pattern and'd gotten themselves involved in marriages of almost complete dependency, and then as the dominant partners, the men, died off, there they were, all those women, suddenly expected to be completely *in*dependent now. Having no choice except that, really. No choice, no preparation, and after all those years, no protection, either. What they might've preferred didn't matter. Not one soul in the whole spinning world cared.

"Well, that was what'd happened to Virginia, had been in the process of happening to her long before that lovely June Sunday when Tory and I'd driven down to David's champagne open-house and then, not close to tight but wined and dined and nicely-mellowed, on over to Westport to Virginia's. Just a casual 'right-down-here-in-the-neighborhood-and-thought-we-might-as-well-drop-in' call, and if that doesn't teach me never again to make another visit like that to *any*one, *any*where, *any*time, no matter how long I may live, then I am beyond even a chance of reclamation, let alone hope of measureable improvement. You might just as well lead me out of the barn now down to the back forty, and have the hired man shoot me point-blank in the head. And then fire another one, just to make sure, we really did get it all over with.

"Virginia was out in the yard," Dennison had said. "She was really good with flowers, good enough and knew enough so that if she hadn't put her mind to not becoming one, she could've become a really preachy pain in the ass on the subject. Like one of those anally-compulsive men who's obliged by the rules to retire when he hits a given age even though he doesn't want to, but being the type he is, he sees it coming and prepares, years ahead—as Brennan doesn't seem to've, at all, and that may be another part of his problem; or: another problem: that he's suddenly realized he's still facing flatfoot retirement flatfooted, and there isn't enough time left to do much about it now. So when they finally give him the watch and kick him out he knows an indecent amount about golf, or flyfishing; bridge, stamp-collecting—which he'd never call 'philately'—or some other goddamned thing that then becomes the only thing he does, and all he talks about. A guy in my wing in Vietnam had a father-in-law that he really got along with fine while the two of us were there and the old guy was back here and working every day, but then we both came back and the time went by, and pretty soon, it seemed like, the old man retired. What'd been up 'til then a nice, pleasant, *interesting* hobby that the two of them'd shared, became the old man's total occupation, and now here was Billy with his wife, her name's Rachel, and three teenagers, two of them in college and the third one headed there, his own career to think about and get as far as he could in, before his own time was up, so he'd have a decent pension to look forward to, at least, and his father-in-law wouldn't leave him alone, would not give him a minute's peace.

"Birding," Dennison had said. "The old boy'd always had a soft spot in his heart for spending a May morning tramping through wet pumpkin-vine underbrush, spying on prothonotary warblers catching errant woodstocks, and that was all right then. But once he was completely on his own, he did it every fucking *day*, and a good part of most nights. Billy'd be in his office at Three-Em there, out in Minnesota, getting his work done, he was general counsel by then, and the phone'd ring on his desk: It was Ted, and it was important. So he'd interrupt his train of thought, stop what he was doing—because he did like the old man and Rachel's mother, too, something might've happened to her—and pick the phone up to discover that his dear wife's father'd just added to his Lifelist a least-plum-busted dingbat, very rare 'round Chapel Hill, at least at that time of year. 'This kind of entertainment,' Terry told me, 'well, put it this way: No matter how much you like watching the birdies, or your loving father-in-law, it can get on your nerves very fast.'

"Well," Dennison had said, "Virginia had the potential to become that kind of pest. She knew just as much, at least as much, about flowers as Billy's father-in-law knew about the birds, and she could've done it, easy. But she didn't. It was something that she did, that she'd always done, and that she'd always liked doing and knew how to do very well, so she did it. She belonged to three or four of the garden clubs around Taunton during the years that she lived there, and then when she moved down to Westport she found one or two down there, and she would go to them from time to time. When the winter started to run down every year so it was getting on toward spring, she would make arrangements to get herself to the Flower Show in Boston, one way or the other—couple years, Tory took her—and those were pretty much all the things she did about what she liked to do. With flowers. All of them. And that really was all of it, too. Because she liked growing flowers for that, for what it was to her. Not as something she could use to make a damned nuisance of herself, to bedevil other people with.

"So when you saw her outdoors or in, working on her plants, something to do with her plants, you knew that Virginia was happy," Dennison had said. "As happy as she ever got, anyway, up to her ass in dirt. And that day, the Sunday in June, when we turned in her drive and went up toward that goddamned house, and I saw her standing there beside the front door, just standing there and looking down at this flower bed she had there, these beds of beautiful tall, white and yellow, blue and red, flowers,—what they were I couldn't possibly tell you to this day, and of course they're all gone now, just as dead as she is, even after only one year of no one taking care of them; that's all it took—on both sides of the door, I looked up that drive, and I saw her just standing there and looking down, and that was when I knew. That the time had come. Now it was all over. What we'd known was coming: It'd come, and now it was there.

"Because that's all she was doing, see?" Dennison had said. "She wasn't working on them. It'd never struck me until then, that I'd never seen her just, well, doing what I guess I would've done, if flowers'd been my thing. Just standing back and looking at them, enjoying what my work, all my skill and care and hours, 'd made come from the earth. No, there was always something more, she was working on. But not now. Not that Sunday. Now there was some reason, what it was I didn't know, and specifically, well, I never did find out exactly what it was, but something had been working on her down inside there, and now it'd finished what it'd set out to do to her. May've had a slight stroke; may've fallen and had a real hard time of it; getting up: any one of those things, it could've been. But something clearly had happened, and she was not going to put on her knee-pads and her cloth gloves and get down her hands and knees again and take care of her flowers any more. And she knew it. That was the end of it. She couldn't do it, grow the flowers, anymore.

"She had this look on her face that I'd never seen before, when she heard the car come up and turned around. The closest I've ever come to describing it to myself is *surprise*, and it wasn't surprise to see us—we quite often dropped by, or at least Tory did. No, this was almost a look of . . . of astonishment, I guess. Wonderment, maybe? I don't know. A kid-on-Christmas-morning look, only what was on her face was not delight—more like dismay. Virginia knew what I knew, too, and she'd found it out just like I had. It was like she'd just happened to stop by, 'd seen herself standing there by the flower-beds at the door, and quite unexpectedly found out. She hadn't been prepared either. Even though she'd also known that it was coming, lots better'n I did.

"Well that, my friend," Dennison had said, "that is the sort of thing that I think must've happened to Bob Brennan while you were away, that none of us happened to notice because we were all around him every day. It was too gradual. I think what you've come up against is Bob Brennan still in the aftermath of suddenly discovering that something he'd never even dreamed could happen to anyone has happened to him, and he's still trying to come to grips with it."

"Have you got any idea what it is?" Dell'Appa had said.

"I haven't yet," Dennison had said. "I'm going to need more'n you've gotten so far, this feeling of uneasiness, or whatever the hell you want to call it, from reading his reports. You're going to have to get a closer look at him'n you've had so far, in the flesh, and do more thinking, too. And then bring me some more data, more details."

"Okay," Dell'Appa said, "but just so long's we both understand it's more than just a 'feeling of uneasiness' that I'm getting, from reading the reports, hardly talking to the man at all, I think there's something seriously wrong. On what I've seen in those reports—actually, more like what I haven't seen that I'd expect to see, and what I have seen that I never would expect to, not from this guy, not from him— something I never saw any sign of in this guy's makeup before's happened to him, and it must've been pretty dramatic, too. Traumatic, even. It's changed the way he looks at things. The way he thinks."

"Well, this happens to people," Dennison had said. "In all lines of work it can happen. And does. Not a bit unusual, either. Very common, in fact. For it, to have it happen, I mean, to someone who's been in law enforcement all his adult life. Especially when his separation date's coming up, and knowing that's more or less's gotten him started taking stock of how he's spent what he's got to see now's been most of his useful life. Like it or not. He's already receptive, he's in a relatively-receptive state, a taking-inventory, stock-taking kind of thing, and then suddenly he sees something that he never saw before. Or else maybe it did, maybe many times, but it so happened every time that he just never noticed. Maybe just wasn't paying attention. His mind was always, you know, off on something else. But now it isn't, and he's positively stunned. Something happens right in front of his eyes and this time, by God, he notices. It just *staggers* him, so much so that he starts to rethink all the basic underpinnings, the premises and principles, of the job that he's been doing. This job that's been most of his whole adult life, the *way* that he's been doing it; what's been that he's been doing. What it all really means."

"Some kind of a midlife crisis there?" Dell'Appa had said. "Male menopause or something? That what you're getting at here, Bry?"

"Well, yeah," Dennison had said. "Yeah, I guess that'd be, it could be, something like that. Maybe. One way of looking at it."

"Yah," Dell'Appa had said. "Well, okay, I guess. Very touching and all that, and I'll do my best. But I got big reservations about this, Brian, okay? Having him still staying on this case, working on it any more, now that it's my baby. Big bad reservations, and they bother me already. I wanna be on record here about this from the gun: There's something wrong already here, with the job that Brennan's done to date with this whole Mossi case, and it bothers me. A lot.

And what bothers me even more is that not only am I not sure just exactly what it is that smells wrong about this file, but I also don't know how to pin it down without alerting Bob that what I'm doing is not only taking over the case from him but, in addition, trying at the same time to figure out how it got so mortally fucked-up. How come he either *let* it get that far sideways, or *made* it get that way. And if he did it on purpose,—which I've got to say right now, in case you didn't guess, I think has to be the explanation here; it's the only way that I can see that any project this important, in the hands of a man with his experience and brains, *could* get so monumentally fucked-up—then: How come? What's the explanation here? What the *hell* is going on?

"The man's not stupid, Brian. I never said he was. No one's ever heard me say I thought Bob wasn't smart. I think he's mean. I don't like him. Those things I've said many times, but never that he's stupid. He can't fall back on that excuse and no one can use it for him. No one who knows him'd even try. When he broke me in here, back when I first came in, the time that I spent with him back then taught me to hate his guts. I know,—hell, I even knew back then, because the old hands told me—it was nothing personal. 'Bob Brennan's always hazed the greenhorns. It's just the way he is.' And at the same time he was making my life miserable, I was seeing him do the same things to the other rooks. He made Cannon grovel, just doing everything he could to break another young guy's spirit—and succeeding too, more than a little, I think, much as I hate to say it. Well, I hated him for that, too, hated him even more for what he tried to do to me, even though it didn't work, because it really *wasn't* personal, on his part, see? It was systematic, programmatic, individually institutionalized meanness. And on some other guys it did work.

"Now I know, I hope, I must've calmed down some, all the time I've been away from here, away from him, but even having that in mind, I think that maybe I still do hate his guts, hate his fuckin' guts. But: about his brains there's still no doubt: I *know* that man's not dumb, and he never has been, either.

"So," Dell'Appa had said, "that makes it kind of important, doesn't it. To figure out as fast as we can what it is that's got me so worried about him now, and do it fast enough to stop him from making my nightmare come true. Whatever that damned nightmare may be."

"Ah, Harry," Dennison had said, "now let's not get, you know, too down-hearted here. Most of our worst fears, you know, never do come true."

"The ones that don't come true aren't the ones that worry me," Dell'Appa had said. "It's the goddamned ones that do, and were before you had them."

7 Short Joe Mossi's progress through the rest of that first day convinced Dell'Appa that Brennan's reports were trustworthy, and therefore likely to be useful, in at least one major respect: if Brennan stated that on a given day what he had observed "the subject Mossi" doing had accorded "with the subject's customary and usual Tuesday routine," it almost certainly had. Dell'Appa by himself and doing sixty-seven miles an hour in the maroon Lexus SC300 coupe he had signed out of the seized-motor-vehicle pool, following Joe Mossi southbound in his old gray Cadillac on Route 24 in Brockton, so stated aloud. "There's nothing wrong with old Bob's vision. This guy may look like the chief assassin in a horde of minivan-size Mongols, which he certainly is, but he's as reliable as disorder and early sorrow, by God.

"The files say Brennan followed him every Tuesday the past year, except when Bob was on vacation, and then back there in July, when Short Joey went away, took Danny down to Swift's Beach down in Wareham. And every Tuesday, Brennan reports, Short Joey did his Tuesday thing. Well, what he saw Short Joey doing all those Tuesdays is what I'm seeing done today. He saw Danny off safely on the Seven-forty-eight. Then he continued on up Dockett Street and turned right onto the parkway, heading for Marie's. 'So why Marie's?' I say to Brennan, 'Why not the Dunkin' in the Square, there? Was good enough for us.' And Brennan says to me: 'Because Short Joey *likes* Marie's, on account he likes Marie. So if her doughnuts aren't as good as Mister Dunkin's there, well, to Joey that don't matter: he's not friends with Dunkin'.' And sure enough, bet the ranch on it, Marie's was where he went.

"'He'll spend an hour, ninety minutes, havin' coffee with the guys, seeing what might be in the papers, keepin' up, what's goin' on. And also, of course, yesterday's results and the card this afternoon, down at Coldstream there.' And that's exactly what he did."

Dell'Appa's microcassette tape recorder kit from Radio Shack included an optional, unidirectional, lavalier microphone fitted with an alligator clip that he could attach to his lapel so "I can be Yuppiecop, and dictate while I drive." He could also use it while he read through documents, studied texts or did surveillance.

"I seldom take notes," he had testified once, when asked to produce them at a hearing of a motion to suppress evidence he had obtained by means of electronic surveillance—defense counsel had pleaded insufficiency of probable cause for issuance of the bugging warrant—"any more than I overheard your client's conversations by shinnying up the drainspout and listening-in under his eaves. I'm an investigator at the shag-end of the twentieth century, not some quill-and-inkpot court-steno out of *Bleak House,* and I work like what I am."

He had conditioned his acceptance of the Department's combination job-promotion/permanent-transfer offer to the Detective Branch upon written assurances that he would have "access at all times to as much clerical assistance as is necessary for the efficient and satisfactory performance of assigned duties." The civilian administrator, publicly- and showily-designated by the Secretary—also a civilian—to "beef up the Department's investigative capability on a hurry-up, crash-basis, not only updating its operations in all technological respects, but making sure as well that they remain thereafter, at all times in the future, in an operationally top-notch, state-of-the-art condition" had fully understood neither the art nor its then-current state, and had therefore gravely underestimated the cost of the Department's compliance with Dell'Appa's condition. When the oversight became apparent, the administrator had first informed Dell'Appa by brusque memo that "unforeseen budgetary limitations will henceforth require advance divisional approval of all expenses of transcription, but in no event to exceed total cost per operative of $100 per week. Please allow minimum three working days for processing such requests."

Dell'Appa had dictated a memorandum of reply to the administrator: "New regulation and procedures inapplicable to this operative," it said. "Read my contract. No typing, old or new." Five weeks thereafter, to the day, he had received an administrative memorandum by which he had been "hereby advised" that he had been "temporarily-separated, forthwith, from Boston central office, for detachment to western field office, for exigent assignment on case-by-case basis, detached duty period not to exceed 12 consecutive calendar months, inclusive of such periods of earned vacation or sick leave as may fall within said 12-month period."

He had consulted Dennison about the memorandum.

"I've seen it," Dennison had said, scaling it back to him across the desk. "I'm copied in on all administrative decisions that affect the operation of my branch. Not necessarily *consulted* before they're made, but fairly-faithfully informed about them after they've been made, before they're to take effect. *Just* before, usually. Just barely before."

"So I take it then, this isn't unique?" Dell'Appa had said.

"What makes you ask that?" Dennison had said.

"A suspicious nature, I guess," Dell'Appa had said. "Not that I'm subject to frequent fits of domination by *post-hoc, propter-hoc* frenzy, least so far as I'm aware, and I don't think I'm any vainer than the next man, but—"

"Oh, but you are," Dennison had said, interrupting. "A good deal vainer than the next man, as a matter of fact. Not necessarily 'the next man here,' because after my sixteen months so far in the Bomber seat my own guess is he was right when he claimed he'd bossed more divas'n the Met's ever seen, but still, certainly a good deal vainer than the next, *ordin*ary, guy. Oh yes, old chap, quite so."

"Well," Dell'Appa had said.

"Good heavens, man," Dennison had said, "you're not taking offense here now, are you? There's nothing wrong with it, with being vain, if you've got something to be proud of and you use it. Just don't make yourself ridiculous, pretending that you aren't. That's all I was suggesting."

"Yeah," Dell'Appa had said. "Well anyway, without some reason to think otherwise, what I started out to say was that it's pretty hard for me to look at that memo without seeing just a hint of retribution in it, you know? A little whiff of the old grapeshot, a bit of a taste of the lash? Oh, nothing *coarse*, mind you, nothing like the bad old days, when I understand a man with a fresh mouth on him could come back to his desk on Thursday night and find out he'd been reassigned to the North Adams barracks, full-pack, back onna road again, him and old Willie Nelson, effective Saturday. Collective bargaining hasn't been a *total* loss. But it still looks to me quite a lot like what it used to be. Like a banishment, I mean. Though maybe only to me. Mom always said I was too sensitive sometimes."

"Of course," Dennison had said.

" 'Of course,' " Dell'Appa had said.

"Sure," Dennison had said. "You think he's given you one good swift boot in the croagies. Well, you're exactly right. He did. You laid some hard attitude on him a while ago. That 'fuck-you,' wise-ass steno-memo. Right off he didn't like it. He was thoroughly pissed-off. The guy spends all day fighting budget battles with the other agencies—thinking he's protecting us guys, who then turn around and laugh at him behind his back for calling us 'my troops,' ungrateful wretches that we are—and then when he puts in a cost-cutback plan that's purely for show-and-tell, a 'leaner-meaner' pufferoo that nobody expects will have any more real-world effect than if he'd merely cleared his throat and said he might actually *have* to do something, some day, that would really cut costs in this place, one of his own people rises up and gives him the speedy finger. You can bet he was annoyed.

"But he's the new variety," Dennison had said. "When his breed gets pissed off, it gets just as pissed off just as fast as the old wardogs we were used to. But then it doesn't do anything. Not right off, like they used to—explode—and that's where the difference is. It's on a delayed fuse or something. Sneaky's more its style. It wouldn't choose that word, though; that would not be sneaky. It calls what it does 'just taking some time to think this whole thing over, turn it over once or twice in my mind. Look at all the angles.'

"Those angles, though, do not include whether it's right, whether it's *appropriate*, for it to be pissed off. It always knows when it is, just like as we do: 'Whaddaya mean, " 'm I pissed off"? Naturally I'm pissed-off. Anybody would be.' No, it wants the time to think about what'd be the best thing to do, what'll not only cut you off at the ankles, or at least no higher'n the knees, but also perform the amputation in such a way that you won't be able to do anything about it afterwards, to get even. By dropping dimes on the media or something, so the papers every morning and the TV every night'll get all worked up about 'numerous reports of a crisis of morale among seasoned long-time members of State law enforcement agencies merged in the new Department.' 'Secretary Said "Out of Touch." ' 'Harrumph, and harraw, and all that shit.' Oh, the new breed wouldn't like that at all; that's why it thinks: to prevent it. But it's smart, and sooner or later it thinks of something that looks like it might be a way to safe revenge. Then it chews *that* over, overnight, and if it still can't find anything wrong with it by morning, then finally it does it. By which time, of course, you've just about forgotten what it was that you did in the first place that set the whole damned thing in motion. So your feelings're hurt when you're justly punished, and you come running in tears to see Brian.

"Sadly for you, that changes nothing. All that thought and stuff's worked. The new breed turns out to've planned revenge well. You *have* been cut off, neat and clean. 'And you can't do a blessed thing about it, you fresh punk, so how do you like that?' "

"And that's the reason then, for it," Dell'Appa had said. "You're telling me that that is what it is for."

"Far as I know it is, yeah," Dennison said, radiating innocence. "Why, can you think of another one? Or don't you think that that one's enough, giving the bosses the finger?"

"Yeah," Dell'Appa had said. "Well, all right then. Consider me chastised, and properly so—if you wanna insist. On to the next thing: what do I do about it?"

" 'Do'?" Dennison had said. "Just what the hell do you think you *can* do here, boy? You got very limited options. You've got a written order from the Secretary's secretary, detaching you from *here,* and dispatching you out *there,* and it tells you to go out there and *sit,* and *stay,* out there until you're called to come back here. Or else for a year, whichever may come first. Now I may be wrong, of course, but that doesn't seem to leave you a whole lot of room for improvisation. So if I were you, and I wondered what to do, that's what I would do. I would go out there, where I've been sent. Or else I would resign. Them's the options, baby."

"Well, no," Dell'Appa had said. "No, I didn't mean that. What I meant was, I guess: What can you do now?"

"*Me?*" Dennison had said. "What can *I* do now?"

"Yeah," Dell'Appa had said.

Dennison had shrugged. "Same thing I was doing when you came in here," he had said. "Finish as much of my afternoon's work as I can before quitting-time comes. Drop it in the Out box. Then put what's still left of it back in the In box and light out for the territories. The In box being where a good chunk of what's in front of me right now was when I came in this morning: because that's where I put it yesterday, when the quitting whistle blew and I dropped the pick and went home. Those environmentalists, boy, they think they've got the lock on recycling stuff, and when it comes to wine bottles and other dead soldiers, well, maybe they actually have. But when it comes to recycling work, work that I really don't want to do, I can make a stack of it last longer'n a little kid can stow a Belgian-cheeka Brussels-sprouts 'til his mother gets distracted so he can feed the veggies to the dog."

"Cut it out, Brian," Dell'Appa had said. "You know what I'm talking about. What can you do?"

"I take it neither one of those two options that I mentioned really appeals to you," Dennison had said.

"No, they don't, as a matter of fact," Dell'Appa said. "I've got this little house in Whitman that I can't afford and a woman that I really like lives in it. With a little boy she says is mine and he looks like he might be, too, every now and then, when the headmaster lets him come home for vacation, so I, his own father, can see him for vacation. And every day when the late afternoon changes into the blue hour, or if it's already night when the guy that I've been following all evening finally decides that it's time we both went home, I *like* going back to that house where I live with those two people.

"That's gonna be mighty tough to do, boss, if I'm out in Northampton every night when the cocktail hour comes. If I'm ninety miles from home, and I've got to be back out there when the sun comes up next day. What'm I supposed to do then, when that's what's in front of me, huh? Say: 'Hey, no problem, buddy, you got investigators in place out there, boundin' around all over the joint like a buncha beagles chasin' bunnies, but for some reason, the other, you want me out there instead? Well, *sure*. Happy to oblige, old pal. This'll be fresh cake.' No, I don't think so, Bry—I don't like this idea at all."

"But at the same time," Dennison said, "you don't want to quit."

"No, I don't," Dell'Appa said. "I went through a lot of specialized training and education on top of what I already knew about the technology stuff so I could do this kind of work. Now I'm to the point where I can do it, and I like it, and I'd just as soon not quit."

Dennison had dropped his voice an octave to the broadcaster's message-from-our-sponsor depth. "Very commendable, son," he had said. "If more of our young people would only take your attitude toward public service, this society of ours would be—"

"Oh shut up," Dell'Appa had said. "This thing isn't funny to me."

"It sure damned-right-well isn't," Dennison had said in his normal voice. "And it damned-well shouldn't be, either, because what you're doing here now is facing the kind of decision that can make or break your career. The wrong one turns you into instant dogfood in this outfit: 'dead-dried meat, just add water.' You might as well just go ahead and quit right now if that happens, because no matter how long you hang around afterwards, after you make that mistake, you'll always be the sad-sack guy in the office; every unit's got one: 'He came in here? He was golden. Had all the talent in the world. Just had talent to burn. But for some reason or other he never did manage to amount to much. Never did understand it, myself, why he never went anyplace. Maybe just one of those poor-bastard guys, never did catch the right break.'

"See, Harry, this is a test that you're facing now, and you've got to treat it like one. You had a solid record in the blue suit with the tunic and the hat on, worked hard and showed good judgment when your judgment was called for. And didn't volunteer it when it wasn't, which is at least as important. And even more important, you had real *friends* in uniform, decent people generous enough so that when they saw a nice young fellow working hard and doing a good job, they made sure the word got around to some place where it'd maybe do the kid some actual good, ginger his life up a little. Get him a real place to shine.

"You're not here because you're smart and honest, Harry. Let me tell you that right now, case you're under that illusion. You wouldn't've lasted here long if it'd turned out you were stupid and you stole, this's true, but you're still here so it must be you didn't. But that still isn't how you got here, Harry, no sirree. You got here 'cause you had *friends.* Not only did some senior officers, whose word on talent counted, see right off you had it; they also liked you well enough, had faith enough in you, so they wrote your name down on one of their secret lists. And those're real short lists, my friend. It's an honor when you make one."

"Yeah, yeah," Dell'Appa had said, flicking his left hand away from his face, "this song I've heard sung a great many times. Never did like it that much, learn how to dance to it, either. Let's cut to the chase, shall we, Bry?"

" 'Yeah-yeah' nothin'," Dennison had said. "There's a lot of happy horseshit in this business, Harry, and I'll never be the one to tell you different. But the mistake smart guys like you make—well, maybe *mostly*-smart guys like you make, because sometimes you are *stunningly*-stupid—it's your very favorite, is when you get to thinking that it's *all* bullshit, you know? That it's never the real thing. And then when it *is*, when it's really the real stuff, when some veteran, some guy who probably trained you and's always been the first one to start laughing when some jerk began slinging the crap; when that guy you respect starts talking about loyalty, hard work, and having balls, and *always*, always going through and doing what you said that you were gonna do, you go into your guffawing mode: no hemming, just plain haw-haw-haw.

"But this time you notice it's not all the same. 'Something's different,' you think, and it is. No one else is doing it. You're laughing all by yourself. And that's when you start to realize: Oh-oh. Somewhere along the line here, could just be, you made a major-league mistake. You look around, and, *damn*, that's what it is, all right. Your worst nightmare came true. You're standing there by yourself, and you're the only one who's laughing. You laughed in the wrong place. Or you might say, if you liked, that you stepped on your own dick, 'cause that's exactly what you did.

"That's when the people who're jealous of you, don't have your ability, intelligence, but're still dangerous because what they do have's just enough to let them see they don't and you are better, or who maybe just don't like you—and as hard's it is for guys like us, really nice, great guys, for us to believe a thing like that, there're always some who don't—that's when they know they've got you. And they really *have* got you, too; boy, have they ever.

"Now I'm not saying the Assistant's one of those people. And I'm not saying it's the Secretary, either, that he's the one who's your enemy. Although he could be—either one of them could be. All I'm saying is that now you know for sure that there's at least one out there, a real saboteur. Somewhere in this outfit, there's at least one someone who's decided that he bigtime doesn't like you, and therefore does not wish to have to watch any more good things happening to you. Or *she* really doesn't like you, and is just as out to get you as any man could be.

"Either one; doesn't matter; the effect's the same. Your long-term career outlook just sneezed a violent sneeze. It may be coming down with something which could lead to something worse. More dangerous, I mean. Maybe even fatal. Because as you found out today, when you got your messages and mail, took them to your desk and read them, whoever this person is has either neatly muttered a bad word about you where the Secretary or his faithful Indian companion could hear it, and it worked, or else the one who doesn't like you's one or both of those two people, and didn't need a prompt.

"I myself tend to doubt it's either one of those fine gentlemen. Being as how they're both butt-sucking, glad-handing, bottom-feeding career-type politicians, they've got stations far above ours. They've got lots of dignity, *mucho* dignity, in fact. *God,* I mean, these guys're so dignified, they've got *bearing.* Their topcoats are of fabric woven from the chest hairs of the camel. Can you imagine how many bare-chested camels there must be, going topless out there, shivering like mad, freezing their asses off out there in the Sahara, while the chubby Secretary and his portly deputy walk like ducks down Beacon Hill, nice and warm in camels' hairs, to lunch at the Parker House? Hundreds, thousands of them. Millions even, maybe. Camels all over far-away Arabia, wearing sweatshirts and wool mufflers so pols in Boston can keep warm. And they *are* warm, too. They've got that *special* warmth, that *inner* warmth, the kind you get from knowing you've got tassels on your loafers, you don't even have to look; the Commonwealth buys lunch for you and pays for all your gas. You can park anywhere you like—hydrants, cross-walks, doesn't matter—and certainly not the least of it, you're,"—Dennison hushed his voice—"*a member of the bar."* He spoke normally. "It ain't Hog-heaven, maybe, but if you are a porker, natural-born to wallowing, little grunting now and then, those surroundings aren't half-bad.

"So, what're we to guys like that, humble guys like us: Can I ask you that? No: Can I *tell* you, then? Sure, I can, you ask polite. Hell, even if you don't; I'll do it anyway. Absolutely. As fleas to wanton dogs are we, they bite us for their sport. *Common drudge* is what we are, synonym for *piece of shit,* career professional policeman. No possible threat to them. Unless one of them should get stupid at the same time you get lucky, so you come up with enough PC to get a judge to sign a paper that'll let you look at all their bank records. But: nah, that'll never happen. They're 'way too cute for that.

"And anyway, to you personally, like I say: Doesn't really matter; either way, you've now been ordered out of the cozy cushioned chair you've had, right here by the fire. and with no ceremony whatsoever escorted out to the distant anteroom. Where the footmen, trades-men, peddlers, and tinkers remove their muddy boots, and humbly— no complaints allowed—respectfully, wait 'til they're summoned. Beckoned. Nodded to. Whatever. That's where you are now, my would-be heir apparent: plunked down on a hard bench, seated in a nasty draught, and you'd better realize it too. Put a sweater on real quick, and tomorrow wear the woolies even if they lie to you and say

114

it's coming summer. That's merely the weather forecast for the outside world, where everybody else is. Much colder where you are, and will be for a while."

"Until I learn to keep a civil tongue?" Dell'Appa had said. "Are you really telling me that I've been sent down to Pawtucket, demoted to triple-A, because I sassed somebody? Hurt some asshole's feelings? By just doing my damned job, the best way I know how? I can't believe it, Brian.

"Partly I mean it's impossible for me to believe in the abstract that any bunch of supposedly-mature and reputedly-intelligent, presumably-adult professionals, engaged in work that every one of us at least seems to believe is difficult and important, that we could ever've reached the point where we're allowing ourselves to be managed like a goddamned junior-high sorority, like kids still in training bras, tying up the phone. The bad boys wouldn't look at us and shudder, fear and loathing in their hearts, if we'd've let that happen to us; they'd've laughed us out of town.

"Then partly from my observations, and I'm pretty good at those if I do say so myself: since the only person I've met since the day I came in here strikes me as obviously unbalanced, unbalanced enough that I wouldn't really dare to predict what he might decide to do in a given situation, maybe even deranged, the only one of those would have to be . . ."

"Bob Brennan," Dennison said.

". . . my estimable mentor," Dell'Appa said, "the very same indeed. But while he might be mean enough, or maybe *perverse enough,* to fuck up this office on purpose, he doesn't happen to have the kind of executive position that'd give him the leverage to do it. Praise Jesus; say: amen."

"Amen," Dennison said laconically. "We may be a sorority, like you say, but when Bomber was our Great Den Mother, he took good care of us. And since I've been Den Mother, I have followed his example. I don't say this group is perfect, or it's been perfectly bossed, but so far as I've seen, up to now, at least, there's been no heavy damage done that looks permanent to me. Which I would say had been done, if Bomber's departure'd somehow not so incidentally led to Bob's elevation. But it didn't. And it won't, I can assure you, as long as I'm the one in charge."

"All right then," Dell'Appa had said, "what you're telling me is that I'm right and it's not Bob, but somebody still did it to me and I'm stuck with it."

Dennison had shrugged. "That's the gist of it," he had said. "You've gotten your penance. You can either grind your teeth and do it, or you can leave the church. Simple."

"Lemme ask you," Dell'Appa had said, "if it was you in this position, in the situation that I'm in, what would your choice be? Obedience? Or leave the Order? Apostasy, I mean. Which one do you think you'd take?"

"Now?" Dennison had said. "At my age? I'm not really sure I know." He frowned. "That's something like the trick baseball question, you know? 'Considering how bad major league pitching's become now, the lousy fielding you see all the time, whaddaya figure Ted Williams'd hit if he was playing today?' And of course the right answer's 'Two-eighty, two-eighty-five. Somewhere in that neighborhood.' Because as third-rate, incompetent and lazy as the competition is these days, 'you've got to keep in mind the guy is over seventy years old. He's had one heart attack already, minor one, I guess, and when he was on TV last year he looked really out of shape.'

"So: what would I do now, if I'd gotten myself into the same kind of fix you're in? Well, it's kind of hard to say, and I'd want to think it over, but I think when I got finished, I'd probably resign."

"You would," Dell'Appa had said.

"Yeah," Dennison had said, "I think so. No flat, resounding statement, no 'You can all go fuck yourselves; I don't need this kind of shit.' But I think I probably would take out my retirement papers, fill them out and send them in."

"But you think I should stay," Dell'Appa had said. "You think you'd probably quit, but I should hang in here and eat the shit. That's what you're really saying."

"No, it's not." Dennison had said. "It's not even remotely like what I'm telling you. You're not thirty-five yet."

"I'm getting pretty close, though," Dell'Appa had said. "At least three days now, every week, clearly at my back I hear Time's winged chariot hurrying near. I feel something hot on the back of my neck, too; could be the spittled breath of the horses."

"Age ain't pitchin' horseshoes, son," Dennison had said. "No leaners; close don't count. Next May I turn forty-seven. That doesn't make me 'close to forty-five,' all right? It is reasonably close, just about as close's it is to forty-seven, but what it *makes* me's forty-six. Eight years and a half from 'Bye-bye, now; thanks loads' from this outfit. When you get to my age, you'll find you're runnin' the stables where the steeds come in to rest up and the fresh teams get hitched up. They don't have to hurry any nearer, not a bit, when it's my attention they want. Those horses've moved in with me.

"So that's the first big difference between us," Dennison had said. "The years really change your perspective. If they don't you've got something wrong with you, because they should. So if I were in your place, with my first choice doing a full grovel and kissing ass right now—and also looking like I really mean it, which is the *real* hard part—because that's the only way there is to save a great career doing something that I like and that I'm really good at; and with my second choice being to tell them: 'Stick it up your ass,' I'd most likely take the second. Because I'd be giving up about a third as many years in this work as you'll be giving up, if that's what you decide to do, and I've got my reputation made and cast in cement. With that record I can get myself a new job that will pay me slightly more than I'm making now, and the only reason I don't take it now is that I'd get hurt retiring early on my pension from this job.

"You haven't been in long enough to get that kind of security yet, so you've still got it to get. That's a big-big difference, Harry. If each of us's got twenty-five thousand dollars to spend on a car, and I can get myself a Porsche for that money, I'm not being extravagant. But if for some crazy reason the Porsche people tell you that same car is going to cost you four times what I'm paying, a hundred thousand dollars—they don't like your looks or something, so your money's not as good—you should be committed for observation if you buy the fucking thing.

"And besides that factor," Dennison had said, "there's another difference in our situations. Maybe even more important, when you come right down to it. There's a reason, you see, for my ability to analyze your problem so quickly and incisively, and with such confidence. In fact I'm just a bit surprised that a bright lad like yourself hasn't already figured it out for himself."

"You've got to be shittin' me," Dell'Appa had said. "A well-behaved fellow like you are, such nice table manners and all? You actually fell in the toilet?"

"I am not shitting you, not a bit of it," Dennison had said. "And I went in head-first, just like you did. I'm not saying what I did was *exactly* the same thing you've done now, or that I was *precisely* the same age as you are now when I fucked up good and proper. But the similarities are too big to overlook, and the differences're too small to matter."

"What'd you do?" Dell'Appa had said.

"Hah," Dennison had said, "not a chance. Time and the gradual hardening of the arteries have combined to dim the memories of those of my superiors who witnessed my youthful indiscretions. Disrespectful acts, to be sure, but mitigated nonetheless by the fact they'd been committed in nothing more than sheer momentary excess of boyishly-exuberant, animal high spirits. In other words, if you think I'm gonna relive all of that embarrassment for you now, a good three-almost-now years since the last witness to it got shitfaced at his own retirement party and thanked me for driving him home afterwards by reminding me of the whole humiliating episode, in ignominious detail, all the way down Route Three to old Cape Cod, well, you've lost your mind, boy. There's no other explanation."

"I can find out, you know," Dell'Appa had said.

"Not where you're going, you can't," Dennison had said. "So if you try you'll have to do it somewhere around this end of the world, and if you do that, *I'll* find out, and I will take offense. Whereupon I'll then proceed to fix your ass so good you'll never get it back here. Your kid'll have children of his own, swimming in your pool in Whitman, begging Doctor-Grammy Gayle to tell them once again the story that's a legend in your family, bigger'n the one about good old Rip Van Winkle: how Grampy Harry left for Hampshire County one day, on a big hush-hush assignment, and never did come back.

" 'That was the last time that we ever saw him,' she'll say, with a tear in her eye. 'None of us ever laid eyes on him again, the rotten son of a bitch, no-good, skip-town scalawag. Not once after that fateful day. He's with God now, kiddies, down there with his God.'

" 'But God isn't *down* there, Grammy,' " the kiddies will then clamor, 'God's *up* there, in Heaven, with the angels. It's the Devil who's *down* there in Hell, Doctor Grammy, with the bad men: all the bad men and the Devil.'

" 'Don't contradict *me*, you fresh little bastards,' Doctor-Grammy Gayle'll say to the kiddies, giving each of the tykes a smart cuff. 'Doc Grammy knew her old Harry lots better'n you did and needs no cheap lip from you ilk. Harry had his own God: he worshipped the Devil, he did. That's what "full of the old Harry" means.'

"And, coincidentally enough, that is now exactly what you've got to convince the Man or Someone Who Knows Him that you really aren't full of. That you're basically an extremely nice guy, and if you somehow gave *him* the impression that you're a real wise-ass, and a rule-breaker and scape-grace, which in fact you are, in spades, that was totally inadvertent and entirely incorrect. Or, in the alternative, if someone else, some malicious, underhanded, lying, treacherous sneak, deliberately gave him the impression that is what you are, well, all you can say is that you really regret that and you're sure he knows, from his own experience, it's pretty hard to go through life in this kind of job without picking up some enemies along the way." Dennison had made wet kissing sounds, like someone calling a cat.

Dell'Appa had sighed, slapped his palms on his thighs and stood up. "Okay," he had said, "what's done is done. No help for it, I guess. It just seems awful strange to me, is all. I came in here fifteen months ago. I survived Bob Brennan's hazing without even getting in a fistfight with him, let alone shooting him or tampering with the brakes on his car. I took over that Salem arson thing that'd gone nowhere for almost a year, had Cannon going nuts, got it modeled, and now right after Christmas it's going to the grand jury. Wrapped up. Finished. Complete. Last couple weeks I've been doing what you told me, pulling up all the data that we've got on those small-banking interests, and we've really got a lot of it, to see if it looks any different when we get it integrated, as of course it will. It's begun to already. And now all of a sudden here I'm getting shipped out for more seasoning in the minor leagues.

"I dunno, Bry," he had said. "I still don't really know what to make of it. If it wasn't you sitting there, if it was someone that I didn't know and trust like I do you, who was sitting in that chair right now and telling me what you just told me, that it's strictly personal, just someone that I happened to piss off without even knowing I was doing it at the time, and he's getting even now, I would almost have to think that there was something funny going on. That the reason for this memo, for the decision to do this, this sudden so-called 'detachment,' has to be that I've gotten someone somewhere very fucking nervous about something he's been doing for a good while, or he did 'til pretty recently, that made him a lot of money—but that no one's found out about yet. And he doesn't want them to, either. That's why he's been so careful to cover his tracks, up to now, and he's done a good job of it, too. I don't even know myself yet what it is I've gotten into, that in time'd lead me to him if I kept on with what I'm doing.

"As I won't, of course, keep on, not if I'm going to be out there in Northampton, catching someone in the sheriff's office padding county purchase orders, for eighty pounds of powdered eggs to feed the House inmates breakfasts in August, when they only used seventy-two. Invoicing fifty gallons of green-vomit paint to redecorate the basement of the courthouse when the job only took eight, and the other forty-two weren't even green paint; those were the cans of various colors chosen by county employees having their own homes redone. Using the labor of ten of those inmates who didn't eat all of the eggs, and who promised not to run away if they could have conjugal visits while they were out on the jobs."

"Well, hey," Dennison had said, "that's pretty serious, I think. We can't have stuff like that going on. Tolerate that kind of official naughtiness, at taxpayer expense? I don't think so, Mister Holmes. You may think it's chickenshit, compared to the awe-inspiring, stupefying grandeur of what you're maybe, could be, doing, even though you don't know what it is yet, or who might be involved, and maybe never will. But if the citizens in western Massachusetts snap their evening papers open some fine night come this summer, and discover on the front page a big story about how Harry caught the county boffins with their paws in the cash drawer, those taxpayers will be very pleased, and they will glorify your name.

" 'We want Harry,' they will cheer, at the band concert that evening. 'All right, *Harry*, way to go, catch those thieving crooks.' They'll shower you with rose petals at the Eastern States Exposition, if takes you 'til next fall, and line up to shake your hand. 'Hey, Harry, you're our main man.' 'Harry-*kid* there, gimme *five*.' 'Harry, move your family out here from Whitman, okay? This's where your future is. Retire from the outfit and throw in your lot with us. We'll give you fifty grand a year, a Mercedes for your cruiser, and your official wardrobe will be Giorgio Armani, Armani minimum. Give 'em all hell for us. We can't afford to have those crooks picking our pockets while we pay them for their time.' "

"We can afford it a hell of a lot better'n we can to close our eyes to the kind of funny business that I still think might be going on here," Dell'Appa had said. "If there is someone who wants me to be somewhere else and pronto, and he's in a position to do that, that is dangerous, Brian. That kind of power? Enough to get me out of here in one fucking big hurry, no waiting until after Christmas, and keep me out of here for as long as it takes him to either shut down whatever he's been getting even richer doing, or pull up stakes and move it, hide it better somewhere else? That ain't no old video game."

"*Ahh*," Dennison had said, his voice guttural, his right hand brushing the suggestion away, "you're hearing the mermaids sing, Harry. Becoming a conspiracy junkie. Seeing a plot behind every bush, finding schemes in old coffee-cups. Beginning to think you're man's last best hope. This 'detachment' may actually turn out to be the best thing in the world for you right now. Not meant to be, no, but still it could be, a good personal thing for you, I mean. Let you decompress after your first year in here, recover your wits and your bearings."

8 "Short Joey's a regular law-abiding citizen," Dell'Appa said to the microphone as the turn signal began to flash on the right rear fender of the Cadillac. "We're still a good five-eighths of a mile north of the One-oh-six exit ramp, but he's slowin' on down and movin' on over into the right travel lane, just like a safe driver should. No sudden snap decisions for our boy here, no reckless-move stuff for Joey. Not after all of these halcyon years—'cept for the handgun reports, of course; the sharp cracks of the skulls being shattered, the crisp snaps of the fibulas breaking. No reason to change his ways now."

Joseph John Mossi's history in the files made him fifty-one years old that day, three months shy of his fifty-second birthday. Both Teresa Coppola and Luigi Mossi had been born in the United States; the six-room apartment on the first floor of the three-decker residence at 73 Pittman Street, West Roxbury, where Joey and Daniel had grown up and where they still lived, had been Luigi and Teresa's first home together; when she had been taken to Boston City Hospital for the last time, in 1988, she had left from that address.

She had done so very reluctantly, having been fearful of hospitals ever since, she was sure, the nurses had somehow damaged Daniel when they'd taken him from her at birth. "I can't get it out of my head, that's all, you know? I know something happened, one of them must've dropped him or something. Someone gave him the wrong medicine. And then when they see what'd happened to him, my poor *little*, brand-new baby boy, then, oh boy, I'm tellin' you, then they all got really scared. 'These people, they find out, they'll kill us for this. The dagoes, that's what they do with things like this. It's just the way ghinnies think.' So they all got together, see? And they protected each other. They all used to do that stuff then, cover up when they made a mistake. Especially when it was one of us. Did something, and they don't even think about it, not for a minute, that they ruined someone's whole life. As long as it ain't them, that it happened to."

She had agreed to do that, go in and submit to the tests, only after she'd been worn down by weeks of nonstop nagging by Short Joey and her husband, who knew very well that irrational fear was the real reason for her resistance, but could not mention it and thus force her to confront it because she knew they knew and did not give them the chance. "Sure, Ma, we know it's nothin', but even so, you still gotta go, you know? Just have some tests, make sure. It's only for a couple of days, and then you'll be right back home here okay? And we'll all have peace of mind. You just got to do this thing."

The morning after she left the house, the surgeon who made the small exploratory opening in her lower abdomen saw that the cancer which had started in her pancreas had metastasized to occupy the liver as well, and promptly closed her up again. But back in her room that afternoon she began to bleed internally, so that when she went back to West Roxbury the day after that, her transportation was the charcoal-gray Ford station wagon that J. S. Cardinale III employed as a service wagon in the undertaking business his grandfather had begun.

The old gray Cadillac displayed very little lateral lean on the ramp leading off Route 24 onto 106, recently-resurfaced two-lane blacktop stretching southwest through what had been mostly dairy-farming country until the 1980s. Then suddenly-prosperous, New Age, Quality-of-Lifers had discovered it as promising territory, virgin for construction of new brick-and-silvered-glass plants and office buildings, none of them exceeding thirty feet in height and all scrupulously designed to blend in with and complement the natural terrain. The kind of buildings, Dell'Appa had thought upon first noticing them scattered in the rolling fields around Northampton, that God would surely have included in the Pioneer Valley landscape, if He'd only had a little foresight, thought ahead a little to the day when His highest-ranking material creatures, His Yups, would require harmonious shelter during kicked-back working hours—along with, of course, on-site facilities for toddler-through-K2 day-care, lunchtime exercise, and quiet rooms for thought. Working hours in working places holistically and wholesomely far from madding crowds of ex-tremely-numerous people who still drove old cars on leaded gasoline; salted fatty foods (bernaise-sauced, marbled beef; deep-fried, un-ranged, unskinned chicken) and ate them; smoked cigarettes (mostly filtered, as though that really mattered); drank hard liquor (some-times neat); jogged not in midroadway, during twilight hours, nor worked out at least thrice a week on formidable machines; heard the chimes of midnight and cared not a whit for whales; distance from such people: that had been what they craved—*God,* what they *had* to have. What they'd contrived for themselves out in California, repli-cating moving east, and what they now had for themselves right here, in West Bridgewater as well—*yes,* well, exactly what they had.

"Pal Joey," Dell'Appa said to his recorder as he settled the Lexus into the Cadillac's 50-mph groove, "he's a meticulous man. His car may look like a piece of shit, eight or ten years old and it's needed new paint for at least six, but the way it's handling for him it's got at least four new Monroes on the corners, maybe eight, nice new heavy-duty shocks. And I bet when I get a chance to look those tires over, they'll be near-new, topline, Goodyears-or-better, with plenty of tread on them. Joe Mossi's a right careful man."

By the time Luigi and Teresa had set up housekeeping, in Boston's wet-wool heat of August, 1940, Luigi's parents had either become the owners of the building or legally surrendered to possession by it. The senior Mossis, Dominic and Philomena, had occupied the third floor as their first and only marital residence for almost nineteen years. Each month for sixteen of those years they had managed to hoard another mortgage payment together, almost always perilously close to the date after which Mr. Scannell at the bank would have called them in again for another dose of humiliation. He would have lectured them once more, as sternly as his reverential demeanor would permit, and warned them once again of the ever-brooding, mausoleum-stinking specter of foreclosure looming over them. Then he would have made what had been too hard to do on time that first and only time, in April '28 (when Philomena'd been flat on her back with the flu for the first three weeks back in March, unable to bring any money home)—make the regular payment—two brutal dollars even harder, terrifyingly harder, by imposing the penalty charge. That had never happened to them again, but neither of them had ever forgotten it. And neither did Luigi. He remembered it, too. Too young to understand it when it happened, at not-quite three-years-old, he had passively acquired from his parents, as soon as he was old enough, so vivid a recollection of the ignominy that for the rest of his lucid life he had personally suffered the aftermath of that disaster, and in pensive moments picked away at the crusted emotional scar.

That degradation had been the reason why Dominic and Philomena had thereafter commenced to assemble their next bank payment the morning after making the one that the next day would become currently due, the day after that overdue, and the day after that one delinquent. At least as far as Mr. Scannell was concerned. Frantically they reported to each other the rents they remorselessly collected from their tenants on the second and first floors, grimly calculating weekly whether it seemed likely, as they always feared, that everyone who lived in their house would be laid off in a week and thus become unable to pay their rents.

Each of Dominic and Philomena's tenants became partners in that apprehensiveness soon after they moved in. They did not have much choice. They tended to be fortyish couples, the majority of them childless, who had heard that the Mossis managed a quiet, respectable place and didn't show much interest in documentation establishing either whether they were legal aliens or had been legally married—or if so, to each other. They also tended to move as soon their circumstances improved even slightly, so long as the additional money looked like it would be enough to permit them to live somewhere else, "aw right, *any*place else," equally clean and well kept. "No hurry, you know? But we're lookin' around. We got our eyes peeled, you know? With some luck, a little bigger. Maybe closer the Square, get the groceries home, huh? Anna subway-stop, right? Make it easier, wintertime there."

It was not because they did not respect Dominic and Philomena. They always said "the owners're good people. Heat's good inna winter and the place's kept up, you know? Always painted and nice, nobody makin' a lotta damned noise alla time, fightin', playin' the TV, when you're just tryin', get some sleep there." But they considered themselves also to be good, hardworking people, even if they didn't mind admitting that they did try to take a little pleasure out of life. They felt some resentment at what seemed like constant dunning. Sad-eyed (he also had unusually-long ears, with proportionately-large lobes), soft-spoken Dominic ("da bloodhound"; the tenants found his mournful inquiries entirely bad enough) and narrow-eyed, sawtooth-voiced Philomena ("craziness, aw right? An' *worse*. You wouldn't believe her, this woman") worked them in relays. Correctly perceiving themselves to be less well-off than Luigi's parents (but refusing to see also that they were far less determined to become much better off, and that this might account in part for the financial imbalance), the tenants really didn't like this. So they had left as soon as they could, usually after four-plus years or so at 73 Pittman, without either bitterness or nostalgia.

Philomena and Dominic had always seen them off without regret, renting out their apartments to newcomers who moved in the day the veterans vacated them, the new occupants not knowing from first-hand experience what they were in for, the Mossis resigned by then to the familiar fugue, starting the cycle again. As long as they kept on paying the rent, the people who came to live in the house could think any damned thing they liked. So long as those rents, combined with their own wages, covered the mortgage each month, what anyone else, outside of the house, cared to think of its owners would be all right. Luigi adopted that attitude too, as soon as he was old enough, and in turn passed it on to his sons. At least to one of the sons.

The senior Mossis combined those rents with every nickel they could sequester from their own earnings at hard physical labor. Luigi's father worked as a teamster for a man whom he correctly described to his own friends as "a biggah meanah bastard, even though he's a goombah himself, ghinny rattabass," who when Dominic first went to work for him had just begun converting his horse-drawn cartage service (specializing in deliveries of heavy machinery) into a fleet of moving trucks. Philomena did scrubwork in the downtown-Boston financial district, washing stone floors with a fifteen-by-four-inch brush with coarse three-inch yellow bristles, pushing a three-gallon galvanized-steel pail of cold, soapy water ahead of her as she proceeded through the corridors on her hands and knees. They doggedly practiced self-denial every day (except Sundays, when they defiantly relished a bottle of Gabbiano and got slightly tipsy on it, Dominic when the mood was on him sometimes singing "Santa Lucia," off-key but with enthusiasm), and so greatly had they impressed their son with the rigorous virtue of their lives that before Luigi had reached the age of fourteen he had made up his mind that he would do everything he had to do to show respect to his good parents by living just as they had, except for as many small improvements as God might permit him to make. His son Joseph in time developed a similar-but-not-identical ambition; he wanted to make larger improvements, and he was not interested at all in whether he might have God's permission to make them, or would have God's approval afterward of the means he had employed.

"The thing I realize about this guy," Brennan had said in the morning, "heck, not just him: about this whole bunch, the longer I'm studyin' them, you know? Is that there is always continuity in what he always does, and there is always the same kind of nice and gradual development in everything they always do." Dell'Appa and Brennan had paused long enough at the curb on the boulevard just down the street but still within view of Marie's Coffee Shop to watch Mossi park the old Cadillac at the curb, lock it up and go inside. Then Brennan had started the Blazer again, to deliver Dell'Appa to the

127

parking lot at the MBTA commuter-rail station on Rust Road in Dedham where he'd left the Lexus that morning.

"He don't do anything sudden, you know? Like he won't just, he won't do the same thing at the same time every day, like: 'Hey, it's ten-thirty, so now I'm gonna do this.' No, not like that. *Usually* he will, and he'll fool you. You get to thinkin': 'Well, then this's when he must always do this, then.' But then all of a sudden, no reason at all, he won't do that anymore. And there isn't any reason either. That's just not what he does, how he goes about doing things. The things he usually does. But he's still orderly, you know? Very orderly. We'll go over Dedham now, and get the car, and like I say, the guy is smart. And he knows I've been on him, and that when I bring him here, he's here for coffee and he goes inside, that when he comes out again and looks up or down the street, I'm gonna be here. He expects it now, that I'm still going to be right here where I was, when he went into Marie's. Like I was his shadow.

"And he knows this. He knows it because when I first started gettin' on him like this, it was after when I went in to Bomber and I told him: 'Hey, I'm not gettin' anywhere, you know? Talkin' to this guy's old pals. A good half of them, for Christ sake, they tell me they don't even see him for a hundred years or so and they're not sure he's still alive. Shit, they're the ones that're askin' *me* alla questions about him, for Christ sake. I know more'n they do about him. I'm not the one askin' *them.*'

"And he looks at me and he says, fuckin' Bomber, real sarcastic like he could be sometimes, fresh bastard he was, right? You know what I mean, when he'd say something but he wouldn't really mean it. He looks at me and he says: 'Well then, you asshole, quit wasting your time then. If the people that you're talking to about the guy don't know, don't know what he's been up to or who he's up to it for, then they don't *know.* So show some initiative for a change, for Christ sake. Go back to basics. Start following the guy around. 'Til when he goes out inna morning and he don't see you around, he's not sure he's fully-dressed. And then that way you find out for yourself.'

" 'Well, Jesus Christ, Bomber,' I say, 'I mean, I know we can do this to a guy if we want to. Wake him up inna morning, make sure he's off to school, and then at night we bring him home an' tuck 'im in. I mean, I know we can do that and all, we can put a tight tail on a guy even though it is, it's gonna, guaranteed to piss him off, the minute he finds out we're gonna do him. Every time he goes out, that the guy leaves his house, there we're gonna be, sittin' there lookin' right up his ass. But Jesus, Bomb, do it to this guy? Are we sure we wanna do that?'

"And he says, this's Bomber, he says to me: 'Aw, what's the *matter, 'oo scared?'* Oo scared of the nasty big man? 'Fraid he'll sic his lawyer on you?' And I say, 'cause it's *not* that: 'Nothin' like that, Bomb, you know that. You know that I'm not scared of nothin'. Except maybe cancer or somethin'. Cancer, yeah; cancer'd scare me shitless. But no, not afraid. It's just all I'm just thinkin's the time and the money. What's all of this gonna cost? And not just in money—in time. We really sure we wanna, put this much of that, of either of them things, into this guy? Into *him?*'

" 'Well, *yeah,*' Bomber says, 'least, *I* think we are.' Which naturally means, since Bomber's the boss then, you can bet we are sure. We *know,* we wanna do that. 'We can't lose, we invest in this case. Joe Mossi knows what we don't know, and what we—what *you,* fuckhead, all right?—what you want to find out. He can't help but tell you, right? He's gotta know himself, what he's doing for somebody. So he's gotta have a way, a way that he finds out, what he's supposed to do. Has to.

" 'Now what is it we already know? Or at least we can be pretty sure. The feds've taken down too many of the old ginzoes with the mikes inna vents and the phones, the minicams aimed at the doorways. So all right, you still with me here? We already know, we're at least pretty sure, it's not gonna be phones that he's usin', he is not checkin' in usin' phones. Unless they are both using pay phones, him and the guy he checks in with, in which case they're usin' the same three or four, and changin' them every two weeks. Which I doubt on account of it'd just get to be too much, too much of a pain in the ass.

" 'Okay then, that's the first thing. That is the first two things that we know, or we're pretty sure of at least.' I say to him: 'Whoa, Bomber, slow down here. I'm not getting it now, I don't think. The first thing I got, that we already know. The second thing I don't see yet.'

" 'Well for Christ sake, Bob,' this's what Bomber says, 'they're not writin' *letters,* each other. They're not passin' notes, like in school.

So, if they're talkin' each other, which they've got to be, they've gotta be face-to-face, am I right? They're not meetin' down at office, 'cause the mikes and cameras. We'd know that if they were, if that's what they were doing, 'cause we'd have 'em, home-videos, right? And we don't. Therefore they're meetin' some other place, Mossi and either the guy he works for, or some other guy, also works for him. Some new guy we don't know about yet. Well that's what Short Joey'll have to tell us, tell us by showing us, right? Since he won't do the right thing and just tell us. If we follow him, he will do that. Because he won't have any choice. Sooner or later he'll have to, and then we'll know what we want to know.'

" 'Well,' I say to him, I says: 'But Bomber,' " Brennan said, " 'he doesn't *have* to, I mean. You're just assuming he does.'

" 'No I'm not,' Bomber says, 'no such thing. This guy we got, what do we know? For starters, we know at least this much. We know that he did not inherit no fifty million dollars from his long-lost cousin that invented toilet paper. And yeah, we know he likes the puppies, goes the track once every week, and he could've gotten lucky, even killers can do that. But nobody down at that track, *nobody* including him or any other hoods that might've dropped by, no Episcopalian bishops or anybody else, has hit a Pik Six—or a twin trifecta, even— lately for the kind of dough that'd let him live forever, 'thout a pay- day now and then. Some day or night soon, *some*body's gonna walk off with a lulu jackpot, high six-figures at least, maybe seven, most likely some deserving fat broad with brown teeth, dips Red Man, and bowls overhand: every Tuesday night, men's league down New Beffa; every Thursday, men's league up in Lowell. But so far not our man that we know of, so this guy needs dough to live.

" 'Okay then: How much dough? A little? A lot? Somewhere in between, I think, based on what we know. Closer to a little 'n a lot. There's no flash to him, this I know. He's got no big-spending habits. I think the last time he's in Vegas was in Sixty-six or so. Went to see an Elvis show because the blonde that he was screwing then, her tits and her other thing, the thing his thing liked to visit, they all just hadda see the King, there. But her poor hopes got dashed. The King didn't see her. Fucked somebody else that night, I guess. Or maybe had ice-cream and speed. But that was the last time Joey did that, did anything that high-priced like that.

" 'But so what? So fuckin'-what if he's frugal? This ain't no yuppie spendthrift we got on our hands here maybe, but he's got a TV set, I bet, and most nights he watches it. It warms my heart like a brown-'n-serve roll, his retarded brother can work, but somehow I doubt the kid brother brings home enough money to stock up the fridge. Joey likes a can of beer? Danny likes one too? Has to pay for all their beer, just like all us working stiffs. At night the sun goes down on his house. Just like it does where we live. There goes more electrical, and in the winter it gets cold, unless he pays for oil. Or gas. There's taxes on that house, too, and that's one thing about taxes: you may not like 'em, anymore'n anybody else does, but by God you're gonna pay 'em. Hitman or not: doesn't matter. The Cadillac, the car he's got? Well, he drives a Cadillac, and that's all anybody needs to say about that. It's old, maybe, and if he bought it second-hand he didn't pay much for it. But it's still a Cadillac, and that means you can *hear* the gas just sluicin' through that baby while it's only sittin' waitin' for the light to change. And that sound you hear is high-test, pal, which spells money, my friend, good old American money.

" 'He's got to get it somewhere,' Bomber says. 'I know he's got the rep. I also know he deserves it. Hell, back when he's still in the ring, fightin' undercards on greasy Thursday nights inna fuckin' roller-rinks, winners getting twenny-five, losers gettin' ten or maybe gettin' nothin'—if you saw what he did to people then, that he didn't know and nobody that he worked for'd told him that he really didn't like, even though he'd never seen the guy before that night, in those days for that money, you wouldn't need to be a bad boy now who just got the boss pissed off—you'd give him some room yourself. On general principles, such as living a long life and being able to walk through it, *see,* an' chew your food and stuff.

" 'I saw him box,' this's still the Bomber talkin', 'I suppose this must've been now thirty years or so ago, back when they still had a lotta fights during the week, and guys would go to see them. I saw a lot of young fighters comin' up—I wasn't married then, settin' a good example for all you young studs in here by goin' straight home every night—or thinkin' they were comin' up, at least. They had all the good moves. The rollin' shoulders when they walked, the shirt too tight across the chest; you shook hands, they mashed your fingers, happy-horseshit stuff like that. Made believe they're sparring with

131

you, they run into you onna street. Shadow box if they're out just walkin' by themselves. Every wakin' minute, every fuckin' day, they were bein' fighters, that was all they thought about.

" 'Now most of these punks,' Bomber says, 'where most of these kids're concerned that was just about all the thinkin' they were up to anyway. Couldn't've handled much more'n that, even if they'd wanted to. These guys were not people you would've called real competition for a Thomas Edison, or that Socrates or anybody like that would've seen, a major threat. The big event in their families was still Great-great-uncle Bobo's birthday, they still celebrated that. That glorious day Bobo the Great was born into this world with real opposable thumbs. Thumbs that nobody in the family before'd ever seen on one of their own, that he could move so he could grab *ahold of things*, you know? And that made him the first one in the family, the very, very first one, that could stand up and walk around, on just his back legs alone.

" 'Well, you couldn't really blame them. That was one big day for them. Since then they'd learned all kinds of things. How to live in a house, if they didn't get home from the barroom so drunk they just passed out and spent the rest of the night inna car. How to use forks and spoons to eat their food, at least now and then, like if they were in too much of a hurry or something. Drink water from a glass. Instead of just sticking their faces, their snouts in their dishes, rippin' meat with their teeth offa roast pigs. Drinking out of the toilet, like their ancestors always did. Thanks to Bobo the Great, they even learned to wear clothes sometimes, like if they were going out, cover up their private parts. Go out lookin' just like humans? They thought that was pretty nice.

" 'Stupid guys in other words,' Bomber says, 'but guys who still would've been completely harmless if it wasn't for two things: they had cocks and they were strong. The cocks made 'em want to fuck women who didn't necessarily have any real enthusiasm about letting them, and who had boyfriends or husbands who happened to be around, handy, and felt just like their women did on that particular subject. And the strength: That made them think that if the particular woman that they decided they wanted to fuck, on a particular night, if she either wasn't interested or her boyfriend didn't go for the idea, well, that didn't matter: They could just punch the boy-friend's lights out and fuck her anyway.

" 'Or they could also get dangerous if they felt like it for some other reason. Decided they had to show off for some broad, hadn't decided yet maybe that they wanted to screw her, just wanted to hear her say: "Oooh," or something like they saw Marilyn Monroe or Rita Hayworth, maybe, saw a movie-star do in a movie. So since there was only one thing they could do, that they thought was really outstand-ing, that'd have to impress any broad, them being a fighter and all, this meant that some guy must be laughing at them, and they had to fight him. What they would call "teach him a lesson." Some guy who didn't even know them, prolly didn't even realize they're on the same earth with them, let alone the same barroom. But that didn't matter. When they were lookin' for a "fight," which was what they called those charades, that was all they needed for an excuse to punch his face in, knock his teeth right down his throat. Real pains in the ass was all they all were, colossal pains in the ass.

" 'Until the night finally came when they climbed up through the ropes and inna the ring for an opponent who'd been up already. Maybe even'd been up for a while, too, not just for a cup of coffee. Before his bell got rung too hard once or twice, or whatever'd hap-pened to've been too many times for him, and so now he's back on his way down. A guy like that, one of those old, experienced hands that isn't just a brawler and he really does know how to box, long past the point where he's fighting on adrenaline, or some thought of being champ, well, when he comes up against one of those tough young kids who's won a lot of fights in bars, taken it into his head that because he took a drunk's best punch and maybe blocked a couple more, he's a natural boxer?

" 'One of those old guys, maybe even ranked once, I can tell you,' Bomber says," Brennan said, " 'he can show a new kid there's an awful lot he doesn't know. And since the reason that he's on the way down is because most likely three or four guys higher up've already shown him how much faster and stronger—and most likely younger, too, rubbin' it in—they just happened to be'n he is now, his last few times out he's been takin' a poundin'. One bad lickin' after another. So this's a real pleasure for him, you know? To take off his robe and see this young spring-lamb shuckin' and jivin' right there. It'd be all he could do to hold himself back, maybe carry the kid for four or five rounds if that's what his manager said the backers'd like—all smart boxers like happy backers.

" 'So, as long as the kid had enough actual talent to make it look good that long, and keep at least most of the people from booin' and throwin' things into the ring, shoutin' bad words like "tank" and "the fix," that was what that journeyman did. He'd waltz around for as long as he could, not really hitting the kid a clean shot but mostly making sure he didn't get careless and let the kid hit him with a lucky shot, until it was time to go home. Knowin' sooner or later, whenever he wanted, he'd rock the baby to sleep.

" 'And then, when it was that round, six or seventh if the kid hadn't stumbled his glass chin right into a light flickin' jab and the next thing gone flat on his ass, the old guy'd just come out and go to work on him. The same way the meat-carvers used to slice up those big juicy, steamboat roasts of beef, under the hot red spotlights at the real good buffet dinners that they used to have in all the restaurants for six bucks on Sunday nights? Almost the very same thing. He'd just take that young punk apart, the old guy would. Usually didn't take him long, either, before he had the kid's handlers—who'd most likely seen it coming, knew that this'd be the night and so they'd bet against their boy, at least had that consolation, some extra money comin' in—throwin' in the sponge and hoping at the same time they'd be able to find a Takeout Transfusions Window open some-place at that hour of the night—assuming their boy didn't bleed to death first.'

"I dunno if you'd be too young to remember this, Harry," Brennan had said, "but do you remember Chuck Davey? That kid, back in the Fifties, I think it was, Big Jim Norris, James J. Norris, was com-missioner back then. Same as all the rest of them, the ones that came before him: just the outfront stooge for Mister Grey, Frank Costello, guy who really ran the game. But, 'Gillette Cavalcade of Sports,' every Friday night there? That was big stuff then, and I do, I remem-ber that. They sold some kind of beer on them too, I think. Just can't remember which kind.

"Well, anyway, that's the kind of thing that Bomber reminds me. How things were, back then in general, when he gets his first look at

Short Joey. There's fights on every week then, every single week. Not all for championships, of course, couldn't have one every week, but still the fights were on and you can imagine what that did. They were eatin' up fighters faster'n new fighters could be made, faster'n they could grow new ones, than it's humanly possible for them to turn new fighters out.

" 'I remember,' Bomber says, 'that time they groomed this white-hope college-boy—least that's what they claimed Davey was—like he was tryin' to be Miss America, or something. Which with the amountah talent he had as a fighter there, and how good-lookin' everybody said he was, was what he should've been doin'. 'Stead of pretending really to be a genuine contender for the middleweight crown. As they called it then, which I never understood where that came from. I saw any number of championship fights, every division, I bet, never once saw one single crown once. But anyway, cripes, that Davey fight, I bet more the high-rollers got new Cadillacs off of bets they made against that kid that night, when they finally had him ripe and ready for the slaughter, 'n they did from bettin' on the Reds against the Black Sox back in Nineteen-nineteen there. It was that big a lock.

" 'I forget who it was they got in to do the execution,' Bomber says. 'Kid Gavilan, maybe. The first Sugar Ray? I dunno. Doesn't matter. What whoever-it-was did to that poor college-boy was the closest thing to mayhem that most people who'd led sheltered lives'd ever seen before. You know how the wise-guys always take the money off the straight guys and the squares? How they always, always, do it? Always do it the same way: by convincin' the square guys, that they wanna clip, as many's they can possibly get, that because they liked all these nice fat suckers so much, well, they couldn't help them-selves, and it's ended up now that they've taught the pigeons so much, let them see the inside story, that they now can't believe they did this. But it's obvious: the suckers aren't suckers anymore. Now they prolly know as much, these former suckers do, maybe even more, about this little crap-game with the loaded dice as the guy who loaded them.

" 'And you know what those suckers do? What they actually do? They *believe* it, can you believe that? They actually go and believe all this shit because it just confirms exactly what they know, because they're so smart, they all knew themselves all along. It just goes to show how smart they are, how much smarter they are than these stupid wise-guys ever even thought of being. And so those suckers get themselves right into that crap-game, or whatever it happens to be, they can't hardly fuckin' *wait*, to show off how much they learned. *And:* they lose their fuckin' *shirts*, naturally. And to the same wise-guys, naturally. 'Cause that's how God intended it, ever since the world began, and so that's always been the way that it's always turned out. And God has another good belly-laugh, His ninety-third-billionth-and-tenth one, most likely, if anyone's been keeping score, and that's how they always do that. I figure that by now suckers must be good for the environment or something: they not only suck up all the shit—they enjoy doing it so much they pay money for the privilege. We should breed them, I think.

" 'Anyway, that's what I figure's probably what is going on, the first time I go see Short Joey. That this's a new one, a local Chuck Davey, they're starting to bring along here. First it's already been him against some the other bar fighters and maybe some club boxers, which I didn't see him in because those bouts I don't go see. All they ever are is fistfights, really, fistfights with gloves on, never really any good or worth watching at all, unless you know the guy and he's a friend of yours. Which this guy Mossi never was, and so I never went, but I still know that night he must've won them because here he was. Not Madison Square Garden, no, but still an honest-to-God real boxing arena. So he had to've fought well enough in them so that he impressed at least some people, because now there he is, on a real legit boxing card. Well, as legit as those cards ever were, back then. So what I'm seeing's probably his first or second dance with one of the has-beens, or a guy that maybe for a while one time looked like maybe he could be, but for some reason never was. If he does all right this time, and maybe a few more times, then I'll be seeing him again a lot. Because the people who control him'll start moving him up in grade, and he'll be taking on the usual string of the liveliest members in the Bum-of-the-Month Club. And he'll win and he'll win and he'll win.

" 'That's when he'll start getting the big play in *Ring* magazine. In six months he'll be on TV. Eighteen months after that, five or six more of so-called "big fights"—that he wins, naturally, because if he loses before he's supposed to the guy who beats him is certified to be dead before morning, although maybe not found for a week, and all his opponents will know that. Then when those're over, and all the geese're fat, that's when they'll set up the kill, and he'll lose like he's now supposed to. But the wise-guys'll be fat again, like they've always known they should be, right?

" 'Then I see that perhaps I am wrong,' Bomber says. 'This Short Joey's a whole other ballgame. This kid's the real goods, he was. The first time that I happen to see him, this's in the early Sixties, Sixty-one or -two, in there, and I don't know where the hell it was. Prolly some place they had onna the North Shore, maybe in Salisbury maybe—that's where I was at the time, workin' out of the Essex DA's. But no, now I know: it was most likely the Alhambra Forum. Off Route One northbound there, up in Danvers. We used to go there quite a lot, couple of times a month at least. So we're all up in there this particular night, four or five of us, prolly, he's the third fight that's on the card. Nothing great, but for the first time ever that anyone who knows much about boxing's gonna really get a chance to see how this kid does in public, well, it's sure nothin' to be ashamed of. *Some*one's got confidence in him. Someone thinks he's got something, might make some people some money.

" 'Now, like I say, I may know what's goin' on generally here, before this fight gets underway there, but I never heard of this kid at that time, naturally, because there's nothin' about him to hear then. I mean: What's he done? So what's to hear, I don't hear, that I missed? Nothin'. And that's why it's nothin'. He's this new kid? Well, sure. That all of us already know, word got around fast in those days, too, if you're paying attention. But that's really all that he is, far as any of us knows, a new kid comin' up. *But,* and this's the real question here then: 'Is he *on the way up?*' 'Can he really fight some? Or he is just another palooka?' That's what we wanna know.

" 'I go in and I figure he is,' Bomber says, 'another palooka, I mean. Ten years he's another stewbum, like most of 'em turn out to be. Bums with no teeth and the watery eyes, runnin' noses, just hangin' around. The street-corners at night, the old trainin'-gym days, 'til someone takes pity and tells 'em: "Go clean out the men's room, Brylcreem. Do a real good job onna shower room there, Lysol the floor down good, and then when you're finished go in and see

Richie, say I said give you two . . . Nah, what the hell, make it three bucks." Next step's out onna street beggin' quarters for good old musky. Thunderbird or white port or who knows? That's the route most of 'em take. But then, like I say, I see him. And this kid's no pushover, no sir. He's in with a guy who's seen better days, but knows how to box, and this Mossi kid's still holdin' his own.

" 'Now I don't mean he's refined or he's classy. He isn't. He's no boxer, you can see that, and he'll prolly never be one, because for one thing he's too old. Even the first time we see him, he's already twenty-two or so, and that's too late, be getting started, learning all the things he should've learned, five, six years ago. What's the most he's got left, if he's lucky, ten or twelve years at the outside? And that's if he's lucky. He's not, he's through in three. And it's always hard, anyway, for an older guy to learn something. He gets to a point where he thinks he's too old to be a kid anymore, and that's when it's gonna get awful hard for him to start to learn anything again. So, all right, you can see he's never gonna be a boxer, he hasn't got the time, but he knows how to brawl, all right, and when he finally gets inside, starts goin' to the body, that's when you begin to see it: 'Jee-*zuss*, can this kid *hit.*'

" 'That kid hit, the only fighter that I ever personally saw before I saw that kid, who could hit like that, was Rocky Marciano. I mean it: Rocco Marchegiano. Well, Short Joe Mossi, the night that I saw him everybody who was there knew he was never gonna be a boxer. Even if he had've been still young enough back then, to maybe take it up and learn it, it would still not've been something that you thought was maybe gonna happen. That it could. Because, he's fightin' that night as a middleweight, all right? And he was, that's what he was, a middleweight right then. But as he gets older, and everybody knows this, he's gonna bulk up some more, just like everybody does. So, if he's twenty-two or so now, and he's a solid middleweight already, one-sixty and all muscle? When he's five or six years older, guarantee it he'll be close, right around one-eighty. Easy. And this'll only be if he really works at it, keepin' the weight down. And also if he *can* do it, keep his weight down without sacrificing too much in strength, which a good many people can't do. Fighters especially, but also jockeys, too. Can have a hard time doing that.

" 'So, he's a middleweight maybe, now, the night I first see him, but sooner or later what he's gonna be, no matter what he does, is a light-heavyweight. At least. By the time he's crowding thirty, in other words—if he's still even fighting then. Which, and this may surprise you, considering what I already told you, that this kid hit like a truck, like a fuckin' goddamned *train*, even that night, I first see him, I didn't think he would be. That power that he had? It's not gonna be enough, never gonna be enough. Because he isn't big enough. He's just not big enough. He had all that mass he had just packed together on this body—which was where he got his power with those just massive muscles; had this huge enormous ass on him, like Jim Ed Rice used to have when the Sox first bring him up; remember how he'd get it into his swing and just crush that fuckin' baseball, just *destroy* it? Well, that's what this Mossi kid had then, a butt on him like a Clydesdale or something, and when he hauled that right arm back, and cocked it, and he's just watching, ready, waitin', and then he sees his chance and *throws* it, shit, he practically comes right off his feet, he's up on his fuckin' toes when it lands, up on the toes of his right foot, like he's just pulled himself right offa the floor and into the air just usin' all that power that he had in his ass. I tell you, it was pretty close to bein' the most astonishin' fuckin' thing I ever seen before in my whole life. It was, no exaggeration here now, *fuckin' beautiful*.

" 'But, and this was the problem, it still didn't matter. It wouldn't. And you could see that, right then, that same night. The body still wasn't big enough for the work he wanted to do, and it was never gonna be, either. He couldn't've been much more'n, I'd say, five-eight, maybe nine inches, but that would've been the maximum. He wasn't no five-foot ten-inches tall, no matter what they said. Which meant his arms, his reach, his fuckin' wingspan, it wasn't long enough. He did have long arms, sure. That's what they always said when a kid came up who had it in every other respect, had it in everything but his size, how big he was: "Yeah, but lookit his arms. Got arms on him like a gorilla. Knuckles scrape onna ground when he walks." "Yeah, but that's not because his arms're so long; for this kid it's that his legs're too short—the ground's up too close to him there." For the rest of him, the legs were, I mean. Probably his arms were about what you'd expect on a guy six feet tall, maybe a little more, but not much. Thirty-four-inch reach, say? Never be enough.

" 'So it was too bad, but it wasn't gonna happen, not even from Day One. He was never gonna have the kind of reach that'd let him stand back at the right range and fight light-heavyweights. Or a heavyweight, obviously, too. Not with a reach like that. Put him up against a guy just as powerful as he was, which the real ranked light-heavies and heavyweights were, at least back then, and most likely a real boxer, too, with two or three more inches of reach? Guy like that'd just stand back in the next town over and beat the shit out of him from there. The only way he'd ever have even a chance of beating someone like that'd be if he could somehow get himself in under what was coming at him all the time, and hit the bigger guy so hard before he could react that even if he only got him once the hands'd have to drop. And then he could just wade in. Not saying that that couldn't happen, or that it wouldn't happen, but not more'n twice. By then at the latest it'd be over, because the guy he met up with would've had a manager who would've seen this kid fight, and therefore would've known how to defense him: never let him get inside. And after that day, night, he would never get a rematch, because by then it'd be obvious to even assholes what to do.

" 'You see what I'm tellin' you?' Bomber says. 'Short Joey Moss had one tough break: got born with a body the wrong size for doing what he could've, and he would've, done with it, if he'd've had the right-size one. No question inna world about it. He would have been a champ, champion of the world, wearin' that big Hickock belt with the diamonds and jewels on it—worth twenty-five thousand bucks, I think it was they said, they used to claim back then; that would've been, in those days, two years' fuckin' salary for a successful man— doin' *anything* he wanted. Just struttin' through his life, every day of it, for all the rest of it. People always would've known him. He would've always seen them nudge each other, right? When he came into a room.

" ' "See that guy, just come in? That guy over there? That there's Short Joey Moss. He was champion the world." That's what they would've said. And if anybody ever asked me whether I think now, seeing how he's ended up, what his life's turned out to be, all the real bad things he's done—that we fuckin' *know* he's done; we just can't prove them yet—if I think part of the reason might be that he got pissed off at God, or fate, or just bad luck, whatever did it to him, and

140

decided to get even? Yeah, I do think that. You can bet I do. That's what I would've done, I think; I think I might have gone and done something like that myself.

" 'So,' Bomber says, 'if people're afraid of him now, I've got to think they're right. I'd look out for him myself, I was in the kind of business where I might piss somebody off who tells Joey what to, and who to do it to.'

"And that's sort of the way, I guess," Brennan had said, "the way I've started feeling myself. That now that I've been watchin' this guy so long day and night like I have, and he knows it, knows what I'm doin' to him and not once's done something to show that it's getting to him in the slightest, I feel like I've gotten to know him a little, you know? Know what it is, makes him tick."

"And as a result," Dell'Appa had said, "you don't want to arrest him any more." He had paused for an instant after he said that, but Brennan had not responded. Dell'Appa had sighed. "That's not a healthy attitude, Bob," he had said. "That's not a good way to think."

9 "Well, if you'd followed him all the way down there," Gayle said that evening. "What is it, about, from Boston? Thirty-five or forty miles or so?" They were eating beef stew that he had made and frozen two weekends before, dipping pieces of French bread into the broth and washing the food down with red table wine. His general responsibility for cooking on the weekends had been among the changes they had improvised in the course of the western Massachusetts detail, found comfortable and pleasant, and for a while at least saw no reason to change.

"Something like that," he said. "Little over, little under, an hour, the time you get out of the city and all."

"Well," she said, "I don't see why you're surprised if he made you right off. You said he's an experienced criminal."

"Oh, he is," he said. "Not a nice person at all, and he's been at it a good long time now. Been at it a very long time now, in fact, 'way longer'n Carson had the 'Tonight Show.' Heck, if you count when he was breakin' in, breakin' legs, 'fore he moved up the ladder to doin' more permanent work that doesn't take as long to do—though the jobs can be, almost always are, a lot noisier—he got hired before Jack Paar was let go. And if anybody, any one of us—the good guys, I mean—during all those years could've nailed him even once, gotten him for even one of those, ah, *projects* he's completed so successfully, he would've been doing life by now. Maybe many lifes, on-and-after lifes, no question in the world. He'd have so many lifes even cats'd be impressed. So yeah, I would say he's experienced all right. Uh-*huh.* Yes indeed."

"The projects being the people that he's killed on orders from higher up," she said.

"Yeah," he said. "He may've also made some people very tardy, meaning 'late,' *sua sponte,* as the kay-jay judgie-wudgies like to call it, when they decide that if the court doesn't get cracking and interfere in the proceedings pretty soon, 'on its own motion,' it's begun to look as though the defendant might actually be convicted."

" 'Kay-jay,' " she said.

"Bomberspeak for 'knee-jerk,' as in 'knee-jerk-liberal,' " he said. "That's the contraction; full-dress is 'kay-jay-ell.' Used to be almost an office password, back when I first went in there. Although now that I think of it, I don't think I've heard it once this time, since I got back. Not at all. Either the judges've shaped up or institutional memory's fading away along with the guy who invented it. One of the two.

"Anyway, Short Joey's got enough status, seniority, juice, whatever you want to call it—meaning all the people in his regional branch, including the ones at the tippy-top, 're afraid of him enough, as they've got damned good reason to be—that if he wanted to take somebody out who *hadn't* violated established policy, disobeyed official orders, ratted, mortified a caporegime or some other pompous bozo—moved the folding-metal funeral-chair and put his own car into the boss's favorite parking space on Richmond Street in the

North End or something—he could do it. On his own authority. Without any more approval than the common courtesy to mention to the boss the afternoon before the evening that he was gonna do it, that that night it would get done. The bosses generally not having been the kind of laid-back, what-the-hell guys who would've featured it if someone'd left them standing there with dumb expressions on their faces, looking silly, because none of them knew Rinky the Dink was gonna get dead 'til somebody let it slip later. After Rinky'd started to spoil. But as long as he didn't embarrass them like that, doing something only an asshole'd do—which he isn't one—well, everything would've been perfectly cool. They would not've ordered him not to; it would've been all right.

"So, we *think*—which means we're pretty damned sure, as sure as we'll ever be without a resounding guilty verdict, *and* a sentence, and him off safely rotting in the pentitentiary for his many wicked deeds —that he's done eleven guys in the normal course of business. Which would be evidence enough, if we just had some evidence, that he's been an industrious fellow indeed, *proof* he's not a nice person at all. But we also have to keep in mind that he could've done somebody who was dumb enough to hurt his retarded brother, or just pissed him off personally, say, and those decedents, too, casualties of any volunteer work he might've done, they'd have to be added to his Lifelist, as the birders like to say. And that he *would've* done some other somebodies, too, and did, most likely, I guess, if he ever got provoked. If what Brennan believes is true."

"You mean the business with the pool-cues," she said. He nodded. "But isn't that also in the files? That's what you told me last night."

"Sure is," he said, "but Brennan-the-guy-who-told-it-to-me's also Brennan-the-guy-who-put-it-in-there. In the files. Now there's no doubt in my mind that when Bob wrote that report, he believed that what he put in it was the solemn-gospel truth. And that, when he recited it to me today, somewhat, ah, what—*improved?* Yeah, *colorized* a little, like the old black-and-white movies that TN-TV shows now, all tarted-up, but basically the same story, that he still believes it's true. But that doesn't necessarily mean it *was* true or it *is* true, true when he wrote it down then, or true now, when he tells it—either one of those times. Somebody Mossi works for, maybe

Mossi his own self, could've made the whole thing up, years and years ago, and then when it was ready, put it out on the street.

"See, a guy in Mossi's line of work, it's to his advantage, have a lot of urban legend floating around out there in the world about him. How mean and cruel and absolutely merciless, how cold and relentless he truly is, when he goes out on a job. The more cheap hoods who get convinced, just by the gaudy patter, that anyone who happens to piss off a boss that Joey works for is as good as dead. The boss who can call up Joey if somebody hurts his *feelings*, forgets he's a man of Respect; or, God forbid, the guy who's stupid enough to piss off Pal Joey *himself,* well, anyone who does that should just go from wherever he is when he does it right on down to his nearest funeral parlor and ask for Salvatore. 'Sal knows about these things. Sal's the man to see.' Pick out the box he likes best, to be laid out in. Sit down with Sal to work out how many nights he'll be waked and all the other petty details. Whether there's room left in the family plot or he should tell the wife, if he ever sees her again, to go down to the cemetery, buy another lot. And whether he wants that lovely young girl, Donna Ventre, that junior cheerleader with the gorgeous hogans on her from the parish high school, to sing 'Ave Maria,' which'll be an additional fifty bucks on the tab, he does—no more'n twenty of it'll actually wind up in Donna's wallet, but that's probably just as well; she'll only spend it on cigarettes anyway, and ruin that lovely voice. Or if it'll be okay with the family, he thinks they'll be satisfied, if the song's just played on the organ at the Mass. Which is included in the hundred-twenty-five that you got to pay anyway, for the church.

"The more guys that think that way, the more wise-guys there are who're far too smart to ever fall for those stories about albino alligators in the city sewer systems, because they themselves, *personally,* 've never seen one, but're smart enough to believe a really scary story about Joe Mossi, because they *have* seen *him,* quite naturally the fewer guys there'll likely turn out to be who annoy the boss on purpose, bother Danny Mossi, or otherwise call Short Joe's attention to themselves."

"The age of public relations," she said. "We've all got to hustle, I guess. Even the murderers advertise. Do they have a rating code, maybe?"

"I don't know," he said. "If they don't, they should. Three little revolvers next to the guy's listing, right? That'd mean he's the best in the business. Very expensive. No credit cards. Closed Sundays, all major holidays, except on emergency basis. No checks, credit cards: strictly cash, half in advance, unless you're a regular customer; balance payable in full on delivery. Extremely inconvenient terms for delinquent accounts. You get casual with this gentleman, he won't stop at just ruining your good credit standing and canceling all of your accounts; what he'll do is cancel *you*."

"Is he?" she said. "The best in the business, I mean?"

"If he isn't," he said, "you're not gonna catch me or Brian—or Bomber or Bob, as far as that goes—admitting it any time soon. For a good many years now he's managed to avoid every trap we've set up to catch him. So either he's pretty damned good or we're pretty damned stupid, and that more or less determines our opinion. Publicly we think he's Bre'r Fox."

"Well then," Gayle said, "if you have to say he's that smart then you have to admit he must be pretty good by now at such things as noticing when someone's following him. He could've just been watching in the mirror today for Bob Brennan, when by luck he spotted you. Wondering what'd happened to Bob, since he's been so used to having him around all the time. Like a guardian angel or something. Of course without knowing how many other cars happened to be on the road, besides the two of you, once you'd left Twenty-four, I don't really know . . . And then, when he didn't see the Blazer, but he did see whatever you were driving, however distinctive that might have been, taking exactly the same turns and everything . . ."

"I had that new Lexus coupe the narcos nabbed from that contractor up in Newburyport," he said. "It's either *very* distinctive, because you know what it is, what it can do and how much it costs, or else you don't know what it is or any of those other intimidating details, and you don't give a shit either, so to you it's not distinctive at all. To you it looks exactly the same's every other one of those hippy new coupes designed in a wind-tunnel: like a slope-nosed, fast-moving, four-wheeled, Fabergé egg."

"Oh," she said, "I didn't know you had that. How'd you like it?"

He shrugged. "It's a nice car," he said. "Course how much I like it's really not much more'n an academic question, considering that buying one of those units for our very own wouldn't leave us much more'n pushcart-lunch money out of forty grand. Which the last time I looked was approximately twenty-five grand more'n we should even think about spending on road-going trinkets."

"That much," she said.

"Times've changed," he said. "The best things in life now cost plenty." He paused, then said slyly: "Unless you'd want to consider, say, setting our little boy free, and then investing what we're spending on his incarceration on some root-tee-toot hot wheels."

Without shifting her gaze she smiled a very small smile and said: "Which you, of course, much rather would."

"Uh-huh," he said. "Car or no car, I still would."

She shook her head twice, very slightly, hardly moving it at all. "We've been through all this a hundred times, Harry," she said, her voice soft and caressing. "You agreed to it when we were first deciding whether to get married. The Abbey's a fourth-generation tradition for boys in my family. We all feel very strongly about it."

"I know," he said, "but it isn't in mine. I agreed to it, yeah, but before I knew, really knew what I'd signed the kid up for. He was always at home when I got home at night. Even last year, while I was out west there, yeah, he was asleep, by the time I got home. But still, it was better'n this. I could look in his room and *see* him, at least say 'Good night' to the kid. Now I'm back home again, every night, and I don't even have that much—at least it was better'n this." He hesitated. "I wasn't ready for this, that's all, Gayle. I just wasn't ready for how it would be, when we really drove up there, and left him and came back without him. I know your father and your brothers all went there . . ."

"And all of my nephews, too," she said. "Don't leave them out of this either. All five of the nephews were Abbey."

"I know," he said, "and I don't deny they're all good men now. Maybe if some of Roy's cousins were still there, if maybe he had them around, to sort of back him up, you know? Maybe then I wouldn't feel this way. But seven years old? Jesus Gayle, when the kid's just turned seven? He's barely seven years old? I dunno, I just think it's too soon, now. Now, now maybe I know what I didn't know then, back before we got married: Seven years old is too early. Seven is just too damned too young. To be sent to New Hampshire alone."

She sighed. "We're not going to reopen this, Harry," she said. "I don't want to go through it again."

"Life sucks, and then you die," he said.

"And when you get up in the night," she said, "it's always three in the morning, and somebody's left the seat up."

Route 106 westbound met 138 southbound at a four-cornered intersection occupied at each angle by a one-story retail establishment designed and constructed in confident reliance on two invariable characteristics of persons traveling by motor vehicle. The first is that such persons welcome if they do not in fact absolutely require at every such four-way intersection a choice of familiar products—gasoline and engine-oil; nationally-advertised fast foods; the usual packaged products available in franchised convenience stores—the vast majority of said products either to be pumped or poured into their motor vehicles, or to be ingested, chewed if necessary, and swallowed into their bodies. And that such persons will therefore appreciatively interrupt their journeys to purchase the products at a profit to the thoughtful businessman. The second principle is that without exception the end products of *all* liquids or solids sold to and consumed by travelers consist solely and entirely of virtually-invisible gases and vapors just as odorlessly insubstantial as those of the gasoline burned in the engines.

Mossi, ignoring both principles, caught the traffic-light changing to green in his favor and turned the old gray Cadillac left onto 138 southbound without hesitating at the corner. "Fine, fine, excellent," Dell'Appa said. "Our man's kidney and bladder functions are in good working order, apparently unimpaired by prostate enlargement so unfortunately common among men of his age. No indications of frequent need or urge to urinate, so no need to stop and beg some pimpled kid for access to a private toilet. Shows you what clean living'll do for a chap." He followed the Cadillac through the turn, allowing a woman approaching eastbound on 106 in a blue Dodge 600 convertible to turn right and precede him behind Mossi's Cadillac southbound on 138.

The asphalt parking lot between the westerly edge of the road and the white buildings looming over the Coldstream dogtrack was broad and deep enough to accommodate around 2,500 cars. Since it contained no more than 300 shortly after 11:00 A.M., when Mossi entered it from 138, to Dell'Appa, continuing southbound on 138, it looked enormous, as though started there by someone who'd intended to pave the entire town, maybe the whole county, and had made an impressive beginning, too, until he'd either lost interest in the enterprise or run out of asphalt and quit. Mossi disregarded the painted lines marking off lanes and spaces and took a diagonal approach to the two-story clubhouse west-southwest of the roadway, the old Cadillac hurrying by itself across the man-made desert to the parked cars huddled near the clubhouse like some mechanical buffalo galloping to rejoin a familiar metallic herd. Dell'Appa, slowing down, drove about half a mile south of the last entrance into the lot before easing the Lexus over onto the shoulder, allowing the cars behind him to pass so that he could make a U-turn and return alone to Coldstream.

"Well, okay," he said to Gayle, finishing his stew, "no harm in trying, I guess. The thing of it is, with Mossi, I mean: I'd already given him time. He's an experienced evildoer, sure, but even though I was born yesterday, it was early. Getting there two hours before post-time for the first race, he wouldn't've had any trouble parking up close to the main gate, and the amount of time I'd given him before I came back and drove in was more'n enough to've let him get out of the car, lock it up and then go all the way inside."

"And therefore, just for that reason," she said, "wouldn't've that been just what he *wouldn't*'ve done? Done all of those things and just gone right in, precisely because he would've been smart enough to know that was just what you'd be expecting him to do? Would be depending on him to do? And so he didn't? Instead he waited, just inside the door, or whatever they've got there, where you couldn't see him when you drove up, but he could watch you, doing it."

"Well obviously," he had said, "obviously that has to've been exactly what he did do. Because the only thing he actually knew—not even knew, really; 'suspected' would've been the closest he could've come to 'knowing,' really being sure, up until then—when he saw the Lexus come into that North Dakota of a parking lot there, was that maybe the person in the Lexus was sitting in on his tail for Bob Brennan today, and that was why he'd seen the coupe but he hadn't seen the Blazer in his rearview since Marie's."

"But when he *did* see that," she said, "saw the Lexus pulling in . . ."

"Oh, sure," he said, "no question. Those cars aren't that common. Oh, it would've been *possible,* sure, course it would've, for somebody else, just by coincidence, to've driven a maroon SC Three Hundred up from Providence, coming from the opposite direction he and I'd both just come from, pull into the track not ten minutes after he did and the other forty-thousand-dollar maroon sled'd gone by, *toward* Providence. Possible sure, but not bloody likely. No, once he'd caught me being cute, so he wouldn't catch me, well then, he'd caught me, hadn't he? And any doubt he might've had about whether I was Brennan for at least today—remember that silly show Dave Maynard used to have on Channel Four, and then Five, on Sunday mornings? The one where fat little girls who couldn't twirl batons came out in pink majorette costumes with stiff little skirts that stuck out all around them, like their own personal toadstools, the white shako hats and white boots, and they proved it?"

" 'Community Auditions'," she said. "The little fat girls always wore glasses with red frames that they had to keep pushing back up on their noses, and you could see them moving their lips, counting the beat, while they did it. And they always dropped the batons. Community Opticians was the sponsor. And the big-breasted girls who played the accordions that all the nasty-male viewers at home always hoped'd catch and pinch them."

"They also had guys who played accordions," he said. "And looked damned near as foolish. And guys who sang, too. There was one kid once who tried to sing 'Feelings,' like Barry Manilow did, and I guess his hormones must've just kicked in or something, because you could see he had feelings, all right; if he'd had any more'n he was obviously having then, his zipper would've burst."

"Nerves," she said. "Stage-fright doesn't affect everyone in quite the same way. Some find it all quite exciting. Arousing, even."

"Yeah," he said. "Well, Maynard used to have to sing 'Star of the day/Who will it be?' at the beginning of the show, and that's what Mossi should've been doing when I got close enough to the glass doors at the entrance for him to check me out. 'Tail of the day/Who can it be?' "

"Did he recognize you?" she said.

"Doubt it," he said. "In fact I'm ninety percent sure he didn't. Because what way would there've been for him to do it, to've seen me before, so he could? When I was in Boston on my first tour, keep in mind, most of the work I was doing kept me in the office most of the time. Making the models of that stuff that was going on on the North Shore, first the fires and then the bank loans. And then when I finally did get to go out, all by myself,—after I promised, cross-my-heart-and-hope-to-die, that I wouldn't talk to strangers or get in any strange man's car and go for ice cream with him—and actully *do* a little field-work, well, you know what happened then. Soon's my own data-acquisition and collection made it so what I was getting was beginning to resemble the data that I needed, even if it wasn't a perfect match for it, I was out on my butt. No sooner did I reach the point where I knew the investigation was being done in the right way, because I was *doing* it all myself and I at least knew what I was doing, than somebody got a hair across his big fat ass, became extremely nervous, and ordered me transported to the colonies. So, where would Mossi've seen me before, for him to've made the connection?"

"A murder out there, maybe?" she said. "He was out there planning a murder with someone, and somebody pointed you out to him, a bar or some restaurant or something?"

"Possible," he said. "Might've happened but unlikely. West of the Blackstone Valley's a different jurisdiction for them, the New York–New Haven–Hartford–Springfield axis. Worcester's in that orbit, too. Everything east of Worcester's New York–Providence–Boston. Portland, too, now of course, with the drugs expanding that market. They do import talent from other families, other jurisdictions, now and then, if for some reason or another there just isn't any way that the regular shooter could do the job without getting caught. But it's unusual, and besides, nothing like that happened while I was assigned out there.

"So: No, I don't think he actually knew who I was, the minute he saw me get out of the car and start toward the door. But he knew *what* I was and what I looked like, some kind of a cop or other, and since that's all that really concerns him about anyone he sees around

151

him a lot and doesn't know, that was the only important thing anyway. So once he got that taken care of, he could sort of melt back into the stream of people moving around inside there, sitting down, handicapping, having their coffee or something. Make himself as inconspicuous as he could, watch me watching him for a while.

"He wasn't standing at the entrance when I went in and bought my grandstand ticket. I didn't actually see him again, in fact, until after I came out of the men's room and spotted him down by the automated betting machines. He had a gray-blue down-vest on over a red plaid flannel shirt, some kind of dark wool pants, new-looking tan work boots. He was looking straight toward the men's room exit and talking to another guy. Soon's he saw me he nodded toward me and said something—'That's him there now,' most likely, or: 'That guy in the tweed sportcoat that just pissed down his leg, I hope.' Something along that line.

"The other guy, he was wearing a blue blazer, tan pants, pink dress-shirt, striped tie. Slim, one-forty, maybe; five nine or five ten; forty-five or so; wavy, prematurely-grey hair, originally black; all very dapper and clean-cut, you know? Plays a lot of golf, I think. Cheats on his wife now and then, but nothing *excessive.* Only when he's out of town, and then only if she's a married woman who's got something to lose too. One of those Smilin' Jacks that always looks like the reason he never takes a seat on at the Ten-o'clock Sundays is because by staying on his feet he's always all ready to grab one of those long-handled baskets lined up against the wall at the rear of the church, before anybody else can jump up and get it, and smile at everybody when he helps take up the collection. Or: he can't wait 'til he comes across his next old-lady-on-a-street-corner, so he can help her cross the street, and maybe also give her a little free advice that'll help to ease her mind some and maybe get her to come in and have him draw up a new will for her—naming himself her executor, of course; one will, but at least two fees.

"And why does he look like he does all these things? Precisely for that very reason: because he does them, day in and day out, and when those're the things that you do, you develop, you *have* to develop, a repertoire, a regular fuckin' *wardrobe,* of appropriate smarmy expressions—one to complement, individuate, and enhance, each of the groveling actions. Because he's *been* doing them so often for so long that the years of strain've remade his whole face, just like your dear mother said was gonna happen to you if you didn't stop sucking your thumb. Reset all his teeth, too, just like a set of braces. Realigned his facial muscles. The poor fellow now has no choice. If he tried to snarl at you in gargoyle hatred, he'd look like the second alto in the Choir of the Guild of Saint Cecilia, buttering up the soprano with an unbearably angelic, rich harmonic counter-point to her show-off solo in 'Adeste Fidelis,' midnight Mass on Christmas Eve.

"So those're all the expressions he's got left now: the ones that go so well with the thoughtful and considerate things he started doin' twenty years or so ago, when he first opened up his law office and started what's become his thriving practice over there in East Ingrati-ate, where he didn't know a soul: so everyone would like him. And that is exactly what they did, too. The nice people that he did those nice things for, they so nicely saw he was a nice young man, and they all thought that that was nice. So they brought him all their business and made him very prosperous, as he is today. And today he's even nicer, if that were possible, always very careful not to be showy about it, all his wonderful good fortune, which in other words means he makes damned sure he never, *ever*, reminds any one of those nice people he sucked in so easily of some fuckin'-rich-Jew-bigshot, be-cause if he does they'll drop him like he'd become a goddamned *snake*—and that's mighty hard for him to carry off, too, because deep down what he thinks is: It's fuckin' *grrrr-eat*, how easy it was for him to suck them in, and it proves he's fuckin' *smart*. So, being smart, what he was doing today was showin' off for his friend, the nice professional killer, how seriously he's takin' the guy's question, he takes a real good look at me. While I look back at him, of course, memorizing him just like he's memorizing me. And then he frowns and shakes his head, which means: 'No, I dunno who the bastard is offhand, but I'll see what I can find out.' A favor, of course, which I'm returning to him even as we speak faster'n he can possibly perform his for me, because there's nothing in the memories his office com-puter can access but boilerplate legal shit, so he's got to resort to the primitive phone while my machines ROM the whole world. And then both of them turned their backs on me, and I bought a program and a newspaper and another cup of coffee, which turned out to be dishwater and lukewarm-dishwater at that, went on up the ramp into the stands."

"You did?" she said. "Weren't you afraid he'd take off or something? Once he knew you were on his trail?"

"No reason to be," he said. "In the first place, it didn't matter if he did scoot. The reason Bomber Lawrence told Brennan in the first place to get off his ass and start tailing Mossi, and he told me this himself, old Bob did, was because anything one of us saw Mossi doing might be something that he did we hadn't known about before. And Mossi today'd just done that. Shown me that he's cosy with a guy we didn't know about before—not in connection with him, anyway. So when I get his name and so forth, get all that pinned down, even if he's harmless we'll still know one more thing about Short Joe Mossi'n we did before I went out of this house this morning.

"Now probably what I learned today won't turn out to be important. Most of us know a lot of people who have absolutely nothing whatsoever to do with how we make our livings, and this guy's most likely nothing more'n an acquaintance of Mossi's who's got no idea in the world why a guy in my line of work'd be interested in him. But there's still the possibility that who he is is in fact important. The theory's been all along that Mossi doesn't go to that dogtrack just because he's nutty about dog-racing. It's obviously not against his religion or anything, because if he didn't like it at all he would've picked someplace else where anyone who had a reason to want to see him, to discuss something confidential, would know he could always find him Tuesdays and Thursdays, every week, except if he was sick in bed. Or away on vacation, naturally."

She laughed. He looked at her quizzically. "No, no, nothing," she said. "I know it isn't funny, that this man's a hired killer, but it just sounds so funny, that's all. Almost like he's an orthodontist or something. If he had a secretary or a receptionist she could take a letter for him to his customers. 'Our office will be closed for the month of July to enable our staff to enjoy their summer vacation, so we won't be able to kill anybody for you between June thirtieth and the first of August.' "

"Yeah," Dell'Appa said, "but that's what makes this kind of case so frustrating. These guys are actually fairly well organized, considering that the managerial system that they use is still basically a feudal

154

autocracy that hasn't been significantly changed, updated, since the thirteenth or fourteenth century, really. And this is a big global operation we're talking here. Someone like Brennan, or like me, as far as that goes, it's altogether too easy for someone like us to get tunnel-vision working on a file like this. Get so narrowed-down and focused-in on Mossi, or on Franco, assuming he succeeds Nunzio like everybody thinks he will when the old man goes to jail—as everybody seems to think he's going to; word is that the feds've really nailed him good—that you lose sight of what they really are: the local branch of an international, diversified conglomerate. Agriculture, mining, raw-materials handling, manufacturing, international development and distribution, transportation, construction, entertainment —cripes, are they ever in entertainment—labor-management relations, banking, governmental relations: hell, you name it and they're in it, all around the world."

She looked skeptical. "Agriculture?" she said. "You aren't telling me the Mafia's really like a big Grange or something, are you? Farmers who happen to shoot each other if things don't go right, there's a drought or something?"

"Well, you tell me," he said. "Opium comes from poppies that're cultivated like any other crop, and that's where the heroin comes from. The people who harvest the coca-leaves in the Andes aren't doing work much different from the ones who harvest coffee-beans, and Juan Valdez maybe doesn't exist, but if he did he'd be considered a farmer. Marijuana grows like the weed it is, but the quality stuff's cultivated just like any other plant. During Prohibition the mob had a considerable interest in cane sugar, malt, hops, barley, corn, you name it. Looks like agriculture to me, ma'am."

She did not say anything. "So, like I was saying," he said, "you lose sight of what they are, the people in the mob in Boston. They're not a free-standing, sort of romantic, contemporary version of Butch Cassidy and the Sundance Kid and the good old Hole-in-the-Wall Gang. A bunch of raffish characters with names like 'Nathan Detroit' and 'Nicely-Nicely' who sing songs about love and shoot crap to the innocent delight of all looking on. No, Damon Runyon was a fucking liar. These're the real hoods we've got on our hands here. What they are, the people you see and know're in the mob, they're the staff of the Boston *office* of a big international operation that grosses billions a year; supports thousands of employees, entrepreneurs, and more-or-less-independent contractors—who'd better not start acting *too* independent or they're liable to become subjects of contracts themselves, wind up *dead;* influences the governments of most industrialized countries and pretty much runs several of them; most likely's never finished a fiscal year in the red, unless you count the blood; nets an annual profit as big or bigger than the combined earnings of half the corporations on the Fortune lists; and's got all that loot invested in things all over this world that no civilian in his wildest dreams ever thought of.

"So, when you start treating those people like office workers and managers of a small regional company, or partners in a local business —good old Al there, your bookie in the barber shop, you've known each other so long now that to you he's no different than Sylvester, your genial neighborhood pharmacist who not only makes up your allergy prescription every May but also recommends this new ointment, just came on the market, that's so great for hemorrhoids— you're just being a pliable jerk. You don't see the conglomerate when you look at Sylvester, though there is one that'll sue you if you bounce a big bad check off it and you don't make it good. And you don't see, either, the organization behind Al that has a man who comes around if you don't pay your losses promptly, menaces you good, and if that don't pry the dough off you damned quick, who'll put you in the hospital at no extra charge. These guys ain't folk-heroes, you know? They are really bad men. But evidently folk-heroes's what they'd like to be, what they want to be, and so that's what they always pretend."

"And you think that's the explanation for what he did," she said. "You think he was trying to insinuate himself into your good graces, so you'd lay off of him? Sounds kind of far-fetched to me."

"Well," he said, "maybe it isn't the real explanation, but I'd be willing to bet, if it's not, that the real one looks a lot like it. Short Joey Moss, keep in mind, isn't like a lot of the stereotyped muscle that you hear and read about, bruisers who can squeeze anything out of anything except the ideas in a book. The guy is not dumb. Now I'm not saying he'd be able to articulate what his plans are, in any scholarly sense, nothing like that. All I'm saying is that whatever he had in mind today when he did what he did was proof that Bob was right when he said this guy never does anything without a good reason for doing it, and the simple fact that he's done it before, that it's been one of his regular habits, part of his usual routine, is not a good enough reason. He may seem to learn more slowly than some autodidactic polymath who decided to invent instant photography one Wednesday morning because he didn't happen to have anything else to do that day, but that's not because he's slow of wit. It's because he only learns empirically. If he doesn't see it, or hear it, or otherwise encounter, some observable phenomenon that can't be otherwise explained, then he'll never have an explanation for the event, or ever think about a way to prevent or replicate it.

"But, if he *does* happen to observe or otherwise experience something, whether it's one event or a series of related phenomena, and it looks to him like his own interest may be involved, well, then, he'll puzzle it out. It may take him an agonizing while longer to figure out the causes and effects than a more sophisticated, trained, and systematic intellectual would need, but that's perfectly all right. It's all right because he's got lots of time, always as much as he needs. He's the man who decides when everybody *else's* time is up; nobody else rushes him.

"Now, what I think about this guy is this: I think the way he saw today's events unfolding, as opposed to the way you or I or Brennan might've seen them, is to begin with, with himself as the victim. Maybe that's too strong a word; the person acted upon. The one being stalked, the passive party to this transaction. Brennan and I being the people who're active in the whole equation, were the ones acting on him. So what he did after I went up the ramp into the stands and left him talking to his friend was start thinking about how he could turn the equation around. So that he'd become the actor and I'd become the object.

"It didn't come to him right off. That was why, after I'd picked out my seat, second one in from the stairs to the left of the ramp, four rows up in the second-tier section, gotten myself settled, figured out how to turn on and tune in the little Quasar TV on the swivel stand in front of me—so it'd show me the Coldstream closed-circuit programs, late scratches, program-consensus selections, all that sort of thing, instead of some late-morning talk show about the special emotional problems and unsatisfied needs of transvestites still in the

157

closet that came on when I turned the set on—he was by himself below me outside, leaning on the fence between the track and the concourse, trying to think up some way he could throw sand in my gears. Then after maybe half an hour, forty minutes more've gone by, he's staring at the track, watching people getting ready for the first race at one o'clock and by now it's long-gone noon, he decides he's thought of something. He turns around and faces the clubhouse. He starts scanning the people, all of us, who're sitting in there behind the big windows, the sissies who don't like God's sunshine and breezes, like second-hand cigarette smoke much better.

"He was very methodical. He started with the non-smoking tiers, the first-tier level next to the big window, at the end furthest away from me. To my right. I'm down near the end, at the left, down where the two betting windows are. And he's of course still outside now. And what he did was search that whole section for someone he thought he might recognize. Such as, for example, me. Didn't find me, of course, because I'm up with the addicts in Smoking, but that didn't faze him. When he came to the end of the first tier he raised his head, just like it was mounted on a typewriter carriage and he was starting a new paragraph or something, began working his way along until he came to where I was. Give him credit: for an amateur who most likely doesn't get to do much of this kind of work, not that much call for it outside of jobs like mine, he's pretty smooth. When he spotted me he didn't let his eyes linger. Just a little hesitation, barely noticeable, and then he went right on.

"That was just about the time that the waitress showed up to my seat, working her own way along the inside something like Joey was, from the outside, and asked me if I'd like something to drink or some lunch. Well, I told her that since I'd already sampled the delicious coffee that they serve to innocent bystanders there, I'd like to have tea. And a pastrami sandwich. She was a nice kid, year or so out of high school, maybe, and . . ."

" 'She wasn't built bad at all,' " Gayle said with elegant weariness, "so you were just checking her out some. I know, already, all right? I understand you look at girls. Well, better'n the other thing, I guess, so long as you don't do anything more. So, if I happen to be around when you decide you've got to reassure yourself that you've still got that world-famous charm, well, since I don't have much choice in the matter I'll sit through the performances. But spare me the reruns, okay?"

"*Cheesh*," he said, "all I was was just saying—"

"I *know* what you were just saying," she said. "All *I'm* saying is saying: 'Don't say it. I already know the routine.' "

"Yeah," he said. "Well, when I looked outside again, clubhouse's starting to fill up gradually by now—wasn't really cold today, not for this time of year, sun out and everything, but just the same, didn't look like that many people were that interested in all that pure fresh air and so forth—he was gone. The next time I saw him was when he came down the stairway behind me, stopped at my row, and took the seat right at the end."

She laughed. "Is this a normal thing to have happen when you're following someone?" she said. " 'Now do you really mean to tell us, Miss Muffet, that this spider you were following came up on you from behind and sat down right on the tuffet beside you? Does this sort of thing happen often? And does it happen to others, do you think? Or is it in fact quite unusual, perhaps even confined just to you, because you'd been leading him on?' "

"If it is normal," he said, "I must not've had any of the normal experiences so far, until today. And that includes even ever having run into an older investigator who ever had it happen to him and then mentioned it to me."

"Well," she said, "tell me, since you've hooked me now: What did this remarkable fellow do next? Did he introduce himself formally?"

"Not exactly," Dell'Appa said. "He said: 'Can't figure it out. You sure don't look Irish to me.' "

10 "I'll bite," Dell'Appa said. "Why? You supposed to be, to get in here or something? Only Irish can come to this track? 'Cause if so, what're you doing here?"

"No," Mossi said, "I didn't mean nothin' like that. It's just that I know you gotta be some kinda cop, and most of the cops I know around here, that's what most of them always are." His normal conversational voice had a black-velvet texture that a neon-Elvis could have used for singing ballads.

"Irish," Dell'Appa said.

"Yeah," Mossi said. "So, well, you know, I was curious and all. I'm out there by the rail, after I see you inside there, you know?"

"Yeah," Dell'Appa said. "I saw you out there, seein' me inside here."

"And I go out there, I'm wonderin', naturally,"

Mossi said, " 'who's this new guy I got now? This new guy they got on me now?' 'Cause, this guy that I know, that I see down inna front part, the lobby, there, you're comin' out of the head? He's been around a lot—he's been around *here* a lot, too. And he never saw you before. Didn't know who you are. Recognize you. So he can't help me out here. So, there I am. I am out there, all right? I'm standin' out there on a nice sunny day, not too cold—it's nice, you know? And I start thinkin': 'Hey, what's goin' on here? What'm I doin', out here like this, pullin' my dick over this guy? Because pretty soon now, you know, it's gonna be winter, snow and it's cold, stuff like that. Won't wanna be out at the fence then, not when that's starting to happen. So, nice day like this, right? What am I worryin', who this guy probably is? He's prolly a nice-enough guy, nothin' to worry about. No, what I should do here, the first thing I do, I should see if he left, he's still here. And if he didn't, I'll go up and ask him. What harm can that do, I do that? It's not like he's got ferrets with him, he'll put weasels down in my pants, here.' So that's what I do. I turn around, look: Here you are."

"I saw you," Dell'Appa said. "I saw you when you were doin' it."

"Well, I know that, all right?" Mossi said. "I seen you see me, looking for you, and I spot you. An' then Judy comes up, you start talkin' to her, and so that's when I come back inside."

" 'Judy,' " Dell'Appa said. "I don't know who Judy is."

"The waitress, there," Mossi said. "The kid you order your lunch from. Or whatever you talk about with her."

"Oh," Dell'Appa said, "Judy's the waitress. Okay, I see then. Glad we've got that settled and all."

"What?" Mossi said, frowning. "What is it here, we got settled?"

"Well," Dell'Appa said, "how the fates brought us together."

"Oh," Mossi said. He grinned. "She's a nice-lookin' kid, am I right?"

"Who?" Dell'Appa said. "We still talkin' about Judy here?"

"Yeah," Mossi said, "Judy. The kid you was talkin' to there, just before I come in. She's really a nice-lookin' kid. Also a very nice ass. I dunno if you notice that. Prolly you do. Very nice ass on that kid. But also a just plain *nice* kid, you know what I mean, what I'm sayin' here?"

"Well, that's good to know," Dell'Appa said. "Now if she can just get back here with my lunch before it's time to order dinner, that'll be even more welcome news."

"Yeah," Mossi said. He sounded sad. He put his elbows on the countertop and clasped his hands together, making a cushion of his forearms to receive his chin, which he lowered onto it. He was silent. He reflected.

"Oh," Dell'Appa said, "so I guess I'm supposed to take it she must be, that she's a friend of yours. Friend of the family or something. Okay, if the food's cold and she forgets the tea, like it looks like, it's gonna be, I'll overlook it, all right? I won't say anything mean to her, all right? And: I'll still tip her heavy, okay?"

Mossi grimaced. He grunted. Without raising his head he said: "Not that. I just know her, is all. I don't care what you do, what happens between you and her."

"Not what?" Dell'Appa said. "I must've fallen behind in the reading or something. I don't think I know where we are anymore. What page it is that we're on now."

Mossi sat up straight. He had smooth olive skin that seemed never to have been creased by worry or sadness. The third tooth back on the left from the front of his upper jaw was either a completely-artificial canine implant or a major filling; it had been fabricated of a dull-silver metal that resembled lead but could not have been: lead would have poisoned him. Old mercury then, maybe, the color, but it could not have been mercury either; mercury would not have held its shape. Whatever it was, from where Dell'Appa sat it was the inert centerpiece of an expression of habitual mourning on Mossi's face each time he opened his mouth to speak. Steel, perhaps; maybe the gray slashing tooth was surgical steel.

"She's," Mossi said, thousand-yard-gazing out the window-wall, "she's going with this kid I know down Pawtucket. I doubt you'd even know him."

"He got a name?" Dell'Appa said, smiling. "You never can tell—I just might." The waitress named Judy emerged from the ramp with a tray that appeared to have his lunch on it and turned to her left, toward his seat.

Mossi sat up fast. He grinned. "You know," he said, "you just might." He reared back in the chair, squinted, and appraised Dell'Appa. "So whadda you now, thirty-five, thirty-six about? Some-

162

where in there? Yeah, that'd be about right. And that'd make ya, lemme think now, year or two younger'n him." The waitress looked up at the two of them and smiled brightly as she started up the stairs. "And most likely married by now, you too, right? Still livin', the first wife and all?"

"Oh yeah, she's still livin'," Dell'Appa said.

The waitress entered the third row in front of them and smiled at Mossi. "Hi, Joe," she said. She reached over the front rail of the counter and put a paper plate with a napkin under it in front of Dell'Appa. "Your pastrami sandwich," she said, taking a plastic-covered cardboard cup with a Lipton teabag on top of it from the tray and placing that to the right of the sandwich. "And your check, sir," she said, putting a bill in front of Dell'Appa. "That'll be four-eighty-one, please."

Dell'Appa moved in his seat to reach his wallet. "Judy," Mossi said, "been a while since I run into you here, see you and everything, you know? Everything's going good for you?"

She nodded happily enough, her expression suggesting things had been at least good enough so that she hadn't given much thought to them. "Uh-huh," she said. Dell'Appa gave her a five-dollar bill and a single. She began to fumble in her uniform-skirt pocket for change. "I been drawing a lot of nights lately, helping Gineen with the baby and stuff."

"That's okay," Dell'Appa said. "No change."

"Timmy's still good and everything, right?" Mossi said.

To Dell'Appa she said prettily, dimpling: "*Thank* you," and then as she turned to Mossi she hardened her face like an old pro. "Timmy's still *fine,* Joe, perfectly fine. The last that I saw of him, at least; week, maybe ten days ago. They finally decided: they're namin' the baby for him, you know that? Like Gineen wanted to, all along. Ever since she found out she was pregnant, in fact, she wanted to name it for him. It was him that didn't want to, but last week he finally gave in."

"Well," Mossi said, "but that doesn't mean, it's not like you're sayin', you're not worried about him or somethin', are you?"

She sighed. She shook her head. "No, Joe," she said, "I'm not worried about him. I'm not worried about him at all. When he's around, and I got a night free, we go out and we have a good time.

And when he's not around, or he is but I'm booked, then we don't, and that's just fine with us."

"Because if you was worried or something," Mossi said, "I'd introduce you here to my old friend, who's a cop, and he could maybe help you out some. Except I still don't know what his name is. His first wife's still alive, but that's all."

She looked at Dell'Appa and chuckled. "Is that true?" she said. "You're a cop?"

"Yeah," he said, "I'm a cop."

"And you're friends with him," she said, nodding toward Mossi, "this guy here? You two're friends, like he says?"

Dell'Appa extended his right hand. "Sure," he said, "if he wants it that way. It's just sort of too soon yet, to tell. Though so far it seems like we're doing all right. My name's Harry Dell'Appa."

She shook. "Judy Comiskey," she said, "pleased to meet you."

"What rank're you, Harry Dell'Appa?" Mossi said. "You must have a rank. All cops've got ranks, they got to have ranks. It's part of their names, I think sometimes."

"Sergeant," Dell'Appa said, "sergeant. Detective Sergeant Harry Dell'Appa then, all right? Call me 'Sarge,' if you like. It's okay."

"Fine," Comiskey said, "and still nice this time, too, second time I meet you today. There's anything else you want here today, just catch my eye, okay, Sergeant?"

"Will do," Dell'Appa said.

She put the chill on Mossi again. "And can I bring you anything, Joe?" she said. "My next trip up here, I mean?"

"I'm all set," Mossi said, and when she'd gone away, shook his head and said sorrowfully: "Too bad. That's really a thing that's too bad."

" 'Too bad,' " Dell'Appa said, biting into the pastrami sandwich, "what's too bad?"

"Ah, nothin' new," Mossi said, "just: they're just kids. They don't know. The guy that she's goin' with? He's not a bad kid, not a bad kid at all. But that's still what he is: He's a kid. Don't matter, he's older'n she is, okay? He's still inna same category. Nobody can tell him a thing. You look at two kids like that, she isn't twenny yet, sure, yeah, they're havin' some fun. Why wouldn't they be, havin' fun? He's got some dough now, can take her out places. They have a few drinks, see a show." He pinched his eyes narrow. "You been around, guy your age, you know, you're doin' your kinda work. You probably know, I'm talkin' about, how guys your age will do this to kids. Takin' advantage of them. Of nice young girls, don't know what they're doin'."

"I have heard of that happenin'," Dell'Appa said. "I have heard that that stuff goes on."

"*Yeah*," Mossi said heavily. "And then afterwards, where do they go? Well, there's a lot of apartments, a whole shitload, apartments. It's not like they're that hard to find. He's probably got one down in Providence there, one that he's got with a friend. Studio, maybe, one bedroom, they can each take their girlfriend to. Fuck. Wife, sure, okay, she wouldn't like this, she found out what he was doin'. So she wouldn't, okay, well then lemme ask this then: how is she gonna find out, huh? 'Less he knocks the other one up? She isn't, that's how, long as everyone's happy, the girlfriend is who I mean here: just as long as nobody gets mad. Which he thinks that nobody does. Just like all of the other guys that did it thought too; all of them thought the same exact thing: nobody'd ever get mad. 'Til one of their girlfriends actually did, she finally got mad and said: 'Okay then, so what's it gonna be here? Gonna be her or gonna be me?' And that is the question without no right answer. No matter what the guy says, he is gonna be wrong, and somebody's gonna be mad. Maybe two some-bodies: mad. And this's not even with guys screwin' sisters; this's just guys with two broads, not even related each other. With sisters, oh brother, I never seen that, but *ka-boom*, that is what I imagine. The H-bomb's what we're talkin' here.

"But that didn't happened to Timmy right now yet, so naturally what does he think? He thinks—with his dick of course, not with his brains—he's havin' fun, this real big hot shit that he is, pokin' both sisters at once, and plenty of money and everythin'. And he is, stupid fuck, he is havin' fun, and he will be, too, 'til he gets caught. That's what he don't realize, see? Then that cock of his'll, *bam,* right in the meatgrinder, and that won't be no fun at all, then. But, what it is that he's finally doin' these days, that's where all the money comes from? That I'm not tellin' you, right? Don't go gettin' that idea or nothin', but this thing that he finally came up with, don't matter no more, some people don't like him, too much fresh mouth on him there.

165

With them, without them, he don't give a shit. Don't matter a good shit to him. He don't need the old paisans no more now. He can do what he wants without them, and he's getting rich doing it, too, he can hang onto some of it there. And they don't even know what it is."

"What what is?" Dell'Appa said idly, chewing and dunking the teabag repeatedly into the hot water.

"Don't talk with your mouth full, all right?" Mossi said. "It's not polite, and anyways, I wouldn't tell you anyways and I already told you that, that I wasn't gonna tell you." The public address system began to amplify a sandpaper voice reading lists of information about the afternoon's racing card. "The point of it is here that the two of them're not only not acting serious about anything, they don't even see how there's anything that they should even be serious about, you know? People've been shot, they've gotten shot, over this kinda stuff, you know?"

He looked sharply at Dell'Appa. "Or do you know that? No, prolly you don't know. How'd you know? You're the same age's he is, you're prolly still just as fuckin' stupid's he is. Here's this guy that's thirty-five, thirty-six years old, and he don't even understand he's way too old for a kid her age, that's what? prolly nineteen years old. And that's his wife's sister to boot. That's what I'm talking about. What they're playin' with's dynamite here. So, but that don't matter none to him, does it, and you seen her: don't matter to her. But . . . and that's all I was sayin'."

"I see," Dell'Appa said absently, reading the program, still chewing his sandwich. The meat was unusually gristly. "You got anything good here, this after?"

"*What*," Mossi said, nasally dragging the word out, "what's this you're asking me here now?"

"I asked you," Dell'Appa said, looking up from the program and chewing pastrami, "you got anything good here this after."

"You *are* asking me," Mossi said.

"Well, yeah," Dell'Appa said. "I mean after all, you're the expert here, right? You're the one that comes here every Tuesday, Thursday afternoon. Been coming here since Truman was president, I guess. Not me. I've never been here before in my life. Which's been my oversight, I can see that now. This's a pretty nice place. It's very comfortable here. But I didn't know that 'til you showed me the way down here today. So it's not like I planned on this happening or anything, you know? Had a chance to do much homework on the dogs or anything. How they've been doing and so forth, which ones've been going good. So I'd know which ones I should be betting on, if you happened to come up and sit next to me. Like I'd come into this expecting that, that we're gonna strike up a conversation like this—or rather: *you* are, 'cause you did the strikin' up here—the first day I take over the detail."

He paused and studied Mossi for a moment, holding the sandwich as though struck by a thought in the process of taking another bite. "Because, you know, when I was going over the files and all, the reports Bob did on you, I didn't run into a reference, least yet, not one single reference, where you and Bob ever did that. Had a conversation, you know? Like you and I're having today, here. Nothing like that at all. And he was with you lots of days. He was with you a long time. Therefore I wasn't prepared, to take over that aspect of this." He hesitated. "If that was an aspect of this, I just didn't know about there." He hesitated again. "So," he said, "was it?"

"What?" Mossi said.

"You having conversations with Bob," Dell'Appa said. He raised the sandwich again and held it ready to bite. "A conversation, just one conversation, or many of them, a whole bunch. Either one. Regular chats between you two guys, regular heart-to-heart talks. Or just one talk once. Either one." He took a quick bite of the sandwich.

Mossi snorted. "Me?" he said. "Talk to Brennan, you mean?"

"Well, yeah," Dell'Appa said, having chewed and swallowed quickly. "That's exactly what I mean, yes indeed. Did you and Bob Brennan go steady?"

Mossi stared at him. "Do they know about you," he said, "back in Boston, I mean? Do they know that you're two-thirds nuts?"

Dell'Appa nodded emphatically. "Oh *yeah*," he said, "absolutely. Matter of fact there's several of 'em'd tell you two-thirds's an understatement. *Big* understatement." He laughed. "But nutty or not, Mister Mossi," he said, "I can still keep track of what's goin' on around me, and you still haven't answered my question. Did you get to be pals with Bob Brennan?"

"I knew who he was," Mossi said. "Him and me never talked in my life."

Dell'Appa finished the sandwich and wiped his hands with the paper napkin. He nodded while he was chewing and swallowing. "Okay then," he said, "that's out of the way. I'm feeling much better about this. I still wasn't prepared for this meeting we're having, but from you tell me, I had no reason to be. But still, since we're having one here, what looks good to you then? Any hot dogs, so to speak? I don't want to look like a chump here, don't know what I'm doing or something."

Mossi glared at him. "You son of a bitch," he said. "Is this what's behind this all then? You takin' over for Brennan on me? Is this why they're doing this thing?"

"Doing what thing," Dell'Appa said. "What thing is it that they're doing?"

"You know what they're doin'," Mossi said. "Don't give me that shit, all right? You come from that place and you work for those guys and they tell you what you're gonna be doing. Just like they tell Brennan, too. And that's what it is, and you do it. So Brennan's gone off now, they're takin' him off, and they're putting you on in his place. So don't try to tell me, don't act like you don't know, exactly what's goin' on here, 'cause you do. Me, I don't know, that's why I'm askin' you, but you an' Brennan, both of you know. Fuckin' government. It's always the same thing, every damned fuckin' time, you deal with the fuckin' damned government. And it don't matter which government, either. The State or the city, the feds: doesn't matter. Any one of you fuckin' damned bastards. The guy that you're dealin' with always plays dumb, like he fuckin' doesn't know what he's fuckin' well doin', don't know what's goin' on. And most times he doesn't, the fucker, he doesn't, because of he is an asshole and he wouldn't know if he did fuckin' know—wouldn't make no difference to him. But sometimes, like now, the guy really does *know,* like you know but you're not gonna tell me, and that's when I really get mad. Playin' Mickey the Dunce on me here."

Dell'Appa laughed at him. "Oh for Christ sake, up yours, Mossi, all right? Cut it out, willya? Just ram it right in the satchel, right in the old barracks bag. And stop actin' like a big asshole. We're both big boys in this now, all grown-up. You do what you do because it's what you've been doing so long now you can't even remember, any more, the other things you did, you're so highly-respected in your profession, whatever it is that you call it. And I know that. I can even understand it. Just like I know damned well you've got to figure that even though Bob Brennan's got a lot of years on me, a lot more time in grade, and you don't even know who I am or where the hell I came from, I must have something on the ball. Because if I didn't, I wouldn't've been assigned to take his place, chasing a gentleman as highly respected as you are."

Mossi glared at him. "Because if you don't," Dell'Appa said, "then I'll just have to assume here that either you're just getting all upset because having a guy your age replaced on your case by a guy a lot younger'n you are makes you start wonderin' if pretty soon you'll have to start wearing Depends or something, because you'll be pissing your pants. Or else all of this, this whole performance of yours here today, it's all just something you're doing to be funny. On purpose. Because if it isn't, if all of this is supposed to be for real, you oughta go to see someone real soon. Some guy who examines heads, you know? Professionally, I mean. To see if there's anything in them. If this's your idea of a tactic. Off-balance the tenderfoot here, his first day on the job."

"Look," Mossi said, clearing his throat, his voice dropping and becoming extremely guttural, "lemme try and see if I can help you, help us both get something straight here, all right? Because I really think we oughta. I don't know anything about no tactic-shit, or anything like that. What I know is that for a long time now I've been . . . well, what it was was, the way it actually went there, was quite a while ago I get outta bed one mornin', and I go to start another day of doin' what I always do, my regular routine. It's nothin' real excitin' but now I'm used to it, you know? And so I don't mind it now. It's what I always do. Make sure my brother's outta bed, he gets dressed and eats his breakfast. See, I don't know, you notice this, you're sittin' there with Brennan in that blue-and-white truck he's always drivin' there this morning, like you most likely must've been, get a look at me—but my kid brother Danny, see, just because he did something yesterday all like he should've, got himself out of bed an' eck-cetra in the morning, all that stuff just like you and I do every day without nobody telling us, well, this don't mean that he is gonna automatically do that same thing today. 'Cause maybe he won't. So I have to make sure he does it, does things like he's supposed to, okay? Doesn't let himself get off the track.

"See, Danny's what they call 'mildly retarded.' When he's having a good day. And when he's had some bad days sometimes, like everybody's had, one time or another, and I've had to take him to the hospital for some help, get him some help there, then they say, some of them've said 'moderately,' that he's 'moderately retarded.' Like when you have a bad time for a few days or so, even a couple weeks or so maybe, like everybody seems to at some point in their life even though they don't like it much, it's because you're not as smart as you usually were.

"And," Mossi said, frowning, "an' this *worries* me, you know? Really bothers the hell out of me. When I hear them sayin' that. Like it isn't that he isn't really what he is on days he's good, and they said he's 'mildly.' It's like when he gets a bad day that is what he really is, and he's 'moderately' then. That really scares me. Because if they can do that, if they can change what he is just by saying different words, then they could change him from 'moderately' to 'severely,' and then from that to 'profoundly', say he's 'profoundly retarded.' Because those are the four kinds of 'retarded' and that is the worst one. Well, if they can do that, just change what Danny is by seeing him when he's not as good as he usually is, or by having somebody see him on a day that's not so good instead of someone who has seen him all the other times, when he's been like he always is, they could put him away. Scares the shit out of me, they could do that. They could take the kid out of the house where he lives, and they could then lock him up. That's what I'm afraid of. And that's what I don't want to see happen, and so I look out for the kid.

"You see what I'm saying here? It's like, it'd be like you come down here to the track quite a lot and you generally make out all right, usually go home with a few dollars, you won fifty or a hundred bucks or so. Then on some other days, maybe, you only won twenny, but another time, perfecta, the double or something, you're up three or four hundred bucks. And on days when you lose—you're like everyone else; everybody's got days when they lose—you don't generally lose that much either, no more'n forty or so, seldom take too bad a hit. Because you been at it long enough now, you got enough experience, you can usually tell when you're havin' a bad day like that, pickin' the dogs, and they're always gonna come along, so you know. And you see that soon as it started and you're keepin' your bets down all day. Plus which, either way, win or lose, at least you had a good time, right? You relaxed, maybe had a few beers, you go home and you're feelin' good. And what is that, you do that? That's 'healthy.' That's 'normal.' That is the way an intelligent man like yourself spends a day off, relaxin', enjoyin' himself. A man should know how to relax.

"And then one day you don't. You get hammered. Get the shit kicked out of you. Well, the assholes at the hospital, they would say that was because you happen to be a very stupid person, that is what you are, and you should probably not even go out by yourself, all right? You see? You got skunked onna dogs, lost your fuckin' shirt, and then you got shit-faced on toppa all that, and the reason was: you are dumb. Not: that you pulled up dumb, on that particular day. Not: that that day you weren't smart like you usually are, so you got your head right up your ass, but next week, even tomorrow, maybe, you'll be just fine again. No, nothin' like that, nothin' like that ever happened, you went home, good night's sleep, and tomorrow you're gonna be fine. No: 'No more racin' for you. You're incompetent to take care of yourself. We're puttin' you inna home.' And they can do that too, if they want. They got the power to do that. If there's nobody else who looks out for you, that's exactly what they can do.

"Now I myself, I don't exactly buy that, that way of thinkin' at all. That they should be able to do that, even though I know they can. What I think is that when they say that Danny, well, that he's 'mildly,' the doctors and the nurses and the asshole social workers, they don't know what the fuck they're talkin' about. And when they say he's 'moderately,' well, they don't know what the fuck they're talking about then, either. But I'm not gonna argue with them there, because either way it don't much matter: Danny needs a little *push*, little *nudge*, there, to get him started inna morning. Like you got to turn on the TV set and set it to the channel that you wanna watch before it'll show you the program that you wanna see. Then he's usually all right. And as long as he's all right, and I'm lookin' out for him, well, they can't put him away."

"What's he do?" Dell'Appa said.

" 'What's he *do?*' " Mossi said. "That what you said, 'what's he *do*'? Whadda you care what he does? Whadda you care where he goes? You gonna start followin' Danny or somethin' now? That what you got on your mind here? Get him all fucked up like you've been wanting me, only with him, might be easier, somethin'? Because you don't like his big brother, don't like what you think I've been doin'?"

"*Hey,*" Dell'Appa said, "take it easy, all right? You're the one, wants to get things straight here? Let *me* see if I can help *you,* pal. You're right. I followed you here today, just like Bob's done a lot, the past year, and unless something happens that I don't expect to see, I'll be following you tomorrow, too. On days, if there's a day, days, when you turn around and you don't see me sitting on your tail, well, you can safely assume those days I had some other bright idea, something else I thought of doing that might get me closer to you faster, 'n following you that day would've, and so I'm off doing that. Doing the very best I can to collect enough information about you so that some day, some day very soon, I'll have the pleasure of walking out of a grand jury room knowing in a day or so, by the end of the week, there's finally gonna be a warrant out on you, and the end of your illustrious career is on the way. In case you had any doubt in your mind, that is what I am doing. And I'm very good at what I do. You can ask any number of guys. You can find them all clustered in two or three places, run by the Department of Corrections.

"Now," Dell'Appa said, "my guess would be that you're pretty much aware of this, that you knew what Brennan had in mind to do to you, and now that I'm behind you, in his place, what I've got in mind. I bet you don't like it, this little task we've set ourselves, or our bosses've set for us. I can even go so far as to sympathize a little bit with you: I don't mean weeping salt tears, or anything like that; just that I know I wouldn't like it either, I'd be annoyed too, if I had the law on my tail all the time. I wouldn't like it at all.

"But just the same, my friend, you know *why* I'm here, and it's not because I've got, or anybody else's got, a hard-on for your brother. You know who's to blame for all this unwelcome attention you get. The guy that you shave every day and drive to this track twice a week. It's that Joe Mossi guy, Mister Mossi, sir; he is the one who's to blame. All the bad things he's done've reflected on you, and now you're paying the price for his deeds. You knew why Bob was on you before me, and you know why I'm on you now that Bob isn't. And that if you outlive or outlast me, someone else will show up in my place. Not because your brother got a bad break in this life. No, because of what you've done.

"And knowing that," Dell'Appa said, "knowing that we're on you, every day, you still choose the places you visit. Which happens to be, in this instance at least, just in case you haven't noticed, *public,* you understand that? This here's a public place, and we've not only got as much right to be here as you, we've got a better one in fact, these here being state-licensed premises. So if you insist on privacy when you consort with known felons, and others not-as-yet-known, you picked the wrong venue to meet them. If you're serious about it, wanting us folks off your ass, you're gonna either have to join a snooty club, or else pick some business associates who don't mind if you're seen going into their offices. And also won't mind if we then decide to get warrants, to find out what you talk about there."

Mossi did not say anything for what seemed like a very long time. Then he put his hands on the counter and stood up, very slowly. "You asked me about dogs," he said.

"Well, you're here a lot," Dell'Appa said. "You should know."

"Error Kennel," Mossi said, standing. "Any dog that's Error Kennel. Not always the class of the field, but always reliable dogs."

"Era Kennel," Dell'Appa said, "I would look for those dogs."

"Willya lissen, for Christ sake, for just once in your life?" Mossi said, leaning. "Not 'Era,' like in 'E-R-A.' 'Error,' awright? Like in baseball. Very good dogs, Error dogs. Good bloodlines and schooled right, the whole bit."

"Okay, 'Error,' " Dell'Appa said. "Error Kennel, I mean."

Mossi slapped both palms down on the counter. He heaved a great breath. "Yeah," he said. "You got any more questions, here, kid?"

"Certainly," Dell'Appa said, "sure. Are you blowin' smoke up my ass here?"

Mossi straightened up. He flapped his upper lip over his lower.

He let his hands hang at his sides. "Do me a favor, all right, kid? Just do me one simple favor. Talk to Bomber, okay? Ask him that question. The one that you just ask me there."

"I don't know if I can do that," Dell'Appa said.

Mossi played to an audience unseen. He shook his head. He rolled his eyes. He whooshed air out of his lungs. He leaned forward and put his hands down on the countertop again. "You're pissing me off here, all right?" he said. "You understand that one simple thing? You really are pissing me off. I don't want to do nothin', nothin' that hurts nobody, all right? I never did. You can ask Bomber. You got to learn here, how to do this, how to do things inna right way. Everyone else, except maybe you, we're all gettin' older here, fast."

"You finished?" Dell'Appa said.

"Am I finished?" Mossi said. "*Yeah,* yeah, I'm finished, you asshole, all right?" He jabbed his right forefinger at Dell'Appa. "It's you," he said, "*you're* the one here, that should worry about bein' finished. Whether he's finished or not yet, and should maybe get offa the pot. Go back and see Bomber again. Ask him what he thinks. Get yourself squared away here, you finally learn, how a man treats a man with *respect.*"

"What I'm saying," Dell'Appa said softly, "all I'm trying to tell you here, is that I'd really like to do exactly what you say. As far as talking to Bomber, I mean, as far as that's concerned, yeah. But in the first place, I wouldn't be doing it *again,* like you suggest, because I've never done it *before.* And in the second . . ."

Mossi interrupted with another snort, rolling his eyes again and raising his hands. "Ahh," he said, "no wonder then. Of course you're an asshole, an asshole for good. You're all of you assholes for good. And assholes're all that you'll ever be. Never talked to the Bomber at all."

"Bomber retired before I came up," Dell'Appa said. "I never worked under him, all right?"

"Well Jesus, for Christ sake," Mossi said, "what difference does that make, I mean? He forgot how to talk once he retired? He move to the North Pole or somethin' and didn't get a phone line put in? He isn't dead, is he? No, he's not dead—I woulda heard if he was. One of the guys would've told me. Would've been a big party or something. Fireworks and drinks and a band. 'Hey, Bomber Lawrence's dead. I'm buyin' drinks for the house.' That's what alla the guys'd be sayin'." He chuckled. "But no, no, there wasn't, wasn't no party like that. So then he's still alive, gotta be. And you can't go and see him, or somethin'?"

"No," Dell'Appa said, "nothing like that. He's still right where he always was, summers at least, only now year around: with his wife down there on the Cape."

"Well for Christ sake then, asshole," Mossi said, "ask somebody who did work with him, give him a call, introduce you. Tell Bomber that you're this new asshole kid and Short Joey said you should see him. Bomber'll know who that is. He'll recognize my name right off." Mossi nodded, agreeing physically with himself. "We go back a long way, Bomber and me. Bomber's one of my fans 'way back when, I was still gettin' fights around here. He maybe don't wanna see no more new cops now, now that he got retired—already seen all the assholes he ever wanted to meet, back when he hadda meet assholes. But he'll see *you*, if you tell him that. Use my name, just like I said. Tell him I said to give you some pointers."

Dell'Appa sighed. "Look," he said, "just shut up for a minute and listen to me here now, okay? It isn't because I didn't want to meet Bomber when I came in, or that I really wouldn't've liked to've talked to him since he retired. Just for the reasons you say. The guy's a national legend, all right? From Boston to Honolulu, every cop in the whole great big street-clothes world knows who you mean, you say: 'Bomber said once,' they all listen. Maybe even bigger'n that, you think about it—the RCMPs and the Scotland Yard guys, the French Sureté know him too.

"So," Dell'Appa said, "it's not as though I've avoided the guy, or don't think he could've taught me a lot. The point is, he can't now, on most days at least. Can't teach anyone now. The Bomber most days can't talk anymore. He can't remember, most of the time, either. The way I understand it, it's gotten to the point now, it's advanced so far, that most days he doesn't even *know* he doesn't know, anymore. Which I hope is true, because from everything I heard about the guy, it'd be absolute torture for him if he understood now what's happened."

Mossi stared at him. "You're shittin' me, aren't you," he said. "You've got to be shittin' me here, tellin' me that kind of shit."

"No," Dell'Appa said, "no, I'm not."

"The Bomber's gone goofy," Mossi said, "right? That *is* what you're tellin me, right? He lost all his marbles and stuff, got simple in his old age. He don't know his ass from third base anymore. You expect I'll believe shit like that?"

Dell'Appa shrugged again. "Doesn't matter to me, pal," he said, "what matters is whether his wife does. His wife and his family there. And they *do* believe it, I know. They won't let anyone see him."

Mossi nodded. "Okay then," he said. "Yeah, that's okay. That'd explain a whole bunch of stuff." He laughed like a big dog barking once. "He oughta come outta retirement," he said, "like Sinatra there's always doin'. What is it they say? Oh, yeah, I remember: 'That's him all right, forgotten but not gone.' That's what the Bomber should do now. He'd fit right in with you young assholes here, if he really don't know which end's up.

"Still, inna way," Mossi said, "inna way it's kinda too bad, he doesn't know what's going on. Because if he did, it'd be good for him, because now at least, he would know. He'd know what it's like, to be someone like that, if he knew anything now, and knew that's what he is himself. And needs someone to look out for him."

11 "It's an interesting approach," Dennison said in his office the next morning. "We can do a paper on it for the next 'Frontline' show on the Mafia, huh? 'Confrontational Aversion: Strategic Surveillance Techniques,' something along that line." He removed his Greek fisherman's black wool cap and gray stormcoat and hung them on the hook behind the door. He clapped his hands together and rubbed them briskly as he went to his desk and sat down. " 'Our theory is that the best initiative for surveillance of the standard-issue stone killer is to get him all riled up as fast as we can. Coddling these chaps just doesn't work.' I can't say I ever heard of it before, and I'm not entirely sure I would've suggested it myself, approved it in advance if I'd been asked. But since I wasn't . . ."

"Well, but I didn't have that luxury," Dell'Appa said. He sprawled in the chair facing Dennison's desk. "Of consultation, I mean. Bob didn't give me any inkling, any reason to expect, either when I talked to him or from reading his reports, that I was going to have the guy all of a sudden right there in my face, the first day I took the handoff. So it wasn't like I could've seen it coming and asked you what you thought I should do when he did it. I hadda improvise, make it up as I went along."

"Yeah, yeah, I know," Dennison said, leafing through his messages, grimacing as he discarded them and picked up the handset of his telephone console. He punched in a two-digit number. He listened for about a minute before he replaced the phone in its cradle. He shook his head, his face showing sadness. "You know," he said, "in my next life I am definitely going to have to give more thought to the decision of what to be when I grow up. I called the Great Bloviator yesterday afternoon, we finally started getting tapes that look like at long last we can grab Buddy Royal. Which if we can'll reduce the *E. coli* count of the human sea around us by at least, oh, say, six percent."

"The guy that runs the chop-shop by the train station there?" Dell'Appa said. "Brennan says he's just a little piece of shit. Gave me a whole big song-and-dance about him yesterday morning, how he beat up his first wife and his second's the town's community-snatch; his friends're all laughin' at him, shootin' him birds all the time; and now, just to cap it off, sort of, his business's gone in the dumper. Guy's so hopeless he can't even get himself indicted for something respectable."

Dennison looked puzzled. "Bob told you that?" he said. "Where the hell'd he get that idea?"

"From the tapes we've been getting, he said," Dell'Appa said. "That's what he told me, at least. He said we finally got around to getting the bug in, after all these years he's been buying hot cars, and now we're gonna catch him red-handed in the act, put a stop to it once and for all. And what happens? Nothin's what happens. Now nobody's calling him up anymore, sell him Porsches so hot they're still smokin'."

"Bob's not on that case," Dennison said. "He's not assigned anything anywhere near it, not even back-up on that lash-up. Buddy

178

Royal's Cannon's case. Connie Cannon's got his name, John Finn helping him. And the stuff you're tellin' me Bob's tellin' you there: that isn't part of the case. That's just fiddlin' and diddlin', the normal, usual bullshit you'd get off of any businessman's phone line if you tapped into it in the lags between major transactions. Got basically nothin' to do with the stuff that we're after, the real meat of the case. But even if it was connected, that still doesn't tell me what the hell Bob doing's with it. He's got nothing to do with Buddy Royal. It's none of his detail at all."

"Oh," Dell'Appa said. "Well, I dunno then. All I know's what he said to me. Which at least sounded like he really knew a lot. Sounded very well-informed."

"He shouldn't even've been monitoring those tapes," Dennison said. "Hell, he shouldn't've even known they were coming in. You sure he said: 'the tapes'? That he not only knew *about* the tapes and what was coming up on them, but he knew it *from* the tapes? It couldn't've been just some scuttlebutt he happened to've picked up around here, heard at the coffee table or something?" He paused. "Not that that wouldn't also disturb me, I thought Connie'd been being that careless, but it wouldn't concern me as much."

"No, 'from the bug' is what he told me," Dell'Appa said. "He told me for a long time, good many years, everybody knew what this Buddy Royal guy was doin', takin' in hot cars for parts. But it was just that nobody seemed to have time to get a bead on him and croak him. Until finally Buddy's turn came, his number'd come up, and we got the mike in, and then, apparently just as we got it in, all his suppliers went out of business, all his buyers went broke. So as a result all we're listenin'-in on's Buddy's friends callin' him up and yankin' his chain—how his new wife's fuckin' every guy in Boston, and six or eight other towns too, all the way the New Hampshire state line."

Dennison raised his eyebrows. "Okay, if you say so," he said, drumming the fingertips of his right hand on the desk and glancing at the phone as he spoke, "but it beats the hell out of me where Bob got his information. Which is fortunately wrong, irrelevant, actually, but that still doesn't change a lot about the basic . . . Goddamn you, Terry, call back."

"Why you need the Bloviator?" Dell'Appa said. "If you're getting what you went in for."

"Because we haven't got enough yet," Dennison said. "The quality's all right, really first-rate, nasty stuff, nothing wrong with it at all. But the warrant ends tomorrow night. So we need another one, right? An extension, I mean. Whatever the hell they call it. So, yesterday afternoon, when I find out what we're getting, which is what we went in for in the first place, the whole reason for this thing, I check back on the paper and find out it's dead at midnight Friday. *Ergo,* we need another one, and I call Terry on the phone." He shook his head.

"Terry isn't there," he said, "and this's not that late in the day. Three-thirty, quarter-four. Terry's secretary doesn't really know where Terry is. I can tell because when Terry's gone out to do something that he should've come back from doing at least two hours ago, she always says: 'Terry isn't back from court yet.' Which is what she always also says when that's really where he is, and she knew he'd get back late. But when she thinks he isn't still in court, that he's wandered off someplace, she says it in a different tone of voice. She says it like she isn't telling you something; what she's doing's asking you a question. What she's really saying is: 'I'm almost sure that Terry's having coffee someplace, goofing off this afternoon. But if I tell people that, even though they already knew it, and Terry finds out, he'll get mad. So if I say he's in court, will you pretend you believe that for me, please?' "

"Jeez, Brian," Dell'Appa said, "you're a hard man on a guy, aren't you, here. Aren't you the guy who practically made it a tradition in this place, that when the thing you're working on's started making you completely nuts, you tell whoever else's around to say that you're out doing fieldwork, and then you go down to the aquarium? Aren't you the guy who invented that?"

"Only the aquarium variation was mine," Dennison said. "The original theme was by Bomber, back in the days of afternoon baseball when ballgames were feasible workdays. But I think the aquarium's better. It's climate-controlled and open all year, two definite advantages for the harried Boston executive, and I for one find it soothing. No man should go through life without porpoise. And anyway, when you've reached stymie on a thing, it helps to visit something, any animal, that looks sillier'n you've made yourself feel. The Red Sox don't, anymore; all that bunch does now is look stupid. Penguins and harbor seals fill the bill, if an innocent free-play period's called for."

"Well," Dell'Appa said, "how do you know Terry hadn't come to stymie too, just like you have, so he either had to go fuck off or else check in for observation?"

"I don't," Dennison said, "and it wouldn't matter if I did. Because even if he did have a good reason, he should've timed it better, for a day when I wasn't going to be the one who had to talk to him."

"Oh," Dell'Appa said, "now I get it. Yeah. Well, I can see where that would make a difference, now you've explained it and all, all of the ramifications. If your elevator's stuck three floors from the top, it's okay to go out and play—unless Lieutenant Dennison might decide to come looking for you. In which case, postpone it 'til you're sure."

"Right," Dennison said, "the whole secret here—" His phone rang and he seized it.

"Yeah, Terry," he said, before the caller could possibly have greeted him or identified himself, "where the hell've you been?" He listened. "Never mind 'the traffic this morning,'" he said. "In the first place I don't believe you—I know very well what held you up was you overslept or you were getting laid or something. And in the second place, it was yesterday when I had to talk to you anyway, so where the hell were you then?" He listened again. "Okay then," he said, "I forgive you. Not that I believe any of that cock-and-bull story you just told me there, but leaving that aside, what we need here's either an extension of the paper that we've got on Buddy Royal, or a new piece of paper entirely. The one we got now dies twelve-oh-one Friday, and we haven't got as much shit in our bucket to plaster all over the motherfucker's I'd like to have, you take it in before the grand jury."

He paused. "No," he said, "I don't care. Doesn't matter a rat's ass to me. If you think a whole new one'd most likely be safer, by all means let's get a new one. I'll send Cannon up to see you *instanter,* chop-chop. Make a new affidavit up pronto. Judge'll give you another closed session? This morning?" He nodded. "Okay then, good," he said. "That's very good there. Yeah, I'll send Cannon right up."

He depressed a different button on the console, lighting a new line. He listened. He said: "Connie. Yeah. I got him. Just now. No, I don't know where he was. He told me he was at the Social Law Library, but of course we both know that's a lie. You ask him, you have to know. See what kind of answer you get." He listened, grinning. "Connie, Connie," he said, "you don't ever listen to me. I keep tellin' you, you aren't listening. You've got to stop, you've just got to stop, lettin' guys intimidate you just because they got law degrees. You got too much respect for attorneys. It's not healthful." He began to laugh. "Corporal," he said, "that is not language appropriate for use by a professional person for description of other professional persons, of either gender, is that clear? Correct. So, when you see Terry . . . yes, right now of course, go on up . . . correct, you are not to call him a cocksucker, 'kay?" He nodded. "Correct," he said, "you can't call him that bad name either."

He replaced the handset in the cradle and smirked. "I *love* this shit," he said, "every bit of it. I *live* for this part of it, that's what I do. This's the part that I live for. Takin' down some guy like him. You get a guy like Buddy Royal, a no-good, scheming-little, dirty-pants, snotty-nosed *bastard,* thinks he's so goddamned smart and we're such fuckin' stupid dummies, we not only cannot catch him doin' what he's really doin', we're not even smart enough to know what it is? I *looove* takin' those assholes down. It's like havin' ice cream and cake.

"All these goddamned *years* he's been sittin' out there in that clapped-out, fly-blown shop of his down next by the railroad tracks there, laughin' with his good-for-nothin' rat-ass buddies at what jerks we are, and how he's of course immortal—*that kindah stuff pisses me off.* Especially since, as a matter of fact, in Buddy's case here, he was right—we couldn't do steam-shit about it."

He nodded. He crooned. "Yeah? Well now we can. Okay now, Buddy, laugh your ass off, gloat all you want, but make sure you're finished in a couple weeks or so, the outside, 'cause when the grand jury gets through hearing those recordings, you'll be on your way to the penitentiary, my friend, and what'll happen to you in that place you aren't gonna like a bit, not, at a fuckin' bit, at *all.*"

"What?" Dell'Appa said. "What's gonna happen to him?"

"Well, the usual thing, I assume," Dennison said. "The usual bridal reception and shower, daisy-chain and the conga-line the boss cons always put on, when the new baby fuckers come in."

" 'Baby-fuckers'?" Dell'Appa said. "I thought Royal's a car-thief, a high-grade, superfly car-thief. Midnight Auto Supply. One of the best ones around."

"That's what everyone thought," Dennison said, now just smiling. "That's exactly what everyone thought. They thought it because while Buddy's a born-to-run sleaze-bag, Buddy Royal's clever, and that's what he wanted them thinking. Well, clever he may be, but he isn't as smart as he thinks he is, or he's managed to make people think. Put him down for just standard-bred cute."

"At doing what?" Dell'Appa said. "If everybody thought he was dealin' in hot cars . . ."

"Harry, Harry," Dennison said, "didn't it seem kinda funny to you, when Brennan or whoever it was first started tellin' you about what a car-thief Buddy was, and everybody knew it, that we hadn't been able to *catch* him? Considerin' how smart you know we are, and what public heroes this would've made all of us, if we'd collared one of those kingpins whose larcenous trade's driven everybody's car-insurance bills right out of sight? If everybody knew Buddy's doin' this, all these years, and if the Governor and the Secretary, both of those fine gentlemen along with the AG, too, would've had a simulta-neous orgasm—'The earth moved for *me*, dears; was it good for you dears, too?'—to hold a news conference the day we hauled him in in irons, why the hell weren't we smart enough to postpone catchin' one more boring drug-smuggler, which'll make us one small headline on page forty-six for one day when we pull it off, and put a full-court press on Buddy, 'til we had him in the can? Had his head on a pike. They would've given us a day in our honor, had a parade down Com Ave. for us, if we'd've done that for them. So why didn't we, then?

"For the obvious reason," Dennison said, "and that's another rule I learn from Bomber: If you can't catch a guy doin' what you know he's doin', and you're satisfied you haven't lost your grip, then maybe it's because you're wrong; he isn't doin', mainly, what you think he's doin', only now and then.

"Mainly he is doin' somethin' else, which you don't catch him doin' 'cause you never look for that. It's like the guy who went out through the factory gates every Friday night for thirty years, pushing a wheelbarrow fulla straw. And every Friday night the same guard pawed through the straw and never once found a damned thing. So the guy finally gets to retirement age, and his last Friday night on the job the guard at the gate says to him: 'Aw right. Tonight I'm not even gonna search the barrow. Just tell me: I know you've been stealing something all these years, what the hell were you takin'?' And the fella says: 'Simple. Wheelbarrows.'

"Well, that's what Buddy's been doin'. Buddy does take stolen cars, and he does cut them up. And he does sell the parts, and that's all illegal, right. But the point is that Santa Claus, that lazy bastard, works about half as many days a year doing what he does as Buddy works at dissecting hot cars, see? Buddy's a chopper, yes indeed he is, just like the guy you knew in high school was the biggest swordsman. He's done it, yeah, but not often; just something he learned how to do a long time ago, he's a kid—now more like something he can do if he likes when things're slow—to fill up time. All the rest's talk: what he wants people thinking, not what he's got going down.

"All those parts," Dennison said, "almost all the parts he had—and he had a lot of them, a real big inventory; always had plenty on hand—were perfectly legit, as more'n a couple of our guys found out when they busted in on him three times, Buddy splittin' his pants, he was laughing so hard, makin' idiots out of the cops. It's selling *hot* parts that's your felony, Jack. *Second-hand* parts, salvage and scrap? Why, child, those're perfectly legal.

"That was why we couldn't catch him doing it, doing what the whole town knew that he'd been doing all along: he wasn't doing it. Buddy'd made it all up, by himself, what he is and what he's been doin'."

"Yeah," Dell'Appa said, "but why would a guy do that then?"

"To camouflage the sewer-business that he's really doing," Dennison said. "Buddy's a regional distribution manager here in a child-pornography ring. Stuff gets made outta state, mostly out of the country. Europe, the Orient, someplace—Central America maybe. Not that the same product isn't made here, right here in this great republic, but the feds're real tough on the scumbags they catch, so the high-grade filth is imported. Then it gets shipped in to Buddy and people like Buddy, and they store it here, for reshipment. Buddy reships in trucks full of crushed junkers, crates of parts leaving his place. The reason we never found what we were lookin' for, hot parts, was because hot parts weren't there. And we never found what really was there, because we never looked for it."

"Brennan, then," Dell'Appa said slowly, "Brennan then doesn't know this. Because if he did, he would've told me."

"And that's why I'm damned glad he didn't," Dennison said. "For one thing, he's got no reason to know it, and . . ."

"And what's the other thing?" Dell'Appa said.

"You got me thinking, the other day there," Dennison said, "when you were doin' all that pissing and moaning about how Bob's files on Joe Mossi don't measure up, and how come. I didn't agree with you at the time, but when you said you couldn't understand how a man with his background could screw up a case so completely without doing it on purpose, having that in mind, it sort of stuck in my mind. At first it was 'Nah, Bob wouldn't do that. Bob wouldn't go inna the tank.' But then I'm driving home that night and it's still naggin' at me, little different perspective, that maybe you could be right. 'Cause, no question my mind I believe you, all right? What you're telling me's in Bob's files. I believe you that somethin' is wrong. But what?

" 'It couldn't've happened by accident,' I think. 'If he did it he did it on purpose. But what the hell could that purpose be? What'd make him do that, for Christ sake?' I think: 'Why would Bob Brennan leave out stuff from reports when someone like Mossi's involved? If he's not afraid,' and I don't think that Bob's that, 'and he isn't corrupt,'— I'd be very surprised if he was, much pride as he takes in this job— 'then what on earth would've been enough, make the guy say *scrotum diem,* just flat-out bag the job like this?' "

"You come up with any answers?" Dell'Appa said.

"Hell no," Dennison said. "It's your job to come up with the answers, once you've raised the questions for me. And don't think I don't appreciate it, either, you alerting me like you did there, just because in a few short days or so I start pushing harder on you for them here."

"Oh, great," Dell'Appa said. "First you give me an assignment that develops bad personal habits—I was never a gamblin' man and I sure can't afford to become one, and now you're expecting *results?* I may have to start filing grievances here, keep putting in new rules like this."

Dennison laughed. "How much of a beating'd you take?" he said. "I knew a guy once that followed the dogs, followed them faithfully, done it for years, and he claimed he didn't even like it. Never had liked it, in fact. He said the only reason that he did it was that there was a dog-race within driving distance, where he lived, every day, every night of the year. He wasn't married, never had been, so: no kids. No relatives left, he lived alone; didn't like watching sports on the weekends and he didn't like staying home nights. So that's why he followed the dogs. 'I maybe drop eight bucks, I maybe win ten. I can afford it, and either way, right? Gives me something to do, I'm bettin' the dogs, besides sit by myself drinking beer. I said: 'You drink beer at the track, don't you, though?' He said: 'Sure, but that's not alone. I'm not alone when I'm there.' I always figured he was proba- bly just scared of sex, with women, with men, either one. Or maybe not scared exactly; maybe just not interested. I mean, I could be wrong, but I wouldn't *think* a man's chances getting laid'd be that great at a dog-track."

"Jeez, I dunno about that," Dell'Appa said. "The kid who brought me my lunch yesterday looked to me like she'd be good for it, and it wouldn't've taken much either. And then there was this broad, I'd say forty-five or six, took the seat right next to me after Mossi left; she was *very* friendly. Very anxious to make sure a newcomer to the place —well, at least someone she hadn't noticed around there before, and I got the distinct impression there aren't very many she doesn't notice, on arrival—felt right at home right off. 'Hiya, handsome,' she says to me, nice black-hair dye-job, not too much eye-stuff on, got a butt hangin' out of her mouth, 'didn't see you around here before. Anyone usin' this seat?' "

"Ah, yes," Dennison said. " 'Well hel-*lo*, sailor-boy, feel like havin' some fun? Like buyin' a drink for a lady?' "

"No, not like that," Dell'Appa said. "Sister Mary Fred: no, she wasn't that, but she wasn't a working-girl either. More in the nature of looking for company: not really shopping, just browsing. But there's no law I ever heard of that says when you're just looking you have to rule out more'n that, and there's no harm in choosing new company with that possibility in mind.

"My, my," Dennison said, "still drivin' all the ladies nuts, are you, Harry? Girls just won't leave you alone? Must be all you can do, keep your ego under control." He paused. "But you'd better though, hadn't you, pal? Don't want Gayle making any more calls now, do we? 'Where does Harry go nights to get supper?' 'Gee, Gayle, we assumed he went home.'"

"Brian," Dell'Appa said, "don't start lettin' your imagination run wild with you again, all right? Everything's kosher with Gayle nowadays, no suspicions breaking loose now out of hand. The waitress's a teenager, twenty at the most. Sure, a good-looking-enough kid, but no blushing-violet stuff; this one's tougher'n a loanshark with a pocket calculator, just waiting to find out how far she can get in this world, on her back with all her clothes off, except maybe a garterbelt, something. Right now, according to Mossi, she's markin' time, floor-showin' the merchandise much as she can, memorizin' her lines for when she's the star of her own little *la vie en rose*. Time being what she's doin's walkin' on the wild side with her sister's husband, two-bit hood from someplace down in Rhode Island, Pawtucket'd be my hunch, gettin' her thrills'n chills that way, meetin' and greetin' the players.

"She'll get a better offer pretty soon, doin' that, and three or four years from now, she's moved up in grade a few times, been the girlfriend a few different guys, nothin' too serious, nice and relaxed, some of the older ones, you know? Guys with a dollar to spend and the yachts, all of that stuff like that there—'Hey, take it easy, relax'— doing what'll amount to some discreet high-grade hookin'? This is a comfortable life. She'll be on retainer through all this, of course, no dime-a-dance stuff, so no one'll say that it's hookin'; boss don't like it if you call his girl a whore. And somewhere along the way, 'cause she's a thoughtful girl and this kind of work is seasonal, doesn't last at all, she'll latch onto a protegé, some boss's protegé, strike up a friendship with him. So when the boss's through with her, ready for a newer model, the kid'll be able, make brownie points with him, takin' her off the man's hands. The boss'll think he thought it up."

"Uh-huh," Dennison said, "well, a short career, perhaps, not very appealing to anyone outside of the life, but a merry one, still, I suppose."

"You think she'll actually mind?" Dell'Appa said. "I knew a

woman, sophomore year of college, we happened to draw the same English class. And she reminded me some, well, this kid yesterday reminded me of her a little, 's what it actually was. And we got to know each other, this's long before I met Gayle, and finally it got to the point where looked to me like it'd become a question of what the hell we were going to do next. Because she was really a good-looking girl, and I was getting involved with her. So, the way I looked at it was: Were we either going to break up, or were we going move in together and see what we had. So I told her that, and she said, well, she guessed that meant we were going to break up, because even though she really liked me a lot and all, and there was no question that the sex'd been, well, certainly acceptable—the physical attraction was unquestionably there—she had other things to think about too. She was from almost the same kind of family background as mine—she didn't actually use the term, most likely just didn't occur to her, but she would've if she'd thought of it: *wage slave*—and while she certainly wouldn't say there was anything wrong with that kind of life, wrong with going to work every day and earning a salary, even a pretty good one, like my father'd always made, because you had to if you had an eating habit, that wasn't what she had in mind as a way she intended to spend her life. So she was keeping herself unattached—which for her meant frequent sleep-overs, yes, but no long-term shacking-up—as she went along, until she either found what she wanted 'or I turn thirty,' she told me. 'After which if I haven't found the kind of man I've got in mind, I'll have to start lowering my requirements.'"

"Christ," Dennison said, "she say she hoped you'd reapply if you were still interested and nothing'd turned up that met her requirements by then?"

Dell'Appa laughed. "Well, she wasn't *quite* that cold-blooded. Almost, but not quite. She just took a very practical point of view about her body and everything else she had to offer. 'My ass is my principal asset. That's what I've got to trade. If I'm going to get anywhere impressive in this life, I've got to peddle it very carefully, real conservatively, and that means only to somebody that I really do like a lot—I insist on that; I'd never screw a man I didn't really like, as I happen to, you—and who also has a lot of money. Which you happen not to.' It was all very calm and dispassionate and all, and I had no trouble at all understanding what she meant.

"And that's what this kid yesterday reminded me of," he said. "When her career as a bimbo draws to a close down the line, I'll bet, she really won't mind at all. She'll actually feel quite relieved. She's like most of those broads, when she gets to that age she'll figure she's got enough jewelry anyway, plus all the fur coats she needs, and if not being greedy means she won't have to suck cock anymore, as she's already decided a long time ago to stop doing as soon as she could, the instant she got the option, well, that is a deal she can live with. Which her new husband won't know just yet that her personal plans will include, of course, but hey, tough titty, huh? Life's full of unpleasant surprises—ambitious young hoods get them too.

"So the marriage'll get off on the wrong, ah, foot, and it most likely won't ever recover. Okay, so it won't last—so what? Lots of marriages don't, and besides, it's beyond her control. Her choices're limited. It's not like she's got a choice here between the gunsel and some tinhorn saint that just left the priesthood, you know; for all practical purposes the only kind of guy that she can hope to marry is one that knows already not only knows all *about* the other hoods she fucked and sucked, but knows all the hoods personally and for years's been getting, what, a blow-by-blow bedside account, I guess it'd be, of her whole career. But that's okay, probably, because he's got to be caught just like she is. Can't let it bother him, that he's known all along what her job, ah, entailed, any more'n she could let it bother her while she was doin' it; what he is's the cock-equipped gender model of her, the muscular part of the same overall system that gave her a living for pussy.

"So she'll give it a shot, get married the first time, the big wedding and all, boss'll pay for the Cancun honeymoon, and six months later she and her hubby won't be speakin'; he won't be comin' home nights. Two or three years later either they'll be permanently separated, or maybe even divorced, and she'll be livin' on the alimony while she pokes the tennis pro and tells anyone who asks that she's still in love with what's-his-name, the wise guy she married back there that she can't even remember what he looks like anymore. And ten or twelve years down the line, still lookin' very good, very sharp, she'll maybe get married again, but this time to some rich divorced guy about fifteen years older she met and screwed on a whim—out at the country club one night. 'What the hell, huh? Who knows what'll happen? Older gent like this, nice and refined, ain't like he'd *hit* you or something—and if he tried it, you'd deck him. So the worst thing'd be, you got a bad lay. Well, hey, so what, huh? That's all right: you'd've still gotten laid, and gettin' laid's never all bad, you got any talent at all.'

"Cripes, even Mossi warned me about her. Although not for my sake: for hers. She's in the training stage now, being groomed for the rest of her life. She doesn't realize it all yet, like Joe Mossi does, so she doesn't understand she maybe shouldn't have a fling with a cop, that that could hurt. Be like losing her virginity before the Hollywood producer ever saw her. Could ruin her entire career. That was what he had in mind."

"The den mother, then," Dennison said, "the dame with the black hair and butts."

"*Huh*," Dell'Appa said, "now there I could get into some trouble, without even noticing at first. I got to talking with that woman, neither one of us knows what the other one's last name is and still wouldn't be sure if we'd introduced ourselves with them, and within fifteen minutes we were yakkin' away like we'd known each other for years."

"Yeah, those're the dangerous ones, all right," Dennison said. "It's the same with everyone, too. Men and women, makes no difference, either one. Once you reach a certain age it isn't how much skin's exposed or how flat the tummies are so much as it's hittin' it off like that, you know? Hittin' it off leads to gettin' it off. Most people, heck, the mystery went away some years ago, and no matter how much bragging somebody's doing, I doubt there's many middle-aged couples that'd really *want* to spend the day getting laid eight or nine times, even if the men could still do that many shows in a row."

"Or ever could, for that matter," Dell'Appa said.

"It's never nice to dispute the accuracy of an older man's memories," Dennison said. He paused. "Especially," he said, "when the reason that you met a lady for the first time might be because an older gentleman's memory suggested to him that you might enjoy it. As you obviously did."

"Like who, 'older gentleman'?" Dell'Appa said. "The hell're you talkin' about, Brian? Some guy tryin' to set me up?"

"Sure," Dennison said, "that's exactly what I'm telling you, at least to think about. Something that could happen, and happen any time, even if it wasn't involved this time. The badger game's been around a long time you know, ever since Samson got involved with the hairdresser there, and there's a reason: it works. Wouldn't be too surprising if Mossi decided to try out a little of the neighborhood poon-tang on the new boy on the block, see if that was his weakness."

"Mossi doesn't know anything about me," Dell'Appa said. "Didn't even know who I was. Only what. He did know that I was a cop."

"Yeah," Dennison said, "well, I don't wanna shock you or anything here, but as much as it may surprise to you hear it, you wouldn't be the first cop, or the only State cop, either, who'd ever let his glands take over decisions his brains should've been making. Mossi if he sent her over could've figured: 'Hey, maybe the guy's got a weakness.' Anyway, learn anything from her?"

"As a matter of fact, yeah, I did," Dell'Appa said. "For one thing that when Mossi recommended a certain group of dogs, the ones from Error Kennels, he wasn't giving me the swerve. I said: 'Don't come here that often, myself. Don't know my way around yet. Guy I know said: "Bet Error's. They give you your dollar, every day you need your dollar." He givin' me the leg there?' She said: 'No, those're good dogs. Don't always win but nobody's dogs do. Error's'll give you a good race.' So I bet 'em, and damn, they're both tellin' the truth. I won almost forty bucks there."

"Turn it in at the Evidence locker," Dennison said.

"Fuck you," DellAppa said.

"Funny name for a kennel though, huh?" Dennison said. "Who owns it, Don Buddin or some other guy, played short like a man fightin' bees?"

"No," Dell'Appa said. "It's a father-daughter combination. He bankrolls it. She trains the dogs. Everett R. Rollins, Olivia Rollins. 'It's her fulltime job,' my new girlfriend tells me, 'dogs're what this lady does. She's very good at this, too. You come down in the morning some time, see her out there schoolin' them, you know? Very nice hand with the dogs. Figures of course. Just what you'd expect,' talkin' out of the side of her mouth, one Marlboro after another, 'we're better at nurturin', stuff.' Then she gives me this look and says: 'Right? That's why we're so good with men. That's what all men're too—dogs.' "

Dennison snickered. "Yeah," he said, "she'd be dangerous all right."

"Maybe not quite as dangerous as the dog-lady's daddy, though," Dell'Appa said. "Last night, I got home, I modemed his name up into the system here. After all, he's a registered breeder and so forth, his kennels're licensed, all kinds-ah rules in that racket. Must be some files on him, right? You bet there're files, files up the gump-stump. Stuff was all ready this morning. Waiting when I came in. This guy's also a lawyer, practicing lawyer, and I think I saw him yesterday. The guy in the blue shirt with Mossi. I think furthermore I now know why Joe goes there, visits the track twice a week. I think he goes there to see Rollins."

12 "Well, yeah, he does that, he sees Rollins," Ernie said. "But also the dogs, they're half his. It's not only Ev Rollins he goes there to see, and that's why it's on Tuesdays and Thursdays: their dogs mostly race on those days." The thick wooden door made it relatively quiet in the chapel/conference-room/library on the third floor at the rear of the main building at the Plymouth County House of Correction, but Dell'Appa could still hear the muffled distant din of over five hundred men locked up together in cellblocks designed to hold about three hundred, their shouting and heavy footsteps on the black steel spiral staircases and corridor balconies in the central guardhouse, the intermittent crashing of the steel cell-doors opening and closing, tier by tier.

"I dread it," he had told Gayle the night before.

"As many times as I've done it, as many times as I've gone in, it's never gotten one bit easier. I'll never get used to it, if I lived to be a hundred and went in every day religiously, like some monk singing vespers or something, I still'd never get used to it. I hate everything about it. The noise; the stink, hundreds of men all jammed in together, good many of them probably none-too-clean when they were on the loose, but at least then they weren't all packed together in a closed space; they were separate and out in the open air, and if they did start to cluster indoors, well, you could still get upwind of the bastards; spending at least eighteen hours of every day, stacked in bunks crammed in two to a room that isn't big enough for a single in even a second-rate flophouse; yellin' at each other all of the time, runnin' their TV pillow-speakers just as loud as they can; sweating and hawking, belching and farting, greasy-meat and vile vegetable gases, jerkin' off in their blankets; takin' a shower in too much of a big hurry to get really clean, so they don't take a dick up the ass, couple of times a week, max; the crowding, the being-confined all the time—Jesus, I hate all of it. Every time I go in I'm scared to death the guards'll get confused, let the guy out that I went in to see and make me stay to finish his time."

"Most people do," she said. "Hate it, I mean. That's why it's such good punishment. Well, pretty much the best we've come up with so far; put it that way—for most people, just the idea of being locked up's enough. And especially people who've had some secondary experience with confinement, visiting naughty relatives or something. They all hated it too. Well, all but a few of the ones I've had any contact with, at least. There were those two strange women that I saw out in Framingham, of course, those two who claimed to be witches and also claimed not to mind being in jail, but then they were all-around strange anyway. World-class strange. And who knows? Maybe they really were witches. Not Hallowe'en witches, I mean; real, honest-to-God, witches—after bedtime they were dematerializing themselves, flying out for a night on the town."

Ernie Nugent was a thin sallow man in his late twenties. He had long, dull, black hair that he appeared to have combed only with his fingers, and his face was narrow under it. His torso did not fully occupy his clothing; both the collar of his dark-gray cotton work-shirt and the tee-shirt under it gaped away from his neck and collarbone.

His eyes were grayish-green and lifeless, deeply-socketed like com-
mercially-stocked samples of diseased tissue preserved for laboratory
studies in pathology. His facial muscles were restless, paramecial,
randomly moving the flesh around his mouth and on his forehead
without any apparent purpose of communicative expression. "Him
and Rollins've been partners in them dogs six-eight-ten-twelve years
now, I guess. Long's I 'member, least. Ever since before I've known
him. Knew Ev Rollins, I mean, and that was back that summer there
when Tyson got lugged out in Indiana there. For rapin' that black girl
that was in the beauty contest."

"That wasn't that long ago," Dell'Appa said.

"What," Ernie said distractedly, as though asking solely in order
to appear polite. He sat in the oak chair across the broad dark conference table from Dell'Appa, his back to the safety-glassed–barred
window overlooking the exercise yard and the two-story annex beyond it where the trusties were housed, closer to the crop fields and
the pastures that they tended inside the chain-link perimeter. A
steady gray rain ran down the glass; it seemed to dissolve the fluores-
cent light in the room, so that it was leaking out through the wet
window into the dull sky beyond, above the cyclone fence and the
concertina razor-wire, and Ernie, monochromed and insubstantial,
looked as though he might be able to leak out along with it, if he
wasn't carefully watched.

"That Tyson got convicted in that rape case," Dell'Appa said.
"That wasn't twelve years ago. Not even close to it."

"No?" Ernie said. "Huh. I thought it was. You know? That's what
I thought it was." He spoke softly and almost wonderingly, inspecting
each of his words before fabricating the sound of it from the idea he
had in his mind.

Dell'Appa cleared his throat. "Well, it doesn't really matter" he
said. "What concerns me's not so much when Joe Mossi bought his
interest in the greyhounds as what else he does with Rollins."

" 'With Rollins,' " Ernie said.

"Yeah, with Rollins," Dell'Appa said. "Is Rollins his lawyer for
him? Does he handle his legal work for him?"

"Oh, geez," Ernie said, looking worried. "I wouldn't think he'd be
doing that, no. I mean, maybe he could, but I doubt it."

"Why?" Dell'Appa said. "Why would that be so far-fetched an

idea, a lawyer doing the legal work for a guy that he's partners with? Rollins is a lawyer, isn't he? Be the most natural thing in the world, I should think, him doin' Joe's legal work. 'Stead of him going out, hirin' somebody else, payin' out money, you know? And plus: They already know each other. So that'd be another advantage—better'n tellin' someone else all his business."

"Oh yeah," Ernie said, "there'd be that, I guess. That could be, I suppose. That they could be doin' that there."

Gayle had asked what Ernie had done "to get him locked up in the first place. Is he some kind of career criminal, like this killer you're after? Or was this just an unlucky break? A temptation too strong to avoid, so he snapped and he did it, got caught?"

"Oh no," Dell'Appa had said. "He's not in for anything he *did*. He's been *charged* with doing something that they haven't gotten around to trying him for yet, but what he's in for right now's for *not* doing something. A federal judge told him to do something, and our Ernie wouldn't do it. He was quite impolite to her honor. He told her to go fuck herself. Or might as well've, at least."

"Gracious," she had said, "what brought that on?"

"He didn't think they were treating him respectfully," he had said. "What they'd done to him was catch him cashing winning pari-mutuel tickets, big bets good for large amounts, five hundred on a longshot that then leads from wire to wire, or two-buck bets on the exotic wagers—Pik-Six, all that stuff. Good for even larger. You cash one of those things, and you've got a year to do it after the winner comes in, you have to show identification and sign all kinds of tax forms before you get your money. And you don't get all of it, either. They withhold income taxes for you, a convenience it's not likely most appreciate."

"Phony ID?" she had said.

"Oh no," he had said, "it was Ernie's ID. His Social Security, too. And the taxes they took out went on his return. All of that was in complete good order. That wasn't the problem at all. The problem was that the tickets weren't his. So the winnings weren't either, you see."

"Oh, he'd stolen the tickets then," she said.

"Nope," he had said, "no, he hadn't. Hadn't counterfeited them, either, which's also been done by bad boys. He didn't get them from their owners, didn't even know who they were, lots of times, and the owners usually didn't know specifically that he was the guy who was cashing them, but that was perfectly all right with them. They'd turned them over to a gentleman name of Chico, Chico Pell. Chico's sort of a, well, I guess you could say he's a factor. Chico handles investment accounts; paying and receiving. Most of his accounts are receivables. Some, but not many, 're payables. Most of the time he collects. Everyone trusts Chico, all the sportin' bloods. They invest in their expectations of the outcomes of athletic contests among humans and also contests of speed and ability of beasts, such as horses and dogs.

"Chico is a bookie, mostly, but he's also an obliging, full-service kind of fella who keeps fungible people like Ernie around on his dance-card to perform other small services for his clients. They appreciate the extra attention, and they show that by paying Chico to provide it.

"One of those services is ten-percenting: in exchange for ten percent of the actual net-, not face-, value of a major winning ticket, Chico will have one of his flying squad of Ernies pretend to be the rightful owner of the ticket and collect the lovely boodle. Ernie's an obliging lad and a hardworking one, within reason, but because very few of his financially rewarding occupations can be found on the books of any corporation or other business entity with a taxpayer-ID number, and none of his usual employers—very much including Chico—makes it a practice to withhold income taxes, Social Security, health insurance, or anything else from his wages, Ernie's annual gross income reported to the IRS and the State Revenue Department consists solely and entirely of what's withheld from his gambling winnings and reported by the tracks. All the rest of his cash is off the books.

"Ernie's Ten-forty-EZ tax return—I assume it's the short form he files—says he's a gamblin' man. *Gambler's* his stated occupation, what he says he does for a living. It's fairly hard, of course, for anyone to make a real good living off of gambling unless he not only works very hard at it but becomes very good at it, and also's as lucky as hell. Certain kinds of gambling, I guess, lend themselves better'n most others do to being someone's principal means of support, because if they didn't the casino operators wouldn't worry so much about blackballing card-counters from the blackjack tables. And high-stakes poker and bridge, I guess; skillful players with steel nerves can do pretty well. But pari-mutuel betting? For most people, a real sometime thing. They lose a lot more than they win.

"Now," he said, "the law says you can deduct what you lose from what you win, but only to the extent of your winnings. So if you lose ten thousand bucks during the year but win five grand in bets taxed at the track, you can deduct only half of your losses. Which means that if you earned the other five grand you lost, by digging ditches or something, well, tough shit; even though it's gone, you blew it at the track, you still owe the income tax on it."

"Doesn't seem quite fair, somehow," she had said.

"It's a tax law, Gayle," he had said. "If it were fair it'd be a contradiction in terms. And to the Ernies of this world? Unfair, yeah, but they can live with it. They don't play fair themselves. They're used to the cracks and the crevices, you know? That's where they spend their whole lives.

"What the Ernies do for the Chicos is bamboozle Uncle Sam into taxing the fat tickets at the low rates that apply to the Ernies' tax brackets. They're not going to come in below the poverty line, practically dare the lawmen to say: 'What's this, then? No net income at all?' And then run a net-worth on them, come after them for tax-evasion? That's how they hooked Al Capone, for Christ sake, back when the earth was still flat. Uh-uh, nothing showy and stupid like that. But you can be damned sure they're not going to top out, either, thirty-one-percent marginal bracket. Their adjusted taxable incomes, after deducting their losses, 're going to come out, oh, between twenty-three and twenty-seven thousand dollars, if a person could live their lifestyle on that, as they make damned sure some straightshooter they know actually could, 'cause he does.

"And that's really all that they need. The federal hit they're gonna take, depending on whether they're single or married, it's going to be somewhere between thirty-six-hundred, forty-eight-hundred bucks a year, all of which of course they more'n likely will've paid when they cashed the bets at the tracks. Which means the Big Uncle in Washington there will've collected somewhere between sixteen- and eighteen-percent in taxes on those bets, that otherwise would've gotten whacked almost double that, if the rich guy who really placed them'd collected them himself.

"It's a really sweet deal all around. Ernie looks like he paid that seventeen percent. But it really didn't come out of him; it got creamed off the top of the fat-ticket payoffs, and those payoffs weren't his. Far as Ernie's concerned, the only effects on him of cashing, say, fifty-thousand in tickets were first he could deduct twenty-five thousand of his own gambling losses, and then second pay no taxes himself on his fees for cashing the tickets. Which'll usually run anywhere from two to five of Chico's ten percentage points and are always under the table."

She had looked uncertain. "Pete Rose, Cincinnati," he said. "Remember that case, Charlie Hustle, Reds local hero goes down? Sure you do. Guy had a street named after him, the boulevard goes to the ballpark. So then he got himself sent to the can and barred from baseball for life, the can for breaking the law and the game for breaking the rules. What started him down the long slippery slope wasn't betting on baseball; it was when he had some buddies cash a couple Pik-Six tickets at a racetrack to cut the taxes down, and he got caught at it."

"Ahh," she had said.

"Well," he said, "that's the kind of goodies Chico's fat-cat customers get from buying that service from him. Guy with a winning ticket for, say ten-thousand dollars, it costs him ten percent of what Ernie nets, say nine-hundred bucks, so his own net is eighty-one hundred. If he'd cashed the ticket himself, in his thirty-one-percent bracket, doing everything upright and kosher, his net would've dressed out at sixty-nine hundred. By going off the books with Chico, paying Ernie to take his place on them, he's pulled half of the teeth out of the jaws of the tax-bite.

"Now what the feds'd had in mind when they went after Ernie was not to take a piece off of him; he's small-time stuff. No, what the feds had was a strong desire to put *Chico* away for a long rest. They thought Ernie might be helpful to them in this enterprise by providing sworn testimony about certain illegal gambling transactions that he'd carried out on orders from Chico. They invited him to come in and have a nice chat with the grand jury present, first taking the precaution of assuring his attention by obtaining an indictment charging him, not Chico, with using interstate telecommunications facilities to violate a State law, to wit: setting up and promoting a lottery. Ernie was registering a few purely local bets himself, sort of on the side, but that's a federal offense if you use a phone to do it. But he hasn't been tried for it yet.

"Well, Ernie was shy. He said he understood they most likely've got him pretty good on this pisspot charge that'll get him thirty days, max, as a first-offender, probably not even that, but if that's how they wanna spend their time and the taxpayers' money, bringing guys in and convicting them on diddly-shit like that, well, he'd take it like the good sport he's always tried to be. But as far as telling anybody any stories about this guy Chico they kept asking him about, that he didn't recall knowing and really wasn't even sure he'd ever heard of, he said in the first place he'd never been much of a storyteller anyway, and in the second place, even if he had been a well-known raconteur, he didn't know any stories about any guy named Chico. So, if it was all the same to them, the feds, he thought he'd just as soon not do it and would like to be excused.

"The feds said apologetically that in fact it *wasn't* all the same to them, that their feelings would be hurt if he took that attitude, and that he would not be excused. That while they'd *so* hoped it wouldn't be necessary for them to insist, resort to stronger measures, and not just begging and pleading, either, if he didn't change his mind and voluntarily avail himself of their kind hospitality pretty damned quick, they'd jolly-right-well feel compelled to. And then in short order, he'd feel some compulsion himself.

"Well, he didn't, avail, and they did, feel compelled, compelled to have him compelled. They went into court and got a grant of immunity for him, guaranteeing that nothing that he said in the grand-jury room could be used in evidence against *him*, unless he took to perjuring himself, and then they hauled him in there and started asking him for all sorts of stuff about Chico that would've been more than just terribly embarrassing for Mister Pell to've had come *out;* it would've put Mister Pell *in*. Which would probably annoy him very much.

"Ernie reminded them that in the first place he wasn't sure he'd even ever heard of this Mister Pell who seemed to fascinate them so, but that even if he was sure, if he recalled knowing this guy, some stories about him and some things he might've done, he still wouldn't like to talk about them—because if he discussed Mister Pell he might inadvertently waive his *own* constitutional right not to incriminate *himself,* which was very precious to him. And the feds said: 'No yah won't, ya shit, you've been immunized, so ya *can't.* Now *talk,*' and he became terribly distraught and burst into tears, or something, so they took him down before the judge and she patiently admonished him that if he persisted in what she viewed as real impudence, she was going to take it as meaning that he didn't take her wishes seriously, behavior she would be inclined to deem contemptuous. She therefore ordered him to return to the nice ladies and gentlemen of the grand jury and have a pleasant conversation with them, answer all their questions, and sent him back to do that.

"Well, he went, there being a sizable U.S. Marshal on each side of him with a good grip on one of his elbows, but he took the Fifth Amendment again and once more didn't converse, so they drug him back out and in before the judge again and this time she was *pissed.* 'Okay for you, Ernie, you little turd,' she said, or words to that effect, 'I'm gonna hold you in civil contempt now, and you're goin' off to the hoosegow, my friend, until you decide to start talking or this here grand jury expires.' And that's where he's been ever since."

"He's afraid of this Chico," she had said, "pain and pleasure, is it? Chico'll hurt him if he talks, and reward him if he doesn't. Have someone like this Mossi character shoot him, or beat him up or something."

"Well," he said, "that's what it'd look like to the average person, and the result's the same as if that was the explanation—he won't talk about Chico—but that's probably not exactly it. These guys, Chico could get him hurt if he got Chico in the shit, but most likely if he did Chico'd be so busy trying not to get the guy *he* works for in the shit that if anybody did something to Ernie, it'd be to frighten Chico. Bolster his resolve if it developed a sag. No, the real reason that Ernie's so quiet's most likely that the feds didn't give him a big enough problem. Theoretically they can keep calling him back every time one grand jury expires and a new one's impaneled, getting him cited again when he won't talk. But as a practical matter, they won't. They'll lose interest in tormenting him, light on someone else to pester, and in time he'll get out. And he knows this.

"When and if they do try him on the racketeering charge, which they have to do within six months of when they got the indictment or he can get it dismissed for lack of speedy trial, and he duly gets convicted, the judge isn't going to send him back to jail for another month or so—he'll get time served, or a suspended, and they'll have to let him out. He knows that, too.

"Ernie's in the can because someone either lost his temper and got such a hard-on for Chico that his judgment was impaired, or else got so distracted by some other case or overwork he just didn't use any judgment at all, never thought the thing through. A good fierce lawyer'd see this, hit the USA with a barrage of motions, get Ernie habed up into court and begin to eat the rug that his client's in the can either by reason of prosecutorial mistake or by abuse of prosecutorial discretion—misconduct, really. Using the contempt process to hit the guy with a heavier punishment than the one for the crime he's charged with. Either way, Ernie in the can's no cosier, and what the government's doing to him doesn't look any prettier; so, a lawyer who could get the court see it either way'd get Ernie either tried and then released, or just plain released."

"So he's basically wasting his time, then," she said.

"Basically," he said. "He'll make a few brownie points with da bigga-boys dere, but the principal result of what he's doing's to get him six months for not talking in lieu of two months, max, for bookin'. He's doing four months more'n he needs to."

"So he's being a fool," she said. "He's making a fool out of himself. Has he thought about it this way? Does he also know that?"

He did not say anything for a moment. "Probably not," he said, "I would say: most likely he hasn't seen it that way yet. I've never fine-tuned this particular bozo, but extended sequential reasoning, beyond the first convolution? Isn't generally one of the breed's major skills. And subtlety almost never is."

"Well then," she said, "if you want him to tell you something that at first he's going to resist telling you, you might be able to discombobulate him a little by helping him to see what's actually going on. That he's making a fool out of himself, at considerable discomfort, without real hope of gaining anything from it. Get him mad at the people he works for—who, after all, got him into this fix and don't seem to've helped him much to get out of it so far, get him this lawyer he really needs. Who knows? If he won't talk to become a good citizen, well, maybe he will for revenge."

"You know," he said, "I think I will do just that."

"You, uh, you like it in here then, do you, pal?" Dell'Appa said. "Food isn't bad, and so forth, you got a nice room with a view, a comfortable bed, entertainment's okay? They put in the new wine-cellar yet? Or still makin' do with the old one?"

Ernie regarded him the way a large and ordinarily-confident cat registers the presence of an indolent bull-mastiff resting nearby just out of paw-slugging reach. He shrugged and said: "It's all right."

"You like it here, then," Dell'Appa said. "Nothin' special, but basically okay."

Ernie raised an eyebrow. "Yeah, basically okay," he said.

"So you're in no hurry, get out then," Dell'Appa said. "Don't miss gettin' laid and all that shit? Goin' out with the guys for a few?"

Ernie sighed. He shifted in the chair. He shook his head once. "You jerkin' my chain for?" he said.

"I'm not jerkin' your chain," Dell'Appa said. "Hey, for all I know you're gettin' laid more inside here'n you're used to gettin' laid, you're onna street. How should I know what flavor you like? Could be why, you don't wanna leave."

"You're jerkin' my chain," Ernie said. He exhaled heavily. He steepled his fingers and stared at them, frowning. "I dunno why I get all this shit," he said. He looked up. "I really don't. Been here fifty-three days now, nothin' to do, can't go out and do nothin', and also got no end in sight. What am I, for Christ sake, Hitler or somethin', you're bustin' my stones alla time? I'm really worth all you guys' time here, am I, fuckin' with my life like this? Christ, I didn't *kill* no one, did I? Least nobody that I can remember."

"Yeah-yeah, go ahead," Dell'Appa said. "Play the violin for me."

"Bullshit, the violin, violin," Ernie said. "Stick the violin right up your ass. You guys're makin' me *toast*, without provin' I did anything, even. The federal guys, they come down once a week, and I get brought up in this room. And who do they think they're foolin', they tell me they're doin' a favor, have me brought up here so nobody sees me, the guys onna tier, none of them know what I'm doin'? That I'm seein' the feds once a week? What is this, a *joke,* somethin', huh? I tell those guys *nothin'*, nothin's what I'm tellin' them, an' everyone in here, everyone else, all the other guys know it. Because if I was, I was tellin' them somethin', I wouldn't be still in here now, would I? No, I'd be back out onna street. Because what did they put me in for? *Not* talkin's what they did me for.

"I know all you guys think we're bad guys. Okay, so go ahead, think that. But Christ, that don't mean that we're stupid, we can't figure a fuckin' thing out." He wheezed an imitation laugh. "I say to them, I told them this. I said: 'Hey, we're not dummies, for Christ sake. You got us inside, yeah, we know you did that, but we didn't leave our brains in the safe-lock, we came in.'

"And then, what do they do to me then? They say: 'Hey, that's okay, we know that. Everything's still cool with us. Wanna smoke or a Coke?' And they think I dunno what they're doin'? Shee-it. Keep me up here an hour, I'm not sayin nothin', I know what they want guys onna tier to think there: I'm spillin' my guts out up here. Well, I got bad news for them then: the guys don't. 'At's the oldest trick inna whole fuckin' *book,* an' everyone knows all about it."

He forced a laugh. "And now you come in here, now you show up. The Staties're seein' me too. You guys keep this up awhile longer here, CIA'll be comin' in too. I'll have to start holdin' regular hours, appointments an' stuff for you assholes, I get any more popular here. 'Now lessee, on Mondays the Feebia's here, and Wednesday is State-Police day. So how about Friday, that good for you? I think I can fit you in then. You like mornin' or afternoons better?' "

"Look," Dell'Appa said, "the routine's pretty good but you're the one who's wastin' my time. It isn't me wastin' yours. I realize that you've got plenty to waste here, but I'm here to do business, all right? So let's see we can do some of that."

"What: business?" Ernie said. "What the hell can you do for me? I'm here on the federal contract. They're payin' my room and board thing. They stashed me here 'cause it's closer'n Danbury, any place else that they got, so it's easier to come down here every fuckin' week and bust my balls for me. Feds the only guys, can come in'n let me out. You, you're a State asshole, can't do nothin' for me. And that's what I just told you, all right? I'm not stupid, okay? I know some things too. And this thing's between me and them. It isn't between me and you."

"We've been known to make a deal now and then, you know, pal," Dell'Appa said. "Least you would if you're not really stupid. We talk to the feds—they talk back."

"Oh, right, willya give me a break, man?" Ernie said. "Just gimme one fuckin' break. The only times you guys talk to each other's when one of you wants to fuck someone over but can't find a way to do it—there's no crime you can charge the guy with. And that's when you call up the feds, or when the feds call you up, and say: 'Hey, we wanna fuck this poor bastard over, but we can't find no way to do it. We really don't like this poor son-of-a-bitch—see if you can de-ball him, all right?' And you do. Those're the times when you talk."

"Jesus," Dell'Appa said, "this's like trying to talk to a stump, for Christ sake. Who the hell do you think you are? Some kind of celebrity gangster, your life's on TV Sunday nights? Get offa the hopper, my friend. No one gives a shit about you. You know who up in Boston knows how long you've been in here—fifty-three days did you say? Nobody. You're the only one who's been counting. As far as the rest of the world's concerned, you don't even exist anymore. They've forgotten about you up there.

"You know what happened to you, little man? You pissed somebody off, back two months ago, made some busy fed take notice of you. That was one dumb mistake. Whoever it was noticed you for a day and said: 'Hey, who is this little shit? What's with the attitude here? He needs a good kick in the balls.' "

"Bullshit," Ernie said, but his gaze wavered. "They wanted Chico and they thought, they thought I'd give him to them. Well, maybe they will get him, but they won't get him from me, and that's what they know now and that's why I'm in here now."

Dell'Appa laughed. "Is that so?" he said. "Is that really fuckin' so. You know what you've got, Ernie? You've got the faith of fuckin' martyrs. Only yours's not in Jesus; yours is in your government. You really think that what they tell you is what's really goin' on? And that if it happens to be what is goin' on today, it'll still be what they're doin' eight weeks from today? Boy, the politicians must love you. You're just what they always hoped for: the guy who not only hears what they say when they're running for the office and actually believes it, but goes right on believin', after they're elected, that is what they're gonna do. Infuckincredible. It's a good thing for you, my friend, you weren't born with a pussy, I think—you'd still believe that all the boys'll still respect you in the morning. You're such a perfect asshole you oughta pose bare-ass for the new proctologists."

"Ah, fuck you," Ernie said, moistening his lips and making small quick movements with his hands back and forth on the table. "Just fuck you and shut up."

Dell'Appa chuckled a few times. "You know what you were, you jerk?" he said. "No, you're weren't always wrong. When they got you indicted and hauled your ass in, yeah, they were after Chico. They did have a hard-on for Chico, just like they still've got one, and sooner or later either they'll get him or else we will, and Chico'll go to the can. Well, fifty-three days ago, or whenever it was that they bagged you, one of those feds who's been after Chico'd had the idea you could and would sink him. As you certainly could, but as you've refused to do. This kind of disappointed the G-man, because if you'd've been nice enough to come coco with him, he could've closed Chico's file that he's bored with now because he's been on it so long, and start chasing somebody else. But his attitude now, since you've managed to convince him you're not going to help him out after all, has got to be: 'Hey, what the hell? You win some, you lose some. It was still worth a try. And the guy is a stat, another sure *guilty*, to go in the yearly report.' He's working on some new approach, now; he has been for over a month."

"You prolly don't even know what the fucker's name is," Ernie said, frowning and using the fingers of his right hand to rub the tips of the fingers on his left. "The fucker who put me in here—you don't even know who he is."

"That's right, I don't," Dell'Appa said. "And I don't need to know, either, need to know who he is. Because I know *what* he is, and once you know that you don't need to know which one—they all think and act just the same. They're just like us, Ernie—we're all alike too. Everyone has to study the book, and then everyone goes by the book. Just like you guys're all alike too; you just go by your own different book.

"Your problem is that in our books there's nothing about being friends with people who go by what's in your book. So that's why you don't find us generally friendly, 'less you're being real nice to us. Your teachers in Sunday School may've told you baptism put you on a first-name basis with Jesus. For all I know, maybe it did, and you are. But not where the feds're concerned, you aren't; He's got no reciprocity with them. If you're not helping them, as you aren't, then they aren't gonna know you from the next load of goats. They don't even know you as *Nugent*. You'd be lucky to rate a 'hey, you.' You ought to be grateful they still come to see you—judge must've ordered them to."

Ernie snuffled. He rubbed his nose with the first knuckles of his right hand. "You don't know, though," he said. "You're just fuckin' sayin' that."

"No," Dell'Appa said, "no I'm not. You've got that part wrong. You're the one 'just fuckin' sayin',' the one who doesn't know shit. Unless you're lying to me, of course, as I think you are, so you do know that I know, that I'm *not* just fuckin' sayin' any fuckin' thing at all."

He smiled. Ernie's gaze wavered. "Sure you do," Dell'Appa said. "What I'm telling you's the truth, and you know it is. It hadn't crossed your mind until you heard me say it to you, which was of course part of the reason that you didn't want to hear it. Made you feel pretty silly, right? This great pose that you've been striking, standing up and going through, real go-through guy for Chico, how impressed the feds must be? Pretty devastating, must be, realizing after all this time that here you've been putting on this big fifty-three-day act for a bunch of total strangers, and the no-good heartless bastards haven't even watched you, up there on the stage, since the end of the first week or so. Now you know where you lost your thumb; it was up your own ass all the time."

Ernie did not say anything for quite a while. He licked his lips and looked away from Dell'Appa's face, glancing back at it every ten or twenty seconds, until he saw Dell'Appa pronate his left wrist and use his right thumb and forefinger to activate the stopwatch function of the Seiko. Then he fixed his gaze on the watch. Forty-three more seconds went by before he cleared his throat. Dell'Appa pushed the button to reset the stopwatch at zero. "I can't talk about Chico," Ernie said. "I can't talk about him and I won't."

"Chico doesn't interest me," Dell'Appa said. "If Chico gets asked to the junior prom by anyone this year, it won't be me who sends his corsage; that'll come from the Effa-Bee-Eye. We won't ask him to dance unless and until the Bureau says they've broken up, and everything's over between them."

"Because Chico did stuff for my father," Ernie said. "He was real good to my father. And also real good to me."

"Doesn't interest me in the slightest," Dell'Appa said. "Joe Mossi's the guy interests me, in the final analysis, all the way down the line. The meantime, of course, also who he hangs with, and what he does with them. Also: why. Everett Rollins, for instance. Ev Rollins."

Ernie licked his lips again. "I'm, ah," he said, "I'm missin' lunch while I'm up here, you know." He jerked his head at the Seiko. "They got separate feeding times for us here, you know? We don't eat with the other guys here; population eats after we do. I don't go with the other guys in isolation, I don't get to eat 'til the next meal. I get pretty hungry, that happens."

"Which no doubt spoils your memory," Dell'Appa said. "Yeah, well: not to worry. I'm on good terms with Stan Graham down here, known Captain Graham for years. I've been in this hotel many times. So I mentioned to him, I reminded him when I called yesterday, that I hoped if we did hit it off, you and I, it wouldn't cause you to skip meals. He assured me it wouldn't, just as it hasn't in the past when I've interviewed inmates here before. They'll have a meal waiting for you."

" 'Cause I really *am* gettin' hungry," Ernie said morosely. " 'Sides, I would rather, I like to eat with the guys. No fun, eatin' alone."

"*Aww,*" Dell'Appa said, "and you see so little of all your playmates, locked up with each other all day and all night. Gimme a break, willya? You guys'd win an Olympic gold medal, if team-synchronized jerkin'-off ever became a recognized sport. This here, what you're doin'? It's much more important 'n tradin' your cookies, his cake. This's your future we're talkin' about. Precious days outta your life. Tell me a tale of Joe Mossi. Tell me what you know about him."

"I still don't know what you could do for me," Ernie said. "You didn't tell me that yet."

"Fuckin' A-Y," Dell'Appa said. "Fuckin'-A, I didn't do that. That isn't how we make deals. I do that and then I walk outta here after,

after you give me nothin', and you call the ACLU. 'He said he'd get me out and then get me a pension, and make sure all my teeth'd get fixed. And a date with Madonna, besides. Sue him and sue him again. Make the judge make him get me out.' Right. Up yours, pal. You tell me what you've got that you can give to me. I'll think about it overnight and then I'll get back to you, what I can trade you for it. You don't like it? Fine by me. Rot your ass off in here. But that's the way the deals go down. Ain't no other way."

13

"What I did was the night shift down at Reno's onna Lynnway," Ernie said. "I was the night-man down Reno's, I went in there, 'cause that's what everyone was—first went in, after he trained. 'Cause no one wanted it, see, eight until four inna mornin', on account of it fucked up their love-life something awful for them. So every time somebody leaves, one of the older guys finds somethin' better, gets called back on a job he got laid off of, maybe their wife gets a job so they don't need to work two themselves no more, well, that meant guys that're still there and'd been Reno's longer, all of those guys'd move up. If they didn't like their particular shift, see? The night-guy'd draw the early-shift then, come in four an' then he'd leave at noon, and whoever got hired to take the old guy's place'd be the new night-guy again. It'd always been happenin' that way.

"Until I come along. With me it was different. I was a new kind of night-guy for them, different 'cause I kind of liked it. It didn't fuck up my love-life for me for the plain and simple reason because I didn't *have* no love-life, okay? I am like sixteen years old. Not actually old enough, be pushin' a hack, didn't have no hack-license or nothin', so when someone comes in, from the city or somethin', sees me sittin' around when I'm there—which is, after all, it's eight hours a day and five days a week, so you know it's got to happen there sometimes, I'd be in there when someone comes in—Reno tells them I answer the phone. He don't tell them I'm drivin' a cab. And when I'm still workin', on my shift, all right? But I'm just between fares, or somethin', I don't wait out in front inna seatah the cab, like all the rest of the guys, read the paper or somethin' like that. I come back to the office, shut it down and go in. I read the paper in there. Before two A.M, I mean, I do that. After that you're still gettin' the fares from the after-hours joints, sendin' guys home in them that aren't too drunk to drive—they're too drunk to even stand up. But who's gonna turn Reno in for havin' me do that? Havin' me drivin' to pick up the stiffs, huh? I'll tell you who'll do that: nobody, uh-uh, nobody's gonna do that. Nobody wants these drunken guys, drivin' themselves home, killin' all kinds of people, so nobody wants no one to know, and nobody turns Reno in. For havin' me do that there. And that's what I know about that there.

"But so anyway, if that's what I'm doin', doin' that alla the time, how'm I sposed to have any love-life? I'm not in school anymore since my old man goes inna can, my mother and I got no money except what Chico sends over, maybe half what my father was makin', so all right, okay? Nobody hadda tell me or anythin'. Nobody hadda come and say to me, you know, tell me I didn't have no choice there: I hadda go to work—I could figure that out by myself. But, you wanna tell me how I'm supposed to get a love-life, I'm not meetin' no girls, with no girls and no money to spend? There's a way, well, all I can say is I wished someone would've told me back then, when that was what I was doin'. Because I couldn't think of no way. So for me, though, because of that, I'm actually givin' up nothin', I'm not gettin' laid anyway, bein' the night-guy's not really that bad. Wouldn't've been that way for anybody, but for me, it was pretty good.

"You get better tippers at night, that was one thing. You don't get so many old ladies. Not so many old-lady pickups, the plaza, the market, the drugstore and all that shit, the kind that the day-drivers get. Not too many widows on Social Security're gonna tip you real good. The old men don't tip you good either, most of them anyway, at least. They still think a quarter is serious money, like it used to be, they were kids, tank-ah gas cost them two bucks or so then. You believe that? I wasn't sure if I did. You know. That's pretty hard to believe. But I had a fare, told me that once. When he was still growin' up, that's what he said, he said it was twenny-five cents. For a gallon of gasoline, right?" Ernie dropped his voice an octave: " 'And that was for high-test, young man,' he says to me, meanin' I guess, he meant *premium* by that. He swore he was tellin' the truth. 'I can tell you, young man, a buck was a buck then. A quarter meant somethin' in those days.' Well, maybe he was, tellin' the truth, but that still didn't change nothin' for me: Guy can't make no money on quarters if that's what he's gettin'—maybe could once, but he sure can't now.

"But anyway, no, that's not what I'm sayin', at night's when the spenders come out. And also, the whores make their out-calls—none of them use their own car, naturally, because who wants their ex-husband, payin' alimony to them 'cause they haven't got a job, or maybe they aren't even really divorced yet, they're still in a custody fight, somethin', maybe? Well, how is *that* gonna look then, he sees their car, their car's at the motels every night, like they're workin' in housekeepin' there? He isn't gonna believe that, you know, that they got this new job makin' beds. Not after what she told him at least, what the thing is she likes to do best, what she called it her *specialty*, when they was married, when she was doing it, him."

"Or their boyfriend, puh-*haps?* Maybe someone else, a cousin they're maybe related-to? Their sister-in-law who never did like them? Their ex-mother-in-law? Oh, she would just *love* seein' that, that mean old bitch, catch them out puttin' out down the beach. She'd go straight home and take out a big ad in the paper, whole fuckin' full-page announcement: 'My ex-daughter-in-law's a no-good fuckin' *slut*, she's a *tramp*, like I said all along, peddlin' her ass for cash every night the Imperial Inn. She accepts major credit cards, too.' Or even one of their regular customers, maybe; he wants to pretend she only does it with him—he knows she's out sellin' her hole every single night, just makin' believe she's only his girl. Fucks him every Thursday because she loves him so much, the money that he gives her's just to buy her her own candy and flowers, those garter belts he likes on her so much—not to pay her car insurance, get new soles put on her shoes and keep the telephone turned on. So, the whores don't, they don't drive to their tricks; hired pussy takes cabs to the job—and the johns pay for their cab-ride home, too. Which they also book before they leave the car, so that way they'll have an excuse to get out if the john wants more than he paid them for, or he decides to turn mean: 'Oh, sweetie, I can't let you do that to me tonight—that's my ride honking outside right now. Bye-bye now—don't forget your sweet Tootsie.'

"Not that the whores are that good-ah tippers, unless they got to know you real good, they got so they trusted you and like that. But then quite a lot of them want to tip you in trade, and it's pretty hard payin' the landlord with blow-jobs—unless he's the one gettin' blown. Which're the principal thing that whores do, by the way, what they always told me was the thing that they got the most call for. I had this enormous black whore that I got so I knew pretty well, drove her around lots of nights, and she was just about the ugliest-lookin', fat-lookin' fat skag that you ever seen in your life. A hell of a nice broad, she was really nice, get you laughin' like you'd never stop. It's a wonder I didn't put the cab inna drink onna Lynnway some night, she got me laughin' so hard. She thought all of her customers were just perfect assholes, the things they all asked her to do, 'but if they've got the money, I'll do them.' But she was still, she was really very ugly. She must've weighed six hundred pounds. The first night I picked her up and I was going out to get her, Reno happened to be in there and he told me: 'That's fat Rita. Make her sit in the middle the back seat.' See Reno didn't always take what you'd call the best care of his cars, didn't always have new shocks put in quite as soon as he should-ah, so as a result they didn't ride right if you got an unbalanced load. 'You let her sit to one side of the cab, the front wheel on the opposite side'll lift half of the road and the headlight on that side'll look like a small airport beacon, pointin' right up at the sky.'

"So I liked Rita, like I say, but I could not imagine how she ever got a customer. Who could get it hard, lookin' at her? So I asked her one night and she told me: 'Blow jobs,' she said, 'I could suck a basketball through a hundred feet of top-grade fire-hose, and if somebody pays me, I'll do it. I suck cock. That's my motto. That's the motto of all of us girls. Cock-sucking's our stock-in-trade. "Cocks will be sucked here for money." Don't pay any attention to any the girls that tell you they are different, that they got their Mercedes and they got the mink coat doin' somethin' different to men, because they're better, because that's a fuckin' lie, kid, just a fuckin' lie that they maybe wish was true, but it never, never is. I don't care if they look like Marlene Dietrich when she was only fifteen. What we make our dough offa's suckin' dick. You show me a good-lookin' kid that don't mind what she puts in her mouth, I'll show you a good-lookin' kid who can get you the deed to Japan in three years, she plays her cards right in this world. If middle-class white broads, and rich ones, if they ever start doin' that, takin' their men's cocks into their mouth, us workin'-class girls of this world'll be out of business. We won't have nothin' to do.' So, I maybe couldn't pay for nothing with those blow-jobs I got in tips, but they were good at it, knew what they were doin', and a blow-job a night's not that bad a tip, either, for a horny kid with no love-life at all.

"And, bein' the night-guy, what I could do, I would go right home from work, hit the sack. Because how many people're there to hang out with, you get off work at four inna mornin'? You see what I mean about that. And my mother's sacked out, collecting her Zs, which is also a good thing for me, because like my old man was always sayin': my ma never nags when she's sleepin'. So she's not on my ass alla time, drivin' me nuts like she did him so bad I think in a way he might've kinda looked forward—a little bit, you know?—to going to jail like he did. Cut her nagging to one day a week. And then when I wake up, eleven or so, my mother's gone off to work there, I got the whole place to myself. I get showered, get dressed, I have somethin' to eat, and then I go over the track. I go over Suffolk, all right? The weekdays. And onna weekends, when I am off—which's also why I like bein' the night-guy; night-guy gets all his weekends off; Reno's got another guy, just works the weekends for him—I also go over to Wonderland there, so: horses days, then the puppies at night. I like

214

goin' the track even then. I guess you could probably tell that, huh? I always liked bein' the track, people, excitement and stuff.

"Well, that's how I met Short Joe Mossi. I'm over the track there, forget which one it was, one or the other, and it's just the usual thing. I'm hooked up with someone, you know, like you do, I run into some guy that I knew, and he knows a guy and we're talkin'. An' that's all we were doin'—nothin' particular goin' on. And Joey comes up and he knows one of them, and so that's how I meet him. He's just 'Joey' to me, that's all he was—I didn't know him before. I never heard of the guy.

"The four of us shoot the shit for a while, this'n that, you know the routine, had a beer or had somethin' to eat, but nothing too serious, you know? Just a few guys over the track. And I see him again, from time to time there, Suffolk and Wonderland, too, and it's: 'Whaddaya hear?' 'Hey, how's it goin'?' The usual stuff like that there. And that's all I know about him.

"Now by now I am workin' for this other guy," Ernie said. "I'm still over at Reno's, I'm still night man there, but now I got this other job. Well, not really a real job, exactly. I just do things for him now and then."

"And this would be Chico, of course," Dell'Appa said. "Odd-jobs for him at the track."

Ernie sighed. "Look," he said, "you know what I told you, all right? You know what I already said. I told you my father goes inna can, draws a Concord Twenty, all right? He thinks he'll get out in a couple of years. That's what everyone does, ten percent, am I right? If they draw MCI Concord. So naturally that's what everyone thinks, and so he thinks that, too, that that's what's gonna happen to him. Except he doesn't get out in two years like he thinks—gets the heart attack first, so he dies. And everyone's sorry, naturally, because most of them liked him, all right? And nobody even expected it, either. He was just barely forty years old, and looked like he was in pretty good shape. But he did drink and smoke a lot, that doesn't help, and I guess it could've been that.

"So, but that don't change nothin'. Once he's dead, well, now everything's different. He wasn't at home, of course, he's doin' time, so it wasn't like he wasn't there: All of a sudden, boom, he's not at home—he didn't come home anyway. No, but what it was, like, this still meant that there was a change. Back then, at least, still some of the guys would still do the right thing, if a guy that they knew went away. And, it wouldn't be much, maybe, but you still would know that if you ran with them and if you got hooked there, and then you stood up and went in, well, your family'd have food onna table, all right? So you knew they would still be all right on that kind of thing, there, as far as that was concerned. They would still have enough to eat. And the landlord would not throw them out, or like that, so they wouldn't be out onna street. Because he would know that if he did that, then someone would come to see him, someone he would not like seeing, if he did something like that to your family, just because you were in jail and they got behind on their rent. Even though when you got out, naturally, you would still owe the rent. And the guys that still did this—and not all of them did—but the ones that still did it took pride.

"But once the guy's out, once he's out of the joint, then that was the end of it, okay? They done all they're supposed to do. Jesus, I mean, you got to be reasonable—how much can you ask a guy, huh? How long can you ask them to do this? Guy doesn't get out, he dies inna can, what's his rabbi supposed to do then? It isn't their fault that he died. And he's not keepin' quiet for anyone now, so now what're they doin' this for? Give his family a pension for life? No, you can't ask for that. They're all really sorry the guy died inna can, 'course they are, because look what he did for them, with him not talkin', or otherwise they would've been going in too. Themselves, just like he did, they would've gone in with him, too. And so, they appreciate it, and the money is how they show that. But Jesus, the guy's dead now. Bein' sorry don't make him alive; there's nothin' they can do about that, and sooner or later, there's no way around it, that money has gotta end sometime. It just hasta come to an end.

"So," Ernie said, "that meant that I hadda find some more work to do, you know? Somethin' else I could do to get money—more money, I mean. Because my mother, she's still workin' too, but wait-ressin' don't pay that much and she never liked hostessin' there, keepin' track of the help, customers always pissin' and moanin', all of that shit and so forth. She said it gave her a headache. So, but it was takin' what she makes and almost all what I bring home, from bein' the night guy at Reno's, takin' almost all of what we both make just in what it's costin' us to live. And I'm eighteen years old now, you know what I mean? It's not like I mind gettin' my spine sucked out three or four times a week, any time that I want, actually, but I think there should be more to your life'n jump-inna-backseat, quickie blow-jobs between fares in Reno's second-oldest cab. Sure, I'm a still a young guy, that's easy to say, but I'm also, hardworkin' guy too. I also deserve to have a good time, have a few laughs for myself. Well, as you probably know, been a young guy yourself, you've been one too, you got to have money for that. You can't have a good time without money, if you deserve it or not."

"What the fuck's that supposed to mean?" Dell'Appa said.

"*What?*" Ernie said, whining.

"What you just said, about bein' a young guy," Dell'Appa said. "What the fuck was that for?"

"*Noth*-in', wasn't for anythin'," Ernie said. "I was just sayin', is all, you would know. You been a young guy yourself, weren't you there? Well that was all I was sayin'."

"Yeah," Dell'Appa said. "Yeah. Well, go ahead. Watch your ass though."

"Yeah," Ernie said. "Jesus, I didn't mean nothin' by it." He coughed and shook his head, clearing his throat. "I wished they wouldn't let the guys smoke in here. There's too many of us in one place. I never had this, onna street."

"Yup, there it is, I just knew it'd come up," Dell'Appa said, "only a matter of time here: 'cruel and unusual punishment.' I think you should bring a civil rights suit. Same judges that put all of you guys in here could change what they say judgment day: 'I'm sentencing you to the maximum term of two-and-a-half in the House, and also you gotta quit smokin'.' That'd shape some of the real bad bastards up in a jiffy, make them see the light in a flash. 'No, no,' they would say, 'don't say that to me. Don't tell me you're gonna do that, make me quit smoking for just killing people. I'll be good, I promise I will.' Or you could get yourself convicted on what the feds've got you for, which could make you eligible to get sent to a genuine federal prison, ree-formed and improved all at once. No smoking in federal stir, no sirree; feds don't want you missin' out on any of the interesting programs and activities they got planned for all of their guests, not doin' all of your rightful time, droppin' dead 'fore you've done the full hitch. Good robust, healthy prisoners, that's what they want, attractive, well-nourished inmates, suitable for all occasions both public and private. *Mens malo sed corpore sano.* Little Latin for you there, son, no extra charge whatsoever: 'His mind's pure unadulterated evil but his body's Sanforized and won't shrink from anything, foreign or domestic.'

"Feds only want very pure people in their penitentiaries these days, only the best class of prisoners. It's *much* harder gettin' into the federal calabozo'n it is makin' it into Harvard: if doin' federal time is your cherished ambition, well, you're gonna have to get a haircut and *behave* yourself, as well, and no fuckin' backtalk either, like your parents and your prep-school teachers may've taken from you because they won't stand for it. Practically got to file an application in writing, include three references, none of them members of your immediate family or addicted to any harmful substances, who've known you for at least ten years, have never seen you naked or expressed any strong desire to do so, and can testify persuasively with clear elocution to your good character, high moral standards, abstemious habits, and do it without mispronouncing any words. And then submit to an interview, neatly-dressed, jacket and tie for boys, girls with neatly-braided hair, no slacks, culottes or jeans, before they'll even consider you. They're very particular about who they let in these days, don't want the wrong type of person gainin' admission and then turnin' out to be a bad influence on their other residents. And then, if you *do* get in—it's provisional, of course; they think you *might* be a deserving person who will benefit their program; in the federal system, see, you do the probationary period first, and if you pass that, well, *then* you get to do the time—and you start look to them like you're might be thinkin' of maybe pullin' your Johnson bar there, they give you a rubber glove right off, a clean towel to wipe up the mess. And God help the guy who fucks you up the ass: they take him downstairs and heave him headfirst into a vat of boiling Lysol. Teach *him* some fuckin' manners. Shake their heads over his conduct. 'Don't this asshole know about AIDS?' "

"Yeah," Ernie said. He looked worried.

"Anyway, anyway," Dell'Appa said, "you prolly knew all of that anyway. Like you were tellin' me: Joey."

"Yeah," Ernie said, "tellin' you about Joey. Anyway, like I was sayin' there, it was right around then that Joey was lookin', someone who could help him out. Nothin' really permanent, anything like that —just a guy who could give him a hand for a while, 'til he got a few things straightened out."

"Have you got any real notion at all," Dell'Appa said, "of just when this might've been? Try to leave Tyson out of it this time, you can."

"Tyson wasn't around then," Ernie said. "I don't get it. This had nothin' to do with Mike Tyson. I never heard of him then."

"Glad to hear it," Dell'Appa said. "Mike Tyson seems to bother your brain. Mike Tyson confuses you. *Timor* Tyson *conturbat . . . vos?* Ah the hell with it: just try to leave him out all the time. Just stick to: when did all stuff this happen with Mossi, that's all—do the best you can with just that. When you did this work for Joe Mossi."

"Well, I can tell you 'about,' " Ernie said. "It was right around when . . . it was pretty soon after my father, like I told you, he'd just died doin' time up in Concord. And I was eighteen, like I said. So that would've made it ten years or so ago, right around ten years—or in there. And another way I know, another way I can tell, was that it was right around the time there, pretty soon in there, when they just'd found Chuckie's head. It was after that. Not *right after* that, but pretty soon, you know?" He fluttered the fingers of his left hand. "Right about in there, I'd say, three–four months or so. Guys were still talkin' about Chuckie's head then, when Joe asked me to do some stuff for him, so I would say it would have to've been well, about, less'n six months after that."

"This would've been Chuckie Damon's head, am I right?" Dell'Appa said. "The head in the box, the Hitachi TV box, in the car in the alley offa Stanhope Street, up behind PD Headquarters there?"

"Yeah, that's the one," Ernie said. "The head in the box in the red Oldsmobile, turned out to be Chuckie Damon's. Both of them belonged to Chuckie. First the car, and then after, the head. All the guys were really surprised. They all knew that Chuckie wasn't around, and like that, that wasn't what was surprising them there, that they didn't see him for a while—I guess it was six or eight months."

"More like six or eight weeks, if I've got it right," Dell'Appa said.

"Yeah?" Ernie said, looking thoughtful. "Yeah, well, I suppose, it could've been that, coulda been six or eight weeks. I thought it more'n that, though. Could've sworn it was more'n that. Because, you know, there was that about him. Chuckie was like that; he was *always* like that, and everyone all knew it, too: go away for a while, then come back. Tell all the guys he had somethin' come up, hadda go outta town for a while and take care of it. Took him longer'n he thought it would. If he would've known, how long it would take, well, then naturally he would've said somethin'. But the time he finds out, that he realized it, well, by then he was already gone, right? By then he was already gone. Because that's why he went inna first place: he hadda go and find out. So when he wasn't around and nobody seen him, well, what they all thought was that that's where he was, doin' somethin', doin' that all over again. So, when he didn't show up again then for a while, that was of course what alla guys thought: he had somethin' else that come up unexpected, hadda drop everything and go handle it."

"Any of the guys ever say what kind of thing it was that was always taking Chuckie by surprise like that, so he hadda leave town and go deal with it?" Dell'Appa said.

"Well, they *could*'ve," Ernie said. "I didn't pay too much attention, who Chuckie Damon even was back around then. See, I didn't know too many guys then, like I do now, most of them. I only knew some of them, see what I'm sayin'? And Chuckie didn't happen to be one. He wasn't one of those guys that I felt like I knew there, so: what he was doin' or where he went, any of that stuff like that? I honest-to-God didn't know. I didn't pay no attention, was basically what I did then, to anything he might've been doin'. I didn't know the guy, hardly, anything like that or something, I don't think I even met him. Might've seen him someplace or something like that, but I didn't really know Chuckie. Before they found his head and like that, I mean, because after that, of course, then *everyone* did, me included. We all knew who Chuckie was then. But so: Where he was, what he might've been doin'? Just didn't mean anythin' to me. He was just a name that I heard, and in those days you heard lots of names. There was lots of stuff goin' on, those days. Much more'n there's goin' on now. This guy here's doin' this; that guy there's doin' that; some other guys—who knows where they come from? Ba-da-bing, ba-da-boom, they got somethin' else goin', no one else even thought of it yet. Nowadays, Jesus Christ, the whole town's dead. Not a fuckin' thing goin' on now. Except with the coons, naturally—niggers always got stuff goin' on. They got more stuff'n we *ever* had, any of us ever had, goin' on, and it seems like there's more of them, too."

"Right," Dell'Appa said. "That's what all of us guys also think: The spearchuckers're the ones that're doin' all the stuff. Those bastards just don't ever sleep. They're more fun'n four otters in your bathtub in the mornin', when you've got a long day 'headah you, no matter how much they cost. We completely agree with you on that point: nothin' goes down anymore. Not with the white boys, at least. Only problems we got now're dark meat. Wasn't for them you disband the police force. But there is one thing that kind of puzzles us, you know? It's what it was that made all you wile-an'-crazy guys clean up your acts all at once. You all did it the very same time. What was the cue for you all to get born-again? How did the word of the rapture get passed, to every last one of you, without any of us gettin' wind of it? How did all of you know precisely the instant to rid yourselves of the soiled and tattered garments of this tearstained world and put on the shining raiments of Light?"

"Huh?" Ernie said.

"Sorry," Dell'Appa said, "lemme rephrase that: What is this shit that you're handin' me, huh? That nobody's got nothin' goin' on. That's a bunch of crap and you know it. And it's *unnecessary* crap, too, completely unnecessary. The decapitation of Chuckie may've caused a lot of consternation in better circles at the time, especially for the Boston cops who'd been coming up that alleyway and using the back doorway off it for ten days or two weeks so before it occurred to any one of those crack sleuths there to ask what the hell that red Olds was doing there, illegally-parked and all, right under their fuckin' red noses. And then to find out that the guy who owns it's a rather well-known figgah in your higher-rollin' circles who hasn't been seen around very much, and who's been rumored deceased, and *then*, as a *pièce de résistance*, crack it open and see what is in it—the oh-my-fuckin'-word, honest-to-God, missing-high-roller's, personal-favorite, very-own, singular, *head*. That he never went noplace without. Well, yes indeed, it sure did; that did raise a considerable ruckus. But since then much sand's gone over the dam and much water's pissed out of the hour-glass, and now we all know that the rest of Chuckie Damon almost certainly'd been served as the *plat du jour* dinner to the lobsters off of Castle Island, at least a week before his gift-wrapped head turned up at PD Boston. And, furthermore, we know why."

"Why?" Ernie said.

"No-no and uh-uh," Dell'Appa said, wagging his left forefinger. "That is another part of the forest, and not why we're meeting here today. We're not gathered here for me to tell *you* the mysterious 'whys' of things, Ernest, how zebras got stripes and all that shit; no, we're here so that *you* can tell *me*." He paused and shook his head. "I will tell you this, though, my friend: I would bet a modest sum that not a day or evening went by, when Chuckie once again didn't show up for his mail, when Short Joe Mossi missed a single edition of the morning papers, drove a mile without listening to all-news radio, or went to bed without watching the late news, and that as those days mounted up, all those quiet summer days, that noise most ignored in the background being only the nice lobsters munching, Chuckie still unsighted and unofficially still missing, MIA in more sophisticated knowledgeable circles, Short Joe must've been appalled at the shoddy law enforcement his tax-dollars were buying. Here he'd gone to all the trouble and inconvenience of leaving the gendarmes a door-prize right under their beer-blossomed noses, and they don't even know enough to unwrap their present and say 'thank you all out there, very much'? Goodness and gracious, what louts."

"I don't get it," Ernie said.

"No," Dell'Appa said, "well, no, most likely not. I do go on sometimes. Only that it's now common knowledge and's been for several years that Chuckie gave what head he gave—the only one that he had on him, good head or not good, regardless—not because he was real eager to make such a contribution, but because somebody—someone that he knew and trusted, by the name of Joey—shot him in it with a pistol 'fore removing it off him. His head, I mean: removing his *head* off of him. But even though we've known it, and we can guess why Joseph did this, knowing almost certainly that we're abso-

222

lutely right, well, all the same it isn't quite what we've had in mind, and *have* in mind, to prosecute him for. And also, well . . . also because it doesn't quite suit our peculiar needs. We live to have at least one witness, indisputably alive, at a minimum, and ideally also a decedent for whose passing a reasonable jury can muster up at least a twinge of real regret, not one whose assassin they might be tempted to honor at a testimonial dinner. Chuckie didn't qualify on either count. Not as a witness, being dead, of course, but he didn't make it as a victim, either, having been a real bad boy before he got somebody mad enough to make him a real dead one. But pardon the digression. What'd Joey want from you?"

"You think Joe clipped Chuckie?" Ernie said. "You guys think Joe did that, shot Chuckie Damon inna head and then cut his head right off?"

"Well," Dell'Appa said, "not exactly. That's not exactly what we think. What we actually think is that Joey shot him in the head, yes, making him terminally dead and *much* easier to manage, but not that he then *cut* Chuckie's head off—we think that he then *sawed* the head off Chuckie. With a small electric chainsaw—not as noisy's the big heavy gas ones—also found off Castle Island, hitched to what remained of Chuckie's left thigh with the same length of stout rope formerly connecting his much-meatier corpse to the cinder block tied to it, when it first went into the drink."

"But him and Chuckie was *friends,*" Ernie said.

"Ah yes, my little chickadee," Dell'Appa said, "but then, wasn't it all for the best, that way? If you were scouting around for somebody to shoot you right in your very-own, Sunday-best, *head,* and then cut off that head with a chainsaw, well, my dear fellow, whom would you prefer for such sensitive, delicate work? The next stranger you meet on the street, someone whose qualifications—his training, experience, neatness, originality, taste: my *God:* simply *all* of those things, so important on such an occasion when only the very best will do, and that only just barely—someone whom you know absolutely nothing about? Or: a close, trusted, personal *friend,* someone whose work you know well, whose work you've always admired, and who always takes infinite pains? Well, the friend, obviously, I should think. This's certainly not the sort of casual chore you'd want to entrust to some short-tempered, slovenly, ill-mannered, fly-by-nighter who'd be content to do a slapdash, slipshod job that would embarrass everyone. Besides, touch-hole, do you think Chuckie Damon would've let anybody but a *friend* sit behind him in his car on any night when Chuckie knew, at least suspected, there might be a contract on him? Chuckie wasn't your garden-variety-asshole, you know, even though he trusted his pal and that was a big fatal mistake—he wouldn't've thought it was, at the time that he made it. But would he've trusted a stranger? I personally do not think so; I think that's why Joey got picked for the job."

Ernie licked his lips and stared at Dell'Appa. A gust of shifting wind drove the gray rain harder and more noisily against the window. Ernie shook his head once. "Nope," he said, "I don't believe it. Him and Chuckie was friends. Joey would never do that."

Dell'Appa shrugged. "Suit yourself," he said. "You wanna believe Joey didn't shoot Chuckie, and then clothesline him with the chainsaw? Certainly your prerogative. Fine by me, absolutely. What'd Joey want you to do for him, right after they found Chuckie's head?"

"It wasn't *right* after," Ernie said, "I didn't say it was that. I said it was *right around,* after, after they found Chuckie's head."

Dell'Appa shrugged again. "Okay again: fine by me. We'll agree it was *right around, after.* Just tell me what Joe wanted done."

"It was pretty easy, really," Ernie said. "His brother Danny, the retard, he'd just gotten his job, inna financial district downtown. A month or six weeks before that. They were livin' in Roslindale, was it?"

"West Roxbury, actually," Dell'Appa said. "Seventy-three Pittman Street, in West Roxbury."

"Yeah, wherever," Ernie said, "I guess you must know him, Danny, huh? You know him, Danny, the retard; the brother?"

"I've seen him," Dell'Appa said. "Saw him taking the train one day, going to work, I suppose. His brother was shadowing him."

"Inna gray Cadillac, am I right?" Ernie said.

"Inna gray Cadillac, yeah, yeah, you're right," Dell'Appa said.

"Yeah," Ernie said, "well, that'd be him, that'd be Danny all right. Danny's a really nice kid. Well, a *kid:* he's not that, I guess, older'n I am, but still he still acts like a kid, like he's still about ten–twelve years old. And Joey still treats him like he is—which I would guess, far as Joey's concerned, Danny still probably is, always has been 'n always will be: kid brother younger'n him."

"What kind of work does he do?" Dell'Appa said. "Cleanin' up at McDonald's or something?"

"What's that 'sposed to mean?" Ernie said. "I got a cousin does that, this pizza place over in Belmont, and she's happy doin' it, too. Geraldine's a nice kid, she's a very nice kid, and all of the people she works with, all of them really like her. Geraldine is a very nice kid and it's a nice thing that those people do. Lettin' her have a real job like that, that makes her really feel good, like she's a real person and so forth. Their pizza's still shitty, I never would eat it, but that doesn't mean they're not nice. They give Geraldine somethin' to do. She's still stupid but now she's happy."

"Calm down, Ernie," Dell'Appa said. "It's not supposed to mean anything except to ask whether that happens to be what he does. I know at least one of the fast-food outfits's got a program to hire people like that—that's the only reason I said that."

"Yeah," Ernie said. "Okay. No. Danny don't work for no restaurant. Danny works for the federal government there. Down there in Government Center, I think. Somewhere down in there anyway."

For a moment Dell'Appa did not say anything. "Danny works for the federal government," he said. "Okay, that could explain quite a few things, 've baffled the hell out of me."

Ernie furrowed his brows. "Like what," he said, "explain what? Danny works for the GSA there. General Services, you know? Building maintenance, right? Danny's a janitor, one of the buildings, one of the buildings they got. Sweeps the floors and empties wastebaskets; all of that stuff like that. They got one of those job-programs too, GSA does. Hire lots of people like him. Go around to the State schools and all of those places, they'll hire anyone who can work. Danny told me, that time I stayed with him, the ones that come out of the church schools, like he did, or anyplace private like that, they're much better workers, 'because we're smarter,' than the ones that're in public hospitals when they were kids."

Ernie paused. "I laughed when he told me that," he said. "I didn't mean nothin' by it or nothing—just sounded funny to me, this retard braggin' he's smarter, 'n the other retards he works with. I shouldn't've done that, I guess. I guess doing it I hurt his feelings. He didn't speak to me, rest of that mornin', but he was okay the next day —he can't remember most things the next day, I guess, the next day after they happen."

"Good thing for you, if he can't," Dell'Appa said. "If he'd been able to remember 'til Joey came back there, you probably would've wound up with a pool-cue up your ass."

"You heard about that then there too, I guess, huh?" Ernie said. "Yeah, I guess I was lucky in that there. But I would still guess just the same that no matter how much braggin' Danny and his friends want to do, how they're better, they all must be pretty good workers. They must all do a good job, I guess. Even though they do really stink there. They really smell bad, you're next to them. I hadda go in there one day for a thing, one of the government buildings down there? I hadda go in and get something, an office on the eighth floor. And I went in the elevator just as they're all goin' back to their work from their lunch. Whole bunch of them got in with me. I guess that mustn't matter to them, don't bother them like it would me or you. But just the same, even if it don't, they're used to it so they don't even notice it, they still should give them clean uniforms more there, so they wouldn't smell so bad, I think. You get on the elevator with some of those guys, it's like havin' cat-piss in your bed. But, so, just the same, they give them real jobs they can do, and so what's the matter with that? What's the matter with them doin' that?"

"Nothin'," Dell'Appa said, "nothin' at all. Nothin' to do with Danny. But what was it that Joey wanted from you, if we can just move on to that here."

"Yeah," Ernie said. He resettled himself in his chair, so that the base of his skull rested on the top of the back of the chair. "Joey hadda go outta town, see? Had some stuff to do outta town. And . . . I dunno where the hell he was goin', some place out in the Midwest or somethin', coulda been it was Chicago. Anyway, Joey don't like to fly. This's just somethin' about him, he doesn't like gettin' on planes. So when he goes somewhere, has to go someplace, what Joey will do is, he'll drive. I guess he would probably take a train if he hadda, if there was one where he wanted to go and it went when he wanted to go there, but what he likes better is drivin' himself. That's the kind of a guy that he is. Gets in his car and he goes where he goes, and when he's through doin' what he went to do, he gets in his car and comes back. Any time that he feels like it. So that makes him the one who decides when he leaves, when he goes, when he's goin' some other place, comin' back. No one else can decide 'stead of him. I guess he likes doing that or something."

"A good many others do, too," Dell'Appa said.

"Yeah," Ernie said. He nodded. "I guess lots of people like that." He coughed and cleared his throat. "Jesus," he said, "I never coughed so much in my life as I coughed since they put me in here."

"You probably haven't been talkin' enough," Dell'Appa said. "Your throat's gotten dry from not talkin'. You'd taken advantage of the opportunities, feds've been givin' you here, talked more about Chico, they asked you, this problem might not've come up."

"Yeah, very funny," Ernie said. "I said: I won't talk about Chico. I don't know nobody named Chico. Or if I did, what Chico is doin'."

"Joey's the subject," Dell'Appa said. "Chico is not our concern here. What did Joey want you to do?"

"Well, like I said," Ernie said, "Joe said he was goin' away for a while, had somethin' he hadda take care of, and he was lookin' for someone to come and stay in his house with his brother. Because like I said, Danny'd just started his GSA job there, and he didn't have no vacation saved up yet, or Joe would've taken him with him. Because that's what they both always did. If Joey goes somewhere or takes a vacation, he always takes Danny along. 'Cause if Joey don't go, who's he go with? He hasn't got no way to go. Only this time, with no vacation, Danny this time can't go with him. So what Joey was worried was if he's not there, would Danny still get to work all right? And that's what he wanted from me. I get through in the morning to come from down from Reno's and stay inna house there with Danny. Set the alarm-clock for seven o'clock and make sure Danny got up all right. Make his breakfast for him and then drive him to work, this's before he starts takin' the train there, and then at night Joe had somebody else, a woman who lived upstairs from them, to make sure he got home okay, made his dinner and that stuff. He had it all figured out, so Dan would be taken care of."

"And you said you'd do this for him," Dell'Appa said.

"Yeah, I did," Ernie said. "I liked the guy then—like him now. I had no problem with that. It was kind of a pain in the ass for me, yeah, goin' there when I got off from Reno's; sleepin' for maybe two or three hours, then gettin' right up again, drivin' Danny to work. But from there I went home to my ma's in Revere and I went right back to bed there, so I ended up still gettin' just as much sleep, so it really wasn't that bad."

"Right," Dell'Appa said. "And how much did you get paid for this?"

" 'Paid,' " Ernie said. "You mean: how much money did Joey give me? For stayin' with Danny like that?"

"Yeah, that's exactly what I mean," Dell'Appa said. "What'd Joey pay you for doin' this?"

"Well, Jesus," Ernie said, "Joe didn't pay me no money. This was just something he asked me to do, that I was doin' for him. It wasn't like, you know, I was *doin'* somethin', somethin' that was makin' him money, so I should've had a cut from it. All I did really, I wouldn't've done, was more drivin' I usually hadda. 'Stead of just goin' home I got off from work, I went down to West Roxbury there. And then I hadda drive back. But that's really all that it was. Just doin' a favor, a guy that I knew. Didn't call for no skill or like that."

"Oh," Dell'Appa said, "I misunderstood then. I thought you said that the reason you did this was because you were looking for more work. Second odd-jobs, to make spending money."

"Well, I was, doing that," Ernie said. "I needed to make some more money. But I didn't look at stayin' with Danny like something that would make me money. I looked at it more as a favor a guy, who needed a favor from me."

"And who, if you helped him on this occasion, might find some work for you in the future," Dell'Appa said.

"Yeah," Ernie said, "that was what I had in mind. Sure. I knew why he was askin', could I help him out. There wasn't no doubt in my mind. Always before, when somethin' came up, after his dad went in the rest home, and he hadda go outta town, if Dan couldn't go with him, one reason or other, he would have Chuckie come over. And Chuckie would do what I did. Well, like I said, by the time he asked me, I knew about Chuckie, and he sure was not coming over. And I also knew that in the past there, him and Chuckie'd done business. Not partners exactly, but you get the idea. Him and Chuckie'd done things together."

"What does Danny carry in the briefcase?" Dell'Appa said.

"That attaché case he has got, you mean?" Ernie said. "That little red attaché case he's got?"

"Yeah," Dell'Appa said. "What's in it? He's like the Queen of fuckin' England with her goddamned fuckin' handbag that she's always got with her, and I don't know what's in that, either, and I'd like to know. What the fuck that Danny Mossi's got inside the briefcase that he carries every day."

"I don't know," Ernie said, frowning. "I never seen inside it and I never asked him that. Why? Why you want to know?"

"Because I'm the type of guy that likes to know things," Dell'Appa said. "I just like to know."

"Well, I can't help you there," Ernie said, "because I don't know myself. I was just over there that one time, over there that once, after Chuckie disappeared, when they thought he went away. You know what I mean."

"I'm not sure I do," Dell'Appa said. "Let me see if I do get it here. What you're telling me, if I'm getting it right, is that Chuckie and Joe were a Frick-and-Frack combo. Partners in mayhem. A team. An underworld enforcement SWAT team. They worked for the bosses, principally Franco, during the wars of the Irish. When the dumb Micks forgot what the game was about—making money, not havin' gunfights—and got to dukin' it out with each other, instead, usin' sidearms instead of their fists."

"*What,*" Ernie said. "I didn't say nothin' 'bout that. I don't know nothing 'bout that."

"Half-true," Dell'Appa said. "You didn't *say* anything about it, no, but you do know all about it. Everyone who's been around since the turnip-truck rolled through last Wednesday knows all about what went on. The role Franco carved out for himself during the wars was the same as Switzerland's is in world wars: he was the neutral banker for both sides. 'Whyn't you and him fight, I'll hold the coats, and then when you get through, heal the winner and bury the loser, all for a reasonable price. Namely: every last piece of the business you fools're fighting over, instead of running right and making lots of money.' "

"I never heard nothin' like that," Ernie said, shaking his head positively.

"Oh, sure you did," Dell'Appa said, reassuringly, "and you also heard, just like everybody else did, why Santa's elves'd gone to work out of season, the late winter of that year you stayed with Danny in the summer, and'd gift-wrapped Chuckie's head for PD Boston. Because informed and usually highly-reliable sources had it Chuckie'd been gettin' far too chummy and chatty with the homicide division. That he'd been whispering to a cop who was a cousin of his about some of the Irish lads that Chuckie didn't like himself—hated actually, competitors of his loan-sharking business—but Franco wouldn't let him put them out of business—and also out of life, as well, while he was at it. So Chuckie's idea was to have his cousin the cop do the dirty work for him, getting rid of his rivals for him without getting Franco mad at him at the same time. I suppose when Franco found out what skulduggery Chuckie was up to he must've been annoyed. Probably thought it wouldn't be too good for his own business, word got out that one of Franco's bone-breakers was collaboratin' with the cops about some of Franco's own payin' clients. Trading with the enemy, they would've seen it as; a clear breach of neutrality there. So Franco told Joey to scrag his friend Chuckie, and present his head, but no longer talkin', to all Chuckie's friends at the cop-house. And Joey, reliable like always, did as he was told and knocked his pal off."

"I still don't believe that," Ernie said. "You can say it as much as you want to, all right? I still don't believe he would do that."

"Okay," Dell'Appa said, "still perfectly fine by me. You can believe whatever you want, no matter how silly it is. How long did Joey stay gone when he went, while you stayed with Danny ten years back?"

"Little over a week or so, I guess," Ernie said. "I'm not really sure now, it's so long ago, but a week or ten days or so, in there. I got used to it pretty fast, goin' there when I got through work, gettin' up with Danny, the mornin', makin' sure he made work on time, and then goin' home, back to bed. It wasn't like I'd like to be doin' it alla the time, but still, I didn't mind doin' it there."

"And did Joey give you some more jobs?" Dell'Appa said.

Ernie became uneasy. He frowned again, shifted in the chair, straightened up and folded his hands in his lap. He nodded. "Well, yeah, I guess you could say that. It wasn't as though he got me new jobs, but when he had somethin' that might be worth money, a way to make money, he'd let me in on it there."

"Sure," Dell'Appa said, "because now he trusted you now, now that you took care of Danny. He did trust you, too, didn't he?"

"Well, jeez, I mean, sure, 'trusted me,'" Ernie said. "But not just because I stayed with Danny. He wouldn't've asked me to stay with Danny, he didn't, like, *know* me, and trust me some first."

"Sure," Dell'Appa said, "and the reason he trusted you first like that, right off, was because you'd come to him recommended. He knew you were workin' for Reno. And Reno was Chico's own personal laundry-man, Chico's own currency-washer. Chico washed off his dough in the cab-fare deposits that Reno made at his bank there."

"I dunno that," Ernie said. "I never knew nothin' like that."

"Yes you did," Dell'Appa said. "You knew it just as well then and you know it just as well today as you know that I'm sittin' here, this very minute right now. That was why Joey trusted you, right from the start, and why you did what Joe wanted done. Because your boss was Reno, and his boss was Chico, and Franco was Chico's boss, right? And Franco directly, no middleman, Franco was Joey's boss, too. So when Chico'd vouched for you, when your dad went to jail—for not squealin' on Chico, among other things, just like you've been refusing to do for all of these past fifty-three days, carryin' on the honored family tradition here in upstanding praiseworthy fashion—well then, Reno hired you on the spot. Which in turn meant that when Franco's guy, Joey, needed a trustworthy kid, to stay with his brother a while, while Joe went on loan out to Gary, Indiana, to kill a nice fellow there. Guy by the name of Walter Biowker who presented some serious logistical problems to the local hierarchy desiring him to be dead. Walter knew all the local stone-killers on sight, also by habit and method, having done some of that type of work his own self, so setting him up to be get slain, as they say, was no simple task for house-bound. That was why Outta-town Joe hadda go, or someone like Joe in that line of work that Walter'd never worked with, so his face and his work wouldn't be so familiar to Walter that he'd head for the high timber as soon as he spotted the guy coming towards him. Joey said fine, but he'd need a kid who could keep an eye on his brother. Franco told Joey that Chico had someone, a kid that he'd put in with Reno, and Reno'd said he's all right, he'd done good. And Chico's kid Reno'd said that about, well, that had to've been you, didn't it? Sure it did, no one else even came close: faithful Ernie, none other than you, you were that trustworthy lad, unlaid hack of the woebegone countenance. So now, all right? Tell me, quit horsin' around here, what business did Joe send your way, after you'd served him well too?"

"Nothin', I told you," Ernie said, "I already told you that: nothin'. I never went on jobs with Joe. If Joey was even, doin' jobs there, if he was goin' on jobs when I knew him. I never knew nothin' 'bout that. You got to believe me on that."

"I don't *got* to believe you," Dell'Appa said, "and I *don't* believe you, either. You're fuckin lyin' to me. Think you're blowin' smoke right up my ass. Somehow you managed to get the idea you can do that, you can fuckin' lie to me, and so somehow I got to convince you right here and right now, you got your head right up your ass. So let me try this out on you here, and see if it changes your mind: tomorrow morning I'm gonna show up in Ev Rollins's law office, all right? I'm gonna have with me a piece of paper that says *subpoena* on it. Meaning: 'get your buns in before the grand jury in Boston; they wanna hear what you've got to say.' And also says: *duces tecum.* Little more of that Latin for you there; what it means, it means 'and bring all your papers in with you; they wanna look those over as well.' And lastly it will say: *forthwith.* Meaning: 'right now, so haul ass, babycakes; we're not waitin' for you to "lose" any your things, our truck's backed up outside, your door. I talked to Ernie yesterday, we had a lovely chat, and he told me some things that made me stop and think. If what this young man says is true, about you and Joe Mossi—and it sure sounds to me like it is, at this point—you should not be permitted to course dogs at licensed pari-mutuel meetings, much less hold a license to practice law in Massachusetts. And that's just for openers. You could very well be facing jail.'

"That's what I'm gonna say to him, Ernie, very first thing in the morning. All of that clear to you so far?"

Ernie licked his lips again and looked away from Dell'Appa. Dell'Appa deliberately raised his left arm, shot his left cuff, and started the stop-watch again.

14 "Well, I don't know as you could say that he actually *said* it," Dell'Appa said. "Didn't say it to me, at least —I happened to be the only person who was in the room with him at the time when he made the sounds, and I certainly heard what he said, but I don't think I'd go so far as to say it was really directed at me. He wasn't looking at me when he made them, the sounds he was making . . ."

". . . yes, those noises that did happen nonetheless to be recognizable English words," Dennison said, "which was probably not by coincidence; we most likely shouldn't over*look* that here, I think."

"Oh yeah," Dell'Appa said, "they were words, too, all right, they were words. No question of them being that. But when he uttered them he was gazing off into the distance. It was more like he was thinking out loud, sort of talking to himself, in some kind of a reverie, you know? Even though there was someone else there, even though I was also there with him."

"Well, okay," Dennison said, "I'm not sure I follow, but what was it you heard him say then? In this trance-state you'd put him into?" Dennison, arriving home about twenty minutes after Dell'Appa had located the long maple-lined drive leading to the mauve villa in Westport, had gestured to him to wait in the Lexus in the cold rain until he had gone around to the back and opened the house. Then, holding the front door open as Dell'Appa parked in front of it and trotted up the two steps to the entrance, he had said they would "talk in the drawing room."

"Gee," Dell'Appa had said, "I never actually knew anyone with a drawing-room before. There was this kid in grade-school that I knew, had a hare-lip and a cleft palate, but he had corrective surgery and had them fixed. But, a *real drawing-room?* Wow, boy, I am impressed."

"You can go and fuck yourself at your earliest convenience here, you know," Dennison had said, ushering him into it.

It was about thirty feet long and at least fifteen feet wide, the walls and the high ceiling as well darkened by carved fruitwood panels two feet square, the floor dark parquet around the edges of an Oriental rug predominantly pastel-blue. They occupied matching navy-blue leather armchairs flanking a low cherry round table. In front of the table was a fireplace set into the inner wall at the center of the room. The fireplace was tiled in an intricate blue-and-white delft scroll design. There was a spray-bouquet of white stock in a white straw-patterned vase in the center. Across the room behind them there were tall French doors framed with dark-blue velvet drapes, giving out over a meadow sloping away from rear of the house. The rain off the bay of the sea to the south of Westport beat more heavily and steadily against the glass than the rain that had come in over the land against the window of the prison-chapel at Plymouth.

" 'You son of a son of a bitch,' " Dell'Appa said. "And then he said it again: 'You son of a son of a bitch.' Like some kind of mantra or something, something you'd hear an old medicine man say, one of those tanbark-stained, leather-faced, big-mother kahunas, some kind of kachina-dancer, NBA-sized, enormous from where you're stand-ing, on the ground, up on the top of his mountain, tilting his head back with his eyes closed, defying a thunderhead sky, long spear with white feathers at the point in his right hand, and in his left, a long, fat, angry rattlesnake, his shiny familiar, cellular-phone to the spirit-world, coiling, and poising to strike. And then when he's come down and face to face with you on level ground, he turns out to be five-foot-three and talks with a lisp. He tells you he bought his big scary pet snake in a joke shop; fuckin' thing isn't real at all; it's got a spring like a Slinky inside, runs on four double-A, alkaline batteries he hadda buy separately, 'and were *they* a bitch to install.' " He felt chillier than he had at the jail, and shivered inside his tweed jacket.

"And you don't think he was talkin' to you," Dennison said. "You were the only other guy in the room when he said: 'you son, of a son, of a bitch,' after you just got through as good as flat-out fuckin' *tellin'* him that tomorrow you're gonna start doin' the very best that you possibly can to see if you can't get him killed. See if you can't spook Mossi into knockin' him off, and you don't think he was talkin' to *you*? You think he didn't have you in mind, when he said a bad name twice there, and you were the only other guy who was present; that's what you're telling me here."

"Yeah, it is," Dell'Appa said. "If I was in a room, and you were in the same room, the same time, and I heard you say, 'you son of a son of a bitch,' and you even said it in that same soft tone of voice this kid used, I would *know*, the minute you said it, there would not be the slightest doubt in my mind whatsoever, that you, you son of a son of a bitch, were usin' that term about me. Because that is the kind of a son of a bitch that you are, that you just happen to be. You're just not in the kind of person who has got a habit of dreaming himself off into space. But this kid? I don't think so. I don't think he is that, the kind of a person you are.

"You have to have a fairly strong character to be what you are, someone who'd call another son of a bitch, a son of a bitch to his face. And mean it. Especially if it is true, and he knows it, knows he's a real son of a bitch. He's liable to do something to you. Kick the piss out of you, something. Make blood come out of your ears. This kid doesn't have that much fibre. What he said, well, he could've said anythin', really—wouldn't've meant anything more. Anything *either*, anything

235

at all, maybe. He was like one of those guys that didn't want to learn how to play the piano, but his parents made him take lessons, much against his will, and so, okay, he took them, he did it. They were still bigger'n he was, back then, and if he'd said no, just refused, well, they would've beat the shit out of him. But he was still able to thwart them; he never did try to learn how to do it, to play, and his teacher saw this, about the third week or so, so she just sat back and let him make a mess of things, and took her hourly fee. And so therefore he never did. He still, to this very day, doesn't know how.

"But that doesn't stop him from sitting down at it, the piano you've got at home, when your wife's invited him to the very first party he's ever come to at your house—and it's gonna be the last one, too, not because he threw up cold ratatouille on your best pair of pants or down your wife's lowest-cut dress, or grabbed your thirteen-year-old daughter's left tit and said to her: 'That'll be sixty-nine cents for the milkshake, that's the special this week, I hope you got your coupon with you'; no, won't be nothing like that—because he'd never do any of those things. It'll be because no one remembers him, even if he was there, as though when he was there, well, he was there but he was completely invisible—and pickin' away at the keys.

"And noises're gonna come out of that, there, maybe even sound something a lot like a song that exists and that you know you heard, you just can't place it right now. But if that does happen, it'll be just an accident, something offbeat, happened purely at random, like a cloud forming up in a high summer sky that looks exactly like Gene Autry's white Stetson hat. Or when the ten-millionth monkey, the one in the very last seat at the very left end of the very last row, in your private simian typing-zoo, almost replicates *Hamlet* or something, only he doesn't quite pull it off: 'To be or not to be, muhfuck, yaah, *that's* the gefilte fish, yick-yick, and if she can stand it, I can, so play it, yick, you heard me, yick, you asshole you: play it-ah, play it-ah, afuckin-gain, thassit.' Well, that isn't Shakespeare, old pal of mine, and what the guy plays, at your piano, that will not be playin' a song. No matter how much it sounds like one, not inna real sense of the word. It didn't just come to him all at once, he's a natural, he can play the piano; all he's doin' is makin' some noise, that happens to sound like a song. It isn't music if what you had in mind to make when you produced it was spaghetti sauce or something. Intention

236

precedent is critical; you're not cursing a guy when you say bad names unless you intend to curse him, and we first-chop philosophers know this.

"Well, that's what I'm sayin' with this kid. He could've started in sayin' 'Hail, Holy Queen'; recitin' Five Glorious Mysteries; disclosin' his secret of fluffy-light sponge cake, or how your cat can learn to do simple repair jobs, around the house, case somethin' breaks, you're not there. It wouldn't've meant any more about me, had any more to do with me'n the words that he actually said."

Dennison had switched on only the pharmacist's brass floor lamp next to the chair he had offered Dell'Appa as they had come into the room; the bulb added no more than sixty paltry watts to the thin and diminishing, gray, residual, late-November, late-afternoon light collected like airborne lint by the tall glassed doors. Dennison's face across the round table from Dell'Appa was becoming indistinct in the fading daylight and the weak incandescence. Dell'Appa shivered again, this time making no effort to conceal the rictus or keep it from his face. "Are you all right, Harry?" Dennison said in the dimness.

"I've felt better," Dell'Appa said. "And one common feature of every time, I recall feeling vividly better, I recall as well feeling much warmer. Have you got any heat on in here, or are you being respectful to fuel-making fossils, so their sacrifice wasn't in vain? I don't want to be rude with you, here in your very own house, boss, but the truth of the matter's: I'm cold."

Dennison sighed. "Well, I'll tell you, Harry," he said, shaking his head and lightly slapping his right hand on his thigh, "there's two answers, both true, to your question. One is 'yes' and the other is 'no.' *Yes*, we do have the heat on, insofar as anything we're able to do affects heat production in this house. We've got the thermostats upstairs and down all carefully set: sixty-five degrees Fahrenheit, though sixty-two's most likely more what we actually get, insofar as we get *any*thing. But then again, *no*, we do not have the heat on, because no matter where we set the thermostats, fifty-five, or eighty-five, it really won't make that much difference. All we really affect by setting to *bake*, or conversely by setting to *freeze*, are the temperatures in the rooms directly above the furnace, or opening right onto them.

"The oil-burner's under the northeasterly corner of the house.

237

This room occupies the southwesterly corner, which puts it just about as far from the burner as it's possible to get without going out in the yard, so you see what the problem is with it: the heat's all at the other end of the house; there's none left to warm up this end.

"Now why, you may well ask, as we have ourselves, did the all-seeing, all-knowing architect pull a boneheaded dumb stunt like that, putting the oil-burner there? For an excellent reason: a house as big as this, no matter what he did, was going to require a lot of BTUs to heat, and because his client, the rug merchant's son, wouldn't be here for much of the winter—he'd be down in West Palm, I guess, having another house there—he'd want to be sure he had enough oil to last him for months at a time; no fuel-degree-day charts in those days, I guess—you had to order each load. So the design called for a mammoth tank, a thousand gallons of oil—the days when the oil man fills that fucker up are days that your checkbook remembers; whole vacations, fur coats, and new stereo rigs've drowned in that thing with nary a trace. If they'd put it inside, that big bastard would've taken up the whole basement and ruined the billiard room plans, so the architect had it buried in the yard, out next to the driveway there, so the delivery men wouldn't have to drag their heavy hoses all across the lovely lawns. So that made the heat a little spotty, room-to-room? So who cared? The owner never bitched about it—owner was in Florida, the heat came on in the winter, so the owner never knew. Caretakers knew, freezin' their asses off, they're in here takin' care, but since they didn't count, that didn't mean anything—once again: who on earth gave a shit? No one did, that is who, no one.

" 'Ginia did, though," Dennison said, "because she lived here, and since we moved in, so've we. So we do the best that we can. Since the rooms we use a lot tend to be places like the kitchen, the bedroom and bathroom, the library where we both have our desks, those far from the furnace chase have quartz heaters in them. But since this isn't one of those often-used rooms, it doesn't have such a device."

"Okay then," Dell'Appa said, "how 'bout having a fire then, the fireplace? The flowers're pretty, I'm not saying that, but they don't make me feel warm; they mean maybe I'm gonna be dead soon. That's not an idea that I like."

"Calm yourself, Harry," Dennison said. "I'll keep a close eye on you, and if I hear you starting to babble ah green fields, or bidding me put more clothes on, I'll take strong measures at once. But they won't consist of a fire; that's a fake, not a wood-burning fireplace. When we moved in here with Tory's mother, 'Ginia didn't know if it worked. She and Lucy'd never even bothered to try it. Well, it didn't, at least not the way that you and I would expect a fireplace to work— throw some logs in and open the flue. The only thing this thing can handle's one of those electric logs, the fireplace accessory that does for ambiance what pantyhose did for finger-fuckin'. But which wasn't really all that surprising—lots of these old showplace, show-off, homes had vanity fireplaces like this, solely for decoration, no more'n holes in the walls, really, no chimneys or flues attached to them, flaunting the owner's wealth, as demonstrated by his possession of the very latest improvements in central heating."

"Okay," Dell'Appa said, "how 'bout the library then? Can we go in there and turn on the heater?"

"We could've done that," Dennison said, "and it would've been right if we had, but to make it right we would've had to've made our plans to meet here *before* Tory asked her client this morning to come here this afternoon and go over proposals to redecorate the whole first floor of her new house in Falmouth."

"I didn't see any other cars here, I come up the drive," Dell'Appa said. "That's why I stayed in my car; I thought nobody was home yet. How many ways you got into this place?"

"Attaboy, Harry," Dennison said. "Way to go, Harry, old kid. Keep up that full-time sleuthin' shit there, 'case some bastard here's greasin' your goose for you. You didn't see any other car parked in the driveway because there're sixteen rooms on that first floor of Tory's client's house, her Cape house overlooking the lighthouse at Nobska, and ladies of her certain age who've got summer houses with that many rooms in their downstairs, and thus more dignity'n Eastern potentates 'n prophets, perceive no good and sufficient reason to operate their motorcars themselves. They have people they employ to drive their motorcars for them, as, I am sure, they would also have people to handle for them many other such tiresome daily transactions as defecation and micturation, even have their cases of swine flu, if only, God, *only*, they could. Tory's client's chauffeur springs out of the driver's seat at each destination and opens the rear door of her pearl-gray Bentley Turbo for her; when it's raining, like today,—

as it most certainly shouldn't when this lady wants to go out, but then mustn't grumble, must one—he shields her head with an umbrella 'til she's under cover. Then he gets back in the car and goes to where she told him to, does what she told him to do when he got there, and then returns to pick her up precisely at the hour she appointed, thus sparing her the tedium of explaining frequently to lesser breeds without the law, whom she has hired to do still other things, that she must away, and simply cannot tarry longer in their company; her time's too valuable for that.

"Now," Dennison said, "the library, right above us here, heated toasty-warm by no less than two quartz heaters, is certainly large enough to accommodate one person working at the desk at one end and two other persons talking across the desk at the other. I know because I've been in that room when it's done it, accommodated that number, doing those things, very nicely indeed. But that doesn't mean that room is also large enough to accommodate two somewhat volatile and animated ladies, one of them quite refined and fucking filthy rich, and whose contentment is thus quite important to the other one that's married to a goddamned fucking cop who's paid at the poverty level, who are talking about what ladies really talk about instead of baseball and politics: not of good old Mickey Angelo there, as old T. S. Eliot had it when he wasn't petting kitties, giving them preposterous names, but of wall- and window-treatments, carpets and upholstery fabrics, while waving fabric swatches in the air like gonfalons, *and* house at the same time two fuckin' roughneck cops who're dispassionately discussing, in appropriate terms, lowlife finks, stoolies and sewer-rats, and how to complicate their worthless rotten useless lives. You read?"

"I copy," Dell'Appa said. "The kitchen? We could do what the folks who don't work have to do, when their landlords don't fix the heat: turn the oven on, open the door."

"Also off-limits," Dennison said. "In the kitchen are engaged in honest toil—but not too much of it; they're in absolutely no danger of dropping from exhaustion—two gentlemen, not of Verona but from Perugia itself, which is almost just as good, and some would say: even better—who are putting onto the floor, onto the walls and also onto the countertops, the very finest of Italian marble tile in many varie-gated hues, the merest sight of which would, if you were not very careful—or hardhearted, either one—bring real salt tears to your eyes.

"And by Jesus, I can tell you: if the fuckin' tiles don't do it, then the price we paid for them and what these guys're costing us for not working very much could make a ten-foot-two cement-cast gargoyle weep, and then have to go lie down. And if he lay down in that kitchen while those two guys're still here, they'd tile him up, too, just like they've been doing the floor, and the walls, and the countertops, like they learned as apprentices to the legendary Mick Angelo—bet you didn't know until now that he was actually Irish, in addition to being as queer as Tiberius, at least on every third Thursday—helpin' him do the Pope's chapel ceiling. They came here just soon as they finished that job, been workin' those same four speeds for us here ever since; slow; really slow; even slower than that; and infuckin-credibly slow—no discernible motion at all.

"There've been days when I would've sworn that both of those fine Italian craftsmen were dead, that they'd both expired near the sink, or over there, next to the stove. But every time—'Oh no, you're not rid of us that easy.'—they started movin' again. Before I'd had time enough to get someone in, have them hauled away in a rough wooden cart, and dumped in a potter's field somewhere. So they're still out there in the kitchen, stretchin' out this lifetime job even longer, to keep their American work-visas. Those cherished green cards that so many vie for, and guess who hadda go through all the rigamarole for those permits, so those two odious, freeloadin' bozos could come into this Great Republic and move right in with us, live here for the rest of our lives. I'm afraid they're becoming our wards. When they finally get through, if they ever do, they'll head off in their fifties for college and their eventual doctorates in comparative transfixed immobility states, otherwise known as static inertia, and we'll have to pay for that too.

"And you know how Tory sucked me into hiring them inna first place, and then getting them those fucking visas? She tells me that what she's gonna do's use that kitchen as a tax-deductible showroom, the whole house's gonna become one, a goddamned display, and that will mean we'll end up selling the damned thing for much more'n we'd ever get without all the tile and stuff. She says. And she also says: in the meantime she'll be selling boatloads of those tiles to her clients, who when they see it'll all be instantly overcome by frenzies of covetousness, and that when she then takes her lavish commissions, plus what we'll get for the house itself, we'll be filthy rich. Read: when we die we'll have plenty of dough. Which, I start to think —but only after I went for it, naturally; the craftsmen've taken up residence so I've now seen them in total inaction—is about how long it looks like they're gonna take here, most of the rest of our natural lives, but I think now I have it figured out.

"It's gonna be *years* before she gets this atrocity finished, in any kind of shape to put on the market. And that's only *if*,—emphasis: if—, that *is* what she does plan to do, and I'm not livin' here because I got duped in a scam she cooked up with her voice-hearing mother; which, yes, could've happened, it could've; I might not've been paying sufficient attention, had my mind on something else unimportant, putting down a prison riot or something, and they blew one right by me back there. I haven't entirely ruled that one out, either. But if it isn't that, and she does plan to sell it, well, okay, so the two of them didn't bamboozle me, and my pride isn't bruised after all, but still, even then, we're not gonna get rich until we're old. And until we get rich, and get the fuck outta here, we're gonna live in a showroom. I'm not sure I like that idea. I never aspired to be a new car, not even a new luxury car. I like them, I'll own one if I ever can, but for some reason I don't wanna *become* one, any kind of durable goods where things get reversed from their natural order so I become he who works for the building, not him whom the damn building works for.

"And then here's this other thing, too, since I'm finally thinking about it. Now what I got to wonder is: who is it, really cares, if you are rich when you're dead? Which is, like I say, what I think we're gonna be pretty close to bein', when-as-and-if all the fine imported craftsmen finish up. Besides the tax man, I mean, and all of your mean grasping relatives, who, of course, since they knew you were rich, most likely did as much as they dared to, helping to nudge you along on your way—'Can we fetch you a fresh fluffy pillow, Uncle Brian, for over your nose and your mouth?' Meaning: 'Can we fetch *you,* with a pillow? Come on, hurry up, you scrimy old bastard, for Christ sake get it over with, willya? Die and leave us the money.' What the hell good does rich do you then, when you are finally dead—have they got a funeral deluxe you can buy now, get lugged

242

off in a six-tired, limo-style hearse, pool with sauna out in the trunk, wet-bar and TV at your feet?

"Anyway, no," Dennison said, "sad to relate, for us today the kitchen is out, just as the library is. And we're not gonna have our little chat in the master-bedroom, which's the only other warm room. You're a nice guy and I respect the hell out of you, Harry, but I've never thought of you in that way. And besides, even if I did, we don't wanna start any loose talk. But you can see better now, I bet, why I say we're stuck with this house? Fuckin' thing doesn't work for shit, and it costs all outdoors to maintain. But as long as the real-estate market stays down like it's been, we're stuck in it, that's what we are. Payin' a mortgage we can't afford—Lucy and 'Ginia's shares of the overhead, both of them, but only Virginia's Lottery check—and making repairs we can't afford either, improving a place that we don't even like and probably oughta blow up, all of it so that *maybe* some day we can sell the damned thing at a profit of obscene proportions. Which we'll promptly have to turn over to a luxurious resthome. The only enjoyment we'll ever get from it'll be from squattin' our hams eight times a day on polished-maroon, Chinese-lacquered Du Pont bedpans rimmed in eighteen-carat gold, and wondering where we misplaced our lives.

"And then, like a revelation from the heavens radiant, like the angel finally got around to opening the seventh seal, it'll come to us: 'Bomber's Law,' we will think ruefully. 'Bomber's fucking Law's why we dumb-ass masochists went and self-inflicted all that crazy shit upon ourselves. We did it for the *fucking money, just like Bomber predicted.* Yes, we got it, got the money, and the money says we're rich, but it's also proof we're assholes, well-to-do fuckin' assholes who pissed half our lives away, butt-sucking a goddamned house, all to get lots of money. Bomber's Law triumphed again. Woe and more woe, woe on top of that, truly, we is a woebegone pair.'

"So then, you wanna go out to some cheap low-rent bar where at least they got heat someplace, maybe?"

"That's a thought, isn't it," Dell'Appa said.

"Yeah, but not a very good one," Dennison said. "Tell me about this kid here, the one that you tortured most of the day before you came over here to rattle my cage. Get me all excited. Tell me one of the people I got working for me actually did something worthwhile today. I'm easy. That's all it takes. You can do that, I'll buy you a drink. Whatever you like, long's it's beer. You get anything out of this punk?"

"That's a good question," Dell'Appa said, crossing his legs and hugging himself. "You think Admiral Scott, or Roald Amundsen, maybe one of them's got an opinion? They must be around here some place. They'd feel right at home in this joint."

"Quit griping and talk to me, my son," Dennison said. "What'd he say after alleging your dear paternal grandmother'd barked and probably died chasing a car?"

"Started whining about how he wanted his lunch again," Dell'Appa said. "I took that as a good sign, of course; hungry men're much better informers and sources. Empty bellies sharpen up memories, fine-tune the focus control. Oh: also said he hadda pee."

"Good, good," Dennison said, nodding. "It's an inconvenience, I know, we're no longer permitted to converse with our little friends in that cramped-but-soundproof room in the cellar, the one with the naked lightbulb hanging from brass socket, had a beaded chain, at the end of the frayed cord in the ceiling, where so many in the past were persuaded by severe beatings to assist us police with our inquiries, as our English friends so charmingly put it. But times change and we have to change with them. A growling stomach and extreme bladder-discomfort may not seem like an adequate substitute, I know, but to this pampered generation that we're forced to deal with now, well, I tell you, it's damned near enough to make those chaps wonder if Amnesty International shouldn't be advised, if it's true that the crack State Police're treating helpless prisoners this way."

"He wasn't helpless, boss," Dell'Appa said. "He could've gotten relief. I told him he could piss his pants then and there if he wanted. Didn't matter one bit to me. I wasn't plannin' to sit in 'em with him while all that nice warm piss got colder on his ass'n the rain washin' down the window behind him there—which of course made him listen to that, too, the rain, and that made him want to go even worse. I also told him I'd clocked him at eighty-eight seconds of sulking in silence before he stated his urge to take a piss, which made me think that if he really hadda go that bad then he'd been keeping his legs crossed for almost a minute and a half more'n he'd had to. So until he told me he was ready to talk turkey and Mossi and Rollins, in a forthright and meaningful manner, the best he was gonna be able to hope for was that I'd agree to let him open the drawer in the table we're sitting at there, and see if maybe someone'd left an elastic band behind he could twist like a tourniquet around his poor shrinkin' little pecker there, help him at the cost of some additional discomfort —maybe some small risk of gangrene, too—keep his skivvies dry a little longer.

"As for his lunch, I'd already told him they'd save lunch for him, and I meant that. What I'd left out, but what I also meant, and what he either hadn't noticed or just hadn't bothered to ask me about when I told him, which was why I was tellin' him then, was when I'd decide to tell my friend Stanley it was okay with me if they *gave* that lunch to him. 'Because no matter how long they may've been *savin'* a lunch for you, it's gonna be pretty hard for you to actually *eat* it, until they *give* it to you. Which they're not gonna do here today 'til I tell 'em to, that it's okay with me if you eat.' And also: which since he'd pouted for eighty-eight seconds, when I did get around to tellin' 'em it was okay it was obviously going to be almost a minute and a half later than it needed to've been, when I did finally decide to do it."

"And?" Dennison said.

"And then he said 'mothermucker,' " Dell'Appa said. "Put real feeling into it, too, and when he said it he was looking right at me."

"So you think that this time when he said a bad name," Dennison said, "he was in fact calling you by it. You did have that feeling. That it was you that he meant. To whom he had reference to."

"That was the impression that I did have at that time, yes sir, yeah," Dell'Appa said. "I did have that definite impression. But naturally I wanted to be absolutely one-hundred-percent sure, before I did anything rash, and so I said politely to the subject: 'Listen, you cocksucker, and listen up good: I'm layin' the truth on you here. If you even think, *even think,* you're gonna either wheedle me here, *or* you can get me mad enough, to trick me into bangin' on that deadbolt door behind me and tellin' that guard to let you go take a piss, and then eat lunch, so you can figure out some way to con him into lettin' you get in touch with Ev Rollins, so he can start purging his files and destroyin' stuff I want and I know he's got, *before I get what I came here to get,* you're gonna find out what it feels like when your teeth're really afloat and your fillings start washin' away, and also what all the starvin' Africans felt like, before we sent famine relief in. Your know what your situation is today, asshole? Your situation is hopeless; your ass is the grass, and what you see bearin' down on you, head-on, is the big power mower from Hell.' "

"And that was what did it, then?" Dennison said. "That was what made him tell you?"

"I don't think it was, actually," Dell'Appa said. "Gayle knows a lot more about the dynamics that go into this interrogating shit'n I do, and she says what she knows about the whole business, that is most likely shit too. Because nobody really does know. The hardest part of her job, she tells me, is persuadin' the patient: stop lying. But with Gayle this's someone who's *paying her,* paying money to talk to her. And then that person lies to her too. You tell me how that can make sense. But, anyway, she says is that what has to happen first is, first you have to resolve dominance. The issue of who's gonna dominate whom, which chicken's gonna be doin' the peckin'; which one is gonna get pecked. Have to get that all out of the way. Because it's a formality, no more'n that, but both animals need to resolve it, have to, really, before there's ever gonna be any hope at all of them being able to sit down and have a real beak-to-beak talk. And the one who goes into it expecting that he's gonna be the peck*ee?* This kinda surprised me, I admit: he's even more anxious than the one that's gonna be the peck-*er* is, to get it out of the way. And *isn't* upset when it comes out that way, that he's the one gettin' pecked-on, because that's what he thought all along. What he expected would happen.

"So, what I think is that what I was doin' for the first hour-and-a-half or so with this little prick was confirmin' his suspicions that even though he didn't know me, never heard of me before, hadn't known that I was comin', or what to talk about, I was in fact another one of those guys that he didn't even know, hadn't even ever heard of, who was gonna hurt him some where the bruises wouldn't show, and who could do it, too.

"So the first order of business that we had ahead of us, from the minute I walked in, was to establish in his mind that he had no choice at all: he had to talk to me, and give me at least part of—and a very big part, too—of what I came to him to get. It's very important, to a guy like Ernie is, that if you want something from him, that it will endanger him to give, you first *enable* him to give it. The way you enable him to give it is by first convincing him that what he's afraid will happen to him, if he does what *you* want him to—what someone else will do to him for doing that for you—is nowhere near as bad as what will happen to him, what *you* will do to him, if he *doesn't* help you out. And furthermore: that what he fears that someone else will do to hurt him, if he does what you want, is nowhere near as certain to happen, and anyway won't happen as soon, as what he fears that you'll do."

"So first you ease his pain, by giving him a good heavy dose of it," Dennison said.

"Exactly," Dell'Appa said. "At least that's the way Gayle looks at it. What I have to do, to get a guy to talk to me, who doesn't want to talk to me, and who knows his peer group would tell him right off the bat that he *shouldn't* talk to me, is transform him from my worthy opponent into my helpless victim. If he's got any choice, he knows very well, the code says he can't talk to me, no matter what I offer him. But, if he's my victim, he's got no choice, and then he can take with complete impunity any reward that I offer. Or so he can rationalize, anyway.

"So," he said, "here we have Brother Nugent now, squirmin' and writhin' around somethin' fierce, because of course now that he's mentioned it out loud, his bladder feels like it's gonna *burst*. Instead of doin' his best to ignore it, how really bad he has to go, he's gone and told me about it, and naturally that's made it worse. Now it's the only thing he can think about. If there'd been a sink in the room, and I could've held his hand under warm water, he would've told me atomic secrets and how to get three well-balanced meals for four well-nourished adults out of one pound of day-old chopped liver."

"Hell, everybody knows that," Dennison said.

"Sure," Dell'Appa said, "well-nourished adults won't eat chopped liver, no matter how many times it's served to them. They can and they will, go hungry three meals, before they will eat that chopped liver, because they know then you'll get the idea, give up and throw the stuff out, and give them something to eat. But anyway, okay then, he was satisfied. He had no choice anymore. I'd convinced him I'd beaten him. It was okay to give up.

" 'Joey and Ev've got their own breeding kennel they run, this farm down in Mansfield they bought. Well, Olivia Rollins, Ev's daughter there, it's really her that runs it. She's the one, there, that lives at the place, and does almost all of the work, but their money is what's behind it. And Livia's really good with those dogs, boy, even if she is a dyke. Kind of a shame, too, if you ask me—she's really a good-lookin' broad. Her girlfriend, though, Mandy, there, she isn't. She's not a good-lookin' woman. She's not good-lookin' at all. Livia must really likes dogs, boy. She takes care of the dogs all day long, and then her girlfriend at night is a dog, and she is: Mandy looks sort of like *you*.' "

"Mercy," Dennison said, "now there's an unfortunate woman indeed, a truly unfortunate girl. Bad enough to be openly queer, all the grief that that's bound to bring on you, but then also to resemble you?"

"That's what I said to him, myself," Dell'Appa said. " 'Cripes. God help that poor miserable woman—she's got a real cross to bear.' He looked a little disappointed, like what he'd had in mind was to piss me off.

" 'Yeah,' he says, 'well, Olivia that summer there, after Joe came back from where he went, when I stayed with Danny there, that time, Olivia, she had some kind of accident. Dislocated her shoulder or broke her arm, maybe; I forget just what it was. Some kind of a swimming-pool accident, I guess, fell off of a divin'-board, something —I don't really know it was that, I mean; I just know it was something like that. Anyway, what it was was, she couldn't lift nothin', couldn't lift nothin' up for a while. Which, when you're takin' care of dogs all the time like she was, there, she hadda, it wasn't just somethin' that she liked to do, you know, there; this was her regular fuckin' job she did there. Her way, makin' a livin', okay? That Joe and her old man, I thought at the time, they were all the ones financin' her there—this's long before I ever meet Doug, there, and find out he's in with them, too—gettin' her started in, onna career, right after she got out of college. Right after she got out of school.

" 'Well, anyway there, she did have this kid already, a kid that come in all the time, helpin' her feed them and stuff. They had quite a few dogs there, Ev and Joe did. So she needed the kid to help out. It's not only that those dogfood bags can be heavy, they are: go fifty pounds at least, all right? You buy the big bags, you got lots of dogs, because them racing-dogs, they eat a lot. And so, liftin' them, you're a small woman anyway, this isn't no June-weekend picnic, even when your arm is all right. Now Mandy, there, she could've lifted them all right, I think. Mandy looks like she could lift a car up, so you wouldn't need a jack if she was with you and you got a flat you hadda change, but she's not around the place much most days except weekends, so she wasn't that much help. She's got her own job, too, I guess. I don't know what it is. Workin' on construction, prolly, usin' jackhammers and stuff.

" 'And then all of the other stuff, too, that Livia hadda do: muck out the kennels and so forth, the runs, and brush them and give them their baths there. 'Cause hey, these're valuable dogs you've got here. These dogs're worth lots of money. You can't just let your investment in them go to hell there; you got to take care of your dogs, just like you would anything else. But you see what I mean, this's lots of work, keepin' dogs like Olivia is, and it's not easy work, either.

" 'They used to have six or eight dogs, I guess there, running at any one time, Joey and Ev Rollins, I mean, and then they've also, they've got some they're schoolin'; some that they're breedin'; some that got too old to race, they retired them and bred them until after that they even got too old to fuck much. But one reason or other, quite a few of them, *quite* a few of their dogs, when they got too old she just didn't do it, do what they always do. Livia didn't have them put down.

" ' "Well, I didn't want to," this's what she told me, at least. Because I asked her there, see, I see this, she isn't getting that done. Why she wasn't puttin' them down. "That's the reason I'm not," she tells me. "I am the honcho running this business here. I'm the managing partner of this here entire operation; I am the resident HNIC—I'm the Head Nigger In Charge. I also own part of it, myself, and all of the other investors, all of them also approved. So I think if all three of them say we agree, we're going to keep some of our dogs around because we feel like it, even after they've stopped making us money, because they've always been good dogs for us, and we can afford to be good, too, my bet would be: we're gonna do it. We ought to be able to do that, I think, and my dad and Short Joe, and Dougie, him too, they all agreed with me on that. So we decided we would. And that's the whole reason for that. We own this business, and we run this business; our very own private business we've got here. We can do as we fucking well please."

" 'Olivia's really a nice woman,' Ernie said," Dell'Appa said. "Ernie gets very earnest when he talks about his Livia, almost eloquent. I think that's why it bothers him that Livia does not seem to him to be at all of the heterosexual persuasion. He knows it, she's not, but it hurts. 'I know she's a dyke, and her wife or her girlfriend, whatever two broads call each other, her girlfriend looks just like a damned cop, a big fuckin' cop and a mean one.' "

"My-my," Dennison said, "his bladder may've been full and his stomach empty, too, but he certainly wasn't giving up on getting to you, was he now?"

"Ernie was getting noticeably desperate," Dell'Appa said, "moving around so much he looked like he was trying to bore a hole in the chair, usin' his ass for a drill."

"Not a tool well-adapted to the task, I would say," Dennison said.

"Not at all," Dell'Appa said. "And he did seem to've resigned himself to doing this thing that he really didn't want to do, given the fact that it could be in fact pretty dangerous to sink Short Joe Mossi. So I'd already made up my mind that when I'd gotten enough out of him at least to get a search warrant for Everett Rollins's office—and when he said that, 'Dougie,' I thought I was probably gettin' pretty close there, I'd let up a little on poor Ernie there just a bit, and let the kid go take a leak. Under a guard's watchful eye, of course, with no chance at a phone or to chat up his pals. And then too, another factor also of importance, I was reaching the point, too, where even though I'd tapped a kidney on the way in, well, I wasn't close to desperate but I sort of had to take a piss myself.

"But that didn't make Portia right; Portia was still dead wrong: the quality of mercy certainly *is* strained, at least until you talk. He was getting no lunch, nothing to eat, until I'd gotten everything I'd come for. Prison food's not that good anyway, and besides, *I* wasn't hungry. I'd had a full breakfast, before I left home, bacon and waffles with syrup, stuffing my gut to beat the band. I figured it might come in handy, as indeed it was doing. So I said to him: 'Ernie, if I could prevent me from taking a leak, when I really did have to take one, I certainly wouldn't annoy me any more'n I really had to, until I let me get out to the bathroom. So since you have to piss, and I *am* stopping you, I'm really surprised that you're doing that, and giving me little cheap shots. Doesn't seem very smart, from where I sit.'

"'*Yeah*,' he said, slight note of contempt there, and still pretty combative, but obviously swayed by my logic, 'Well, I think she's got a very good heart. When I'm goin' down there to help her out there, the five afternoons and then weekends, I'm still drivin' the cab over Reno's? Well, I'm still a young guy and I'm not in bad shape, but that's a long drive, down to Mansfield and back, and I'm doin' it every day. Drivin' down there as soon's I get up inna mornin', and then drivin' back up again, afternoons, and I'm drivin' the cab all night too. I admit I was gettin' pretty-near beat. It was really knockin' me out. And Olivia, she could see this. Even though she has got her own troubles there, she is hurt and she can't do her work, got her own troubles to think about there, which is why I am doin' what I'm doin', that don't mean she still can't see that I am really *beat*. This is beating the shit out of me. But she's got some compassion, you know? And this, this is unusual.

" 'Like, what most racing-dog people usually do—as soon as a dog's gotten the point were he's no good for nothin' no more, not that this means he's really real old, like you would look at him and you would say "Hey, now that's a really old dog you got there," you know, like you would. You can tell that by just lookin' at them, their nose-hairs, the fur that they got on their muzzle, there? It's all turned all white, they're so old. And like that, that kind of thing. You can tell just by looking at them, that a dog is twelve or fourteen, and that's pretty old for a dog. But a good racing dog, a competitive dog, well, three years's gettin' up there, gettin' kind of old, and then, *four* years, well, I mean, like, *forget* it—by then it's all over, it's time; you gotta face up to it: four years is *old, really old,* for a greyhound to be. So, and there's some women that I guess adopt them, they got this farm that they run, and they put the retired dogs up for adoption, free, no charge for them. For people that don't have a dog of their own at home but they've got kids who want a nice dog, a dog they can play with, you know. And who also I would assume live some place 'way out inna country, dog like that needs a place he can run. But most

251

racing-dog people, what most of them do is they just have their too-old dogs put to sleep, except for their personal favorite ones, big winners that won lots of races—them they might keep around.

" 'The others, though, all of 'em, five out of ten of them at least, for them it's automatic: the old vacuum chamber: put 'em in, take the air out, and *boom:* that's the end of them. They went to sleep. Well, it's not really cruel, you look at it the way that most people who do it, who're actually doing it, look at it. You got to do that, you're runnin' a business, every dog eats a certain amount, and then you got the shots and that stuff? It all costs money, you know. And, hey, all right, huh? You're runnin' a business here, not just playin' with doggies, *"Oooh, lookit dah cute little puppy,"* that kindah kid-shit, fuck that kindah shit, this's *your* way of makin' a livin'. From breedin' and raisin' the dogs, and then racin' them with other dogs, that is how, all right? That is what you are doin'. Not from you're lettin' 'em geddup in your lap, an' then lick all over your face, always tellin' them: *"Hey, geddoffa* couch there, yah gettin' doghair all over"—no, *that* isn't why you're doin' this shit; you're doin' this shit to make money. Well, then, shit, then what it is—what it's gotta be, really, you wanna keep runnin' it there—it's just like what any business'd be: you got to make money off it. Off what you're supportin', what you're payin' the money out, that brings more money back in. Or else, if you don't, there won't be none for you, after you get through with all of it, payin' your overhead, takin' care of expenses, like every businessman has to.

" 'I guess in horse-racing, it's sposed to be different, at least with the thoroughbreds, there. The real thoroughbreds, at least, Kentucky Derby, the horse-races you see on TV. Probably not so much with the standard-breds there, only with thoroughbreds, this's where that'd apply: most people in that, they're not in it expectin', they're really gonna make money. Well, the trainers an' jockeys, the exercise kids, the stablehands, yeah, them, they do. Hafta. Because they've gotta eat there. But the owners, you know, nah, not for them; for them it's not that at all. They're in it for somethin' else. They're in it for the excitement and stuff, and you know, they also really like horses, and they're also rich, so there's that. Those people got money to burn there. So they can do what they like, when they want, and then not care what it costs. But most people with racing-dogs haven't got that, so you see, it's different for them. They got to watch nickels and dimes.

" 'I know Livia said to me, said a couple of times there, Livia said it a lot: "I know these oldtimers, been at it a long time, experience up the gump-stump. So maybe they're right, and that does carry them; that really is how they do it. They've been flying so long, by the seat of their pants, and, goddamnit, no matter what anyone says, all of that shit, it still works for them. Well, what I say's 'Goddamnit, it won't work for us.' And *I* don't care what anyone says: it's too late for us now to bother to learn all that outmoded, otta-date *shit*. We're gonna come in now, we gotta come in, if we're gonna compete, armed right up to our teeth, with everything we can bring with us. Because everyone else who's coming in now, 's coming in with everything *they* got, and they're who we're not only up against now, in addition to all the oldtimers—they're who'll we'll be up against later, the rest of our lives, and we're the oldtimers, when all our oldtimers're dead. Not the oldtimers, much as we love 'em; it's not them we're competing with now. It is *us* we're competing with now, and we got to use what we've got. And by that I mean that I think the biggest thing, by far, my father gave me for this, was not with the dogs, growin' up with the dogs, but when he sent me to college." '

"Now," Dell'Appa said to Dennison, "by now I know what this kid's got, what he knows that I've only suspected. Suspected a long time, and strongly, too, yeah, absolutely I have, but still, no more'n that: only suspected. That's all you can do, far's you can travel, on what you know without proof. But he doesn't know, A, he knows what he knows, because he doesn't know what it means. What its significance is. And he doesn't know, B, 'til he actually says it, I can actually get him to say it, I'm no better off'n I was before, before I laid eyes on him. But the minute it dawns on him, what he's got that I'm after, he's gonna start tryin' to haggle again, and I'm gonna be back at Square One."

"Lovely," Dennison said. "Don't you love workin' without a net down there under you? One false step and you know, and this's the hardest part, too: as you fall to your death, you'll be giving the crowd what they came for, and the bastards won't even say 'thanks.' Not so you'll hear it, at least."

"Right," Dell'Appa said, "so what I've got to do here is come at the kid sideways, like one of those old B-Fifty-Two bombers can do, when they're landin' into a crosswind and there's the wheels going straight down the runway but the nose of the fuselage looks like it's aiming ten or twenty degrees to the left. Or the right, dead on to wherever the wind was. Damndest thing I ever saw, first time I saw that on TV; thing looks like a flying building anyway, it's so damned big, but there it is, all calm and serene, got more moves'n Bobby Orr had. So I said to him: '*College*'? Is that what she told you, what she had goin' for her, runnin' this kennel, was what they taught her in college? Where'd she go, veterinary school, some A and M college or something?'

" 'No,' he says, 'no—accounting. Olivia's an accountant. A real accountant, I mean. That's what she studied in school.'

" 'Gee,' I said, still trying my best to seem like I've got all the time in the world—after all, *I* don't have to pee, 'that's not what I'd choose to as a way to prepare for a rewarding career in the racing-dog business.'

" 'No-no,' says Ernie, 'that's not what it is, that she spends all of her time with the dogs. She does a lot of that accounting work. Besides running the kennel days, I mean. Prolly she spends more her time on accounting in fact, 'n she does doin' stuff with the dogs. The dogs're just one thing she does.

" 'Livia works very hard. She's a very hard-workin' woman. Day and night, work-work-work, she just works all the time, everybody says that. If you don't see her, you don't know where she went, well, you just can count on it, there, that wherever she is, that's what it is that she's probably doing: Livia's workin' again. It seems like she *can't* just sit down, you know, have a beer, catch a little TV, just shoot the shit for a while. No, instead all the time what she has to be doin', always has to be somethin' that's work, something she's got to get done.

" 'And she actually likes it that way. She will even admit it to you: "I got to have somethin' to do, I go nuts, if I don't have somethin' to do." Like she's actually proud that she's like this or somethin', she don't think anything's wrong. When most people would tell you, they see someone like this, someone who's actin' like she does, they can't ever sit down and relax, they would say to you, they would tell you: "Well, then, this person is nuts."

" 'She keeps all the books for the kennel and so forth, this's her kennel there, Error, plus she also does all of her father's accounting work, his law office there, and Joey's taxes, too, Joey has her do those for him. I have her do mine too, even though mine're simple, but I feel better havin' her do it, the deductions and all that shit there. I don't know about any of that stuff. And she only charges me ten bucks to do it; she don't even wanna charge that. "Hey, no," she says, "you helped me out there. Gave me a hand, I was hurt. I'm just repayin' a favor here, is all."

" 'I hadda insist on it, payin' her somethin', that's the kind of person she is. I say: "Livia, no, this isn't right. You paid me, I did work for you. I won't feel right, now, you do work for me, and you don't let me pay you. Next year I won't feel like I should ask you, I'll just do the damned things myself. And then I will get myself into the shit, and then it'll be all your fault. Because you wouldn't take money from me." So she says: "Okay, that's the way that you feel, gimme ten bucks," and so that's what I do. But if I didn't have her to do it, and help me out there, I know what I'd do: all I'd do is fill out the card, even though I would know I was costing myself money doin' that. But I don't know about all them deductions and stuff, and I wouldn't feel comfortable, you know? I wouldn't feel comfortable doin' that. I feel better just havin' her do it, and then I save some money besides.' "

"Right," Dennison said. "I wonder how many of Reno's other drivers and flunkies have this lady do their taxes too, not to mention how many of Chico's. With her working for them Franco and Chico can always be sure that at least their own boys're not courting tax troubles, they all report income sufficient, and legal, and aren't gonna get net-worthed on them. That might be an interesting inquiry there, to prevent boredom this winter, time hanging heavy on our hands.' "

"That," Dell'Appa said, "and a few other things beside that. She keeps the books for a lot of the other dog-people, too, a lot of the other kennels. We're already sure Reno's cab company's Chico's money-laundry; people who own racing kennels would be pretty good cash-washers, too. Ernie said: 'About twenty of them, at least, I think, the other kennels, they use her. Plus which, inna wintertime, matter of fact, she prolly does more the accounting stuff there'n she actually spends on the other, doin' her work with the dogs. During the winter months, startin' right after Christmas, it's like nobody sees her at all. Every minute she's not with the dogs, or maybe doin' somethin' that she has to do. All the nights and the weekends and like that. Makin' out people's taxes for them.

" 'Some of them, like the kennel guys, for example, those guys've got their own businesses, so she has got those that she does. And then there's a lot who just work for a living, which is like most people do, but they also have her do their taxes. Some of her father's law clients, because naturally he would recommend her to someone who he was their lawyer and they needed their taxes done, but also a lot of guys that didn't use him. They never had Ev at all. They just heard good things about Olivia, and how her work was real good, and that's what they're after themselves; they want someone good, do their taxes. Because they're afraid if they made a mistake there, well, they're scared of the IRS, which most people are, everybody I know is. Scared of those bastards, I mean. So they all go to her and say to her: "Here, you do this for us," and that's what she does then, she does that. Fills out their tax-returns for them.

" 'Her clients all really like her, I guess. I know they all keep coming back, year after year, and I don't think they would do that if they didn't. Unless they moved away, or maybe they died, but if it was, you know, something like that, well, then that wouldn't be her fault that they did that, not like it was something she did that made them go find someone else.

" 'Which all of this would make sense, of course; she's a professional accountant there, and that's what those people do. Got a paper says she passed this exam—she's one of them, whadda they call alla those people there, got that, one of them CPAs there. Got it framed up there onna wall in her office, with her college diploma. I guess that's how you get to be that, by takin' some special test that they give you, and you pass it and they make you one. So it's not like the paper by itself means that much; all it does is just say that they did that.'

" 'How about this guy Doug that you mentioned a while back,' I said with elaborate nonchalance, 'did she do Doug's tax return too?'

" 'Oh yeah, she does Doug's,' the kid says to me, 'she did Doug and Laura's returns for years, ever since she got her computer, bigger one'n she'd had in college. That's how she met Doug in the first place, I guess: he sold her computer to her, and then, he found out what she wanted it for, I guess he gave her the thing at his cost, if she'd keep his books for his business. Although it could've been, it could also've been, that they knew each other from school. Like they were in college together, knew each other before, and that was why she bought her machine from him. I know it's a really expensive machine there, I don't even know what it cost. She told me: "Oh, 'bout as much as a small car does, but it does things a car never could." So that could've been it too, I guess. That could be the reason. I guess I really don't know that. I *have* got to go though, I know *that*.'

" 'Well, okay,' I said, 'I can understand that. But just tell me this, if you will: this guy Doug that Olivia's so friendly with, that she's known ever since her school days? Do you know what his last name might be?'

"His forehead's all wrinkled already," Dell'Appa said, "but it wasn't that my question bothered him. It was from the effort of concentrating all his inmost strength and resolve on keeping his ureter closed. If he'd had an odometer hitched to his ass, he would've logged seven miles in that chair.

" 'Yeah,' he said through clenched teeth, 'yeah, I know his name. Lemme think just a second here: Brennan's his name, yeah, his name's Brennan. I met him once, nice-looking guy, maybe six or eight years older'n I am. Lives over in Quincy, that's where he is. The computer guy's name is Doug Brennan.' "

"*Bing*-go," Dennison said softly. He sighed almost inaudibly, sitting there in the gloom, visible only in silhouetted shadow to Dell'Appa, his dusky voice over a hundred years away. "So, you were right all along. All that's left to get now are the details. Oh, shit."

Dell'Appa nodded. The lamp next to him meant that Dennison could see what his face did as he spoke. "Yeah," he said, keeping expression out of everything except his voice and eyes. "Sorry, boss, and I really do mean that. I thought I was right, right from the beginning. It hadda be something like that. I began to be sure, when I was at Coldstream, and Joey said 'ferret-legging.' There's only one person I ever heard say that before it came out of his mouth, and that was our friend, Bob Brennan."

"He got it from Bomber," Dennison said. "Bomber in one of his moods. I know. I was there the same day. When Bob and I were both young troopers, back around the time that South Carolina decided to secede and see how that played up the coast, Bomber got the wind up him one day and told us about how the Highlanders, Scotland and Wales, put hungry live ferrets down the fronts of their pants and bet on who'll stand it the longest."

Dennison chuckled. "It was a really great story," he said. "He had all of us clutching our balls. And it was years later, I guess, 'fore I asked him one day, and I don't know how it came up, what it was that brought it up, but I said to him: 'Bomber, goddamn it, tell me something for just once now, will you? Is that story about ferrets true?'

"And he looked me straight in the eye and he laughed. 'Of course not,' he said, 'I made it up.' And I said to him: 'Why, you bastard, why did you do that to us, nice innocent young guys like us? Because you know that we all believed it. We believed anything that you said.'

"And he said: 'Yeah, I did know that, and that's why I did it. To teach you you shouldn't do that. You should never believe everything anyone tells you, no matter how good he is. He'll lie to you then just for fun.' "

"Yeah," Dell'Appa said, "well that was the beginning, after all these years, of a trail of breadcrumbs that was leading me right home. But then when I *really* knew, when I knew for sure, that I'm right and now we're gonna prove it—which was when the kid said: 'Doug and Laura,' that was when it first hit me: *Right, I was right, and we're gonna prove it, all right. Because once he says it, we gonna have to prove it. Because from now on, we're not gonna have any choice.* I started to hope—and this amazed the hell out of me; not what I expected at all—I started to hope that we weren't. That he wouldn't tell me what I knew he was going to tell me, because I knew that it was going to be what I'd known, I had known all along. I wanted him to say something else, entirely, so I'd never even dreamed of what I knew. The trouble was that I had. It really made me feel sad, and I mean that. I really wish now I'd been wrong. That there was a way that maybe you knew, a way to un-find something out, to un-know something you knew. But I don't think that there is."

"No help for it," Dennison said slowly and still almost inaudibly in the shadows. "He that increaseth wisdom increaseth sorrow. Some days, you get the bear; some days, the bear gets you. Come on, kid, I'll buy you a drink."

15 "Bob did not look good when he opened the door and came into Brian's office," Dell'Appa said to his wife in the golden light concentrated in their kitchen by the thickness of the early December evening outside. The chicken roasting in the oven had been expertly-fattened, and the aroma of it made him salivate. He was trying to hurry the process of opening the jug of cabernet sauvignon, in order to have something to put down his throat until the chicken was ready, so that he left the leaded collar torn raggedly around the top.

"He looked gray and bleached-out at the same time, like an old sweatshirt starting to fray around the cuffs and neck, pile all pilled-up and the shape mostly gone, not quite ready for throw-away yet, but right on the brink of it, 'thout any question—no more'n two washes away from extinction, and then into the rag bag. He looked like a big bag of shit, is really what the guy looked like. It's possible he did have the flu."

" 'Possible,' " Gayle said, "meaning: 'Maybe I'd like to kiss a pig after all, maybe it's not so bad.' You don't think so, that is, that he really had had a virus."

"Approximately that, yeah," he said. "I don't doubt for a minute that he was *sick;* I'm sure he was as sick as a rat. I just don't think he was sick with the flu. It was Thursday when I went down to Plymouth and hoovered the very lint out of Ernie Nugent's navel. Until I left the jail, neither one of the Brennans would've had any way of knowing, any reason to suspect, that I'd gotten anything out of Ernie. The best they could've done, knowing I'd gone down there and the name of the man I wanted to talk to—as of course Bob would've known, working out of the same office, Thursday noon at the latest; he's not a bad detective except when he wants to be, has a motive to be one—was that I must've run up against something that connected Nugent to Mossi."

He had seated the corkscrew firmly and the cork came out of the neck of the jug cleanly enough, but when he poured the first glass the ragged edge of the leaded collar caused some of the wine to dribble over the lip of the glass, so that it puddled on the countertop. He said "Oh goddamnit," put the jug down, used one paper-towel to mop up the spill and moistened another to clean the wine off the outside of the bowl of the glass. Then he trimmed the collar properly around the neck of the jug and resumed filling the glass, concentrating at the same time on not drooling. As soon as he had filled it, Gayle reached deftly around his back and filched it from the counter. *"Hey,"* he said, "that was mine."

"You can pour another one," she said, drinking from the glass. "You just opened it, you know. There's plenty still left for you."

"I know I just opened it," he said. "That's why I opened it in such a hurry and made a mess of it. Because I wanted a glass of wine."

"Mmmm," she said, after rolling it around against the roof of her mouth with her tongue in a parody of tasting a vintage, "this's really pretty nice wine. Considering that it's only cheap crap, I mean. Much better than that other brand of cheap crap we've been drinking. My mouth was just watering for a glass of wine or something."

"Well, you should've opened it, then," he said, filling a second glass. "And this isn't cheap crap, either. This is the wine that the people who actually make all the wine drink with their food in their own homes, not the pricey stuff in the bottles with the hoity-toity labels that they sell to all the doctors and professors in the stores, who if they ever even tried to grow a grape would probably grow it cubical. *Vin ordinaire,* that's what this is, *pour tout le monde ordinaire,* which is what we are. And the person who opens the bottle always gets the first glass out of it. Everyone knows that. That's the rule."

He hesitated and glanced at her. "Not," he said, "that it really should've been strictly necessary for either one of us to've opened another bottle tonight, given the fact that there was a good three-quarters of a litre left in the one that I recall opening last night."

"The rule's so the guests won't be the ones who discover it's become vinegar," she said. "That's why the rule is, I mean. Tell you to be sure to add plenty of oil to it before you pour it over the salad. Well, *I'm* not a guest, I live here. And besides, I was willing to take the chance. I don't think *you'd* give *me* vinegar. So therefore I took the wine too, along with the risk I'd accepted. And it must be prowlers got in, while we were both gone today, and drank all the wine left from last night. 'S the only possible explanation. Good thing for us that's all they wanted, half a bottle of cheap-crap red wine—they didn't take anything else, huh?" She grinned, but then erased it when he did not smile back at her. *"Yeah,"* she said, sternly, *"oh-kay,* back to business, here, Gaylesie. Stan' by your man an' all that shit. You don't think then that before you went down to see him, the Brennans knew about Nugent?"

"Probably not," he said. "Oh, they might've had some dim awareness that there was some kid named Ernie who did things now and then for Mossi, but he would've been no more than a supernumerary to them, far as they'd've been concerned. He'd only met Dougie once, years ago at the kennel. Dougie probably wouldn't even have remembered the kid, wouldn't've known last week if you'd asked him, why the kid'd even been there. That day years ago when Dougie came over to see the Rollins woman about something or other, some minor thing, computer adjustment or something, Ernie happened to be there and she introduced them? That wouldn't have meant much to him then. He'd probably forgotten the kid's name before he got his car-door shut, leaving the place—just another one of those young racetrack-hustlers, a dime for a dozen, an extra one free with each order. Two-dimensional, basically, of no importance to Doug. Part of the scenery backdrop.

"Now, though, *now* Dougie would know if you asked him who this Nugent kid is, how he fitted into the frame, absolutely, and in great detail. But then the only knowledge they had before lunchtime was only that I'd gone to see Ernie. It would've concerned them, sure; I might be onto something or I might stumble onto something. But it wouldn't've been enough to panic them; probably just enough to get them started on the phone. It was still possible, when they first found out, that all I knew about was the Reno-Chico-Franco connection that Joey used to get Ernie to babysit his brother ten or eleven years ago. That would've worried them, naturally, because whoever they talked to would've clued them in that Ernie's not too bright, if they didn't already know that. He might not have brains enough to keep his mouth shut about having worked for Olivia that same summer, and anyway, even whether in fact he'd learned anything damaging to them, as a result of working for her.

"But it wouldn't've thrown them into a state of high agitation, because, after all, why was Ernie in the lockup anyway? For complete obedience to the code of *omerta;* he's in the can for not talking. It has to be somewhat reassuring to find out that the guy who might hurt you, if he talks, is already in the jug because he *won't* talk, and very likely wouldn't know what he knows anyway, because he's fairly stupid. Long as everything stays smooth, no ripples on the pond, well, then everything's cool, and okay. All you've got to do is keep your nerve, your fingers crossed, and also a good tight asshole.

"By noon on Friday all of those things've become much harder for them to do. By then Bob's been into the office and seen that there's lots going on, some of it involving me, in which no one sees fit to include him. The water's all muddy where he is, and there aren't ripples on it, there're *whitecaps* on it. But he's too far downstream, down-current, whichever, from whatever's roiling it up, to see what the hell it might be, and he can't seem to find anyone who'll describe it to him. They all explain: it's nothin' personal, it's just that they're all just too busy, and besides, it's my wild-west show now and I'm in charge, so to find out, he'll have to ask me. And I'm nowhere to be found.

"My guess would be that by twelve-fifteen or twelve-thirty, either someone from Rollins's office or someone from Doug Brennan's bunch has found out that Ernie is gonzo, and now he's been gone a whole day. They took him out from Isolation to talk to someone Thursday morning. The Brennans of course know who this is. But then he missed lunch, and the evening meal, too, and, then Friday morning he still wasn't around, and some deputies came in and packed up all his stuff, dirty clothes and smelly socks, and took it all away someplace else. No one there seems to know where Ernie went. All they know is where he isn't, hasn't been: he hasn't come back to his cell there since I came to see him on Thursday.

"Now both the Brennans are very upset. If Doug doesn't know what all of this means, Bob does; he knows very well. He knows because he used to do it, before he turned slightly rancid. When the guy in the can goes to talk to a cop, and he doesn't come back from the chat, the guy in the can told the cop something hot, and the cop didn't want it to get cold. As it would've if the guy who gave him the hot thing got back in with the wrong type of guys. So by the middle of Friday afternoon Bob has to know that I've gotten the feds to let me borrow Ernie for a while—and why not; they weren't getting a helluva lotta use out of him—and stashed him in a fifty-dollar-a-night suite with a bring-your-own-sweetie-special-hot-and-cold Jacuzzi in a traveling-salesmen's-paradise motel, Mount-Vernon-by-the-Filter-Beds, four big-tall-white pillars—if you wanna, you can count 'em, but there's really four of them—in some South Shore industrial park right next to some six-lane highway somewhere, eighteen-wheelers roarin'-by, day and fuckin' night, and then when the sun is down, rabid raccoons everywhere—I'd think twice if I was you, I went out after dark; couple of our younger and more dashing dudes with shotguns watching CNN, ESPN, and probably dirty movies with him, washing Domino's pepperoni pizza down with Giant Diet Cokes. Oh yeah, them're the days, in the life of your above-average buckaroo, memsahib, and Bob knows 'em himself, knows 'em good.

"What Bob doesn't know, though, is which Days Inn, or Quality, or HoJo it is, or even what town I picked, for a hidey-hole to stash Ernie in, and this is a good thing for Ernie. Because if Bob did, then

Dougie would know, and when he knew, well, Franco would know. And Franco would then get ahold of Short Joey, and say to him: 'Aw right now, we found out, and this's the place. This's where that little shit is, this's the place they have got him. So go there at once and shoot him a few times, and then shoot him two more for good measure.' But what Bob does know now, and knows sure as shit, as sure as if I'd told him, is that I got something real tasty from Ernie, and it's brown-shorts-time now in the ol' bunkhouse, boys, so hunker down and jes' wait 'til your turn comes 'round, in the old three-holer outside. Bob left the office early, around three-thirty, quarter-four. Said his stomach was upset, and that, I am *very* sure, was the honest-to-God Gospel truth.

"On Monday morning, after putting in what I'm also sure was one weekend in Hell with his brother, calling anyone and everyone they could think of who might have some idea of how just much shit was in the fan and just whose shit was involved, and most likely calling upon every bit of Dougie's wizard-hackery to safecrack into the master motel-registries on the off-chance they can find out where the hell I'm bastin' Ernie nice-an'-even on the grille—with a tape-recorder and two VHS minicams running every goddamned minute, case Short Joey *does* find him, and pack him off to meet Jesus, and a steno taking notes, we'll still have his testimony—Bob called the office, on *my* line. Which he had no reason in the world to do except for the one he couldn't admit to: to find out what the hell I was doing, and how far I'd gotten doing it, if I was any closer to *him*—and of course once more I was the man who wasn't there, he had met upon the stair, on Friday; again I wasn't there.

"I was with Con Cannon in the van,—Con was staking out Ev Rollins's office down in Norton and the van's got a secure radio-phone, which the Lexus that I've got doesn't—waiting for Brian to call from the courthouse where he was with the Bloviator, and tell us we had the warrants. Whereupon I'm gonna give Finn a call where *he* is, at Olivia's kennel-farm, get Con started looting Ev's office and then go help Finn toss and pillage hers. So Bob got Rosie at the desk when I didn't pick up, and she told him I was out, as he of course already knew because I hadn't answered.

" 'Then,' Rosie told me, 'it was like the line went dead for a while. I told him you were out on assignment, but I didn't know where, or when you'd be back, and he just didn't say anything, and I said: "Hello? Hello? You still there, Bob, you okay?" Because he didn't sound good, you know? Like he usually does, pretty upbeat and happy, when we talk on the phone—you know, like he's pretending that we're having an affair. Which is, yeah, kind of corny, silly, really, stupid, you know, that Bob plays that game with me. Like I'm supposed to think when he was young, he was, you know, he was getting lots of girls? Which no one would believe now he was, if that was how he hit on them. But he likes doing it, I guess, and he never gets, you know, real dirty, so I don't really mind—I don't think it's funny, I mean, but it doesn't bother me. I guess is what I mean.' "

"Huh," Gayle said, "has Bob, has he always been like that around the office?"

"With the girls, you mean?" Harry said.

"Well, the women," she said.

"Okay, the women," he said. "With the dirty-old-man routine there, though? I dunno, not that I know of. Why?"

"Because what you'd done since you took over the Mossi case must've put him under a lot of stress, and if he hadn't been in the habit of harassing the women before, that would indicate he's undergone a personality change, a shift. And that could be an indication that he might crack, and then do something. To himself, I mean, which I assume you don't want to have happen. Which would mean that maybe you should have him watched, for his own protection," Gayle said. "At least alert his family or something."

"Well, of course I don't want him hurting himself," he said, "but I don't see who could tell me whether he's always been like this, or this's a new wrinkle for him. Rosie can't help me with that one," he said. "She wasn't even there, in the office, I mean, when I went out to Northampton. Carol was there, she had been there a long time, but she retired while I was gone, somewhere in Florida, think I heard. Denise's another one; she would've known, but she took maternity leave just around when I left, and then there was some terrible problem when the kid was born, and she still hasn't come back. And Linda, of course, she was there. But Linda's long-gone, as you know."

Gayle had removed the chicken from the oven and lifted it from the roasting-pan rack onto a platter. She was whisking flour into the chicken drippings in the pan to make a medium-brown thick gravy. She frowned but she did not say anything.

"But you probably wouldn't want me trying to track Linda down to ask her that, huh? About Bob, I mean? To talk to her about that?" he said.

Gayle poured the gravy from the pan into a small green china pitcher. "Oh, I wouldn't mind if you *talked* to her," she said. "Talk wasn't what bothered me."

"Yeah," he said, "well it sure bothered me, the talking you did to your father, and then the talking he did to his buddies from college, that went into politics there. Appointive politics, that is. Had a hell of an effect on me."

She carried the platter of chicken to the table and set it in the middle, between their places. She pursed her lips. "Now stop being silly yourself, Harry," she said. "I've told you, over and over again, Dad never did any such thing. So, once and for all, you really have to get that whole silly idea completely out of your head. He had nothing to do with what happened to you. He was just as surprised as we all were."

"And as *I* have told *you*, over and over," he said, "every damned time you've told me that, I didn't believe it the first time you said it, and I don't believe it tonight."

She went to the stove counter and rubbed her hands with a dish towel. "Yes, I know you have," she said. "Now let's just have our dinner here now, all right? Before it all gets cold on us, I mean. You can finish telling me what this Rosie told you Bob said. Because I really do want to hear all there is about Bob, his new problems, that you've created for him. Not about problems we may've had, but managed to put behind us, or not had, if we didn't, if we never had them, long ago, back in the past."

"Okay," he said, tautly, "we'll just have it your way again. Like we did with Roy, and with the Abbey School; like we do with everything, seems like." She scowled but she didn't reply.

"Rosie said when he tried to start talking again, 'he sounded, you know, kind of funny? Like he wasn't really sure where he was? He wasn't really saying words, just sort of mumbling, kind of. And then I heard him clear his throat and say "Yeah, yeah, I'm still here." And then he asked me to switch him over to Lieutenant Dennison, and I said he wasn't in the office either. So Bob goes: "Oh, is he with Harry, or do you know if he is?" And I said I didn't know, but I thought he was, you and the lieutenant'd been going to meet some-place today before you both came in, but I wasn't really sure and I really didn't know. And then Bob cleared his throat again and said, well, did I know if you were out on the Mossi case, if that was where you were, and I said I didn't even know there was, we even had, a Mossi case, in the office.' Which in fact Rosie doesn't. Except for Brian and the Bloviator, no one in the office, in the field or totally inside, knows what cases we have got except the ones they're working on. 'And he goes "No, no, I guess you probably wouldn't, at that. It's one of those things: you hadda be there." Like I made him feel bad or something.

"'And I asked him if I should have either you or the lieutenant call him when you came in, or you called in, like whether this was some kind of an *emer*gency he had or something, and he said: "No, no, no need of that. Just tell Brian for me, honey, or if anyone else asks, I won't be coming in today. I came down with that damned Rumanian flu Friday night, or whatever the name is that they've got for it this year, and I really don't feel good. So if anyone's looking for me, well, I might be able to come in tomorrow, and I will if I can, got some stuff I want to get cleaned up in there, but if I'm still running a temperature . . . well, just say I'm home, sick in bed, and I'll come in as soon as I can, without taking a chance of giving this damned misery to everyone else in the place."' "

"He was just afraid to face everybody, you think?" she said. "Face anybody he knew in there, I mean? Not necessarily you."

"I don't think he'd quite reached that point yet," he said. "Maybe he was, staying home, playing sick, to get more time to steel himself for the ordeal of what he must've known by then was coming, in his guts, but I tend to doubt it. As much as I've disliked Bob, ever since I met him—really hated him, in fact, at one point—I've never said I thought he was stupid or afraid. If he had medicine that he was going to have to take—and by then he had to know he did—Bob is not the kind of guy who'd run and hide from it. No, he'd pride himself on showing up on time when he had to get it, full-pack, too: clean uniform, boots freshly-shined and all brass polished, for the firing-squad. My guess is it was more likely by then, sometime on Monday, that Dougie and Olivia and the other chirping members of his swarming-beeping nerd-herd'd tapped into some computer somewhere that'd given up some data that we still don't know exist. Which they'd used to make a model of what we were likely getting out of holding hands with Ernie."

"So by then they knew what you were doing," she said. "Where you were headed, I mean."

"Pretty much, yeah," he said. "They had nothing specific to go on from Ev Rollins's copy of the warrant Con'd executed at his office or the one Finn'd slapped on her lesbian nibs there. Bry and I'd had the Bloviator draw 'em just as loose's law allows, but just the fact that we'd picked those particular two places to hit, that alone told them quite a lot. Basically what the paper said was that Ernie was a reliable witness, with a reputation for truth and veracity—which of course everybody's got until he's formally convicted of perjury or major fraud, at least for search-warrant purposes—who'd told us Reno and Chico, and Franco and Joey, and Ev and Livia, were all in cahoots, to do all kinds of mischievious deeds. And that based on surveillances we had conducted, confirming what Ernie had said, we therefore did swear and affirm that there was probable cause to believe that those six people had been, and were indeed still, cahooting, wilfully and maliciously, in the buildings occupied by them and more specifically described as two structures in Norton and Mansfield, in the Commonwealth aforesaid and like that, and that there was therefore probable cause to believe that physical and electronic evidence of the means, equipment and methods employed in and for the commission of the said felonious cahooting, to wit: evasion of taxes due and owing to the Department of Revenue of the Office of the Treasurer of the Commonwealth of Massachusetts, was to be found, practically begging to be found, right there in those very buildings."

"But not mentioning Bob or his brother," she said.

"Correct, naming neither of them," he said, slicing more chicken, "and leaving out therefore our *total* assurance that when we have sifted all the stuff we seized, and've wrung Ernie utterly dry, we'll have lethal proof that those six people had made up an ensemble arranged and conducted, if not cahooted, by Dougie. Franco and Joey and Ev, and Chico and Reno'd all been racketeering along at a rollicking good pace, with no help from modern technology, long before Dougie and Livia'd teamed up together, to kick Franco's operation into hyper-space, warp-speed. But after those two cherubs made their way into the mix, it was digital crime in a different dimension. I mean, Don Vito thought he knew from organized crime, but he never knew nothin' like this. The reason he didn't want nobody, no time, askin' him 'bout his business, was that compared to this generation of vipers, he didn't know what his business was. Bob's brother may look like Saint Anthony of Padua or something, but behind that clear-conscience gaze of those sparkling brown eyes is the mind of a criminal genius."

"Well," she said, "I realize you've cracked a major case and all, a monster case, yeah, but're you sure? A criminal genius? You think he's Rasputin or something? You're saying he's a Professor Moriarty, Sergeant Bob Brennan's kid brother from Quincy?"

"He isn't yet," he said, "but that's purely because he's only been at it a while, no more'n three or four years. If he'd made better use of his time, he would be, but he didn't find his métier right off, right out of college. First he futzed around five or six years, trying various kinds of careers, like a casual shopper who doesn't need anything browsing the suits down in Filene's Basement, seeing if any one of them yells: 'Hey, asshole, buy me.' Little of this, a little of that. The Franco-loop he got into by purest accident, but it was the same kind of accident for him that Saint Paul had on the road to Tarsus, or wherever the hell he was on the way to, when he got knocked off of his horse there. This man'd then found his life's work, found his life's work in that instant. What God'd put him here for.

"Dougie's wife Laura grew up in Wellesley. She'd known Olivia at Wellesley High School, both on the girls' varsity swim-team. They stayed in touch after they graduated. Laura went to Emmanuel, and Olivia went to Bentley. Laura met Dougie at some college-hangout bar during his last year at BU, he was in computer science and she was in Ann Taylor clothes, so it was obvious at once that they'd been fashionably designed to complement each other perfectly. He complimented her and she complimented him, and one thing led smoothly to another, as things are supposed to, for two such perfect, young people.

"When they got married, Laura and Dougie, Livia was maid of honor. They stayed in touch after that, too. So then when Olivia quit her first job—she'd been working for five or six years for Ballard, Weaver and Sales, out of their Minneapolis office, and wanted to come back to New England—and backpacked her career in accounting into her dad and Joe's racing kennels, she naturally went to Doug for microchips and high-speed modems, scanners, everything in sight. Where else, after all, could she get a better price, than from her old friend Laura's Dougie?

"Well, he put it all—and I mean *all*—together for her in that backroom office there. All her stuff'd been, when it came out, absolute state-of-the-art. And it still isn't that old, even now; few new programs and upgrades'll kick that system right back up to top-grade again, Brian can cadge a few bucks from the budget, after we forfeit the stuff to ourselves. I felt like I was raiding the command-bridge of an Aegis missile cruiser. But for the happy fact that I'd suspected she'd have it, and'd dropped that little word 'equipment' into the warrant application and the warrant the judge signed, the gear I saw when I went in there would've made me moan and slobber. But I did have the word in there, so now the evidence includes all the goodies Dougie got her, to do what she'd been doing, and she has instead of them her very own copy of the warrant, plus a lot of newly-vacant desk- and counter-space. That was one very good warrant.

"Yes ma'am, Dougie really did that lady proud. And she knew it, and was grateful, and they remained on the friendliest terms. We know this because if you look at the list of Coldstream Track Records, they print them in the front of the program, the dog that holds them at five-sixteenths of a mile —just over thirty seconds— and also at three-eighths—just under thirty-seven—is Error Kennel's 'Laura's Dougie,' set a year ago. Olivia named one of her very best animals, big blue male sprinter, over seventy pounds, for her friend Laura's sweet young hubby, Douglas Brennan. And a very good doggie Laura's Dougie still is, at least a second better at his best distances most outings than the average animal."

Gayle laughed sourly. "I'm not sure I'd like it, if someone named a racing-dog after me," she said. "With my luck, it'd be a loser. And a bitch, too, of course—throw *that* in there before you do. 'Came in last again, you bitch, ha ha?' " She shook her head. " 'Worse'n average animal.' Uh-uh, nope, wouldn't like that at all."

He had been cutting a large slice of chicken-breast on his plate, making the division neatly across the striations of the meat after first having scraped the concealing gravy off. He stopped for a moment and looked up at her. Her eyes were dull, and her head waggled slightly. He furrowed his forehead and then shook his head. He looked down at his plate again, and resumed cutting the meat. "Aw right, *whaaat*," she said, drawing it out.

He shook his head again. "Uh-uh," he said. "I don't think so." He kept his gaze on the plate and lifted the chicken to his mouth.

"Yeah," she said, "right. You don't think so. Well, I *do,* you got that? *I* think so." She put her fork down and picked up her wine. She stared at him over the glass, and then nodded twice. "Well," she said, "yeah, I got to hand it, you. By sweet Jesus, I do, I hand it to you. I got to hand it to you. Or else nobody does, nobody has to, hand it to you's what I mean. Because by Jesus, they *can't,* hand it to you, because you've already got it. If it's something you want, if it's something you wanted, well then, by Jesus, it's not gonna last very long. Because you will just *take* it, if it's what you want. You don't stand on no ceremony. A little taste-a Harry in the night. Harry was here and he wrecked me.

"And by Jesus, you never change," she said, slapping the table with the palm of her right hand. "You're as constant the moon'n the tides. You decide you know something, no one else knows, and nobody else agrees with you? Everyone else thinks you're nuts? Well, hell, that's all right, that doesn't matter, you don't give a good flyin' *fuck. Nothin'* matters to you, 'cept what matters to *you.* What you think is what rules the world. Nothin' else makes no difference at all. Ahh Rockies may crumble, Gibraltar c'n tumble, but old Harry, he's made-ah stone, an' old Harry, he stays jus' the same. I knew, yes, I *knew,* you went out there, you, you *bassar,* I knew if you ever came back, did make it back here, I knew you would manage to do this. Him. *Something* to him. I knew you would do this to Bob. Zackly *what?* I dinn' know that, an' I dinn' know *how,* an' I dinn' know *when,* but by Jesus, I knew you would do it.

"I said it to Dad, I said it him then, I said: 'Mark my words, he'll come back. He won't stay out there and he won't send for me; he won't do anything like that. He will come back, like Godzilla, he will, like ah fuckin' Assyrian, 'syrian there, inna purple an' gold, you know who I mean, *down* likeah wolf onna fold, his *cohort* . . . that it, it's his *cohort* 'at's gleamin', in purple an' gold, uh-huh, you wait an' see. He will know, and he'll pay us *all,* back.'

"And he wooln't listen to me. None of them'd listen to me. Stupid dumb woman, I guess. What possible fuck could she know? Well, that's all right, I still knew. And I was still right, wasn't I, matter how long it took. And that's another thing 'at there is with you: no time. Time's got no meanin' for you, doesn' mean anythin', you. With you when you get an idea in your *head,* a year could be an *hour,* 'n *hour* could be a *year,* jus' dunn' matter at all, you. Because I knew what I knew about you, and I still know, what I know, an' I know to this very day: I knew you *never* forget. Fuckin' elephant, that's what you are: Harry never forgets. In your former life you're an elephant, or else in your next one, you'll be. One. So . . . anyway, anyway," she shook her head, "I knew jus' what you'd do. An' I was . . . fuckin' right, too." She stared at him, blinking; her eyes were filling up fast enough so that pretty soon it would be not only reasonable but necessary to cry.

"And by Jesus," she said, toasting him with the glass, "give me credit for that, and give you credit, too. Harry, you've *done* it, just what I said, you came back and you've begun getting even. What do you call this, on your mental agenda? 'Item One: Brennan, Robert, Sergeant Bob'? 'Okay, that takes care of *that* motherfucker. Cross him offa the list there, that's *one* down. On to the next entry here.' How many more, 've you got to go, 'fore you get down to me?"

"Go to bed, Gayle," he said, "like you've told me to do, nights when I've done what you've done tonight. Sleep's all that remains for that day, and nothing's very much fun."

She stared at him. " 'Item X,' " she said slowly, " 'Gayle Fairhurst Dell'Appa.' Come on, tell me: I know I'm on it. And now I would like to know. Well, sort of, I wanna—I *don't* really, wanna, but I know I *should* wanna, 'cause I have got *work* to do here, *work,* aheadah me here, and I should get, get started on it. I should be beginnin', gettin' started again here, plannin' ah . . . rest of my life." She lifted the glass and drained it.

"Oh, sorry," Brennan said, finding Dell'Appa in Dennison's office when he opened the door and came in. "Rosie said that you wanted, see me, boss. Didn't just mean to barge in."

273

"You're not, Bob," Dennison said, "barging in here, I mean. I did want to see you, as soon's you came in. And Harry here's part of the meeting. Come in. Close the door. Have a seat."

Brennan frowned. "Uh-huh," he said, "I see." He turned his back partially to them, so that the roll of middle-aged stoutness bulging his shirt at his waist, topping the walnut butt of the old Smith & Wesson snub-nosed .38 holstered on his belt above his right kidney, stood out in better relief, and closed the door very slowly and carefully, not making much noise at all. He turned again toward the desk and smiled, turning his head to include each of them individually, making little mincing steps to the vacant chair at the right corner of the front of Dennison's desk. He sat down gingerly, like a man with a sacroiliac problem he has learned from sharp pain had better not be trifled with, and folded his hands in his lap. He nodded. He smiled again, without showing any of his teeth, chipmunking his cheeks fatly for them, so that Dell'Appa for the first time noticed a general just-awakened puffiness about the man, as though not only the flesh around his eyes but his entire physique had commenced retaining fluids to excess. "Well, here I am, boss," he said, "seeing you seeing me, seeing you, just like you had in mind there. I don't seem to have a scorecard-line-up with me, though, for today's game, you know? Didn't pick one up, my way in. So I'm not sure which one we're playing. Which game I mean, you're playing today."

Dennison looked at Dell'Appa, smiling and raising his eyebrows. Dell'Appa imitated him, adding a shrug. Dennison looked back at Brennan. "You're good, Bob," he said, "you are good. Can't take that away from you, can they."

"Hope not, Lieutenant," Brennan said, preserving the bulging smile. "Man's got to have something, can hang onto in this stormy world. I'd like to think I got that."

"So then, Bob," Dennison said, "you're fully recovered and back on the job, we can take it?"

Brennan relaxed his facial muscles and shook his head once. "Well, I don't know about all of that," he said, "not sure of quite all of that. I'm pretty-well recovered, I guess, from the flu I mean—sure hope you guys don't get what I had. But as for that part about 'back on the job,' I'm not really sure about that. The 'back' part, that's right; I'm right here; you can see me. But the 'job' part, that's harder, that part I'm not sure of. I know when I left here last Friday, I think it was, days all sort of *blend,* you know, with each other, blend *together,* you run a high fever. Hard to say, then, later on, pin something down, when it happened there, which one was which. But I'm pretty sure it was Friday, and I know when I went home to be sick privately, I did leave a job at my desk."

He shook his head and widened his eyes. "It isn't there now, though," he said. "I came in this morning, thought it'd be there, right where it always's been. But son of a bitch, the fool thing wasn't there, and now I can't find it anyplace now; it's just nowhere to be found. I've looked high and low, under this, top of that, well, you both know how it gets, we all had it happen to us, most normal thing inna world. You're sittin' at home and you hear the phone ring, phone rings and you're reading, all right? You know what you do because we all do this, we all do the exact same thing. Once we're past forty, at least."

He glanced at Dell'Appa. "Most of you kids wouldn't know about this yet. But you will, never fear, in good time." He looked back at Dennison. "But you know this, you're one of us older folks: all it takes for it is, the phone rings — we forget what we did with our glasses. Say 'Oh shit, who the hell can this be, callin' at this fuckin' hour? When I'm trynah relax, for Chrissake.' Get outta the chair, take your glasses off, go an' answer the thing. Which as often as not, and we all know this too, it's prolly a wrong fuckin' number.

"Some asshole didn't bother, look it up right, didn't watch what he's doin', he dialed it, so he calls you up instead, bothered you? Well, that's just too bad then, fuck you. He can even get mad when you tell him you won't, look up the right number for him. I had people do that, swear at me when I wouldn't, after they called me up by mistake, like it was my fault or something." He made his voice a nasal falsetto: " 'But I'm callin' from *outta state,* Mister. I ain't got no phone-book for *there.' "* He resumed his normal voice. " 'I don't give a shit—call up Information. That's what they're there for: find numbers.' I show no mercy the bastards. 'No prisoners. Shoot the wounded': that's what I say.

"Back when I was Uniform, had the fuckin' whistle, I used to blow it at those guys. I'd get home from days-on, I got my days-off, keep that whistle right by the phone. And when I would get a wrong-number guy—and we got a shitload of wrong numbers then; our number was almost the same as the priest-house, I think it was one digit off, from Saint Andrew's rectory there. And every Sunday, and Easter and Christmas—Christmas, Jesus, was *awful,* alla the people that go once a year, dunno know what time that anythin' is, call after call after call"—in the whining falsetto again—" 'What time's midnight Mass gonna be?' And I would say, oh very polite, naturally: 'Just a moment, please,' and I'd grab that whistle. Give them a full blast, right in their ear. Although of course I dunno what it did, church attendance, the monthly collection. Prolly didn't help much, the assholes think their pure holy priests're hurtin' their poor ears like that: 'Go to mass there? Think I'm nuts? No, I ain't goin' there; the priest at Saint Andrew's 's crazy.' Priests had've known, they might not've liked it.

"But anyway, that's what you get, you get every time, you just had yourself one of those fuckers, and then you come back, you sit down in the chair, an' it never fails, the goddamned glasses are *gone,* they took off, your fuckin' glasses aren't there. One wrong number, you lose twenny minutes or so, lookin' for those goddamned glasses. You could've been enjoyin' yourself, hey, you even were, that's what you were doin', before that fuckin' phone rang. You were enjoyin' yourself, there havin' a nice, quiet-good time, and now what're you? All pissed off.

"Well, this'll surprise you, I know it will, because I know that it surprised me, I found out it happened, this mornin'. The exact same thing we've all had with our glasses, our car-keys, our left glove, your best pair-ah pliers; all of that stuff disappears, and we get sort of used to it there. It gets so it's almost like: we expect it, that stuff's gonna vanish on us. An' when it does, well, *yeah,* we're pissed off then too, it's not just losin' our glasses that does it, but we're certainly not really surprised. We forget where we put everything, get to our age, sometimes how old we even are. You get used to it after a while.

"But this morning, I am surprised. This's the first time I can ever remember, that I had this happen to me. Had a job disappear, just like that." He snapped the thumb and middle of his left hand, making a crisp report. "It happened my father, a long time ago, he had it happen to him. But in his case it wasn't just his job that vanished, it was a whole fuckin' store, an entire *supermarket,* A and P there, he had disappear on him—they closed down the whole place he worked.

So it wasn't just him, that lost his job, it was everyone else that he'd worked with for years, they lost their jobs, too. People he'd known for thirty and forty, one of them forty-two years? Hey, this was no joke, when that happened. To some of them, all those hard-workin' people, lost their job, outta work, onna street. 'Thanks for all your help, all you done for us here, the past forty-five years, but now get the fuck outta here, willya? We ain't got no more use for you.'

"Well, he didn't like it, my father, I mean, none of 'em liked it a hell of a lot, but at least they weren't baffled, like I am. They at least knew that it really'd happened and it wasn't nothin' that they did themselves, like they were careless or somethin'. Like you're always readin' about, seein' on TV or somethin', some woman puts her baby onna roofah car, while she gets out her keys to unlock it, and then she gets in, shuts the door, starts it up, she isn't thinkin' about it, why should she? It's all, it's all perfectly normal, isn't it? Did her shoppin', got that done, and now she is doin' what everyone does after that: what she's doin' is, she's drivin' home. And she don't even know, 'til some cop pulls her over, her kid's still onna roofah the car there. Well, that's what I feel like I did, like I must've done, there, or something, to have this experience I'm havin' here, havin' this happen to me."

Dennison looked at Dell'Appa and tilted his head. Dell'Appa smiled and shook his head. "What can I say, Brian, that you didn't get through just sayin', huh? This here guy, he really is good. The guy is the fuckin' best that there ever was, fuckin' best inna whole fuckin' world. When it comes to trampin' up dust, and layin' down smokescreens, I'll tell you, no one else I know even comes close, let alone anyone who can touch him, compete with him when he's doin' this. Bob Brennan can confuse obfuscation when he wants; he could murk up an enigma. When it comes to creating total bewilderment out of clear and simple reality, well, there's no one can carry his hat."

"The fuck're you think you're talkin' to here, asshole college-boy," Brennan said, growling, to Dell'Appa. "Who the fuck do you think you're kiddin' here? You think I don't know what you're doin' to me, you're kissin' the lieutenant's ass alla time here, ever since you come back this office? *Bullshit*, I don't know. I'm not stupid, you know. I know there's a knife right in my fuckin' back, this fuckin' minute, and I know too who put that knife there. And whose fuckin' knife that fuckin' knife is. It's your fuckin' knife, you tinhorn cocksucker, that's whose fuckin' knife that knife is.

"I was downah Cape seein' Bomber, yesterday, and I told him what you've been doin'. And you know what the Bomber, what he said-ah me? He said: '*Bobby,* if I was still up there, you know . . . if I was still up there in charge, and I was still runnin' that show, that punk wouldn't be doin' this to you, he *couldn't* be doin' this to you, because I wouldn't've, *let* him do it. I'd've had him stomped down so fast he'd be buyin' used suits, get somethin' to fit him, second-hand-me-downs from circus midgets. They just never change, those damn punks never do, you can tell 'em the minute you see 'em, and the worst thing you can do is forget what you saw, when you saw them, the first time you caught sight of the bastards. Because every time that you thought you'd spotted one, it would always turn out you were right. And that's what it always did, always turned out you were right. Every fuckin' damn time. Every last fuckin' time.' "

"Well, I think we've got to admit it, Harry," Dennison said, "this gentleman's very generous. He doesn't just give you one *plat du jour* problem, either take it or come back tomorrow, he lays out a whole fuckin' buffet." He exhaled heavily and looked back at Brennan.

"Now lemme see, Robert," he said, "where *do* we begin? How to choose from this rich, varied offering? Do I say 'Okay, so you weren't sick yesterday; all right, since we mustn't defraud Mother Common-wealth here—the old girl takes it so *personally,* you know, her own cops get caught breaking her laws—be sure you put that down as *vacation,* not *sick leave*'?

"Or do I say: 'Well, the insult's ingenious, ringing my ailing rabbi up at long-distance not only to endorse your anger at me but to voice as well his own, and very personal indeed, denunciation of me, using you as his proxy'? Or then again, perhaps, I should choose simply to state the most obvious and egregious among the several scurvy and offensive insubordinations you've just managed to commit all at once, in a bunch, and just tell you to your face that your blasphemy of Bomber is a sorry, pathetically-bare-assed, *out-and-out, fucking, damned,* lie, because anyone who's been in touch with him or with his daughters or his wife since a year ago Thanksgiving—as I have, every week, not that I'm the only one—knows our estimable mentor's been in la-la land since then, as vacant and as cuckoo as the purest of the blessed angels in the sky. And the fact that I know why you fabricated that mean and contemptible lie—abject, guilty desperation—doesn't mitigate its nastiness at all; it's men who act like you just did who given self-pity a bad name."

Brennan did not say anything. His face had flushed, gradually becoming dark red, but his gaze did not waver from Dennison's face. "Cut the shit, Lieutenant, all right?" he said in a low voice; it was under his control and did not tremble. "Whaddaya say we quit fucking around here and just get to the fuckin' point, huh? Save everyone's time in this thing, and a whole lot of damned aggravation. You want my badge, my friend? You *got* my badge, my friend. Have someone add up, I've got coming to me, vacation built-up, the bonus for the sick-leave that I never took much of—in all the years I been here I might've taken ten days, max—and I'll go outta here today, retire on terminal leave. You want me out? Okay, I'll clear out, see if some other outfit can still find some use for me, man with the experience I've got, 'sides the AARP, or the Hair Club for Men."

Dennison and Dell'Appa looked at each other and shook their heads almost simultaneously. Dennison focused his eyes on his hands on the top of his desk and frowned, shaking his head again. He looked up at Brennan. He cleared his throat. "Bob," he said, "we've had our differences in the course of working together many years. Would've been a miracle if we hadn't, I suppose, two men with such very different styles, different ways of looking at things and different ways of going about them, thrown in together as long as we have been, over twenty years. But good Christ, man, as many times as I could've throttled you; and as many times, I'm sure at least as many, as you were tempted to use your service revolver to persuade me of your point of view, overcome my stubborness; and as hard as it must've been for you, when I succeeded Bomber in this job I know you wanted . . ."

"More'n 'wanted,'" Brennan said. "I was also told, I was fuckin' all-but-*promised,* by two people over Bomber, that when he took retirement I'd be next line for this job. And I would've had it, too, if this AG and this governor hadn't been so damned determined to just throw out all the tried-'n-true ways that've worked for generations, and the men who've worked with them, all the men who've made them work and were the reason that they did, and just turn the whole division over to the punks like him." He jerked his head at Dell'Appa, then fixed his eyes back on Dennison.

"They didn't pick you because I did anything wrong, or there was something bad in my record. They did it because there was one thing you did so much better'n I did that I couldn't compete with you on it, and I wouldn't've if I could have—kissing civilian, executive asses. The way I was trained in this job, the way that Bomber trained me, I was trained that this is a paramilitary operation that we're involved in here every day, and that we're a kind of domestic soldier, and that's why we behave like soldiers do: because that's what we are.

"Now I know that a lot of asses get kissed and sucked-on in the military, too, especially in peacetime, and I know that pretty often that's what pays off there, but I know too what I was told: it wasn't going to happen here. This was going on merit only, strictly merit, all the way. Wasn't one man, told me that, two men told me that. It was even in the papers, inna gossip columns there, all the inside-political stuff there, that I was the one next in line for this job when the Bomber finally stepped down. And then he did, and it was time, the time'd come for them to do it, to deliver on what they said, give it to me, and what did they do then? They turned around and fucked me, up the front and down the back. That was what they did to me, those dirty rotten bastards: they gave me a royal fucking, fucked me right up the fucking ass.

"Okay, that's the history lesson. That's how we all got here today, in our places here. So here I am, and there you are, with your little stooge here nodding, every word you say, logging-in his smoochies now, so that when you retire, he'll take over your place here and get his own ass kissed, by his own seven dwarfs. I sit here and you guys can double-team me all you want, pound me to a fuckin' boneless bloody pulp, and there isn't one damned thing on this whole fuckin' earth that I can do about it. What a thing to have to say, after all the years of being what I've been in this outfit, what a fuckin' thing to say, fuckin' thing to have to say."

He took a deep breath. "So, that's what I am telling you, you see what I'm saying? I didn't think you'd do it to me, when you got the job. I saw the possibility, sure, I saw it there, that you'd get rid of me, but somehow I thought: 'Brian? Nah, Brian's bigger'n that. He wouldn't do that to me. He would not do that to anybody, Brian and me maybe don't always get along, okay, but Brian wouldn't do a thing like that. Brian is a man.'

"Well, was I ever fuckin'-wrong on that one. There is one I booted, if you want to add those up, and you won't need all your fingers, my mistakes in all these years; I booted that one good, kicked it clear to Mars, when I predicted what you would and wouldn't do, because of what I thought you were, kind of man you were. You're doin' it in spades. Well, Jesus, okay, then I'm fucked then. Go ahead and do what you wanna do, willya? Heave me in the fuckin' street, if that's what you're gonna do: 'Many thanks, all your hard work. Now please go and fuck yourself.' I can't stop you and I know it, and you know I know it. I can't even make it hard for you—you're the man who's got the power. You've got the power now. But for Christ sake, get it over with. Take the money and go home. You won. You had the cards."

Dennison sighed. He looked at Dell'Appa. "I don't seem to be getting through, Harry," he said. "You wanna give it a try?"

"No," Dell'Appa said.

"Look," Dennison said, "try to think of that suggestion as a direct order, a command delivered by a superior officer. Does that help you to gain a better perspective on it?"

Dell'Appa nodded and exhaled. "I hadn't looked at it from that angle, sir," he said. "Yes, sir, I will give it a shot." He shifted in his chair so that he faced Brennan. "I know you know 'em, Bob, your rights, so I'm not gonna Miranda you here unless you make me do it. I've got a form you can sign that'll do it, take care of it, and that'll spare both of us the humiliation of me telling you that you've got *this* right, and *that* right, and then some more rights, after those rights, and you know something? I would appreciate it. I know you don't like me, and you know I don't like you, so there is one thing we agree on, and considering the big bagga shit we're both in here, that we've got ourselves in, that's really not such a bad start. In fact, it's damned miracle. So whaddaya say, sign the form?"

Brennan stared at him the way a middle-aged man contemplates the young gum-chewing technician named Tricia who is about to tell him how to arrange himself for the trip through the CAT-Scanner cylinder. "You know," he said, softly in a sorrowfully-reflective tone of voice, "when you first come in here, kid, I thought that you had some promise. A whole lotta promise in fact. Like I always did with alla the young guys, most of the young guys come in. 'Hey, so he's young, can't hold that against him. You also were young once yourself. He maybe knows something, you didn't notice, didn't happen to catch your attention, you could end up, you learn somethin' from him, somethin' that you didn't know.'

"And that's the attitude I always took, well, attitude that I *triedah* take, anyway, with alla the new kids come in, all of the time I was here, ever since *I* first come in. But Jesus H. Christ, you made it impossible. I couldn't do that with you. You were all over the whole fuckin' *lot* here, into *this*, into *that*, and then it would be somethin' else. I couldn't keep up with you there. I say to myself: 'Jesus H. Christ, who is this fuckin' kid? How'd we ever get by without him? And what makes him think that we didn't, we never got anything done, until he comes through the door and saves us?

"Because Jesus Christ, that is how you were, then. That's how you acted back then, and that wasn't that long ago, either. So, that was the sequence, at least for me, at least as far as I'm concerned, how the two of us there got wrong-footed. You first come in, you're like everyone else; you're someone I don't even know. What I hope is I'm gonna at least like you some, that we will at least get along. Because, after all, I don't wanna get married, you—I'm married to Margaret already, and one Margaret's enough for me. I don't hire and fire here, can't get rid of you; I'm just one of the regulars, field-hands, myself. I got no power at all. I do what I do, and I go home at night, and then the next day, I come in again. Do some more of my usual stuff, kind of stuff I spent yesterday doin'. Because that is the job that I have. I think that's the job too, that you also have, and that you can't get me thrown out of. Well, of course we know that on that one at least, I make a small miscalculation.

"Well, hey, that's how you make reputations. Pontius Pilate may not've been that bad a procurator, we don't know, got no way of knowing, this late date, he got assigned to Judea. But, boy, look what happened when he got his big case, when old Pontius got his biggest case: fucked it up, major-league, big-time. Said: 'Okay, my finding is: Rome's got no beef with him. That means that I turn him loose here. But, all of you Jews there, you want him, you got him. Take Jesus and get the fuck out of here, all right? I'm sickah wastin' my time with this shit, all these petty damned argments you got. Now get him the fuck out of here.' And that's the end of old Pontius there, far as the history books go. That guy is finished, *kaput* and road-kill, kiss his sorry ass good-bye one last time.

"But anyway, chances are, when you first come in here, I'm gonna work with you here. I'm not gonna have any choice, if somebody's brought you in, right? And, life is easier, I always believe, if all of the people who work in one place can get along with each other, you know? If they can just get along.

"Well," Brennan said, "you know, it didn't matter. It just didn't matter at all. A lot of things don't, like that, matter, you find out as you go along. That they didn't matter at all. You got into that business with that little girl there, what's her name, Linda, and she was what, nineteen, eighteen or so, nineteen? Too young for you, anyway, *'way* too young for a guy your age, and a married guy, too, don't leave that out. Which anyway I thought was a terrible thing, and you knew because I told you that. I had the balls, told you right to your face, that you're not bein' fair to anyone here, anyone who's involved in it. Your own nice young wife, a good woman who loves you, or your kid, and quite obvious, no matter what she said, not fair to Linda, not fair to the rest of us, work in this office, can't help seein' what's goin' on here, right under our very own *noses*. Women and men *both*'re talkin'; not like they're all *blind* there, you know, they can *see*—so what do you think that was doin', what effect that had on morale? And for that reason, all by itself, not even fair to yourself.

"Here you are, a young guy, with a whole lotta promise, and you're gettin' a real bad reputation. You don't know what you're doin', yourself. 'Yeah, I know, I know he's smart, even bother tellin' me how bright he is. Or he works hard, I know that, too, or he dresses neat, or even that he's been around. I don't *care* how much talent, guy brings to the job; I don't want him doin' it here. Comin' in and disruptin' my whole operation, chasin' every tight skirt in the place. Next thing you know, I bring him in here, I'll have 'em all suin' *me*. For harassment, just for havin' the bastard around. And you think I want that kindah shit? He'll have me so I'm spendin' all of my time with lawyers who're defendin' *me*, 'stead of on what I ought to be doin' with lawyers: puttin' more bad guys in jail. So, no, nothin' doin'. I don't want him in here, a damn cocksman on my watch, just can't have that happenin' here.'

"So, yeah, sure, I know, I took it upon myself, which you know there was nothin', obliged me, it's not like I hadda do it, I just felt like I hadda, is all. Because this business just hadda *stop*. It couldn't keep on goin' on like it was like that, just couldn't keep goin' on. So then, and then what did I do? What I did was I warned you myself there, and this was early, you shouldn't be doin' what you were. Because it wasn't right, and you're gonna get hurt, a lotta nice people're gonna. And so what do you do, I do that? You do what young guys like you are always're doin': first you denied it, you lied all about it, what the whole fuckin' world knows you're doin', and when I said 'Bullshit,' which was just what it was, bullshit was all that it was, you told me to go mind my own fuckin' business and keep my fuckin' nose outta yours.

"And just the kinda thing that I figured would happen, and told you would happen, well, that was exactly what happened, exactly what I said would happen: you got broomed outta here until Linda got transferred, into the AG's office there, which Linda did not *want* to be transferred to, transferred to that job over there, so she quit— way you acted there, what you did then, well, it all ended up, it ended up makin' her *quit,* and so now she is out of a job. Unemployed. And also, I hear, pretty mad at you these days, because she now thinks the same thing I did, I told you: what happened was all of your fault, guy your age fooling round with her then, when she was still just a kid, before she could even buy a legal beer. She wouldn't rub your dick now, if she ran into you, not if what I hear's true; she would kick you right in the balls.

"And, I dunno how your wife feels about you, after what you did to her there, but without even knowin' I would still bet, Gayle hasn't been able, forget. And she never will be, able to, either; much as I'm sure that she would like to, she'll never be able to do it. She won't be able to ever forget, how you embarrassed her with that thing. With that shitty thing that you did. And I also know, I don't care what you say, you can say anything that you want, but I know that that is the actual reason that you're doing this to me, now, the reason why you engineered it, and why it's all happening now.

"And that is why you got Brian involved: it's all purely because, you've hated my guts, ever since you got caught and detached there. You blame me for all of what happened to you, tellin' yourself it's all *my* fault. I think you maybe got yourself now so you're even *believin'* it, too, you even believe I did all that; I was somehow responsible for it. Well, go ahead, pal, that's what you wanna do, it doesn't matter to me. All that does is show how much of a true asshole you really fuckin' are—can make yourself believe shit like that."

"Well, whaddaya think, Brian?" Dell'Appa said. "My reading of that is that Bob doesn't think he needs to be advised of his rights because he thinks he's just gonna bullshit and brazen his way through all of this, until he comes out whole on the other side, maybe a little rumpled and disheveled, but still with his pension rights and his reputation intact, maybe even a recommendation. So I'd better give him his rights anyway, because if he's gotten that far out of touch from this planet he's not competent right now to decide to waive his rights and therefore needs a firm reminder."

"Ahh, fuck you," Brennan said. "Fuck the whole bunch of you two guys here. Gimme the damned form and I'll sign it." He scrawled his signature largely through, over and around the block provided and scaled it back onto Dennison's desk.

Dennison nodded at Dell'Appa. "Okay, Harry," he said, "having no choice in the matter, I suppose you might as well just sort of outline for Bob's benefit, as a matter of collegial and professional courtesy, what we've gotten so far. And, if he chooses to take some advantage from it, well, that would be a definite plus. From our point of view as much as his own."

"Okay," Dell'Appa said. He faced Brennan. "You pegged me pretty good there, Bob," he said. "That was a stupid thing I did, with and to Linda, and a lot of damage did result, to several people. So you were right about those things. But you were more modest than you should've been about your contribution to that damage, because you and I both knew that I was in the process of breaking it off with Linda, trying to manage it without having her continue to go into hysterics every time I came into the office, when you confronted me. Never have I seen a bottom-feeder striking such a righteous pose about his filthy habit.

"And you also know, although you probably won't admit it now, that Linda's tears were in fact how you'd found out that I was having an affair with her. That until she started going to pieces whenever she saw me, you didn't have the slightest inkling of it. That in fact you never knew anything about the affair at all, until I'd come to my senses and it'd started to be over. And finally, you know very well that Gayle never had a whiff of any of it, any suspicion at all, of what I'd been doing, until *you*, you malignant-fucking-meddlesome-lying-old-cocksucking-shiteating bastard, took it upon yourself, to borrow your self-righteous phrase, to call her up and fill her in, not only with what happened to be true about the whole episode, but also with a lot more gory details that added a lot to the color but didn't happen to be true. In other words, you did the same thing to Gayle that you tried to do to us today with your cock-and-bull story about seeing Bomber: you lied.

"You told Gayle about Linda having to have had our child aborted, for example: admittedly very juicy stuff; but *not true.* If Linda was ever pregnant while I was sleeping with her, or had to have an abortion, she never mentioned it to me, and I think she would've, you know?

"Second example, two-parter: I'd told several people in the office I was leaving Gayle to marry Linda, in one version because I'd made her pregnant, in the other because I loved Linda and I didn't love Gayle any more because she'd put on so much weight before she had Roy and didn't lose it afterwards. Here again, a very colorful tale that certainly would've been interesting, if true, but which in fact was false, in both versions. You sure do have a fetish about pregnancy, though, don't you, Bob? Is that a flashback to your strict Catholic upbringing, when all the bad girls invariably got knocked-up as punishment, had to go and see Aunt Flossie Crittenden? Or is it just that you've been watching too many TV soaps and you've hit overload?

"And, just for a final example here: you told Gayle it was common knowledge around this place, because I'd said it to so many people, that the only reason I'd married her in the first place, and the only reason I was dumping Linda now, was that Gayle's father's rich, subsidizing us now with our kid in private school, and when he kicks the bucket we will be very rich, and that's why I'm hanging in there with my wife: all, to borrow another word from you: bullshit. Gayle's father's a doctor with a surgical practice, and he teaches—makes a good living, sure, but he's very far from rich. Especially after he and his wife, who's a professor, not a Texarkana-wildcatter, got through sending Gayle and her three brothers through prep school, college, and graduate doctoral programs. Which long process, I, not her parents, have already started paying for, our son's first year in private school. Contrary to the bullshit that you attributed to me, you soggy squishy piece of human *shit*.

"But don't delude yourself, Bob, not by any means, that the lies you told to Gayle were just a little *harmless* bullshit, *nooooo*, not by any means." Dell'Appa said. "Quite the contrary, it did a lot of harm. Gayle, who is after all a clinical psychologist, and as a result probably has considerably better defenses against attacks of depression than the average person, was so devastated by what you did to her that she had to delay resumption of her work a full year longer than she'd planned to, after Roy was born, because first with what you'd done to her, and second what'd happened to me—that detached duty; which was a direct result of what you'd done to her, what she'd done in her desperation after you'd made her frantic—she didn't feel she was in good-enough shape herself to be counseling anybody else. And, as you so smugly surmise, she still hasn't been able to put the whole disaster far enough behind her so that we can try to be approximately as content with each other as an average couple might be. Which, if we ever make it, will never even come close to the way we felt about each other before. But hey, what do you care, huh, shithead? You're like the fuckin' mutt that shits and pisses on the Oriental carpet, makes a stain that no solvent on earth short of fire can ever bleach, and leaves an odor that every animal that ever sees that rug will detect on the spot, and immediately shit and piss on that same spot, too.

"But that's just your way, isn't it, Bob, that charming way you have about you. If God makes you an offer to come back in your next life as a rattlesnake, you'll turn him down, won't you, you snake. You'll say: 'No God, it's not like I would mind, you know, being a viper. I was one of those, in my past life. But if I'm gonna be one, a real one this time, I would still wanna be sneaky, to go with the poison, you know? I'll come back as a sidewinder there. So's to sneak up on people from angles. Just like I've always done.'

"As long's you've got a clear picture of what you want to get done,

287

you'll do anything you have to to do it. A year ago, after we'd had our first few little sparring matches, and I'd told you to go fuck yourself a few times, in front of the other rooks, you decided I hadda go. And because I disobeyed what's always been my father's maxim—if you know the hostiles've got rifles in the hills, when they come into town for whiskey, for the luvva Mike don't sell 'em ammunition—it wasn't very long at all before you had me screwed, blued, and tattooed. If a guy's got a weakness, and you want the guy down, you'll find the weakness, and down him.

"So, knowing that, having learned that about you, and you knowing that I'd learned it, why in the world did you go and show me precisely where your weakness was? *Knowing* from Day One, when I came back, I would be out to get you. What the hell is it with you? Have you got a death-wish or something?"

Brennan looked troubled. He shifted in the chair, his thighs bulging in his trousers as he crossed his legs. "I haven't got that many weaknesses, I know of," he said. "Margaret says, she's always said, that I'm no good handling money, so if it was something big we're buyin', she had to be there with me. Margaret says she is practical, there. Margaret says also: I'm not."

He arched his eyebrows and shook his head. "*I* dunno," he said, "that could be, I guess. It could be that she is right. But that's not what I mean, that I know it is. Where she's concerned, I dunno anythin'. I've been married to that woman now, comin' up on thirty years, and to this day two things have not happened, like I always hoped that they would: I have not gotten so I know her better, and she hasn't become better-lookin'. I have to say I never really understood her. Still don't know what she'll do, when she gets it in her head, that she is gonna do somethin', somethin' that she's gotta do. Or any of them actually, any women that I know. Every one of them is Greek to me, like the VCR there: '*Hey,* is there a *button* on this thing, button I can push here makes it do what *I* want? Or is the only thing it does what *it* wants to do, huh? And if there is, will someone tell me, which one do I push? And how many times? Little Vaseline help, there, you think?' I admit it: I really don't know. I still don't really know.

"She told me yesterday, she said: 'Bob, all right? I'm goin' out. Is there anythin' you want?' And I was doin' somethin', wasn't payin' that much attention, and there was nothin' that I needed, anyway. So I just said: 'No, no that's okay, Margaret, I'll see you when you get back.' Little later, couple hours, she comes back, all right? I am downstairs, in my workshop. I said I'd make a cobbler's bench for my son Freddie's wife, Melissa, wants it for her family-room. And so I am doin' that, and Margaret comes back and she hollers down the stairs, she can hear the lathe up there, I know; good hard maple's noisy on that, 'I'm home, Bob, I'm back.' And so everything is fine.

"And that night we're havin' dinner and I said to her: 'Hey, I meant to ask you: you went out this after, when you went out, there? Anythin' particular, or just to get some air?' And she looks at me and she says: 'No, the funeral home. I went down to Quillici's and picked my casket out.'

"I just sit there. I am stunned, a thing which very seldom happens so I don't know what to do. I sit there and I look at her, got a mouthful, baked-sliced ham, we are havin' with pineapple, and I just stop chewin' it. Then I start because I gotta, gotta get it chewed, so that I can swallow it so I can talk to her. And so I do that. And then I say to her: 'For *Christ* sake, what's the matter with you? Are you sick or somethin', didn't bother tellin' *me?* What the Christ is wrong with you, I didn't know about?'

"And she says: 'Hey, calm down, I'm fine, I am perfectly all right. *Nothin's* wrong with me. I just wanted, get it done, have it out the way. It's somethin' we all know there, there isn't any question, that we're all gonna hafta do, and if we haven't done it, by the time comes that it's time, that isn't gonna cancel it, postpone it for a while—like someone's gonna say to us: "Well, darn it, you ain't ready. We'll give you another week, walk around and so forth, see if you can get it done—we'll be back next Friday." No, if the time comes when the time comes, like we know it will, it won't make no difference that we didn't do it there. All it'll mean is that we'll still be just as dead and so forth, and someone else'll have to do for us, the stuff we didn't do.

"'And I just decided, well, if everythin' is goin' up, cars 'n houses, food 'n water, you name it: it's gone up, then that must mean that caskets are up too. Because they don't just *exist*, there—people have to make them, and they need more money too. So what I should do now, like those TV ads all say that sell the cemetery lots—course we already got our lot so we are all set there, and no worry about that—

but we don't have our boxes yet, to put us in, in the lot, I should do like they're always sayin': I should *plan* before the need, seems to be the key to it. Because if somethin' happens so I go ahead of you, well, this's a big expense that you'd have on your hands here, and you know how I feel about you and things that cost big money that you got to have, no choice—you just shouldn't, by yourself, do those kind of things. You're no good at them. And so that is what I did, what I was out doin' today.'

"I couldn't fuckin' believe it," Brennan said. "I can't believe my own ears. Here is this woman, my own wife, Margaret, sittin' there right across from me. There is my plate, in front of me, my beer and my knife and my fork, everything looks perfectly normal, just like it always looks, and unless I have been gettin' some kind of science-fiction story playin' to me through my fuckin' *teeth,* she's just finished tellin' me, calm as can be, she was out plannin' her funeral. Almost thirty years, I've been married to her, and she might as well be from Mars. 'Jesus H. Christ,' I said to her, 'you're fifty-two and you feel good, and you've got your funeral all planned? Don't you think that's a little bit *early?* Have you picked out a dress for yourself yet?'

"She nods her head, she's chewing her food, that's another thing I didn't tell you. All the time this's goin' on, she is still eatin', tuckin' the food right away. 'Yeah,' she says, when she swallowed, 'and all cleaned and pressed. It's the dark-green shawl-collar you like so much, and that also takes care of the jewelry. I think that that's tacky, corpse wearin' jewelry: "You make sure she's got cab-fare home? What if some man-corpse gets fresh with her? She gonna hafta walk home then?" If the jewelry's any good, you're not gonna bury it, because you're a fool if you do. And if it isn't any good, she shouldn't've been wearin' it when she alive, why the hell then put it on the old fool when she's dead and can't defend herself? What the hell's that say about her, huh? "She was so great inna sack that people gave her cheap jewelry? Where'd her boyfriend work anyway, K mart?"

" 'And I told Tommy Quillici—his son, Rick, was with us; I insisted, because after all, Tommy is my age, and he's a man, and there's more hair on the hood of my car than there is on the top of his head. So that means he will die before I do, and so I want somebody who's younger than me, knowing how I want things done, he'll still be around when I'm dead. So anyway, I said: 'And none of that goddamned blue hair-rinse, all right? So with the green dress and then with the hair, I look like a grape-'n-lime Popsicle? Because I do not want that to happen." And they both promised me that it won't.

" 'And we also took care of the visiting hours: one day, that is all, first day after I'm dead, just the evening, seven-to-nine and that's all—that is it. Tommy said to me: "Geez, Peg, just the two hours? You're pretty well-known in this town, you know, Peg. Lotta people're gonna wanna come around when you're dead, pay their respects to your family. That isn't gonna give 'em enough time there, to do it, you know? You don't wanna have two-to-four too?" This's after he tells me that visiting hours are one-dollar-fifty per minute, him and his kid and three freeloading pals-ah theirs takin' money for wearing dark suits, openin' doors and then closin' them. "Not a chance, Tom," I say to him. "If they really liked me, they came around, and they saw me when I was alive. And if they didn't like me enough to do something as simple as that, well then, I'm not lying still at those kinds of prices, so they can apologize when I'm dead.'

"So I says to her," Brennan said, "I says: *Jesus*, 'm I really hearin' you sayin' this? The next thing you'll be tellin' me, you will be tellin' me, you've got mine all planned out for me too. You picked out my casket for me.'

"And she looks at me and she says to me, my own *wife*, I'm not makin' this up: 'Yeah, I did," she says. 'I got that done today too. You want the truth, which you probably don't, that was the real reason I went—to get all of your stuff all picked out. I just did my own stuff while I was there, save makin' an extra trip.'

"I didn't say one fuckin' thing, I tell you," Brennan said. "I did not say one fuckin' thing. I just stared at this woman that I'm married to, I been married to a long time, and I can't believe what I'm hearin'. And I said to her: 'Well, Jesus H. Christ, and tell me the fuckin' truth now: should I eat any more of this dinner here now, or anythin' else that you feed me? Or are you poisonin' me?'

"And do you know, you know, what she said to me when I said that? She said: 'Heck, got no reason, waste poison on you, I wanted you outta the way—an' I *don't* want you outta the way, by the way. I just think what you're doin' is lettin' your old pals, all them loyal brothers of yours, I think you're lettin' them, put you outta the way,

291

here. I think you're lettin' them do you in, Bob. I think you're lettin'
'em kill you. And I think it's just a matter of time here, and not very
much time at that, before they finish what they're doin' to you, what
you are lettin' them do. And they will, you know that, that they will.
They will kill you and use you for bait. And after they do that, after
you let them, well, we'll need a box to put you in. Dispose of the
remains properly. We have to that; that's the law. You know that we
can't, just keep you here, when that happens and you are dead—we'll
have to put you someplace. But you gotta go packed inna box, that's
the rule—they won't take you if you're not boxed.' And that's what
she said about that.

"So now you ask me, have I got this death wish? Well, I dunno;
maybe I have. Margaret's right? I guess I have."

Dennison and Dell'Appa both nodded. *"Okay,"* Dennison said,
"show-time, Robert." Dell'Appa opened his tweed sport jacket and
put his hand on his gun-butt. "Revolver and badge on the desk, if you
would, please." Dennison patted the desktop. "Put 'em right here,
Bob, right here now, okay?"

Brennan sighed. He leaned forward in the chair and unsnapped
the keeper-strap on the holster, grasping the .38 at the end of the
butt with his thumb and forefinger clenched on it. He held it up
vertically as though consecrating it and then lowered it slowly onto
the surface of the desk, the barrel pointing toward him. Dennison
leaned forward, picked it up by the butt and released the cylinder,
swinging it open and tilting the muzzle toward the ceiling. He had to
use the extractor to eject the five grimy cartridges onto his blotter.
He glanced up at Brennan. "Yeah, I know, boss," Brennan said. "I've
been meanin' to clean it, any day now. Looks like I won't have to,
now. Badge's in my jacket. Drop it off on the way out."

Dennison nodded. "Bob," he said, "I hate doin' this to you. I
really hate doing this. But my God, you've gotten yourself into one
smelly peckah-shit here, and I can't do anything else. Hadda dog
once, liked rollin' in stink, just a regular, long-haired, old dog, and if
there was one thing she loved in the world, loved even better'n me—
and Princie there, really loved me, more'n my own mother did; but
of course, then, my mother was smarter—it was a carcass, perfectly
rotted, right at the peak of decay, 'nother dog, or a cat, or maybe a
squirrel—squirrel'd do, that was nothin' else—that got run over or

something, so all of the skin an' the flesh 'n the muscles'd all gone all soft in the sun? And she would find it, usin' her nose, and my Lord, she would go to town on it. She would go totally nuts. She'd jump on it, smash it up, just tear it open, get it spread out in the grass, and what she would do, she'd go right to work on it there: jump on it, kick it, throw it around, toss it up in the air, spread it out on the ground again, roll in it, roll in it, do it all to beat the band. Get her front shoulders right down in those rotten guts there, roll around, roll around, roll around. It was like that dog, when she was doin' that, it was like we would be, gettin' laid. And'd waited a long time to get, too.

"And then she'd come home, and my God, she would stink. We couldn't let her in the house. And we'd say 'No, Princie, you can't come in. You'll have to sleep in the yard.' And then she would look so mournful at us that one of us would volunteer. Go outside with her, turn on the hose, hard-spray her down to clean skin. So we could let her come into the house. And even then, she still stunk a little.

"But Jesus, Bob, you stink to high Hell here, and I haven't got any hard-spray hose to wash you, hard-spray to use on you, here. I'm not sure they even make one. When Harry and the boys served those warrants that we got, they left those machines on and watched them. faxes comin' in from all over the place, and *damn*, what variety there. Did you know Dougie had that kiddie-porno-scumbag Buddy Royal wired into the network he built for that woman?"

Brennan had his head down. He shook it, once. "He had *orders* coming in on it, for Christ sake, Bob," Dennison said. "People who cater to perverts, ordering crates of dirty pictures of little kids getting abused. Kiddie-porn, Jesus H. Christ. Is there *anythin'*, lower'n that? Did you know that your brother, and therefore you, too, did you know you were both in that rotten garbage? *Makin' money off pictures of kids?* Kids with men's hands in their asses? We knew Reno, and Chico, and Franco, them of course, and Short Joe, too; all them nice fellas like that, they were involved in it there. But my sweet Lord, at least they're all self-respecting *gangsters.* Buddy Royal's an *embarrassment.* Buddy Royal's pond-scum. Did you know Doug was tied up with him, too?"

Brennan nodded again. He did not raise his eyes.

"And this was because, at least this's what we've got, because

Dougie got Rollins to get you a *job*?" Dennison said. "In exchange for the job with Track Security—and not much of a job, I must say, thirty-two-lousy-grand a year—Bob Brennan went into the tank? What the hell did you do to your little kid-brother? Grab his dick when he was eleven, and he's got a Polaroid of it? What the hell's this hold he's got over you? You tanked it on Mossi, you tanked it on all of them, and these're all very bad guys. None of this makes any sense."

Brennan raised his head. His eyes were dead, and to Dell'Appa it appeared that all the fluid that had inflated him had vaporized and left him sagging floppy in the chair, like a discarded balloon. "It doesn't now, I guess," he said. "It seemed like it did, at the time. When you got the job I'd been told would be mine, and then I was getting retired, and Harry came in, raising hell. Dougie's my brother for Christ sake. When I found out, when I first found out, what kind of shitheels were his customers, I went and I tried to talk to him. Didn't know about Buddy then; didn't find out about him 'til later. All I knew about when I first talked to Dougie was the drug-guys, Franco's guys washin' the money. But I said to him: 'Jesus H. Christ, you can't do this stuff, Doug—you just can't do this stuff, you're my brother.' And he told me to wise up or else arrest him, but his choice would be wising-up. 'Get some dough for yourself for a change.' What can I say? He's brother. He's sure getting heavy though, padre, now." He sighed. "I dunno, Brian," he said, "I haven't got no excuse. This just isn't fun any more. Is it okay if I go along now?'"

Dennison looked at Dell'Appa. He nodded. "Yeah, Bob, you can go now," Dennison said. "I wish I knew what to tell you. I don't know what we'll give the grand jury. I won't know 'til we see what we've got."

Brennan, standing back to them, goatshoulder-slumped, flopped his left hand at his side, the right hanging limply at the empty holster with the snap-strap loose. "Doesn't matter," he said, "doesn't matter at all. Do the best you can for me, guys. That's all I guess I can ask." He shuffled the rest of his way to the door, the empty holster bobbing on his right hip, turned the knob and went out, closing the door carefully and quietly behind him."

"Happy, Harry?" Dennison said.

"No," Dell'Appa said, "Bob was right about that one, too. It just isn't fun when you win what I won. Even when you wanted to win it."

"You know how the Bomber got his name?" Dennison said.

"No," Dell'Appa said. "I assumed: from the Air Force. He was in B-Fifty-twos, I know? 'Rolling Thunder' or something."

"Nope," Dennison said. "Bomber grew up on K Street in Southie, and he was not a big kid. What he was was a fat little fucker the nuns loved, because he was also so bright, and Jesus, did that ever plague him. So when he's about seven, he's got this blond crewcut that his old man'd slapped on him there, most likely savin' money on haircuts, or like that, hot weather, I know it was summer, and for some reason or other, suddenly that was *his year.* That was his summer to shine. People pickin' on him, wouldn't give him no peace, and they're all of course bigger 'n he was. They're all 'way bigger 'n he was. And well, he tells me, 'I just said: "Aw right, fuck it then. So I'll die. All right then, at least I'll die proud."

" 'It's a wonder I didn't have to have surgery six times, 'fore Labor Day finally come that year. I had more fights 'n Tunney an' Dempsey did, and I don't mean: just with each other. Both of all of their fights, them and everyone else, all of their fights put together.

" 'I lost almost every one of those fights. I was too small, and too short and too hot, and I didn't know howtah fight. But I was the kid that grows into the man that they tell you about in flight-school: "The man to look out for's the man who found out, that he really does not give a shit. Because he will hit you with everything he's got, and when he runs out of *that,* then he'll hit you with his own *head.* He will ram you with his own fuckin' head, and if that kills *him,* killing *you* with his head, well, that's all right, he don't care. Because that is the thing he found out, and at least to everyone else that he comes up against, it is a terrible thing: he doesn't *care* if he dies. There's nothing you can do to him.

" 'And that was the way that I was, that year, that summer when I was seven. Somebody jumped me? Hey, okay by me. I didn't mind a good fistfight, even though I knew I would lose. Losin'd gotten me noplace—the other kids still beat me up, so I might as well do some damage to them. At least I went home, shit all kicked outta me, I knew the other guy hurt too. You can't stop the customers from comin' in, but by Jesus, you can make 'em pay, 'fore you let the bastards get out. And if you can set the price high enough, maybe not quite so many will come.

" 'That was all that I hoped to do: make it hurt so much to beat me black-and-blue, which all of those big guys could do, they'd go beat someone else black-'n-blue when they felt like doin' that, and then they would leave me alone. I threw lefts, I threw rights, I threw elbows and butted, I kicked and I bit and I grabbed, and I took hold of ears and I yanked 'em, yanked 'em as hard as I could. Closed my eyes and then I got hit on 'em? I didn't care; I would've got hit on 'em anyway, if they had've been open, I mean, and I swung as hard as I could. If I missed? Okay, then I'd swing again. And of course the real advantage, edge I had on them there, with the kids that were beatin' me up, was that they didn't know howtah fight either. So every so often I would get lucky, knock one of them into next week. And word of that will get around. You fight stupid long enough, get a few good shots in, pretty soon you're not fighting no more. Guys still see you, you go out for somethin', but they also leave you alone.

" 'So that's how it happened, how I got my name, that summer, when I was seven. "He's in another one, down the beach there, and it's just like the last time was too—he's bombin' lefts, bombin' rights, all over the place. Bomber loses; he don't give up." I knew they said about me. And also what they didn't say, too: 'Yeah, throwing hands. And gettin' killed, most of the time. Yeah, but also winnin', just often enough, to keep the old spark of hope bright.'

"And that, Harry, I think, is what we've got to do. No one said we were gonna have fun here. The pitch was, as I seem to recall it, that what we do here is important. What we do here is worthwhile. And that is our real reward."

"Then, then you mean, Master," Dell'Appa said, "you mean that the monster lives? That he will walk in the world then, and they will know then, what we have done here? He will be called . . . *Fronk-en-schteen?*"

"Yes, my son, and God love you," Dennison said. "And this is also really the year that the Boston Red Sox win the whole goddamned-fuckin' World Series. Oh, and do not forget this, either: Life sucks, and then you die."

"Words to live by," Dell'Appa said.